Signs and Wonders

Also by Melvin Jules Bukiet

After

While the Messiah Tarries (Stories)

Stories of an Imaginary Childhood

Sandman's Dust

Signs and Wonders

a novel

Melvin Jules Bukiet

picador usa   new york

Picador® is a U.S. registered trademark and is used by St. Martin's Press under license from Pan Books Limited.

Library of Congress Cataloging-in-Publication Data

Bukiet, Melvin Jules.
    Signs and wonders : a novel / Melvin Jules Bukiet.
       p.   cm.
    ISBN 0-312-20009-9
    I. Title.
    PS3552.U398S44   1999
    813' .54—dc21   98-47800
                                                                       CIP

Book Design by Cheryl L. Cipriani

First Picador USA Edition: April 1999

10 9 8 7 6 5 4 3 2 1

To Isaac

Prologue

CONSIDER THE CALENDAR. An elegant device, a whole interlocking array of numbers and astrological measurements constructed over time to measure the time spent to construct itself and define the future in the terms of the present. If there is any meaning, why shouldn't it reside in numbers?

Take, say, 1/1/00. Strictly a binary combination, not very complex, but simplicity has its own rewards. Like faith. Maybe it's no accident that the two so often coincide.

With the date 1/1/00 fast approaching, all history seemed in abeyance. In England, parliamentary debate ceased; in the Mideast, warring factions called a truce; in Africa, tribal conflicts subsided; in America's inner cities, crime rates dropped to zero; and in St. Petersburg, the citizens walked along the Nevsky Prospekt under the moonlight, holding hands. Everywhere on earth, people felt that the first moments of the new millennium would determine the shape of the next thousand years. It was a time of personal, ethical, domestic, political, and universal watches. Vows aimed at giving up cigarettes, dieting, saving money, investing wisely, maintaining marital fidelity, and all-around better behavior took on a new seriousness.

The last year had brought forth a torrent of oratory from everyone from presidents and prime ministers to tent preachers crying "Armegge-don" to just about every publication in the world, tabloid, glossy, on-line, or photocopied in a dormitory basement. Many looked forward, made resolutions, issued master plans, while others recollected in smug tranquility as lists dominated the media. The *Times Literary Supplement* dug up the ten most important critics it could find to expound on the ten most important books of the millennium and *Boating* magazine featured the ten most glorious seabound vessels and *Biker* named the ten horniest hogs and hottest mamas from Madame Pompadour to Madonna while *Variety* abjectly confessed that its editors couldn't find many movies from 1400 to fill out its own list. *Forbes* attempted to calculate present-day value in its "Four Hundred Richest People of the Millennium" special issue, which brought John Jacob Astor, Mayer Rothschild, Nicholas Romanoff, Philip II, Clive of India, and Taniko Takowa together in print as they had never met in life.

The very word, "millennium," archaic or highfalutin a decade earlier, became as common as pudding. Bowling alleys held Millennium Competitions—first player to score a thousand points wins—and a Mexican beauty pageant declared Miss High Yield Corn of the Millennium. In Times Square, the famous silver ball set to fall at the stroke of midnight was divided into a thousand little balls that would drop like snowflakes to the crowd below, while parties were scheduled everywhere else to close the last era and hearken the next.

Futurists had a field day. One pundit in the *International Herald Tribune* penned a column listing the ten things we could expect for sure during the next thousand years:

1. A chicken in every pot; the agricultural revolution.
2. A computer in every garage; we're all home alone.
3. War in the Mideast.
4. A cure for AIDS; Ebola in America.
5. The end of cash; haves and have-nots. One group doesn't need it; the other can't get it.
6. Omnisexuality; the erogenous pore.
7. Another war in the Mideast.
8. Beyond the solar system; colonies on Alpha Centauri, a clean, safe place at minus 20,000 degrees.
9. Postliterate culture; books, the dodos among us.
10. Bill Gates will die.

In Paris, a famous Gallic cynic puffed on a Gitane and gave an interview to CNN. "What to expect?" he repeated the question. "Alas," he said, shrugged, and concluded, "Nothing new."

Book I
Providence

Chapter One

"GOD IS THE PROBLEM," Snakes Hammurabi replied. His cell mates had asked him what he had done. Three of them surrounded the new arrival, scenting fresh blood—or, maybe, more likely, money. Snakes dressed well for prison. His sleek Italian loafers, purchased in Florence the week before, seemed to repel the rank yellow pool he stepped in. The liquid sloshed outward from his sole and drained away toward a hole at the base of a slight concavity in the cement floor. If Snakes hadn't been drunk and the entire world hadn't already been topsy-turvy, he might have noticed that his own internal balance wheel tipped likewise. But the phenomenon at his feet was arresting—his softly contoured shoe sat like Noah's ark atop a half-inch Ararat with forty days and forty nights of yellow flood eddying mysteriously down into the sewer of the planet—and he gazed at the miracle his shoes had wrought.

"The gentle sway of Der Good Shit *Lollipop*," the cross-eyed one explained. "It's the only way we can tell when the barge is listing." He was standing between two other prisoners; he was their leader and spokesman. To his left hulked a shirtless giant who resembled a missile, thick cylindrical body with a broad neck that tapered indistinguishably toward a small pointed head. To his right was a wiry man with shoulder-length coils of black hair and a complexion as dark as Snakes's, probably a Turk.

Snakes wondered if he should feel intimidated, and took secret comfort in the knife that the cursory police search had missed; it was tucked into a slot in the heel of his left shoe, a tiny, spring-loaded switchblade with a stone-ground edge.

Then a wave crashed into the base of the barge—it was forty days and forty nights outside too—and even the most experienced of unwilling mariners had to grab ahold of something solid. The bodybuilder tripped on the drain and careened into the far corner of the cell. "Well, sometimes we can tell, anyway," he hee-hawed, and grinned a wide, toothless smile.

"Heavy weather," Snakes sympathized.

"Heavy water," said an old man from the shadowy recesses of the bunk behind Snakes, cackling to himself.

A flash of light burst through a four-inch square of two-inch-thick glass set into the distant wall. The window was so streaked with gull droppings it was practically opaque and only the vaguest tinge of Baltic green could usually be discerned, but the lightning illuminated the cell long enough for Snakes to perceive it more properly than the dim bulb anchored on the ceiling allowed. His new home was eight feet wide, twenty long, with two tiers of three beds, head to toe to head to toe to head to toe, along each wall. Snakes caught a glimpse of images of naked women with large breasts and spread legs stuck to the cinder-block walls.

Four beds were empty; three obviously belonged to his greeting committee and one was reserved for him. Each of the first three had several threadbare coverlets and pillows, while his, like most of his new roomies', was barren. Okay. He'd have to see about that. It was cold in the cell.

Snakes took a seat on the untenanted cement slab cantilevered out of the wall as if it were a red velvet settee at the Kastrasse Lounge, where he had last held court until his recent unfortunate encounter with the law. His long legs extended outward, and he appreciated the match between the exposed green silk socks that clung to his bony ankles and the chartreuse linen pants riding up his calves. Snakes was a dandy.

Most of the men on the blanketless slabs who had not bothered to scope out the new arrival were old, their faces and clothes an identical pallid gray, whether from lack of light or lack of cleansing, he couldn't tell. Suddenly the cell reeked of age and its miseries, scabs and sores, badly digested food and its evacuation, which crusted the rim of the drain. Snakes took a handkerchief from his breast pocket and delicately pressed it to his nostrils to inhale the scent of magnolias.

Another wave crashed below them and the barge rocked and the pool of urine that had overshot the drain came flowing back, streaking the concrete in thin rivulets.

"Looks like we're in for it."

"We're all in for it." The cackler behind Snakes laughed in his dementia. He was the oldest man in one of the upper tiers, which Snakes instantly perceived were preferable, those at the corners more so. Ipso facto, Snakes as a newcomer, along with the inmate directly across from him, behind the welcoming committee—a tall, gaunt man with streaks of filthy hair—had been relegated to the least desirable quarters. Closest to the latrine. Even here, a hierarchy.

The cross-eyed one slapped at the side of the feet dangling in front of Snakes's eyes, and the feet swung as erratically as a straw man's. "Shut up, I told you."

"Shut up, you told me," the cackler echoed.

The cross-eyed one grabbed the leg and yanked the old man down onto the floor. Long white hair shot upward as the body dropped. A flesh-covered bag of bones hit the floor with a thump and rattle of teeth.

Unfazed, the bag's occupant continued, "And I told you we're in for it, and just because I told you don't mean it ain't true."

The cross-eyed one straddled the cackler in parody of one of the pornographic images taped to the walls. Instead of rocking with pleasure or satisfaction, however, he clutched the shank of white hair, hauled the head upward and banged it back onto the floor.

The bodybuilder sidled forward from the corner and stood above them like a referee, but he did not move to interfere, and nobody else on the other beds moved either.

Snakes understood that this was a show for his benefit. He leaned back upon his two elbows and prepared to enjoy it.

The old man chortled wildly even as the cross-eyed man continued to crack his head until either head or concrete seemed bound to split.

Thunder rolled in from across the bay and boomed through the walls and echoed in the tiny room, and the lightbulb encased in a tight wire mesh blinked. Underneath it, the battered old man's eyes flickered like the bulb's and finally closed, and the cross-eyed man turned around, and continued, "You were saying . . . Snakes, you said your name was?"

"Nice to meet you . . ." Snakes left the sentence hanging for an introduction.

"That God was the problem."

"Small enough."

"For a nautical stay."

"Apparently."

From the moment of his appearance before the judge on the midnight-to-dawn shift, Snakes had known that he was not in for the usual trouble that a man in his position was liable to. A deed that ought to have resulted in a desk summons was taken too seriously by the blank-eyed justice who leered down from his bench. "Remanded to *Farnhagen* until further notice," he said, and smacked his gavel.

It was the same in the police van that carried Snakes to the *Farnhagen*. He was kept isolated from both guards and other prisoners as if he were contaminated with a rare disease. During the two hours' transport to the northeast, he realized that he had not been given an opportunity to call a lawyer. Fat lot of good his fat retainer did him here. He felt the bump of the van as it left the road and climbed onto a dirt road and then onto a corduroy bridge and then halted. Only in the ten-step passage from the van through the gate was he granted a glimpse of sea and a breath of salt before entering into the immense structure he was condemned to.

The barge *Farnhagen* sat like a semi-deflated balloon on the surface of the stagnant inlet at Wieland. Its top was curved like a tennis bubble, but down below it consisted of floor after floor of concrete with tiny holes that were all the contact its residents were to have with the outside universe until their release. Built for temporary overflow of the regular prison facilities twenty years earlier, the *Farnhagen* was designated for short-term use and quick abandonment, but the overflow never abated and it sat and sat and deteriorated.

Snakes was checked through a lax security that hardly bothered to pat him down. He could have smuggled a bazooka in with his knife. Perhaps the authorities didn't care, because the prisoners could only harm each other and save the state the expense of their upkeep. His height, weight, and identifying features were noted: 5´8˝, 134 pounds, brown eyes, three-inch scar under left breast.

Next stop was the storeroom, where his watch and wallet were confiscated and logged into a narrow blue ledger, so that they could be parceled out among the civil servants who worked there for precisely such perks. The sergeant in charge of the storeroom noticed Snakes's fancy clothes, but did not issue him prison garb, either because they didn't have any or because Snakes's 32 slim wouldn't fit his own 44 large frame. Perhaps it didn't make a difference because all clothes here, prisoners' and warders' both, were destined to be transformed immediately into *Farnhagen* drab.

Snakes was marched down several long halls, through several checkpoints, until he faced one in a row of steel doors with fisheye peepholes. The guard made a great show of raising his hand to his forehead as if saluting while peering through the hole, until he deemed it safe to open the outer door. Snakes was shoved through into a two-foot anteroom. The door behind him locked; the door ahead opened with a remote hydraulic whoosh, the only evidence of modern prison technology. Eleven pairs of eyes met him from inside the cell where he now—surely temporarily—resided, although some of his—surely temporary—companions had the look of decades of airless, motionless incarceration.

"So, what are you in for?" the Turkish-looking fellow said.

"Peeing."

"It's no crime here," Snakes's new interrogator commented as he unzipped and spattered about the hole, creating a new pool to refill the depression Snakes's fine shoes had displaced.

"It is in church . . . that is, if you don't use the bathroom."

The three men stood menacingly—and not because they were offended at Snakes's transgression, but rather because a man as well-dressed as this one, in stir for an offense as petty as this one, might have something to offer that the guards hadn't already grabbed. Snakes crossed his legs to bring his knife within easy reach of his hand, and began. "I was at the Kastrasse, maybe you know it, in the St. Pauli district, a nice place, good for business and pleasure."

Suddenly cagey, the cross-eyed one said, "I've heard of it."

The Kastrasse was a private club, very private, too private for the likes of this thug. "What have you heard?"

"That everyone who goes there is a pansy."

"Only partially true," Snakes answered obligingly.

The cross-eyed man looked baffled that his insult had been accepted or deflected, he wasn't certain which. "Go on."

"It was a lovely night, was it only last night? Good Scotch, good hash, good conversation, the kind you gentlemen are clearly familiar with, until it was late, and I decided to go home. All good things come to an end. Unfortunately, the bathroom was occupied by certain parties involved in a . . . transaction, so I bade my adieus with a rather full bladder."

"I don't understand him," the bodybuilder whined.

"To pee or not to pee, that was the question, mein Herr. Unwisely, I opted for the latter until several blocks later necessity made itself too keenly felt. I might have done my duty in a park al fresco, but the dew was already staining my cuffs, yet no place in the vicinity was open for business, and my lodging still distant. It was a lovely night, no hint of this storm, and I was strolling. Fortunately, or unfortunately, I noticed a religious edifice, and re-called the legend that such doors were never locked. It was true. It was a large room, and I saw what appeared to be a free-standing pissoir on a stage at the front."

"The fuckin' pulpit."

"I had never peed on a stage in front of, oh, say, a thousand seats, and the idea appealed to me. Imagine those seats filled: ladies with hats, gents humble on bent knee, a first-night, first-rate, first-class audience, and the curtain rises to—"

"Haw!"

"Precisely. It was a case of clear biological need, and I always defer to biology. I did what was necessary, while imagining the house full, and as-suming it empty. Alas, it was neither. A nocturnal believer in silent back-row communion witnessed my distress. Wretch, rather than sympathize with my predicament or shout 'Bravo!' he sneaked outward, flagged a cruis-ing rover, and brought them posthaste. I was caught with my pants down."

"Perhaps you would be so kind as to remove those pants now," the cross-eyed one said.

"Perhaps I wouldn't."

"We are simply requesting to see what you have already presented to the church," the Turk explained.

"I'm sorry, but I believe in rigorous church-state separation. That's a deeply held principle."

"Bruno," the cross-eyed one said.

At a signal, the lumbering giant stepped forward.

"Bruno," Snakes repeated, and extended his hand. "Glad to meet you."

Unsure, the giant looked back at his leader. "Anton?" he pleaded.

"Shake the man's hand, Bruno."

The halfwit thrust out a paw.

Before their fingers touched, the one named Anton said, "Maybe you've heard of Bruno. He's a wrestler. Once known as Le Grand Blond. Sometimes he doesn't know his own strength."

Snakes recalled the newspaper headlines when Bruno broke an opponent's neck in the ring. The fight had been fixed, but not that well, and Bruno was arrested for manslaughter rather than murder. It was a minor charge, brought to sate the public in the same way that the wrestling matches themselves did. The trial was as fixed as the performance. But that was several years ago and Snakes might have thought Bruno would have been released by now. Time off for good behavior and all that. Unless Bruno hadn't behaved.

The big man's hands twitched in anticipation, and Snakes foresaw the vise squeezing his nicely manicured fingers. He removed the utensil from his heel and palmed it, then clasped hands together as if in prayer.

"You're not back at the church. Shake hands with Bruno," the host insisted.

Snakes extended his curled hand.

Bruno began with a friendly pressure that increased gradually. Snakes's fingers were crushed together like layers of cake under a press. He wiggled the release mechanism on the tool, and Bruno yelped and leapt back, a tiny spike embedded an inch in his palm, not quite piercing the far side of the flesh.

The old man on the floor giggled, and the cross-eyed man kicked him.

"Allow me," Snakes offered, leaning forward and jerking the knife from the flesh, releasing a thin spout of red to mix with and tint the yellow on the floor.

Released from his tiny pinion, Bruno swung wildly.

Snakes ducked and the sledge of a fist smacked into the side of Snakes's bed. Swiftly, Snakes moved under the fist and held the tiny knife to the thick neck that looked as invulnerable as a tree, but might yet have bled its own human sap. "Sit," he demanded.

Bruno sat.

"As I said, God is the problem. *You* are not. You I can deal with in my sleep. Next man who tried to touch me gets his balls cut off. Is that understood?" Then he turned to the cross-eyed leader named Anton. "My pillow?"

"Sure," Anton grumbled, and took an extra pillow from his own slab in the top corner beside the door. He tossed it across the room, and Snakes plucked it out of the air. A moment later, unrequested, a miserable blanket also flew, also snagged. Snakes turned his back to smooth them down as evenly as possible on the concrete bed, and then lay, arms crossed beneath his head, to contemplate his future.

Bruno whimpered, the cackler cackled, the others stared into space. Lightning flashed infrequently and the barge rocked upon the waters. Anton said, "Welcome to the pen."

Chapter Two

DAYS PASSED; the storm never let up. The sky bled water.

Even inside the *Farnhagen*, it was so damp that moisture seemed to coalesce out of the air. And all the while the barge rocked and rose higher within the gradually swelling harbor. The men in Cell #306 grew so used to the sway that brief moments of calm unsteadied them. And the light continued to disorient them. Perpetual cloud cover prevented the sun from providing the minor illumination their tiny window had once allowed during the day, and a lighthouse on the tip of the jetty outside the window kept the night from imposing its blanket of darkness. The prisoners lived in a terminal dusk broken only by flashes of lightning.

"God, you said, was the problem." Anton returned to Snakes's original declaration for the hundredth time. "You think He has it in for you?"

Locked away with no papers except those yellowing on the walls, no telly, no prospect beyond the grim sea, no other faces beside the twelve in the cell, the men fed on each other's words. Those familiar with prison etiquette understood this immediately, and the rest adapted swiftly. One's first defining characteristic in stir was always crime. What you done to get invited to this dance. After the traditional, initial "I was framed" song of innocence was sung, the truth invariably came out. Thus, Snakes learned that his companions were more than the usual bunch of pimps and pushers and lowlifes from Hamburg to Danzig.

The north shore of Germany was the nation's link to the world. East lay the decrepitude of the former Iron Curtain, west the cultural gulf to France, and south, beyond the Alps, only the tedious probity of Swiss watchmakers. It was north, where shipping bridged the turbulent Baltic, that commerce and media and money made their home. Oh, the capital might be located safely inland, but shake the nation, like the cement deck of the *Farnhagen*, and all the skyscrapers and sex shops and Snakeses would slide north. Even leave it steady Eddie, as the *Farnhagen* never was, and they'd drift north on their own.

Sure, there were pickpockets in Munich, smugglers in Regensburg, and every once in a while an overzealous disciplinarian dad would kill his child in Bonn, "bon Bonn" the French tourists who crossed the border for kinky medical videos called it, but crime, real crime, crime as a serious dignified vocation, was a northern pursuit. Witness:

Upper left, north wall: Anton Bartsch—armed robber, murdered a policeman during the commission of a crime.

Upper center, north wall: Georg Kiehr—heir to an industrial fortune, serial killer, accused of cannibalism.

Upper right, north wall: Bruno Morgen—wrestler, manslaughter.

Upper left, south wall: Omar Nazzarian—assassin, preferred weapons shotgun and ice pick.

Upper center, south wall: Dietrich Eisenheim—Obersturmbannführer at Bergen-Belsen.

Upper right, south wall: Karl Blobel—kidnapper, murdered a wealthy banker by suffocation.

Lower left, north wall: Erich Langefeld—accountant, stabbed his homosexual lover to death in a crime of passion.

Lower right, north wall: Herbert Glucks—schoolteacher, rapist; his victim killed herself.

Lower left, south wall: Franz Palitzsch—gigolo, poisoned four widows after being named as beneficiary of their wills.

Lower right, south wall: Martin Clauberg—arsonist, responsible for seventeen deaths.

And that was only what they'd been convicted of, and that didn't include Snakes Hammurabi, public nuisance, south wall, lower center. It also didn't include north wall, lower center, the only one whose place was more degraded than Snakes's, the one prisoner who never uttered a word, whose crime therefore was unknown: Ben Alef.

Once again, Anton repeated his question. "God . . . ?"

Again, the cackler, whom Snakes was fairly impressed to learn was the infamous Dietrich Eisenheim, last of the big-name war criminals, interrupted. "He has it in for all of us." Eisenheim's notoriety was as exotic for this group as was Snakes's apprehension for picayune malfeasance.

Anton waved a threatening fist from his bunk and was about to renew the beating, but decided it wasn't worth the effort. His stomach was queasy and he preferred to rest and chat.

Snakes said, "Dietrich's right this time. Not only because I peed in His home, but because every time any of us us pee, we do it in His home."

Bruno, the baffled manslaughterer, looked at the drain, which had backed up and overflowed its small cup, as if to ask, "Is that His home?"

"Might as well be," Snakes answered. "This whole world is a cesspool. You eat, you shit, you drink, you piss, you fuck, you come, you live, you die. That's where He really gets us."

"Do you mean that's when we get to live with Him?"

Snakes took pity. "Yes, Bruno. In Heaven, if you live your life according to His laws."

"I always done unto others." Le Grand Blond wasn't all there. He meekly followed Anton or the Turk's instructions, but had no ideas of his own beyond those he had received at boarding school in Alsace-Lorraine in the early eighties. He was six feet tall by sixth grade and growing too fast for his father, a postal worker, to handle. His mother had died when he was young. Fortunately the state-subsidized Catholic school, La Petite Ecole, agreed to take the thick adolescent year round if he would also serve as the institution's unofficial porter. Thus, between studies, he carried rubbish to the curb outside the school's wrought-iron gates every Tuesday, shifted desks around the crumbling stucco premises when necessary, and dragged the sixty other students' trunks from the van when they arrived in the autumn and to the van when they departed for the summer.

Bruno's muscles were needed because staffing at La Petite Ecole was sparse. Beside a cook and handyman, there were only three teachers in residence in the attic of the "château" surrounded by overgrown hawthorn. Madame Raissa, a pinched widow, taught literature, history, and the other liberal arts, and Monsieur Tatlin taught mathematics and the sciences. Both earned their miserable keep at the sole discretion of the headmaster, Monsieur LeClerc. This admirable specimen of *Homo academicus* filed papers to obtain the relevant government agencies' support and reserved the pupils' biblical studies for himself; it was he who was responsible for inculcating Bruno with the Golden Rule. Beyond that, he saw his mission as similar to the *Farnhagen's*—keep his charges for the duration of their sentence and keep them in line. Otherwise, down came the cane. This solid oak heirloom from some distant, disabled LeClerc was kept in a place of honor upon two brackets over the blackboard. Pink with the blood of generations of bad boys, the cane punished all infractions from the behavioral to the intellectual.

"Two on the knuckles" might attend a latecomer to class; "Three on the back" giggling, fidgeting, or in any way wasting the master's precious time; and, for the most recalcitrant of scholars, "Ten on the bottom."

Bruno never minded the gnat's sting of Monsieur LeClerc's cane, but he flinched sympathetically whenever the headmaster went after one of the other boys. Shunned by his peers, Bruno nonetheless felt their blows more keenly than his own. One boy in particular, Daniel Genser, also an isolate like Bruno, drew LeClerc's most fervent animosity. A frail, bespectacled lad who read straight through the school's single-room library, starting at A, he had made the mistake of correcting the headmaster's pronunciation of "gelaises" his first week at the school. This was particularly ironic, because Daniel was constitutionally incapable of speaking what ought to have been the most basic word in his vocabulary. Anything else from anatomy to politics (he was up to the P's), he knew, but from kindergarten forward the act of proclaiming his own name during roll call reduced the nervous child to a stuttering wreck. This finally led his parents to take him out of public education and replant him in the private domain of Monsieur LeClerc, where he could be properly nurtured.

Other boys romped through Madame Raissa's lessons and totally ignored Tatlin, but they learned to recite the list of Israel's kings or prophets correctly for LeClerc. More important, they knew to sit in craven silence, hands folded, eyes front, during Bible even though they would rather have been playing with their own stick and a ball. But Daniel, despite or because of his intelligence, bored and distracted by the flutter of trees outside the classroom window, could not master this simple survival skill, and was constantly on the wrong end of Monsieur's punitive pedagogical rage.

This came to a head one bad day after a state inspector queried the meagerness of the lunches and, perhaps not so idly, wondered where the money provided for the boys' sustenance went. Monsieur, who relied upon the department's subsidy for his own salary, perks, and peculation, was therefore in an especially foul mood when he strode into class, looked around, and took keen aim at the boy who never mentioned his own name.

Inspired, he began, "We were discussing the early messianic prophecies, weren't we, Daniel?"

"Yes, sir."

"So then tell me, Daniel, which prophet went into the lion's den?"

Daniel gaped soundlessly.

"Who was it? Ezekiel?"

Daniel shook his head.

"What about Jeremiah?"

Silently, sweat popped off the tiny boy's forehead, and LeClerc advanced. He removed the cane from its brackets and stroked its length, savoring every inch. "Who?" I asked. "Tell me who walked into the lion's den, you stupid clod." And the more he ranted, the less the child could summon the capacity to do more than stutter.

"One on the fingers," LeClerc said, and the cane fell. "Now, who walked into the lion's den?"

Still no answer.

"Three on the arm," LeClerc said, and the cane fell again, three times in rapid succession, creating three thin red lines like military stripes on Daniel's soft upper limb as the boy cringed beneath the blows.

But after the punishment, there was still no answer, and LeClerc duly intoned, "Ten on the bottom. Stand and drop."

Daniel rose shakily, and lowered his pants and bent over his desk, exposing two pale, quivering globes.

The cane rose again for its ultimate descent, and stopped, upright. A thick hand from above held the top of the cane as if it were a pencil.

Bruno hadn't been aware of making a decision or tiptoeing forward to execute it, but he found himself in a frozen tableau with the teacher. Each had an arm raised; each held the cane, aiming straight up toward the sky as if waiting for lightning.

Then they unfroze, and the headmaster's free left hand lashed out and slapped Bruno, and Bruno's right hand instinctively responded in kind. Swift as lightning, or a pair of adolescent trousers, the teacher dropped to the tile floor.

Bruno might yet have graduated if not for the cane he still, solely now, held. The other boys stared at him, and he brought the wood down again upon Daniel's tormentor so hard it cracked. Unstoppable in his fit of primitive retribution, Bruno swung at Monsieur LeClerc with the splintery stub. He herded the crawling and bleeding headmaster into his office, where LeClerc summoned the gendarmerie.

Despite his size, Bruno was a juvenile offender, so his prison career did not begin right there. Still, he would have been sent to the reformatory if not for the unaccountable amnesia that struck every boy in the school as they were summoned to the stand. Every boy but one, but Daniel's testimony was insufficient to convict.

Of course, Bruno was expelled. Presumably doomed to a future as a ditch digger, he was rescued from ignominious fate by Kurt Genser, the father of the object of Bruno's towering pity, who managed professional wrestlers and knew a talent when he saw one. A letter with an offer was sent to Bruno's father and gratefully accepted. At age fifteen, with muscles like zeppelins, six three and growing, still unshaved, the newly christened Grand Blond entered Herr Genser's stable and remained its star until the unfortunate accident in the arena led to his rather than Genser's arrest and incarceration. That had been four years ago.

"Feh." The third of the cell's reigning triumvirate hawked toward the drain. He was the one Snakes had pegged as a fellow immigrant to the Federal Republic, but he hadn't yet chosen to introduce himself.

"Been here long?" Snakes asked.

"Long enough."

"A minute's long enough."

"Longer than you were in"—Snakes guessed—"Turkey."

The man smiled for the first time.

"Iran," Snakes hastily corrected himself.

"Omar Nazzarian," the man said. "Just a rug merchant."

"With a little something on the side."

Omar grinned. "Everyone's entitled to a good time."

Snakes crossed his legs. He was known at the Kastrasse as a good listener.

The eighties had been good to Omar, he explained. The others knew this, and Snakes might have figured as much, but Omar's story, like Bruno's, like everyone's, took up slack minutes in the endless expanse of time aboard the *Farnhagen*.

Omar's parents, Ali and Fatima, had left Teheran during the oil embargo of '73. "Things were crazy. There was money, enormous sums of money, billions of dollars pouring into the country for palaces, for monuments, but not for the people." No matter the salary that Ali, a stonemason, took home, it was taxed by the Shah for yet more palaces and monuments, and also prisons for those who disputed the expenditures. Without any class awareness or political agenda, Ali decided to leave when a cousin wrote to describe a much better life in Europe. Omar remembered the debate between his parents. "My mother was fearful. My father said it was an opportunity. Such a modernist."

What this had to do with Omar's presence on the prison barge, Snakes didn't yet know, but everyone worked his own way toward disclosure. Some started the moment the gavel came down; others seemed to need to chronicle all of recorded history until they arrived at the judicial bench.

Omar's parents looked at their small son (he was eight at the time) and wondered if he would be corrupted in the West—never imagining how corrupted he could become. They worried, but finally the opportunity seemed too great to deny, and they fled their homeland in voluntary exile. At first, the new society satisfied the Nazzarians. Ali worked construction on an extension to the Autobahn, Fatima established a good home in a gingerbread cottage in a suburb near the rail line. So far it was loosely similar to Snakes's own journey.

"I went to school, learned the language . . ." Omar paused and peered at Snakes.

Lightning lanced toward the rod atop the barge.

"Yes, so did I," Snakes said. He felt a momentary temptation to lapse into his fragmentarily recollected Arabic, but by now, deeply accented, the mameloshen of Heine and Himmler was embedded in the both of them.

A roll of thunder curled in across the bay, as if the waters themselves were growling the local language.

Omar continued. "I don't know. Maybe they thought Germany was America, the promised land, the melting pot. They tried to belong. They bought a painting of the Black Forest to hang over the fireplace. But there were no fireplaces in Teheran. That's what they never realized, that they weren't still in Teheran. Of course, they found out."

Snakes could almost see where the story was heading. Everyone else in the room had heard it. Some listened for the umpteenth time; some stared blankly at the walls.

As reluctant as he may have been to start talking, Omar found it impossible to stop. "I came home from school one day, book bag on my shoulder. The book bag, individual pouches tabbed for history, for literature, for science—mark of the good immigrant. Well, the door was open so wide that the back was flat against the outside wall. It was a cold day, and I shut the door. My parents were frugal, oil was expensive, the heat waste would have angered my father. My mother heard the door close and ran past me, and swung it open again, and propped it in that position, against the brick wall with a flowerpot. Nice German flowers, nasturtiums. A good hausfrau, she was. 'Don't shut the door!' she screamed. Not like her, a shy, modest women, still a Persian really, only without the veil."

Snakes could imagine the inside of the house, Mitteleuropean architecture, but with the Asiatic touch: a fine rug, perhaps a framed print of a mosque, or a perforated brass lampshade, the smells of pilaf rather than bratwurst. Language changes first, customs next, food never, geography imprinted on an infant's taste buds. Snakes and Omar had the taste for bratwurst now, but deep in their blood lay the scents of cardamom and cumin. "Yes?"

"Oh, tell him," Anton said. "Big deal. There was a swastika on the door."

Omar glared at the colleague who had deliberately undercut the dramatic effect of his story, and if he had had Snakes's knife, blood might have flowed, and the sway of the barge would have twisted the stream of red, left, right, and a twisted cross would have stained the cement. He looked at Snakes and said, "Smeared in shit."

"But," Bruno said, "you weren't even Jews."

"Not exactly the point, Blond."

"But they are, we are, we all are," Eisenheim giggled from his perch. "Everyone on the *Farnhagen* is an honorary Jew. Even me, that's the wonder, the glory of this place. Even me."

Even him, that rarest of all creatures, the Nazi in jail, consigned to prison after the war, more than half a century earlier. Snakes had heard that story already, not from Eisenheim himself, who was incapable of more than hysterical snickering, but in public. Once a year the *Frankfurter Zeitung* ran a feature on Eisenheim: pity the poor bastard, paid his debt to society. Veterans' organizations advocated his release. White-collar crime. Understandable under the circumstances. A life sentence was, in American parlance, cruel and unusual. It was an outrage no civilized nation could abide.

Yet each year the spurious moral lobby of prelates and professors who wanted the community to beat its breast forever inveighed against the pathetic old crank and kept him from parole. Arrested by Allied soldiers as the military liaison in charge of facilitating—and, as the former history student grew fascinated with biology, dabbling in—"science" at the nearby concentration camp in Bergen-Belsen, Eisenheim was by far the longest-standing resident of the *Farnhagen*.

Of course, he claimed innocence, and said in court that those who died from his experimentation were just an unfortunate by-product of research, and that he was a scapegoat. But unlike some weaker colleagues, Eisenheim never denied the tenets of the Reich and ceased to mind jail after the first few decades, and if his supporters had managed to secure his release, he would have fled back to the safety of confinement in a day.

The oldest continuously incarcerated remnant of the Third Reich had commenced his postwar career in Spandau and been transferred from prison to prison through the penal system until the *Farnhagen* barge opened for business. He had been the first customer, had Cell #306 to himself, then watched roommates come and go until, at discrete points in time, one or another inmate stopped going in accordance with some imperceptible selection process. Martin Clauberg, arrested in 1976, was the first to remain, and he was swiftly followed by Karl Blobel. Both were professional criminals, the former an arsonist for hire (and ecstasy), the latter a car thief turned kidnapper whose last victim had unfortunately expired when Karl couldn't bring himself to drill airholes in the trunk of the mint-condition antique Mercedes where he kept the man.

Erich Langefeld ("Gay Lovers' Quarrel Ends in Tragedy!") arrived next, and then Georg Kiehr, heir to an armaments fortune, whose fancy late in a motiveless, labor-free life turned to murder, random and vicious, of homeless men and women. "They died happily," he said, describing to the court and, later, his companions how he lured his victims into the stone mansion built from the proceeds of steel shell casings.

"Kiehr, Kiehr," Dietrich Eisenheim searched his memory when the new felon strolled through the hydraulic door of the cell as if he were entering the grand opening of the Kiehr Pavilion at the Cologne Museum of Art. "Any relation to Helmut Kiehr?"

"Scion," the bored Georg replied, disgusted, and spat toward the drain. All his life, from gymnasium to the society pages, he had detested the inevitable epithet, "Helmut's son," attached to his name. No matter his multiple endowments at the museum or university or hospital, the directors of those august institutions treated him solely as a function of his solid gold pocketbook, which epitomized Germany's postwar economic miracle. Still, he scrawled his name across the bottom of the checks with an aristocratic flourish, because he didn't know what else to do—until he discovered the undifferentiated satisfaction of personal charity.

Living, "if that's what you call it," from limo to salon . . .

"I'd say so." Blobel laughed.

Georg couldn't recall having seen, let alone spoken to, a homeless person until one night, on a lark, he walked from his Berlin flat to the theater. Approached for "spare change" by a creature—there was no discerning its sex—as grimy as he himself would get after decades inside the *Farnhagen*, Georg had difficulty comprehending the request.

"Money, Mac, a bit of spare. I'd give my left leg for a tenner."

"Really? What would a thousand purchase?"

"Name it."

"And what makes you think that I have such assets?"

The creature looked him up and down with a sly leer and replied, "Intuition."

Struck that this was the first person he had ever met who didn't know who he or his father was, Georg opened his wallet and extended the bill with his manicured fingertips, reluctant to touch the loathsome beggar, whom, a minute later, he couldn't say why—a whim—he invited back to his house.

One at a time, Georg took in the miserable and displaced. But he was tender and couldn't throw them back on the streets when he found a new object for his temporary charity. "And so I killed them, but they died happily." Never proved, but hinted at by the prosecutor because of the lack of certain parts when the final few bodies were discovered, was the accusation that Kiehr had eaten his victims—the ultimate delicacy.

The last of the old guard, Franz Palitzsch, landed in 1978 when a career of marrying and mournfully widowering a series of wealthy—not in Kiehr's league—matrons came to an end. After him, the newer inmates were brash and troublesome in their day, but all of them eventually—as would Anton, as would Omar, both in residence a mere decade by the day Snakes arrived—tended to torpor. Eventually their cheeks sagged, energy waned. Eventually they would lose their corner bunk to someone younger, rougher, until they keeled over to be carted out in a sheet.

"So what happened?" Bruno asked Nazzarian, as if he hadn't heard the story a hundred times before.

"Mama cried a lot, Papa comforted her, blamed the hooligans. But I took off. Left the fucking book bag behind and never looked back. You don't know when you're not welcome, that's when you get in trouble."

"But you seem to have gotten into trouble, anyway, if your current residence is any indication," Snakes said.

"Oh, this."

"I assume you're not here for running away from home."

When Omar wasn't more forthcoming, Anton spoke for him. "Nazzarian was caught with a small matter of an ice pick."

"Stealing it?" asked Bruno.

Snakes couldn't say how he knew, but he knew. "In someone's skull, I presume."

Omar shrugged. "I thought it was ice."

"Contract," Anton explained approvingly.

Okay, so now we know who's really dangerous, Snakes thought. Omar lets Anton run the show—why not?—until it counts. That accorded with his knowledge of the world. The quieter they are, the nastier they turn. Except for the human enigma opposite him, closest to the latrine, low man on the totem pole, who never said a word, Snakes was the quietest. But that fellow was the exception that proved the rule. Snakes couldn't put his finger on it, but he knew in a flash of insight as bright as lightning that this man was the opposite of danger.

Anyway, Snakes did not dwell at great length on his companions. He was more concerned with his own situation, which became more unpleasant to contemplate every hour. He had placed note after note, some written, some negotiable, with the food tray to summon his lawyer, and was going quietly crazy. What game did the authorities think they were playing? He knew that the charges were merely the justification for his incarceration, which was so clearly deserved for so many other crimes. But that oughtn't to make any difference. They knew his crime was penny-ante. There were rules. This was Germany.

After their initial attempt at intimidation, the other inmates left Snakes alone. He sat with his knife, whetting it on the cinder walls, and keeping his cheeks smooth, nails clean, flicking specks of dirt from his fine shoes. But the leather was delicate and despite his care the knife nicked the surface, so that the shoes gradually took on a fuzzy, unattractively pimpled appearance. First thing out, he'd chuck them and get new ones, custom. Take a mold of his delicate hooves, fly to Florence, buy new shoes, and toss the ruined pair in the Arno. Or, if he remembered his buddies, he'd send Anton a package.

In the meanwhile he listened to Omar. "I ran off to the city, where there were a lot of young men like me, mostly from Turkey—that was a good guess—but also from Iran, Palestine, Morocco. 'Guest' workers, niggers with no work. Not much play either. You have two choices, starve or serve. I decided to serve."

"Who?"

"Local businessmen. You deliver a message requesting payment on a loan that someone in the goodness of his heart lent to someone else, and there's no payment—how rude—so you deliver another message with a baseball bat. Me, Babe Ruth!" Omar mimed a swing for the fences and paused to appreciate the arc of the ball. "My boss knew skill when he saw it. Took me off the first message, onto the second. From there . . . well . . . one grows in an organization."

"Until the ice pick," Snakes concluded.

"Yah."

And all because he'd come home to see his mother sobbing over a pot of pilaf, a swastika on the door.

Snakes didn't know why, but instead of looking at Anton or Omar, or Eisenheim who once wore the uniform—might in fact still be wearing it under the decades of grime—he looked again at his own stained lime pants and chafing socks, and then looked at the silent mystery man across from him. The man's eyes widened in the dusk. What was the opposite of danger?

"Ridiculous," Omar concluded. "We weren't even Jews."

"Look at us," Anton said. "Two Arabs, two Christians." He counted only himself, Omar, Bruno, and Snakes.

"Not Arab." Snakes tried to explain the difference between Muslims and Arabs.

It was historic, linguistic, cultural. Everyone listened carefully because a lecture on any subject provided a welcome relief from the endless present of life on the *Farnhagen*. Who the hell was Farnhagen that he had this heap named after him, anyway? Glucks's delirious memory of a young woman dragged into a hotel room, Eisenheim's fragmentary recollection of the glory days, Bruno's country education, Snakes's comparative religion: it was all something that life in Cell #306 wasn't—and that was good enough.

The round robin of tale-spinning moved from car thievery to safecracking to the finer points of murder.

"I once took a Jaguar," Blobel said. "Brought it home. Damn thing wouldn't start the next morning. Walnut instrument panel, peach of a sound system, but the engine was shit. Nothing like our Mercedes. Now *there's* a vehicle you can rely on."

To which Clauberg replied, "Like nitro's no good by itself. You've got to have a set of really good tools."

"Nothing like a Mercedes."

"Stanley's my brand."

It could have gone on forever if dinner hadn't arrived. Feeding time was the highlight of the day's routine and since the storm obliterated the sun it was also the only way to tell time. Twice during each twenty-four hour span, at 10:10 in the morning and 6:10 in the evening, the prisoners could hear the external door keyed, twice hear the clatter of a tray of food, chipped plastic plates, and utensils, twice await the slam of the outer door and the hydraulic whoosh of the inner that allowed them to get at the stuff.

The fare varied from powdered scrambled eggs to a rank cabbage broth accompanied by moldy bread to slabs of gray sausage, all served with a tepid, translucent "milk." None was appetizing and, Snakes suspected, none nourishing. Still, ten of the twelve residents jostled each other to get at the grub, but in the end it was always distributed in the same order and proportion. Anton took first, Omar next, Bruno third, and then, after the lions' share was gone, the rest was divided according to the other prisoners' own minor dominion.

"Have some?" Anton suggested on Snakes's second day, when the newcomer had already established himself as superior to most of the long-term residents. Pleased by the recognition, Snakes nonetheless refrained from accepting his due, still assuming that he would be released imminently and maybe have a celebratory Cordon Bleu of appropriate vintage with his counsel.

Two days later, however, in a moment of depressing reality, Hammurabi succumbed to the filthy sausage. Half ground organ, half sawdust, it was the tastiest thing he had ever eaten.

"Not bad, eh?" Omar taunted him.

"If necessary."

The only thing Snakes hungered for more than food was a message from the outside world. But food was the only thing from that world to enter Cell #306, and he devoured the barely edibles as if they were a pardon from the Chancellor.

Still, Snakes never ate before the others. Taking advantage of jailhouse pecking order was the surest way to eventually give in to it. He maintained pride enough to separate himself by refusing to admit that boiled sludge was normal. Steak tartare was normal. Clams casino was normal. Endive salad was normal. Coca-Cola was normal. And so he stood aside until after even Eisenheim thrust his filthy hands into a heap of stringy turnip greens. Then Snakes took out his knife to lever a corner of the mess onto one of the two remaining plates. The last was for the silent man, who left his untouched. As he never peed, the man opposite Snakes never seemed to eat.

And the man didn't have leisure to pick at the remains later, either, since fifty minutes to an hour after the delivery—never less, never more—after the wagon had made its deliveries to Cells 308 through 340, it returned to 302, 304, and 306, and everything that wasn't inside an inmate's belly was expected back. Anton told Snakes the rules. "If you're thinking of keeping a knife, not that these knives would cut butter, don't." He had tried as much his first day in the *Farnhagen* lo those many years ago, and no one had eaten for seventy-two hours. Twice each day after Anton strapped the knife to his calf the door would open to . . . nothing. Fifty minutes later it collected . . . nothing. Finally, he placed the utensil between the two doors, and then another bowl of slop appeared at the next feeding. "Makes you wonder what would happen if a knife fell down the drain or if they, say, miscounted. There's probably a roomful of skeletons waiting for their next meal right now."

"I wasn't thinking of that," Snakes said. He was remembering small moments at the clubs and lounges in which he ate, worked, and played. Remembering Ilsa, his favorite waitress at the Kastrasse, who knew exactly how he liked his martinis, remembering conversations with the Peddler, his mentor and partner. And everything he remembered went to underline how there was something dramatically wrong with his condition here.

It was obvious that the *Farnhagen* was set aside for incorrigibles, but Snakes had had ample opportunity to learn about the penal system elsewhere. He had done small time in several municipal jails along the coast and most of his associates had served at Potsdam or Ludwigshafen, and whether the venues were garden parties or maximum security they all adhered to modern ideas of prison. There was none of this Devil's Island shit anymore. There were lawyers; there was television; there was time in a yard for exercising and weight lifting, and time in a library for self-improvement. But Farnhagen was a cross between space-age technology and a medieval dungeon, and there was neither rhyme nor reason for this group to be set together and set apart, without any end in sight. It wasn't going to be as easy as he had thought. He might have to escape.

Established as no one to fool with, Snakes spent his days ruminating over his condition, doing isometrics to keep up his strength, and listening to the idle conversation that flowed back and forth only when he was too tired for anything else. But even he succumbed to the mealtime mania, and began to look forward to it, for no other reason than to break the endless monotony.

Occasionally, at random hours of day or night, he heard the wet sound of Anton or Omar mounting one of the other prisoners, but even that occurred infrequently, without enthusiasm, as the masters took their way with the slaves. Once, Anton debunked from atop Langefeld and caught Snakes's mild grin. "You want some?"

"No, thanks."

"Share and share alike."

"No, thanks."

"Mind sloppy seconds, do you?"

"That's not it." Many a time he and the Peddler had flipped a coin to determine who would take Ilsa in the back room first, and fifty percent of the time he lost. As with the food, however, Snakes appreciated the recognition of status and demurred from accepting it. Yet he wondered how long it might be until naked human need made Anton's offer enticing.

"Give it time, Hammurabi. A week, a month, any hole in a storm, hah!"

Snakes ignored him and focused on the storm, wondering if it would somehow provide the opportunity for escape.

"Probably take a while till your pecker adjusts to the menu. I think they're putting saltpeter in the food. Didn't used to. There's a lot less sex here than there used to be," Anton said ruefully. "Don't worry; you've got time."

"How long have you been here?" Snakes asked.

"Fourteen years, three months, five days, nine hours, and thirty-six minutes, give or take a decade. Murder."

Anton's story was a simple one. Armed robbery gone wrong, a stupid policeman bucking for a medal, earning it posthumously.

The stories intertwined with each other, this one's murder, that one's theft forming a tapestry of transgression. Farnhagen was an anti-society with its own rules, none of which had to do with the larger world from where food and no messages came. Snakes peed.

"What do think this is, a church?"

He'd heard that before, and bore with it. But suddenly the thought that he might hear the same stupid joke again every day for twenty years made the phrase "fear of God" jump into his head. No, no, he thought. Fear of man was what he felt. Or fear of time. It wasn't the rock slab he slept on or the vile food he ate or even the filth that bothered him, but the endless span of days that turned lime green into gray into black, that turned men into beasts, that, for the first time since the door slammed shut, truly terrified him. But he couldn't show his fear, and he looked to the odd man across from him for inspiration.

"Ben Alef" the tag on the man's neck said, but he seemed as incapable of saying it himself as the boy Daniel in Le Grand Blond's story. Unlike Daniel, the mysterious Ben Alef never said anything else, either. Beside being the only one whom Snakes had never seen rise from his hard plank to pee in God's home, he was the only one who never told his story. Snakes tried to observe the silent prisoner with his dirty, matted shoulder-length hair, face as gray as the cement, deep within the shadowy recess of his bunk. It was hardly possible to say how old the man was; he could have been twenty and he could have been sixty. Only his eyes glittered like those of an animal in a cave.

More and more, Snakes dwelled on the mystery. What did Ben Alef eat and when? Perhaps the man nibbled at the leftover crusts that fell from others' plates like the vermin that crept out of the drain after dark; perhaps he lapped at the puddles sitting on the floor after dark. But that was unlikely, too. Snakes woke to every untoward sound in the cell. And whenever he woke, he saw the same luminous eyes.

When did Ben Alef sleep? He lay there silent and calm and without need, those damn eyes simply aglow. In a universe of encroaching dread, Snakes looked to him for secret advice, and found a strange sustenance.

After three weeks in stir, three weeks of relentless storm, three weeks of the same talk and the same tedious gray sky, Snakes felt his temper fraying. Especially when he anticipated three years or thirty years or three thousand years of the same blunt void, he could have screamed, and would have if it would have done any good. He also knew, as he scraped his chin with the dulling edge of the once razor-sharp blade, that one moment of vulnerability would do irreparable harm. At the next meal, he wouldn't have his choice of the food he disdained, and he would wake a few mornings later with Anton's dick in his mouth. Finally even Hammurabi, for all his preternatural self-possession, found it necessary to reveal himself during an especially violent squall, when the pornography flapped from the walls as if beckoning.

Omar opened the door to the revelation. "Amigo, how about you? What's behind the wild urinator? Snakes, strange name."

"I had strange parents."

"Not a nickname?"

"Not a given name, either. My parents changed it legally several weeks before they died."

"How did they die?"

"Snakes."

He explained that the elder Hammurabis belonged to a cult. They had always belonged to some cult or other, from the earliest Istanbulian days of the late-named Snakes's recollection, but that last one was "Imported from America."

No earnest, striving, would-be bourgeois like Ali Nazzarian, Snakes's father, Hamad, was a comfortably established career diplomat with a secret. Other diplomats had other secrets, but they were usually as mundane as a coke habit or a knocked-up secretary. No, Hamad Hammurabi's secret was not a lust of the body, but a lust of the soul. He was a quester.

Raised in one of Turkey's few modern households, the son of a doctor, Hamad had felt spiritual yearnings for as long as he could remember. Even as a freshman at Ankara University, he was drawn to the students with faith. Inevitably it was forms of Islam that he encountered in those days, as the country sought to educate its youth by bringing the offspring of Sunni Muslims, Zoroastrians, and Kurds to study engineering and science. Virtually chained to a library desk, struggling with quadratic equations for the sake of their nation's future, those children maintained an air of assurance that the purely secular Hamad, who studied languages, noticed and coveted. He took a few comparative religion courses to strive to comprehend them, but the academic approach always seemed to miss something at the heart of their belief.

Hamad's worldly knowledge prepared him well for the diplomatic track he entered soon after graduation. He married Nahid Abulafia, whose father was the Turkish Under Minister of Defense and, after a short stay in the capital, where his only son was born, was assigned to a post in Madrid. There, after the completion of his daily duties in the embassy, he became fascinated with the dense Catholicism of the place—nothing at all like the descriptions in his college texts—and made a trip to Alva to visit the wizened heart of St. Teresa. Surrounded by a busload of American tourists, he stared at the sacred muscle and unaccountably found himself weeping and collapsing to the floor.

This pattern repeated itself all over Europe as Hamad's career advanced. Because of his facility with languages, he was dispatched everywhere from Dublin to Moscow. At each stop, he was exposed to and enthralled by the new and intriguing paths that others took to purity and salvation. This hobby was considered odd, even rather inappropriate, by Hamad's government, but so long as he fulfilled his professional tasks well and kept his proclivities to illumination quiet, he was tacitly allowed to pursue his idiosyncratic personal mission.

"You sure he wasn't a spy?"

"No . . . I'm not at all sure." In fact, Snakes had often wondered the same thing. It could easily have been the case. Why else was the senior Hammurabi shifted every year, every time his son began to feel comfortable in a new school, with new friends and a new tongue? Hamad's ease within diverse cultures made him invaluable to his superiors, whether they were trade envoys or spymasters. But whatever Hamad's ostensible or covert goals, they didn't make any difference to him. All that mattered was the quest, which, when the family arrived in Berlin, led to snake handling after dark on a NATO base.

Germany was the least religious place Hammurabi had been stationed, but by keeping an ear to the ground for any form of authentic or spurious seeking, he discovered a group of American soldiers from some backward region of the States retaining their connection to their home by way of a black market in poisonous reptiles. On reflection, Hamad was not surprised to find this hidden culture among other outsiders. Yet he was an outsider to them. It took months and the use of all his diplomatic skills to win their trust, but finally he was allowed to witness and, eventually, participate in their ceremonies, which he took to with all the enthusiasm he had previously shown for Catholicism or Greek Orthodoxy.

Convinced that this ecstatic communion with the forces of danger was the true path to enlightenment, Hamad changed his son's name and brought the newly christened boy and his mother to one of the rituals. It took place at midnight in a deserted recreation hall. Snakes remembered the khaki-clad soldiers and the elegantly attired diplomat stripping off their shirts and lifting asp after coral snake after rattlesnake from a wooden barrel thick with a coiling mass of iridescent scales and flickering forked tongues.

"Now you, Nahid," Hamad said.

Snakes remembered the way his mother shrank from the suggestion, but as she had danced with peyote-maddened gurus in Majorca and fasted with somber Slavic monks in Kiev to satisfy her husband's strange desires, so she inched toward the barrel. He remembered his father's arms plunging into the barrel and emerging with scaled and dripping streamers dripping from both limbs.

Summoning her own deep faith in matronly fidelity to her spouse, Nahid advanced to the barrel and closed her eyes. Her white cotton blouse was suddenly ornamented with a red-and-green ribbon that moved of its own accord past her elbow toward her neck. But she was nervous, and the snake slithering up her arm seemed to read that. It swiveled its triangular head in the direction of the onlookers, then struck.

Blobel whistled. "Really cuckoo, hey?"

"Rococo," Kiehr drawled.

"My father tried to pull the snake off my mother, but once he was frantic, it bit him, also, and both of them died." He remembered the two of them writhing with poison on the floor, as if they had not merely been bitten by the snakes, but were turning into them. "The group of soldiers wanted to adopt me. They wanted me to stay, but I didn't."

"You found a home in the city," Omar stated.

"Doesn't everyone?"

He slid north, inevitably. Slept in the park with a bunch of hippies as stupid as snake handlers. Shoplifted. Picked pockets. Met the Peddler, but that was another story, another slew of stories. One big score. Six months' leisure. Good shoes. Another score. Hanging out at the Kastrasse. It was a good life. He was a tough hombre; and, more important, most important, he didn't give a shit. His fearlessness gave him a weird kind of immunity, until the night—was it only three weeks ago?—when his bladder had betrayed him.

"You sure that was all they had on you?"

"Well, the search, yes. They might have found certain substances that a lawyer will certainly prove were planted on me. Oh, yes, and certain armaments. Ditto. A shame one cannot rely upon the duly constituted forces of law and order in the Republic."

"A scandal."

"Call the Chancellor."

"Who's the Chancellor?" Glucks, the teacher, insatiable for knowledge, asked.

"Huh?"

"Still Kohl?"

There was something sad, almost touching about the question. But of course, locked up without books or images except for the pornography which filtered into the cell as mysteriously as a draft, Glucks had not seen a newspaper or a television program for years. Kohl had been assassinated six months earlier.

"No kidding! Who did it?"

"Some wacko with a gripe about his pension. Walked straight up to the Chancellor at a reception, blam blam, five hundred witnesses."

"Man! What happened to the guy?"

"He surrendered immediately, so the cops didn't even get a chance to gun him down. Went to trial. Pleaded insanity."

"I'm surprised they didn't put him in with us."

"Right."

"So, um . . ." There was a hesitation in Anton's voice. "What else is new?"

Of course, they were starved for word from the outside. So was Snakes, but he expected—every minute—a different kind of word, something to do with bail or outright dismissal of the idiotic charges. His lawyer ought to have been on this like white on rice. What the hell was taking the Peddler?

In the meanwhile, Snakes, emissary from the outside world, brought the others up-to-date on other current events. Oh, he knew what was going on—until twenty days ago. But what had happened in that period? Did they ever rescue that guy in the mine shaft? What happened in the American election? He, too, was out of touch. A day, a decade—it made no difference. In or out was not a relative quality, but absolute.

Snakes tried not to dwell on his situation as he regaled the other prisoners with stories about the last World Cup, when Germany was eliminated in the semi-finals because of a bad ref, and he described the special election, when Jürgen Grabner, Kohl's undistinguished deputy, won in a cakewalk. "A real law-and-order bastard."

"A man has a right to defend himself," Omar said, nodding toward the weapon with which Snakes idly plucked at his shoes.

"Me, I'm just a nuisance."

"A nuisance with a knife," Omar pointed out.

"I use it to clean my teeth."

"Can I check it out?" Omar asked.

If Snakes refused, or even hesitated, it would bespeak a fear that would become a self-fulfilling prophecy. They said dogs smelled fear, but Omar's nose was keener than a schnauzer's. Snakes had had enough experience in and out of prison to know that one never showed fear. After a certain point, one was never afraid. He tossed the knife across the room.

Omar held on to it, and considered his advantage. Then he said, "Nice blade," and flipped it back. Perhaps he could have cut the newcomer's throat, taken his shoes, but what would it get him?

Shoes.

Perhaps that was enough. He wondered what size Snakes's feet were and said, "So tell us about your problem with God."

"Don't mess with Numero Uno, that's the moral. The army, the police, I could deal with. The Chancellor I could deal with, or a prime minister or a president, or an under-minister of defense. But God is trouble. Or people who believe in God." His eyes rose upward as if to commune with his celestial antagonist, but all they saw was the lightbulb and the striated cement forms that made up the ceiling as well as the walls, floor, and beds.

As if on cue, the light bulb blinked out. It didn't make much difference, because the faint light from the jetty still shone through the cell's square glass pane. Still the rain swept past outside; still the barge shifted upon the rising waters. And it should have been mealtime, but wasn't.

Snakes sat there and grew hungry—or was he imagining it? Or had someone taken a knife at the last feeding?

Hours went by. Bruno did sit-ups and Palitzsch and Langefeld continued their endless, idle chatter about old movies, as persistent and annoying as the rain. Snakes tried to block them out by concentrating on Ben Alef. It struck him again that, after all this time, he didn't even know what the man was in the *Farnhagen* for, and he knew that none of the others knew either. On close examination, he determined that the strange, silent felon was really quite young, probably no more than thirty. There were patches on his cheeks where his beard had never grown in. Yet somehow Anton never bothered this one for sexual congress, though there was something, well, attractive about him. Snakes wondered if he was beginning to feel the stirring of prison longings. But he was wrong; it was real hunger, and the others felt it, too.

"All right," Anton finally declared, when any lingering possibility of misperception of time passed. "Who took a knife?" He paced the center aisle between bunks and looked every one of his eleven companions in the eye. "It won't do you any good, so 'fess up, whoever it is, and be a man."

"C'mon." Blobel whined his agreement. "They'll starve us."

"If we have to, we'll turn this place upside down. We'll look in your ears, between your toes, up your ass."

When there was still no response from the guilty party, Anton began the search. He started with Glucks, bottom left corner under the window. Snakes watched as the tribunal stripped off the pathetic horse blanket and fingered every inch of the miserable excuse for a pillow and made the poor degraded felon remove every stitch of clothing. But there wasn't much more to examine, and the search went quickly. Bruno's bunk above Glucks's was next, and it, too, was searched, in the spirit of equality. Nothing.

They searched Blobel and Kiehr and the maniacally snickering bag of bones that was Eisenheim.

As Snakes's turn arrived, he briefly considered refusing, just to define his separation, but decided it wasn't worth the bother. He undressed with all the dignity possible under the circumstances and folded his stained green pants carefully before grubby paws unfolded them and ran down every seam. Of course, his own knife was there, and there was a moment's pause when Anton considered whether the Hoffritz top-of-the-line item wasn't the sin for which they were being punished. But the weapon had already been in Cell #306 for three weeks and there had been no repercussions, so it was irrational to assume that any would come down now.

Each inmate was duly searched, and by the time they stopped at Anton's own bunk by traveling the cell clockwise rather than crisscrossing it like a shoelace, the place was a mess. Bedding and clothing and the few strips of paper from the walls were scattered. But Anton was rigorous and insisted that the others check his bunk and that he, too, strip.

Then they arrived at the last station, opposite Snakes. Ben Alef was the only one left and had to be the culprit. "Okay, you," Anton said.

There was a pause as the mob of prisoners waited, but the mysterious Ben Alef did not satisfy their need for and expectation of a climax. For the first time Snakes could recall, the fellow stood. He was tall and lank, and his bunk contained nothing, absolutely nothing. But his clothes were still on, and Anton gestured imperiously.

No hesitation, no fear. With a shrug, Ben Alef shed the prison overalls he wore, and they were all that he wore—no shoes, no socks, no stiff brown underwear. He stood, eyes like beacons that outshone the light from the jetty, right hand clasped upon left forearm, rather than, as Snakes had somehow assumed, modestly covering his penis.

There was one discovery: it was circumcised.

And the storm mounted. Lightning flickered as furiously as a disco's strobe. Sound cascaded like waves, one roll of thunder overlapping another, each building upon the last until the men in the cell could not hear themselves. Then, just as the noise was so loud that it couldn't get any louder, it did; the air itself was torn into constituent elements.

They hushed under the onslaught of nature's rage. Needles of spray seemed to come through the walls. Or were those beads of sweat popping out on Snakes's upper body?

Everyone but Eisenheim retreated into his bunk to wait out the storm alone with his own thoughts. But Eisenheim, the most ancient resident, who knew every tic of the barge better than Anton or Blobel or surely Hammurabi, could tell that the *Farnhagen*'s steady back-and-forth motion had been replaced with a novel sliding sensation. He stood at the window, pondering, and then suddenly he turned and declared, "We're moving."

"Ridiculous," Omar snapped, too quickly.

"I tell you, we're moving." Sure enough, from his bunk Snakes could tell that the lighthouse appeared taller than it had until now. He thought it was because the water had risen, the dikes overflowed, but it looked taller yet by the time he finished justifying its new aspect.

Everyone jumped to cluster about the tiny pane of glass in time to see the lighthouse topple under the prow of the newly seaborne vessel. Its beacon shone straight into the cell for a second and then hissed under the surging waters.

The steel cables that had tethered the barge to the continent had snapped; they were floating on the surging waters like enormous dead snakes.

Glucks it was, however, who ran in the opposite direction and began banging on the steel door. "Hey, hey," he screamed, "is anyone there?"

But no one was there at the door, and the only people on the far side of it were those in other cells. Everyone in the village that serviced the prison had been evacuated inland. Everyone who wasn't locked into a cell had fled.

Eisenheim said, "They're gone. We're alone."

Even in the *Farnhagen*, they knew truth when they heard it.

Chapter Three

SNAKES HAD NEVER LIKED WATER. At least not since the blissfully preconscious era of fetal flotation in maternal fluids came to an end at 5:53 A.M., September 21, 1973, or maybe a few infantile bathing sprees later. The child's innate bias was confirmed one sparkling sunny day by the River Lyons, when the business liaison to the Principality of Monaco took it into his head to baptize his family together with a bunch of born-again Huguenots whose spiritual bent he had fallen sway—prey?—to. That was the day the firstborn of the late-twentieth-century Hammurabis learned to hate water.

The sky was clear, the procession to the riverbank festive. Banners of bright red and gold snapped crisply with emblematic joie de vivre. Still a toddler named Samad, Snakes bounced along, enthralled by the colors and the jolly clamor of drums and a goatskin tambourine. He giggled when his serious father waded into the water in his clothes, although Mr. Hammurabi had taken care to remove his elegant Italian loafers first, and when his sad mother followed, but then it was his turn.

"Come." His father beckoned to him, so, trusting, he went. He had no problem splashing in the muddy shallows, until a large paternal hand grasped his head and pushed it under the surface. Suddenly the world was wet. The shock of immersion, the gulp his lungs could not expel without taking in another gallon, hurt and terrified him. Yet worst was his sight of the fluttery rays of sun dancing atop the Lyons—inches, inches too far to breathe. Fingers dangled in front of his eyes like snakes. He cried, but the river washed away the tears.

From then on the newly christened Stephan feared water in any form. Every time the Hammurabis crossed a bridge over the smallest country stream in their Citroën, he held his breath. From then on, his bath was an awkward struggle to keep him in the tub. From then on, he could barely drink water, and to the present he preferred opaque liquids, milk then, wine now, bisque rather than consommé.

Only as a dandy on his own in the world had Snakes learned the virtues of cleanliness and made his peace with regular if repugnant spongings with a damp chamois cloth. Still, he preferred to keep dirt away rather than be obliged to scrub it off, and was fastidious in his habits. He sent his clothes to the dry cleaners because he could not bear the idea of his precious socks and the silk briefs that cosseted his genitals spinning in a dreadful wet vortex. Perhaps hydrophobia, more than his urgent need to pass water, explained why—when the harbingers of the storm to end all storms drizzled upon him that fateful night after he left the Kastrasse Lounge—he ducked into the church.

So when the other residents of Cell #306 pressed themselves against the tiny window to witness the shocking spectacle of the toppling lighthouse, he retreated into his bunk, eyes locked on the drain, which he suddenly knew that he and they were going to go down.

Knives, guns, bicycle chains, garrotes, nunchakus, weapons of all sorts Snakes could face with equanimity. One night a rival in the Bremerhaven drug trade had sent a car to bump him off; he merely sidestepped the careening vehicle, like a matador teasing a bull. Karate ambush, no sweat. Gang warfare, a pleasure. World War, he wished he hadn't missed the fun. But the idea of drowning filled Snakes with terror. His legs curled underneath him and his arms hugged his chest like a straitjacket. His mouth opened like a fish's to gasp at every available breath of air in the dank cell.

"Hey, pisser, don't you realize what's happened?" Eisenheim thrust his ugly face into Snake's horrified focus on the drain.

"What?"

"We've escaped."

"To what?"

It took a moment for the men to understand that their motion was not the delirious sensation it ought to be, like rain for a farmer after a drought. Yes, the world was different one moment than it had been before, but there was too significant a problem for even the greatest optimist to ignore. In a sense they had escaped; that was true, but their prison had escaped with them. They were still locked inside thousands of tons of concrete, and now they were without the support systems that kept it going. They had already discovered that there was no electricity and no food. Up top, there was no steering and perhaps no ballast below. "To what?" Snakes repeated.

"To anything. We're free," Erich Langefeld answered just as a wave thrust the barge over the spit of land that had once supported the lighthouse. A jolt sent the prisoners flying apart like tenpins as the barge smashed the jetty with a prolonged, grating rasp and jagged boulders pierced its hull.

They were free, yes, free to sink to the bottom of the sea. But only Snakes who saw the perennial pool about the drain whirl down in the sudden vacuum created by suction at the bottom, knew how soon that might occur.

Liberated from its moorings, the *Farnhagen* drifted out on the waves.

"Go, baby, go!" Blobel cried.

But they didn't know where it was going; it just went, hour after hour into the night, so when the prisoners' initial fit of enthusiasm passed, they relapsed into an exhausted torpor. In time the fear of endless stasis was replaced with the rising fear of random, or diabolically predestined, motion.

Finally Glucks saw the point of Snakes's pessimism and moaned to nobody in particular, "To what?"

"There are basically two possibilities," Eisenheim replied cheerfully. "Drifting and dying of starvation or sinking and dying of . . ."

Snakes clapped his hands to his ears.

They moved with the winds and waves now, no longer side to side, but front to back, riding the swells.

Even Eisenheim ceased his incessant commentary. Every prisoner resembled Hammurabi or Ben Alef in solitary contemplation in his bunk. Each one was alone with the demons of his past and the uncertainty of his future. Some fell asleep. The space between the bunks was packed with the ghosts of those they had wronged: men robbed, women raped, governments or gods insulted and people slaughtered.

Unbound, at loose upon the waters, and gradually taking on water, the *Farnhagen* rolled farther out to sea. There was no light from within and no man-made light from without; only the flashes of lightning illuminated their cell and only the sounds of the ceaseless storm accompanied their dreams.

Morning came and still the sky was no more than a pale, sodden gray, and still the sheets of rain poured down, and still the seaborne bedlam drifted, perhaps lower in the water than the night before. The *Farnhagen*'s maiden journey was going to be its last.

Anton paced up and down the aisle, his footsteps beating a tattoo concluded and recommenced every time he approached the steel door to the cell with a fist or flat palm to the ungiving metal.

"Sensory deprivation." Eisenheim hooted. "When the mind is not satisfied with its surroundings it tends to create new ones that may not strictly accord with reality." Eisenheim had been involved in such experiments back in '44. Instead of torturing his charges with merely physical pain, he plugged their eyes, ears, and noses, and encased their bodies in blocks of 98.6-degree rubber. Tubes ran in and out of them from machines that provided oxygen and intravenous nutrients and removed waste products, while other machines measured brain waves, just to see where their minds went when denied the nourishment of their senses. The results were fascinating and Eisenheim might have been able to pursue them after the war if he had accepted the conquering Americans' offers of hospitality and immunity. Instead, he remained loyal to his original cause—stood up in court with a mighty "Sieg heil"—and bore the brunt of Allied moral furor while his colleagues went on to Yankee universities and launching pads.

But while Eisenheim recalled his decades of deprivation, the rest of the men in Cell #306 felt a keen sensation: hunger.

Without clocks, with only the eerie disorienting light, 10:10 and 6:10, 10:10 and 6:10 might as well have clanged out on an invisible bell tower. When that schedule was interrupted, they were subject to a Pavlovian response that demanded to be sated. The men took less interest in the course the *Farnhagen* took. Less interest in the unabated storm. More and more the writhings of their bellies occupied them, as if tiny baby white mice were racing about their intestinal tracts, and Anton it was who started talking about food.

"Yo." He addressed Snakes. "Is there still that great burger place on the Richtofenstraße."

Snakes knew the place and nodded.

"Man, those burgers were good. The chef"—he pronounced the word as if describing the master of a four-star kitchen in Paris—"cooked them American style under tin cups to keep in the juices. Served them with a mountain of grilled onions. And the milkshakes, man, they were so thick you had to use a pump to get them out of the glass."

"Couscous," Omar offered to the imaginations of his fellows. "Fine as grains of sand, a taste of heaven."

"Baloney," Bruno said, and everyone nodded in fond recollection of the tainted sausage they had been fed—was it two or three days ago? For only a crust of bread, any of them would have accepted an additional ten years' sentence. For only a bite of . . . anything.

But there was nothing—at least nothing that yet occurred to them—and that lack, like the sensory deprivation Eisenheim described, led to the imagery if not the actuality of food. It also led to an idea that might assuage the brain as it could not the gut. Since there was no food, there must be a reason why there was no food. Blame provided a nourishment all its own.

First, the *Farnhagen*'s masters came under attack. "This damn heap wasn't built to withstand the elements," Blobel complained. "Now, if they had let the contract to the Krupp company, it would have been fine."

"Cheap sons-of-bitches!" Palitzsch agreed.

"Your dad ever build anything like this?" Clauberg asked Kiehr.

"Probably." The serial killer shrugged.

But would more stringent engineering—one more cable, say, or one more thread in the existing cable—have kept the barge in place? Or was there some force at work that led to a more than technological failure?

In the absence of logic, the inmates turned to superstition. The only change in the cell since its ancient days of ease and security was Snakes. Therefore, he must be connected to the change outside. He was bad luck, a jinx. "Jonah," Anton accused.

"No." Bruno explained, summoning the lessons of Monsieur LeClerc's Bible class: the sailors endangered by Jonah's presence were able to save themselves by throwing him overboard, but there was no way to get rid of Hammurabi short of chopping him up and stuffing him down the drain. No, this time they were all castaways in the belly of the whale.

"Fuck that," Anton groused, but stopped short of genuinely blaming Snakes for their misfortune.

Ignoring the ominous murmurs, Snakes looked at the enclosure sure to be his tomb. The striations of the concrete might have been the internal muscular structure of the leviathan, the jutting bunks exposed bone, the drain its alimentary canal. As for himself and the eleven other starved men, they were snacks. Yes, the men were starved, but the *Farnhagen* beast was not, and the creakings of its beams twisting in the storm were just the rumblings of digestion. And the *Farnhagen* itself was just another snack for the ravening sea. And the sea itself was just a bowl of consommé for the infinite God who devoured all.

To satisfy that ultimate being who decreed their peril, Snakes's fellow comestibles might have tossed him overboard if they could, but how? They would have jumped overboard themselves if they could. Instead, another form of sacrifice occurred to them. But nobody dared suggest it yet.

A day later, 10:10, 6:10, another two meals further into absolute famine, the desire for blame turned into a deeper, more specific craving.

Snakes wasn't the first to realize that unless they were rescued soon the only source of food to keep any of them alive was in the cell with them. Taboos be damned. How much longer could they hold out? Each one had had years to learn to adjust to isolation within this singular community. But during those years, their brute needs had been taken care of on the most rigorous schedule. 6:10. 10:10.

Snakes looked around. He was used to examining his companions these last few weeks, but now he considered them not as inevitable company, but as potential food. Bruno's slab of thigh was not an object of sexual appeal; it was a joint, a shank. Likewise, Clauberg's inner organs might be fried upon a grill into shriveled tidbits. He could suck the marrow from Blobel's cracked vertebrae, feast on the sweet meat behind Eisenheim's skull, gnaw on the remains. He could imagine a tureen of Kiehr's blood, red and opaque, to quench his thirst.

The natural—or unnatural—thing would be to start with the oldest and weakest; that would be Anton's way. Eisenheim was oldest, but he would put up a fight, and all of them were weakened by their condition. Blobel, perhaps. Or Clauberg. The problem, as Snakes saw it, was that the Darwinian path of gradual elimination would inevitably lead to nights when he couldn't sleep. Not from guilt, God forbid, but from worry about who might perceive him as appetizing. Guilt had never been a problem in the *Farnhagen* before. They were all guilty. Now they were all hungry. No matter their fear of Snakes and his knife, at a certain point hunger would prevail over caution. If they were going to eat each other to buy another day or week in which they could theoretically be rescued and returned to the safety of harbor—and a new, sensational trial—it was probably wiser to go after Anton or Omar first, although Bruno might well sacrifice himself and would surely provide sustenance for a longer period of time.

Yes, Bruno should be slaughtered first; then Anton and Omar next, on the same night. But how long would they stay good? Whoever became the first meal—or any later meal—would have to be eaten raw. There was certainly no material to light a fire with, and no ventilation to exhaust the smoke. Snakes remembered the steak tartare at Luigi's Brasserie.

Then, as if the sound were emerging from his own two rows of teeth, he heard Eisenheim's molars grinding in anticipation of the feast to come. The old man leaned over the edge of the bunk, his upside-down head winking at Snakes below. "Survival of the fittest, pisser?"

Say what you might about how easy it was for the Obersturmbann-führer to outlive his own prisoners, he outlasted his peers as well. They were dead by now in American Veterans Administration hospitals or South American bordellos or the comfort of family homes in Bavaria. But Eisenheim had also outlasted more recent generations of coequals aboard the *Farnhagen* and was determined to outlast the current crew, too. Snakes grinned back. He knew this game and could play it with experts. But he wouldn't make the first move. That would incur distrust and maybe a communal reaction. Instead, he watched as his comrades' eyes roamed the room, turning human beings into pork chops. He kept a special eye on Georg Kiehr, who had done this before.

6:10. 10:10. A day later he knew that the time had come when Anton woke drooling.

Coward, fool, of course he'd make the worst possible decision. Anton began his daily pacing and stopped in front of the bunk of Ben Alef.

Amid the frenzy of the escape, the silent prisoner never appeared disturbed by his imminent demise.

But everyone else knew what was going on, even Bruno, who stood beside Anton, his stolid, gigantic bulk blocking off any means of escape. Escape, where to? At one end of the cell was the steel door, at the opposite end the thick glass window outside which the cables that had held the ship to shore streamed upward like threads in a cotton candy machine.

But when Anton reached down, Bruno reached down, too, and held him back.

"What's the matter with you?" Anton demanded.

Bruno said, "Eating people is wrong."

Omar put another hand on the broad shoulder. "Morality is fine, Bruno, in its place. Its place is not the *Farnhagen*. Its place is not Germany. Its time is not now. Have some breakfast."

At which word, Ben Alef smiled and reached behind his back and held forth an egg.

It was a pale, perfect ovoid, its shell translucent enough for the next momentary flash of lightning to illuminate the veins. Or, Snakes wondered, were they all hallucinating from hunger? Or under a spell cast by the snickering Eisenheim?

Anton grabbed it. And it was real. Hard-boiled.

Omar said, "Divide."

"In two."

Omar looked around, at Snakes. He did a swift calculation and came to a conclusion. "Yes, in two."

Okay, Snakes thought, let them sate themselves, for now, trick their stomach, for now. A single goddamn egg—wherever the hell did Ben Alef get it? and why didn't it show up in the search for a kitchen utensil?—wasn't going to do anything but put those suckers to sleep. That night, Snakes's knife would make the sleep permanent.

But that night the storm attained heights of frenzy yet unseen. The *Farnhagen* bounced so hard that one prisoner after another was thrown from his bunk to the concrete floor, as if every wave, every five seconds, were another jetty blasted to rubble. In a way they were all like Ben Alef now; with the exception of the single, singular egg that Anton and Omar had devoured, no one ate, and, more pertinently, no one slept. There was no opportune moment for Snakes to put his plan into effect. And by now the barge was obviously lower.

And when it commenced to go down farther the following morning, all thoughts of food were forgotten. No matter the substance of the barge that had prevented any sounds in adjacent cells from reaching #306 for decades, come that last day screams could be heard from the lower levels. Then, worse than the screams, there was silence after Deck One and then Deck Two went under. Cells 101–140 and Cells 201–240 were submerged. Rain, however temporarily, still splattered down upon the single window in 306, and waves splashed up.

Finally, worst of all, a tiny spout of water began bubbling upward from the drain. Mixed with decades of encrusted residue in the pipe, the baby geyser was a pale umber, and Snakes gave minor thanks for that, for the purity of water itself would have been intolerable. Let him die as impurely as he had lived. He waited for the hand of the divine father who was his problem to come from above and push his head under the ordure one last time.

Bruno sat, legs crossed, trying to remember his prayers from La Petite Ecole, while the others prepared to meet their maker in their own ways, sobbing, cursing. Only Ben Alef stood and gazed calmly out the window.

At first the puddle simply increased, but then the fountain gurgled higher, a small penile expansion, and then a spout determined by the pressure from underneath shot up, hit the ceiling, and rained down.

"Showers!"

It was the first word Ben Alef had spoken. How many years had he been here? What crime had he committed? It was the first time anyone had heard his voice.

"Showers!" he screamed, all his silent equanimity gone.

Everyone in the cell was crazy; that much was understood. They had been crazy to begin with and were made crazier by imprisonment and crazier still by their destiny. But the calmest among them was now the craziest. Snakes's first thought was "He hates water more than I do."

"Blazing, flaming showers of the apocalypse," Ben Alef yowled, collapsing into a cringing heap under the window. "Showers!" he shrieked, as the flow from the drain turned into a full-blown geyser. "Showers for everyone. Showers for you." He stared at Snakes, and the newcomer felt as if a knife had been plunged straight through his ear into his brain.

"Showers!" the man continued screaming as the pellets of artificial rain washed him. Rivulets of dirt and decades of grime dripped off his face into the flood, and seemed to make him younger. Shedding years, Ben Alef's skin glowed as luminously as his eyes.

And as he decried the rain inside the locked chamber, the fury outside rose and rose, and the cables twisted into the sky, and lightning struck them. The glowing filaments darted through the air like hypnotized snakes rising from a fakir's basket.

The others stared at Ben Alef, momentarily taken out of themselves and the water that sloshed madly about their feet. Eisenheim it was who reached down to stroke the mourner. But Snakes realized that just as Ben

Alef had never spoken, never eaten, never slept, he had also never been touched before, and he darted out to stop Eisenheim, too late.

Fingers touched flesh, and the cable, fast and furious as lightning or a snake's tongue, struck at the window, shattering the glass into a million pieces. Loose in the chamber, the writhing steel lash also struck Eisenheim's forehead dead center. A black mark appeared there and he toppled into the water, like a lighthouse, eyes rolled up immediately under his lids.

Its mission fulfilled, the whip retreated, yet as it did so the evil, semi-animate thing took out a chunk of wall. Winds and waves swept into the gap.

In the pandemonium, Omar realized that there was no longer a barrier between him and the outside world. He jumped through the gap into the waves, and was followed by everyone else in a pell-mell rush toward a new kind of freedom. Anton pushed Kiehr and Glucks aside to escape; then they jumped, too. For a moment Palitzsch and Langefeld jammed the opening, but Bruno rushed up like a football player, and shoved them and himself through. Only Snakes and Ben Alef and the dead man were left.

"Come on," Snakes said, afraid to reach.

"Showers," Ben Alef whimpered.

"There's very little time," Snakes said.

"Help," Ben Alef begged.

Given permission, Snakes touched him. The flesh was oddly warm and dry, and its warmth coursed into Snakes's own body. Suddenly, he felt at ease.

"Not me," Ben Alef said. "Him." He reached for Eisenheim's corpse, floating facedown in the waters inside the cell, and lifted it to his shoulder and waited for Snakes to pass through into the emptiness and emerged at last himself.

Outside, the rubber covering of the *Farnhagen* sat like a gigantic lily pad upon the waters, and the men who hours before would have eaten each other now assisted the last refugees from the dying barge.

A giant burp, and the *Farnhagen* disappeared beneath the waves.

A ray of light pierced the black clouds.

Book II
Revelation

Chapter Four

Dear Frieda,

The harbor is gone. Utterly gone, the docks, the jetty, the shops, the café, the roads, the telephone poles, or I might have called to give you the good news by word of mouth instead of letter.

Forgive me for nattering, but I feel uncomfortable with this form of communication. The only letters I've ever written have been to institutions. Traffic tickets contested. Tax problems. I once wrote a letter to the Chancellor when the fisheries bill came up. A stupid subsidy to inlanders. They even call it farming. It would destroy the traditions of centuries. Wieland is *here* for men to go to sea. And now they're fish farming in Bavaria. The Chancellor thanked me for my opinion, sent me his photograph, and signed the bill anyway, the traitor.

Sorry for the blots. Everything is damp. I wish we could speak. But perhaps it is meant to be this way, so that my words will remain a testament instead of evaporating upon the air, temporary as the harbor, temporal as the harbor beast. And if I tell you what has taken its place you may not believe me.

They gave us the beast in return for eliminating our livelihood with the fisheries bill. A bond issue passed. Steelmongers arrived. Instead of eelmongers. This is no time for humor.

Okay, so the new prison brought jobs and money, but it cast a shadow on the port. With less competition, fishing should have been easy, but it wasn't. As if the fish shunned the coast once the waters had been poisoned by the hull of the barge.

Over time most of the men of our district gave up their lines and tackle for the ease and pension of state employment. Some moved inland to the fisheries, but most marched aboard *Farnhagen.*

Each morning they marched aboard and each evening they marched off to return to their wives and children on the solid side of the floating dock, wives and children buried now five fathoms deep. My neighbors these men, my friends. Their fathers were our father's friends. Their grandfathers stood shoulder to shoulder with our grandfather in the trenches. They were changed now, no longer men of the sea.

Thus they had no boats when the storm struck. Or none but the pleasure craft they kept in their garages to take out for a spin of a summer's evening to recall their ancestors' days upon the waves. Ah, those boats, made by American manufacturers, where the beer cooler was standard equipment. Now they find out that all fiberglass reacts under stress like a champagne glass flung into a brick fireplace.

Actually glass does not explode. Under pressure it implodes. It's the only thing I remember from high school. No other science, no math beyond what's necessary to calculate what's owed me at the market, and no history to speak of except what we picked up from the old folks who lived it. Then I had Sunday school.

But good, solid fishing boats were no help, either. It was not a storm to ride out to safety. It was clear. Not the weather, but the outcome. Clear as in obvious, not transparent. There was no refuge—except luck. You might as well stand in the square as hide in the cellar. The only salvation was through grace. Did I know this or did I learn it, or did I learn that I already knew it deep in my soul?

One month ago no one in Wieland knew from grace. There we were, anchored in *Farnhagen*'s lee, so permanent it seemed, both it and us. Whereas in reality, both it and us—we? grammar?—were no more secure than a tadpole on a griddle.

Perhaps our town was more akin to the beast than we preferred to recognize. And perhaps we were as great sinners as those abiding within the beast. Falsely flattering ourselves until our boats were loosed upon the same waters.

And what about those poor souls inside—what did we ever know about them? A truck brought them and money rained on our community. We lived off the blood of the down-trodden. They were not innocent, Lord knows, no more than we were. But the more they bled, the fatter we grew.

Yet what made them bleed but their bleeding of us? It's a formula. Every time you steal from Citizen X or kill Citizen Y you give Citizen Z a job. Judges, wardens, guards. Cooks and janitors in the prisons, too; they all need criminals. A symbiotic relationship.

Anyway, the Farnhagen barge encouraged a higher morality in Wieland. Our children seldom became criminals with this huge lesson ever present. Belief is an interesting phenomenon. I'll tell you about it.

How can a sinner believe, or is this language to you too foreign coming from me, Frieda? Do you remember how we used to laugh at the pastor? He seemed old even then. But that was before the *Farnhagen*. And now I am the chastened one, unnerved by the sight my own eyes have been fortunate enough to behold.

Came the storm. Not so pleasant in your portion of the country, and we here, accustomed we thought—how little we knew—to the anger of the sea, we had never experienced such a downpour, an onslaught, an assault from above. My words, they are taking on a specific tone now, but that is the new world in which we live. Let me tell you. My language is inadequate to the task. Let's just say it was . . . impressive. Massive. Destructive. More a natural force than mere weather.

You could see almost to heaven. A gash in the sky, a gush from the ether to Germany.

Those who could flee inland, uphill to Rostock, did. The pastor made it, running fast as his rubber-soled feet could scurry, but the bridge washed out shortly after noon, and the majority was stuck in the lowlands. There was no escape, no more escape than the poor souls inside the beast had had the day before. At first, we fought the good fight. Sandbags, barriers. No help. The dikes held fast and it didn't make a difference. The water rose over the top.

Some repaired to the church, climbed to the rafters, watching the water rise to the shins and thighs and shoulders of the stained-glass saints. Then they prayed.

Some men who had fled the barge at the first sign of trouble returned to it with their families. I wonder if the prisoners knew that their warders took comfort with them. I'd say half the town was on board.

Of course, all that didn't happen at once. It came by stages. First, the rain. Then more rain. So much rain, it simply seemed the texture of the universe. The flood came as a surprise. Even the other fishermen were unprepared—Stern; Schmelling. They forgot who they were and trusted to the land. Why? It had never sustained them before. They left their nets in the warehouse, a tangled worm's nest now that the water has retreated, leaving nothing but mold and mildew and the smell of death. This whole town is dead now, but the good news is that that doesn't matter anymore.

I cannot say why I ran to the shore while everyone else ran away. I claim no special wisdom. If anything, let's call it an inspired stupidity. I set to in my five-meter rowboat. It's my sturdiest. I didn't want to go anywhere in particular, and the storm wouldn't let me. Rather than try to ride out to sea, I enjoyed the novelty of rowing over the streets I had once cycled. That's where I stayed for as many days as my food held out.

Am I dreaming now after a month-long battle with nature, or have I just now woken after a month-long nightmare? I know that these are not the kinds of fancy thoughts you have come to expect from your brother and that you may not trust me with your portion of the property after hearing such blather, but this is the person I have become, and you must know it. The storm and its . . . consequences . . . have transformed me

Just as it seemed likely to continue forever, the storm broke, three days after the beast broke free, and I could see sky for the first time. A shining, glowing pearl of sky, shot with streaks of white—not clouds, but spots of pure, incandescent illumination.

And the water receded, a bit. I aimed toward the house, and only recognized it by the chimney. Its brick top poked above the waves like a reed in a still pond.

I am writing to you from the attic. It's a tiny bit less ruined than everything below. There the floors are buckled, walls crumbled, mud a meter thick in the parlor. I hitched the rowboat to the shutter with a long rope so when the water went down further the boat would not be left dangling, and I looked out to sea, the view no longer blocked by the beast. For a moment there was nothing—no town, no barge, no boats in the harbor, no telephone lines. It was like that for two days. Alone. Then, as I squinted, I began to make out something else.

I had my reward, Frieda. And now I tell you, and tell you to tell yours and tell them to tell theirs, to tell all the good news.

At first it seemed as if one segment of the calm sea was splashing. Yet instead of rising and descending, the curl of foam simply remained solid, like a caterpillar—no, that image is informed by my later knowledge of many feet. Besides, it was, at first, more abstract—a shape, not a substance. At first. For it came closer. It was moving and I could see it better. It was not one, but many. Many men, walking across the water.

I know what you are thinking. Any wine we had was in the basement, buried under water for the last few weeks, ruined by seepage through the cork. No, I saw what I saw at the same distance as, say, two or three or ten football fields. There's no way to describe how the image struck me, but one moment it was a blurry streak, and the next it was just close enough for me to distinguish a line of people walking across the water.

Do you understand what I'm telling you, Frieda? He is risen!

Yours,

Max

Half the planet shifted an inch and the other half was submerged. With each subtle singular motion, cities were inundated, shorelines redrawn. Boats smashed against each other like toys in a tub. Whales were tossed onto beaches. Jetties shattered. Docks flipped easy as playing cards; buoys bounced like marbles on concrete. A million houses from St. Petersburg to Normandy disappeared and kilometer-long bridges were shivered into driftwood.

More intimately, twelve men—eleven breathing—sprawled upon the green rubberized canopy that had flown off the barge during the storm like a yeshiva boy's yarmulke in a ghetto squall. For all their cumulative years asea, the former prisoners had never known the full power of the water surging around and surrounding them.

Now, the enormous green covering of the *Farnhagen* was no more substantial than a skullcap upon the heaving surface of the Baltic.

There was a word for this condition, and it was a voice in the dark that first named it: "Freedom."

Snakes recognized Glucks's accent, and besides, it came from his right, about two meters away. Instinctively, they had recreated the configuration of Cell #306.

"Huh?" Bruno didn't understand.

"It's like the wrestling ring, Blond. You can do anything within the ropes, but you can't cross those ropes. What else is freedom?"

Snakes could think of several answers. Lounging at the Kastrasse with a martini and his shoes up on an elephant-foot hassock, for one. But perhaps Bruno was correct, and he was free. To begin with, this meant that the body had to readjust to exterior space. No matter that they all resumed their prison positions. For the first time since the cell doors had slammed shut, the men could stretch a limb without risk of poking someone else in the eye.

And perhaps it meant a change in manners. Kiehr reached a hand out to help Ben Alef through the jagged tear in the wall of the *Farnhagen*.

And a wave surged up and Kiehr was nearly thrown into the sea. So much for Samaritanship. He should have known; he learned a lesson. That's what made him human.

So Ben Alef staggered onto the raft untouched, except by Eisenheim, his mortal burden slung sideways over his shoulders like saddlebags of gold over a mule. As soon as his foot touched the green raft, the seas underneath calmed.

"Welcome," Anton shouted into the wind, beginning again in a new world, trying to establish the same hierarchy they had left behind.

"Danke," Ben Alef murmured while looking nervously upward and taking his seat dead center, opposite Snakes.

All of them lay flat, clinging to the wet surface as they were borne up and down on the endless rhythm of the waves.

"It reminds me of the rides in the carnival that used to park in the lot by the river every year," Blobel said, and in the night his eyes were alight with the recollected bulbs of the Reifler Brothers Traveling Show.

"I know what you mean," Clauberg said. He loved neon nearly as much as he loved fire.

One by one, the other ex-prisoners' early memories emerged. These were incidents they had never spoken of inside the cell, yet once their bodies were liberated everything that had been incarcerated in their heads came pouring out. Most returned to some primitive fear and thrill. Some darkness, some dampness, some pain or ecstasy, some sex, witnessed, experienced, imagined.

But Snakes refused to relinquish his grasp on current events and, perhaps speaking in the voice of the dead Eisenheim, pointed out, "We're about to drown."

"Thanks for the information," Nazzarian sneered.

"Take a look."

"I don't see anything."

"Exactly." Where the lighthouse had been was ocean. The decks were gone. The town was gone. As for the barge itself, one second the *Farnhagen* was looming in its inconceivable vastness like an iceberg in the dark; the next, it was gone, like the *Titanic*, like Atlantis, like the Jews of Europe. "Nothing. There's nothing out there. You think you've been set free. For what but to die?"

Now the space felt oddly more constricted than inside a cell. Or maybe it was time that had shrunk to the moment. You couldn't anticipate a tray full of something called dinner. You couldn't even expect the light to go on, although it probably would—to a dawn of further nothingness. If this was the state they had all—Snakes for weeks, others for decades—yearned for, they had it, and they were all made crazier by heaven than they had ever been by hell.

Snakes looked at the faces of his companions during the infrequent flashes of lightning. He tried to avoid glancing outside their precarious circle, for fear of the endless nothingness beyond. For though he insisted on compelling them to recognize the fear of death, he was reluctant to face his own fear of water.

"Calm down," Snakes told himself. If he'd ever had to get used to a situation—on his own in the bad section of Hamburg; first time out with a frosty girl; at dinner with a suitcase full of cocaine and a loaded pistol; tossed into the *Farnhagen*—now, now, this was the time to do so.

He wondered if it would have been better to go to the bottom with the barge, together. This way, they were bound to be tossed off—or if they had the tiredness or temerity to sleep they might simply roll off—one by one, abandoned, alone.

Snakes's pants were wet, and it wasn't only water that wet them. So what? He was no longer the dandy who had stared down the institutions of rectitude and depravity with equal contempt. He hadn't cleaned himself since the storm began, and could no more imagine his knife saving him now than shaving him. He couldn't imagine any state other than pure, electrifying fear. It wasn't blood that went through his veins, but fear. It wasn't piss that stained him, but fear. It wasn't thoughts in his head, but fear.

As if in response, an enormous wave the size of a mountain reared like a waking dragon and took them on a roll down into a trough, and up again.

Langefeld clutched his belly and tried to vomit, but there was nothing left except spittle.

"Cheers," Snakes said, glad that he wasn't the only one stricken.

"Man, that was wild. Too bad the old goose-stepper didn't see it." Anton looked at Eisenheim.

Each to his own, Snakes thought. Anton was free, and surely afraid, but he was still hungry. Just like Glucks was free and horny, Palitzsch free and greedy, Nazzarian free and suspicious, Bruno free and stupid. All of them doomed and still precisely who they were.

Snakes could read Anton's thoughts. It was one thing to escape from the tomb; it was another to starve out on the open sea. Did Ben Alef bring the ancient Kraut forth for a snack? Would the salt spray add flavor, make

Eisenheim more palatable? Would it pickle the eyeballs, cure the lips permanently curled back, the gums exposed in an eternal sneer? Would their last act before the end reveal their true nature?

Appetite for life temporarily sated, they could focus on other things: food, memories, dreams. To each his fear, hunger, solitude. Only Snakes wondered how much longer the green raft could float.

"Maybe we could swim to shore," Bruno suggested.

"Which way?"

"Pick a direction, any direction," Omar said.

Giggles in the dark; it was hard to place them.

"Reminds me of the time my cousins were playing hide-and-seek in the summer house," Palitzsch said. It turned out he had come from a more prosperous home than any of them except for Kiehr, had presumably benefited from more of an education, and had gone wrong anyway. His father died young, but his mother took care of him, and when she died he sought out other mothers, married them, and killed them.

So be it. All the animated lightning that tore open the barge had bought them was another few hours before the elements claimed them. They sat atop the gigantic tomb, waiting for the winds to carry them away, chatting.

"So what's the charge?" Clauberg, who used to sit on the upper bunk next to Eisenheim, asked Ben Alef.

Nobody had quite addressed Ben Alef since he had first broken his silence back on board. "The charge?"

"Yeah. What are you in for?"

"In?"

"Well, out now . . . of jail."

There was a pause in which Snakes thought he'd have to explain what jail was, and then Ben Alef answered, "I don't know."

"What do you mean, you don't know."

Ben Alef smiled, a sweet youthful wrinkle that struck Snakes with unaccountable pity. "I woke up and saw you, all of you, as if you had always been there."

And Snakes, oddly, felt that Ben Alef *had* always been there, but Kiehr slapped his knee and said, "That's a nightmare." Even Snakes saw the humor, and their laughter shook the raft.

Nazzarian laughed, too. "Dinner will taste even better." He was contemplating dessert.

They hadn't noticed that their floating craft had taken them out of the storm, but once again a drizzle fluttered down and once again Ben Alef started whimpering. "Showers. Showers make letters. Letters make words."

"But words don't make sense." Nazzarian sneered.

"Start with a cross," Ben Alef chanted. His finger idly drew two intersecting lines in the drops atop the green rubber. "Then add to each limb." He leaned forward and dragged a delicate finger in a right angle from the four points of the cross, and the image twisted into a new form. "Showers," he moaned.

"Look, Benny," Anton interrupted. "Do me a favor: just cut the shower crap. Like how about shutting up for another five or six years."

"Who can tell?"

Was it only days before that Ben Alef's hair was thick and greasy as a shipyard rope, and his eyes were sunk so deeply into black pits that he looked half-human, half-ape? Now those eyes had been cleansed by the eruption in the cell and the despised showers; the hair was a fine wisp. Even his voice was boyish, though spoken with a particular accent, one that Snakes recognized but couldn't quite place. He thought he had heard it before—in a dream, perhaps, or another life.

Although the storm had seemed ferocious from inside, it was actually quite mild outside—unseasonably mild. It reminded Snakes of the mist that was coming down when he had last left the Kastrasse and stopped midway home to urinate. He remembered the church pulpit and imagined a spray-painted image desecrating the walls. And wondered if he had heard Ben Alef's voice in the empty church; but that was impossible.

"Hey, I've got a question, too," Clauberg called out. What were they—shills or a chorus?

"Yes," Ben Alef replied.

"How come the rest of us only have last names, and you don't? I mean as far as the cops go." He referred to the tags they were issued, like soldiers, that said, "Bartsch," "Morgen," "Nazzarian," et cetera.

"Yes."

"You heard me."

Ben Alef repeated, "Yes."

Nazzarian, though he had never shown much inclination to volunteer information, explained, "It's a two-part last name. 'Ben' isn't his first name."

"Yeh."

" 'Ben' means 'son of.' "

"So who's Alef?"

"I don't know."

"You don't know much, do you?"

"No, I don't."

"What sort of name is that?" Bruno asked.

Once again, Nazzarian knew. "It's a Jewish name."

They remembered the lank, tipless penis revealed when Ben Alef had stripped for Anton back on board.

"He must have been a very bad boy. You don't often find Jews in jail."

Snakes thought of the Peddler. A genetic predisposition to manipulation, wasn't that what was said about them, and wasn't it borne out in his own experience? But far from holding that against the Chosen People, Snakes had always found them attractive because of it; he had long since severed ties with his own ancestors' faith—and all of his most immediate ancestor's many, successive faiths—and found truth only in the sub rosa markets in which the secret Jews of northern Europe held sway. Why was theirs the only faith his father never knew?

Maybe it was the thought of his father, or a sudden recollection of the wet grave that waited for the passengers on the precarious lily pad, but Snakes felt apprehension rising, like water.

Okay, at other times in his life he had faced difficult situations and it always helped to focus one's mind. If the situation did not lend itself to analysis, still the action of focusing—on anything at all—honed one's reflexes to perform as needed. So he set himself to ponder what the crime of Ben Alef might have been; yet, rather than easing Snakes, this heightened his anxiety. As if it were the very cause of his anxiety. First, he felt an intuition. Snakes knew that intuitions—like "Someone's watching me" or "This deal stinks"—should be trusted, but this was too slight to be defined until a flash of lightning, clear as the burst that had felled Eisenheim, split the sky into segments. Like a twisted cross illuminating the night.

One fragment of a second and Snakes saw. He remembered the way Ben Alef had stood in the cell, right hand resting gently upon left arm. That left arm was uncovered now.

The man hadn't uttered another word. Yet he bore on his flesh the identification that Snakes alone saw as clearly as he had seen his father and his mother with their arms raised from a barrel of water to the sky, purple-blue marks of a hundred fangs on their arms. Saw in a flash the history of misbegotten faith and the blank stupid eyes of the believers. Saw, and could do no more than surrender.

Usually intuition matured into skepticism into plausibility into considered judgment into evidence, but this was no legal case. Nobody, least of all Ben Alef, was asking for Snakes's affirmation. Yet there it was, despite all logic, all sanity, proof positive, stark as words on a wall.

In the terror of Snakes's new vision, all his terror of the waves had dissolved, but this was not what he wanted, here at the end. No, if he was to die, he would not succumb to the kind of weak-kneed wishful-thinking ecstasy that had sustained pathetic souls through the millennia. No, he'd die as he lived—without a tenet or dogma or credo beyond himself, Snakes Hammurabi, on his own. Pure, raging ego.

Still . . .

Snakes turned toward the faces in the twin rows for confirmation, but none of the others had seen the vision vouchsafed him. Because it couldn't be true. It was chronologically impossible. It was logically impossible. Nevertheless, it was there. No matter that the afterglow of the lightning had faded; he still saw the glow of the flesh.

"I don't know."

"What do you mean, you don't know? Don't give me that innocent shit."

Now, as Snakes turned into the enraged aggressor, an unexpected ally came to Ben Alef's defense. It was Anton who said, "Leave him alone. Can't you see, he's an idiot."

"So are we."

"Now is the time," Ben Alef announced.

"For what?" Snakes said—or begged. He still felt unaccountably warm. At ease. At home on the green rubber lily, as the tidal swell of the Baltic pooled onto its surface and gradually filled its depressions with the weight of salt liquid. The water looked inviting. He opened his mouth to the rain. Opened his eyes to the glimmer of dawn. But the light was not coming westward from the sun, but emanating outward, from Ben Alef, illuminating the circle of raft, a penumbra of sea and then . . .

"Land ho!"

Dawn splashed over the horizon, and hills could be faintly discerned in the far distance.

"Must be five kilometers off."

"More like ten."

"Do I hear twenty?"

"Going, going, gone!" Kiehr hooted. "Sold to the man in the prison fatigues."

Ben Alef stood and looked across the glimmering pink clouds toward the contending sun at the opposite end of the universe.

"Thinking of swimming?"

"Hey, watch it."

Ben Alef squatted and lifted up the slack body of Eisenheim and started to the edge.

"Be careful," Bruno said.

"I think he's serious." It was Omar who was clearheaded now.

"What?"

"Splitsville, mein Bruder. He's leaving us."

And, out of the blue, Snakes made an announcement. "I'm going with him," he declared. This was as much of a surprise to himself as to the others, but he meant it, as much as he had ever meant anything in his entire life.

"I am, too," Bruno said.

"Me, three," Langefeld agreed.

"Are you all kidding?" Glucks cried. The former teacher was the voice of reason. "Hey, look, they'll rescue us soon."

"And do what? Put us back in prison?" Snakes replied. But that was beside the point. He had chosen paths before—off the army base, into crime—and they had been wrong. This was right. The clarity of destiny dispelled all doubt. Intuition had turned into rock-solid faith. He had no choice. "I'm going."

"You're killing yourself."

"So be it. Anyone else coming?" Snakes asked.

Bruno stood and Blobel stood and several of the older criminals hobbled to their feet. Snakes lent a hand to help Clauberg, the frail septuagenarian arsonist.

Ben Alef had already approached the edge of the raft without listening to the argument.

"Anton!" Glucks pleaded, "surely you're not going to listen to this craziness."

After a pause, Anton shrugged and stood, too.

"Omar, Omar, you're not going?"

None of them listened to him. Nazzarian said, "I guess I am."

"If all of you want to commit suicide, that doesn't mean I'm joining you. This is nothing but mass hysteria," Glucks ranted as the remaining company clambered to follow their peers to follow wherever Ben Alef led. "Lemmings."

They were all standing now, waiting for the signal like a line of kindergartners at a corner, waiting for the light to change.

"Wait!" Glucks cried, his own fear of solitude too great to let him remain, jumping up to make it unanimous.

Ben Alef smiled, and shifted Eisenheim onto his shoulders. He smiled again, and stepped off into the dark.

Chapter   Five

AT LEAST THAT WAS HOW Snakes recalled it while he lay onshore, hugging the contours of a pebbly beach with a delirium he had never known in human arms. He was almost afraid to open his eyes, for fear that he would discover he was still adrift or still on board the *Farnhagen* and dreaming of the one impossible path back to life. What did he know of life: a consulate here, an embassy there, a river, a military base, a limited set of bars, pickup and drop-off points, contact names, hookers, lawyers, safe-deposit boxes, luxury apartments, guarded subbasements with secret emergency exits, a church at midnight without an emergency exit, and a twenty-meter cell containing a . . . being . . . who led him out by the light of His eyes in an otherwise dark universe? For all Snakes knew, he was dead.

While his own eyes were shut, the warm pulse of the earth calmed Snakes, and the briny smell perked up his nostrils. He could hear breakers some distance away and suddenly remembered a bizarre walk through the pre-dawn illumination and the lapping water that soaked through his once splendid shoes and tickled his feet. Surrounded by kilometers of ocean— east, west, north, south, *down*—clearly doomed, he hadn't been afraid of water, for the first time since he was four years old. He just followed Ben Alef.

But where did he follow Ben Alef to? Perhaps they had descended a flight of watery footsteps and didn't even perceive the level at which water usurped the place of air in their lungs.

But even if he was dead, his nerves a bundle of retained impression that still buzzed through the slowly disintegrating synapses of his brain, fading yet occasionally sputtering like dying embers in a campfire, Snakes's insatiable curiosity was vividly alive, and he blinked. Crusted sand flaked off his lashes. He wiped his face, and more sand showered off his stubble. All of his senses reeled at the new world, at the luminousness of the beach, at the smell of rotting fish, at the pressure of pebbles and crushed clamshells on his wrist. He was exhausted and starved, but he was indisputably alive. He hauled himself up to his knees and looked around.

Ben Alef sat cross-legged, smiling. At him? The other ten men still lay prone, all of them silent as Eisenheim, stiff as a board in the center of their circle. Perhaps Ben Alef had carried him ashore for a proper earthly burial. The only odd element in the scene was about thirty meters off, where a grizzled local in a shabby suit and visored cap squatted and sucked on a straw.

"This is really weird," Snakes said to the man who had somehow—how?—saved him.

"Not really."

Snakes parsed Ben Alef's syntax. Not really weird, or just not real? He felt a meaning lurking. He felt a deep desire to interpret, to seek out the hidden message beneath the mere vernacular. Yet before Snakes could pursue his inquiries, Bruno stretched and yawned loudly, breaking the moment for potential confidence.

Bruno had an unlined face that betokened no such troubling thoughts as those that disturbed Snakes. He had no questions. He smiled at Ben Alef as might a newborn at the mother who gave him birth. But, of course, rationalists claimed that babies didn't smile. They attributed the facial expressions of infants to gas.

Snakes, a social and historical illiterate, couldn't even say where he had received information about babies or the events of the last century, but one thought led to another, and he hazarded an observation, "No showers."

Ben Alef nodded like a fine teacher at a wise student.

Clauberg stirred, and inadvertently touched Georg Kiehr, who also blinked and stretched, then announced, "I'm hungry."

"Have a little seafood," Nazzarian suggested. Though lying still, he had waked before the others and feigned sleep until now.

"Hmm." Kiehr took the sarcasm seriously and foraged over the beach until he found an intact sea creature washed up in the aftermath of the flood. He examined the thing: several jointed appendages extended from a mottled hull bulging with green meat. Then he popped it whole into his mouth, and made a horrendous slurping, cracking sound. "Not bad," the alleged cannibal judged, while about a thousand miniature black eggs dribbled out onto his chin, and he set forth to seek out more nourishment, not even bothering to leer over at Eisenheim, who might otherwise have provided breakfast.

The dead man's eyes stared at the waves of sand that spread inland. One nostril was buried in the sand; his arms lay at his sides, palms upward. Snakes remembered the sight of those hands flopping beside Ben Alef's thin frame as if gesturing "Follow me" from the land—or sea—of the dead as they crossed the waters. If they really had crossed the waters and Snakes hadn't imagined the whole episode, if he hadn't been smacked on the head by a stray beam of the broken barge and floated ashore.

Snakes kept thinking about that walk as he examined Ben Alef even more carefully than he had in the cell or out on the rubber lily pad in the ocean. The savior was thin. His clothes were tattered, sleeves torn, flesh exposed. In the perfect morning light, with not a wisp of cloud to mar the infinitely blue sky, the image that had only flashed before Snakes's eyes was utterly clear. He stared at Ben Alef's arm.

But before he could summon up the vaguest of historical connections, which must have filtered out of the common culture into Snakes's tiny uncommon corner, and figure out what it meant, the rest of the prisoners responded to Bruno's inadvertent wake-up call.

Clauberg, the oldest living though not the longest-term resident of Cell #306, mumbled, "What was that?"

"Who cares? Now we're really free."

"What?" Blobel repeated Clauberg's question. After three-plus decades of confinement, he was senile.

"Free, Zaydeh."

"What happened to Dietrich?" He pointed to Eisenheim.

"He didn't make it."

The old prisoner nodded thoughtfully and then turned matter-of-factly to the situation: "How do we get out of here?"

Anton nodded. "Atta boy, Pops." It was time to think clearly. The immediate danger having passed, a new danger loomed. No matter the cosmic flukiness of their rescue, the police would not consider it double-jeopardy grounds for parole; they would only find it fortunate that the men from Cell #306 survived in order to be reincarcerated. They'd be shipped inland or onto a new barge that three tugs could be hauling from the works at Rotterdam as they lay on the sand. The new *Farnhagen* would be stronger, less vulnerable to the elements than its predecessor. Georg Kiehr's family's shipbuilding subsidiary would see to that. "Better get away as fast as possible."

But how would they get anywhere? They had no cash, no connections, no charm, hardly any clothes. Blobel said, "You find an empty car, I can hot-wire it in twenty seconds."

"You find an occupied car"—Anton guffawed—"and I can empty it in ten seconds."

"And then where do we go?" Glucks asked. "There'll be an all-points bulletin out on every police radio from Hamburg to Danzig."

"No, there won't," Nazzarian corrected him. "That's the beauty of our situation. The *Farnhagen* is at the bottom of the Baltic with all hands and feet and heads. Nobody will be looking for us."

"Not to mention," Langefeld added, "there must be a lot of damage on shore. That was one hell of a storm. Reminds me of the tornado in *The Wizard of Oz.*"

"So we just steal a car and drive."

"For the border."

"For the capital."

"We can't fit into one car, anyway."

"So steal a bus."

"We should split up."

"We should stick together."

Busy debating the pros and cons of different modes of escape, the professional cons didn't realize that the man who had been squatting at a distance had crept up on them until he spoke. "Wouldn't do you any good. Bridge across the isthmus canal is out."

"Who the fuck are you?"

"Max Vetter."

"What are you doing here?"

"I live here. I'm a fisherman."

Snakes's head jerked toward Ben Alef. Several points of reference were coalescing.

Ben Alef just smiled.

"Hell of a storm, indeed," the intruder continued, "worst one since . . . worst one I've ever seen. You fellows from around here?"

"Pretty close."

Vetter spoke as if there were nothing in the least bit extraordinary about eleven men and a corpse appearing on an isolated beach without any visible means of transportation. For the moment, he didn't give any hint of what he had witnessed. "Well, you're here now, and there's no getting off. For the time being, we're an island."

"Hey, you." Anton nudged Ben Alef. "Can you walk us across the channel, too?"

This was the first time any of them had publicly acknowledged the events of the night before. Until now, it might have been a private dream, which no reasonable man would dare confess to confusing with experience. But these were not reasonable men. Anton opened the gates, and Langefeld entered immediately, "Hey, why not Sweden?"

"Or America?" Glucks said. "Lead us to America."

"Why not Rostock?"

Only Snakes, who had lived and thrived in the mayhem until two months earlier, had any sense of what home to make his way back to, yet even he wondered how eagerly the Peddler would take him in. Snakes was practical enough to understand that just as his partner would glance up from his regular booth in the Kastrasse and hoist a champagne glass at his associate's unexpectedly early return, there might be a fraction of a second of silence in which one could almost hear the gears of mental arithmetic as the Peddler calculated whether Snakes was worth more at large or in stir. And the truly remarkable thing was that suddenly Snakes just didn't want to go to the Kastrasse or anywhere else, and surely not America. He wanted to remain on the ruined beach, happy as Bruno.

This made it even more frustrating that his companions didn't seem to value the moment. By focusing on their own minor dilemma, they were ignoring something infinitely larger than themselves.

"Hey!" Snakes shouted, needing to rub their noses in the amazing truth that ought to have been self-evident. Something had happened, and they all knew it, yet none of these idiots bothered to acknowledge its existence, let alone importance. "Let's not forget that we're here."

Nazzarian took up Snakes's half-articulated challenge. "Lucky for that sandbar."

"Sandbar?" Snakes repeated incredulously. He hadn't been able to see anything during their weird stroll, but he had damn well felt fathoms of water underneath him.

"Yes, a sandbar, formed and then probably swept away, a magic carpet whisked to oblivion."

"There was no sandbar," Snakes countered, weakly.

"What do you think, there was a miracle?" Nazzarian spat out the word that Snakes himself couldn't.

"Well . . ." He looked toward Ben Alef, but the person who should have known better than any of them refused to offer a word in His own behalf.

"No sandbar," Max Vetter interrupted again. "I know this harbor like the back of my hand, every centimeter. I've been sounding these waters since I was a guppy. No sandbar. Look around you." He gestured to the field of small gray pebbles. "No sand."

Snakes was relieved by the fisherman's statement. He had been battered, imprisoned, starved, nearly drowned—ought to have been drowned—and, contrary to Nazzarian's insidiously tainting skepticism, miraculously saved, yet all he could feel was infantile bliss. The fisherman had verified his intuition.

Teasing away at the perimeter of his consciousness was a sense of pure, untainted ecstasy that he had felt only once before. Where? It must have been in the company of his father, the senior Hammurabi, as they walked tiny hand in big hand toward the River Lyons, before the terror of the immersion.

"There had to be a sandbar," Nazzarian insisted.

But Snakes called upon a higher logic. "And even if there was a sandbar, in that whole ocean, don't you think it was a . . ." He still couldn't use the "m" word. ". . . remarkable that we found it?"

"No, I think that was a lucky break."

"You think the lightning was a lucky break, too?"

"No, I think that was electricity."

They looked toward Ben Alef Himself, but the presumed source of their deliverance remained silent. Instead of paying the least attention to the debate, He was looking carefully at Eisenheim.

"Or maybe we all imagined it together." Omar didn't have the precise scientific terminology, but he implied a communal hallucination. History was full of examples of shared illusion in every realm from the patriotic to the financial to the spiritual: witch trials, tulip mania, revolutionary fervor, strange beliefs that swayed crowds. And none was stranger than the belief Snakes felt now.

Educated on the back streets of Hamburg, Snakes didn't have much of a historical framework, but he knew well how people could convince themselves of anything. He also knew that he personally could convince most people of anything. But his skills had always been used purely for his own gain. Now, for some reason, he felt that he, too, had a mission: to convince people, for their own good, that there was a truth as hard as it was necessary to believe. Still, as Omar Nazzarian couldn't use the language of science, Snakes couldn't fully verbalize this new language of faith to refute the attacks of infidels. What about the storm stopping? They would have a direct, meteorological explanation. It had gone its course. Yes, but why? And why was the midwinter weather still so balmy?

And what about walking on water—not only the blunt, astonishing fact, but the sense of perfect tranquillity that came from it? How could Snakes describe the ineffable nourishment of the soul, which hardly required the mind's affirmation?

For a second, he thought that the calm, sweet figure of Ben Alef was not sitting on the same beach, but hovering a single layer of air above it, as He had skimmed over the water while carrying Eisenheim, and, by virtue of the invisible tie that linked all of them, the others, too. What it meant, he wasn't sure. It simply *was*. "He brought us out."

"He's not taking you anywhere," Omar scoffed.

"Well . . ." Ben Alef's voice punctured the dialogue. It was soft, but it was a clarion that called all attention.

Was He denying Snakes, or affirming something yet grander? Why did every utterance from His lips create an echo?

"I cannot take you."

"No!" Snakes cried, and then, immediately, "Yes!" as he understood. Ben Alef could not take them, because they had to take themselves. They simply had to, because the consequences of their failure would be immense. Snakes pondered what might occur if they didn't believe . . . but if they did . . . could the . . . miracle . . . be true simply as a result of their belief?

On the other hand, if they didn't believe, wouldn't that destroy the chance for something . . . significant? There had been a moment out there in the ocean, and when Snakes first woke to a new life back on earth, when the rules did not apply—a moment of perfect freedom. No, that wasn't true, either. There were different, stranger rules that somehow, yes, mirac- ulously, entailed a vaster freedom than any mere government granted its citizens.

But only if they deserved it, and the only way they could prove that was by action in accordance with the new principles. Snakes felt an un- graspable yet unutterably precious idea collapsing, and tried to explain. He babbled about the waters flowing into the cell and through the cell and around the lily pad and under their feet. He couldn't stop himself. He went on about the water raining into the ocean, and the evaporation from the ocean feeding the clouds in an eternal cycle. He was strong when silent; his volubility revealed a new weakness, which meant a new opportunity for anyone disposed to take advantage.

Nazzarian looked at him—and saw this weakness in the man with the knife. If they were back onshore, free in the wild world, a knife would come in handy.

Snakes saw Omar's expression a moment too late. He saw a man who was vulgar and vicious and belonged in jail. But he didn't see what the vul- gar, vicious man who belonged in jail was about to do. His reflexes had been dulled by bliss.

Nazzarian leapt at Snakes.

Caught off guard, Hammurabi fell backward. Then the street- fighting reflexes of his past life kicked in, and he pushed off the man whose fingers were already around his throat.

Omar rebounded and pounced again. Locked in struggle, the two men rolled across the sand into the body of Eisenheim, and then over the body into the space beside the dead man.

Anton smirked and bent down behind Eisenheim. He reached under the limp body and hoisted its weight upward into an upright position. "Look, Dietrich," he shouted gleefully. "You like what you see?"

Jaw clenched by his master's fingers, the dead puppet wagged his head back and forth. "Ja, ja. I like," Anton answered for Eisenheim from behind the mane of white hair. "But who shall win? Any bets?"

And the two dark men, one fighting for life and truth, the other for a gleaming shank of whetted and pointed steel, continued to fight, and Omar continued to win, partly because of surprise and partly because most of Snakes's energy was still going into trying to explain himself. "A miracle," he sputtered into his assailant's face. "The new dominion," he gagged.

Then Anton let the head of his puppet drop and gripped Eisenheim's right arm and shot it upward in salute. "All heil!" Anton shrieked in imitation of Dietrich's thick accent. "I mean hail, the new dominion."

Blobel and Clauberg laughed.

It was the same scene that had played itself out in the *Farnhagen* cell time after time. Snakes remembered his first day, and saw Eisenheim's white hair flying like thread, except this time Snakes was the victim, and he didn't have the Kommandant's strength or crazy stamina.

So, while the audience shouted at the two on the ground, laying wagers and commenting on their technique, Snakes's mind grew blanker and blanker as Omar's fingers dug deeper into his throat. Hammurabi's grip on Omar's wrists was weakening, his brain fluttering in and out of consciousness. In another moment, he knew, he had to succumb.

"Arise," Ben Alef said.

"How?" thought Snakes. He was underwater and all he could see was fingers.

But it wasn't Snakes whom Ben Alef addressed. The direction of His voice was elsewhere. He reached out and touched Eisenheim.

In bright day, without a cloud in sight, lightning struck.

The dead man's eyes popped open.

"Holy shit!" yelped Anton and dropped his burden, and even Omar Nazzarian let Snakes go, while the others stared.

Eisenheim remained upright, and his arm remained upright. From the moment he opened his eyes, he knew where he had been and where he was and what had occurred.

"Oh, my," Langefeld sighed, and swooned.

Eisenheim looked at the eyes of the man whose touch had summoned him from the depths of . . . wherever. They were the same clear deep brown they had always been. Something registered and Eisenheim blinked and saw beyond the eyes, beyond the long hair of confinement and the lineaments of starchy *Farnhagen* diet. He saw a shaven head encased in gaunt skin stretched tight to the skull. He looked at the arm of the deliverer.

Then they all saw what Snakes knew. There was a tattoo, executed in artless aniline blue, between Ben Alef's wrist and elbow. It was a number: 108016.

Unless the number had been self-imposed in a moment of high apostasy at a tattoo shop in a basement in East Berlin, the only human beings who bore this sign were those who had received it at the blazing tip of a

German tattoo during the years 1942–1944. Survivors of those years still lived, having nightmares, writing memoirs, dandling grandchildren on their knees, but they were seventy and eighty years old by now. Nobody of Ben Alef's age was around, nor had they been for nearly half a century, unless one could draw the single extraordinary conclusion. And how could one deny it?

"I knew I saw you before," Eisenheim said. "In Belsen in '44. You came on a transport from the East and went to the showers."

"And now I am clean."

"He is risen," Max Vetter said. "Resurrected."

"My Lord," Bruno gasped, and fell at Ben Alef's feet.

"Yes," Snakes nearly sobbed, putting it all together. "This man is the Messiah."

"Da," Eisenheim said as maybe he had been about to say back in Cell #306 before he died and before he, too, was resurrected by his consummately forgiving Lord. As entirely he had once believed in a god with a toothbrush mustache, he now believed in this new deity, and he knew what he had to do. He spat in the Messiah's face.

Where they slept, Snakes couldn't remember—although they must have camped near the village for more than a day, less than a week. He had no sense of the passage of hours. "December," someone mentioned, but it might as well have been June or 1848. His mind was aswirl with sensation, emotion, and the image of Ben Alef. Nothing else registered, not the weather, not even hunger, though Max Vetter concocted a rough soup from springwater, swamped garden vegetables, and beached codfish. For all Snakes knew, they feasted on the air and the few words that came from their new, or, as Max claimed, newly risen, Lord's clear tongue.

After Eisenheim spat at Ben Alef, Snakes lunged for the ancient killer with even greater ferocity than Omar had exhibited moments earlier or than Anton had showed a month ago, back on Snakes's first day in the now drowned *Farnhagen*. But if Omar's attack had been premeditated, while Anton's was a matter of habit, Snakes's assault was neither deliberate nor dull. He hadn't thought about it; he simply reacted to the shock of the sight of the jet of saliva that dripped down Ben Alef's pale cheek. One second

Snakes was sitting in the circle of wonder, and the next second he was on top of the miserable octogenarian.

He didn't care how old Eisenheim was. Something about those cornflower eyes in the midst of that woodcut face enraged him. Nor was this reaction, which Eisenheim gleefully exacerbated by endless, insistent provocation of everyone he encountered, uncommon. Dating way back from the days when he was kleine Dieti, tearing the wings off butterflies, throwing away the lovely iridescent tissues and keeping the twitching torsos until they expired, he found or created an atmosphere of perverse and malicious depravity. Perhaps that was why he survived the war, because he was too mean to die. Prisoner or imprisoner, it didn't make much difference to him. He thrived in rancor, and didn't really care if it emanated from him or extended toward him, so long as he could breathe the undiluted air of poison.

Snakes's fingers clenched the old man's scrawny throat; he could practically feel his thumbs meeting the rest of his fingers as if the last shreds of meat in the channel from Eisenheim's head to his chest had disappeared and the skin was an empty cloth tube. Still he pressed with all his strength. In no knife fight over distribution of illicit profits in a warehouse in Hamburg, in no gun battle over ten kilos of cocaine on the back streets of Rostock, in no adrenalinized or erotic moment had he ever acted more intently. Eisenheim's hands fluttered and lay still by his side, and still Snakes pressed as hard as he could on the flimsy pipe. He was smelling the final rank exhalation from the pit of Eisenheim's lungs when he felt another hand on his own shoulder, and instinctively snapped, "Bug off! Who do you think you are?"

"I'm . . . not sure."

The hurt in Ben Alef's eyes as much as the warmth of IIis touch stopped Snakes immediately. He bent his head and let go of Eisenheim's throat.

Who, indeed, was this man? The convicts muttered ominously, their relief at finding themselves alive immediately superseded by their doubt about how they arrived onshore.

"He's one of us," Palitzsch said.

"Just another con," Glucks agreed.

"I'm not sure," Bruno echoed Ben Alef.

Omar Nazzarian looked around and realized that most of his companions were too stupid to believe the evidence of their senses, whereas he was too smart. In either case, belief itself was not an option. Besides, nothing had changed. Once again, Eisenheim was dead, innocent blue eyes rolled up inside his knob of a skull—there was no keeping this guy alive—and one of them was guilty. No matter that the killer was the only one of them arrested for a petty misdemeanor; the rest were accessories, and whatever mystery they thought they had participated in was meaningless. The only vital thing was to get out of there.

"How?" Blobel said.

The car thief merely referred to the lack of transportation, but he was righter than he knew. Vehicle or no vehicle, they were bound as if by invisible ropes, still incarcerated in an invisible cell.

This cell, however, stretching to the horizon, was too small. Bang each other's heads against bricks, rape each other, steal each other's food: all okay according to the *Farnhagen*'s unwritten code. Now, however, without bars or barbed wire to restrain them, the limits of acceptable behavior were as vast as the sea, and long-simmering rivalries and resentments erupted.

"How?" Langefeld imitated Blobel's accent.

"Shut up and get yourself a little boy."

One of the prisoners had just strangled another, and all the rest could think to do was to break into schoolyard name-calling.

"Who do you think you are?"

"Wait, wait, wait." Max tried to calm the men. He was not one to speak in public, but neither was he one to see visions, and he had been transformed, and couldn't believe that the visions themselves remained stiffly untransformed—except for the one who had brutally throttled the old man. "You're forgetting something."

"What?"

"What?" Max repeated, astounded. Didn't these creatures understand the gift they had been given? Or were they just too frightened to acknowledge it? If that was the case, it was his job, a job forced upon him, to force them to understand, whether they preferred to or not, and one thing Max could understand was the necessity of hard labor. He spoke simply: "You've just walked across the ocean. And you've just witnessed a resurrection. He"—he pointed to Ben Alef—"saved your lives."

"Who invited him?"

"He doesn't even know who He is."

"But I do," Max said.

"Tell us." Omar dared the fisherman to display his catch, to prove that it wasn't just another fish story. If it's really that-a-a-a-a-a-at big, then lay it on the table.

"For He is the Lord," Max Vetter explained.

There it was. Yet the statement, straight as a harpoonist's rope in front of them, was hard to accept. "Easy for you to say," Anton joked.

"No," Max said, "it's not easy at all. But it's"—he paused, and then concluded—"true."

"I don't know what to believe," Clauberg moaned.

"Just believe what you see," Max said. "I do."

"I don't know what I saw," Kiehr said.

"Then believe what you feel." Max strived to convince.

"What's that?"

Doubts about feelings and doubts about facts and doubts about doubts circled the circle of ex-convicts as none of them could figure out precisely where they stood while standing around the corpse of the Nazi Kommandant. Murder didn't faze them, but freedom did: freedom from physical prison and a dramatic new freedom from more universal human constraint. These were more disturbing than a confinement that also bred security.

"Maybe we should turn ourselves in."

"Maybe we should kill ourselves."

"What's the difference?"

"Maybe Ben Alef will perform His tricks again," Glucks suggested.

"Maybe He already did." Snakes interrupted the fractious argument as he noticed something odd about the man at his feet. Ben Alef had raised Eisenheim from the dead once . . . at least once. Or had he simply carried a wounded man to shore, where he naturally revived? But now Eisenheim was dead again. Or was he? Had Snakes really extinguished life, or had he braked, been braked, a hair before he crossed the boundary from which there was never a return, never, never, never unless . . .

Suddenly the apparently dead man's shrunken lungs inflated with another breath of life, his throat regained its substance, with two large purple blotches in the shape of Snakes's thumbs, and—maybe—reborn for the second time in as many minutes, Eisenheim croaked, "Couldn't bring yourself to do it, could you?"

"No," Snakes admitted.

"Don't worry. You'll learn."

. . .

Further debate must have occurred as they scavenged in the storm-abandoned villages along the shore, but Snakes couldn't remember much; he was too consumed with his own internal dialogue, pondering the events since his arrest, to listen. All he recalled of those strange, early days was the invigorated Eisenheim complaining, "I don't like this."

"At least someone has an ounce of brains," Omar said. "Let's split."

"I didn't say I wanted to go anywhere with you, Black Boy."

"Likewise, Kraut. But I didn't mean we have to split together. I was more inclined to go it alone."

"So go, already." Max, wiser by the day, called Omar's bluff. "Go ahead and we'll stay here, or stay here and we'll continue."

Nazzarian kicked at a stone and glanced at Ben Alef, who said nothing.

Despite the ostensible freedom to peel off, there was no place any of them could imagine to escape to from the history they already shared. The twelve men and Max Vetter were as inextricably linked as they had been when circumscribed by *Farnhagen*'s cinder blocks. Think of an Alabama chain gang. Think of a Phoenician galley. Think of a space shuttle with a couple of aluminum-clad astronauts orbiting the moon. Hiding by day and walking inland after dark, the refugees had no more choice of company and consequence than two drivers speeding toward each other at a hundred and twenty kilometers an hour around a one-lane blind bend, until they arrived at the Kaltenhaven church.

Chapter Six

THE PONTIFF PLUCKED a soft, acorn-sized treat from the crystal bowl on the round café-style table that sat between his chair and the window overlooking St. Peter's Square. Shriveled, puckered, resembling a lichee, the treat dripped some of the jellied solution it had been steeping in onto the table's gray and white marble inlay, which formed a chessboard from a series of interlocking stars.

Immediately, an aide appeared at the Pontiff's shoulder. He was a fidgety novice holding a linen handkerchief to wipe off the liquid. He also clutched two curious metal implements.

The Bishop of Rome extended his free hand and the aide, stunned by the resemblance of the gesture to Michelangelo's deity downstairs, froze.

A strangely youthful snap of the fingers restored his awareness. "Yes, Your Holiness. Forgive me," the aide stammered and presented him with the first of the implements. It was a clamp, into which the elderly man, his face shriveled, puckered, also resembling a lichee, inserted the treat. Shifting the clamp back to his left hand, he then accepted the second implement, a scalpel, and sliced the treat along a raised seam in order to more easily peel the nubby rind off the small, oblong, fruitlike luxury. He folded the skin back from the pinkish pulp interior and squeezed gently.

Not gently enough. The treat jumped out, and he reached for it, and missed, and it bounced onto the table with a liquidy splat. The implements clattered from his frail grip to the floor and the aide quivered with a second's internal debate. Should he stoop to pick up the the tools first or try to help with the gooey treat?

The Pope smiled, lifted the treat between two wrinkled fingers, and popped it into his mouth. Smiling kindly, he said, "Only one a day."

"Doctor's orders, Your Holiness," the aide replied, pleased that he had been so intimately addressed.

"Alas." The Pope, too, remembered his doctor's words about moderation, and gazed fondly at the bowl in which a dozen more treats swam about in sultry solution, like so many eyes staring at him.

"Yes, Your Holiness."

The Pope contemplated the cut-glass bowl. If Urban IX had had it his way, he would have feasted on treat after treat against doctor's orders and spent the rest of the afternoon doing nothing but gorging and gazing at the pigeons in the square.

"Father Immaculato, Your Holiness, at eleven."

"Yes," the spiritual leader of nine hundred million believers sighed wearily. He would do as he must, but for a moment he pondered the nature of the man undoubtedly pacing impatiently in the anteroom, checking his inappropriately elegant Swiss watch twice every minute while waiting for the audience to commence. Like all encounters between the two men, it was bound to be extremely distasteful. The only question was who would find it more distasteful. Surely Urban IX's predecessors, at least those who had occupied the papal throne since Galileo, hadn't had to deal with such things.

"It's after eleven, Your Holiness, and after Father Immaculato there's an American senator and—"

"Listen." The Pontiff interrupted his aide by lifting a jelly-coated finger to call attention to the choir of boys in the background. Their sweet cadences floated on the air like birdsong, the paean to eternal deity as immaterial as the air itself.

"Lovely."

"Yes." Music was the part of his job that never tired Urban. Hymns, chants, madrigals: he loved being surrounded by the rhythms human beings made to simulate the divine music of the spheres. Unlike other popes, he attended symphonies and operas whenever his schedule permitted, and even enjoyed meeting regenerate rock stars who had abandoned their wild, flagrant careers for a more glorious reward.

Born in an isolated mountain village outside Padua, Urban, né Giuseppe Caldino, had sung in choir and simply lived for music until a moment of revelation. One day, the village was blessed by a visit from the regional cardinal. Preparations had been extensive; as part of the service, the choir was to perform "Dei Excelsius." The eleven-year-old Giuseppe stepped forward to sing a one-line solo, but in the midst of that line his high, clear, infinitely rehearsed voice suddenly hit the "wolf tone" whereupon it horrifically, inexplicably jumped an octave.

The cardinal's gently nodding head whipsawed toward the boy.

Giuseppe cringed, barely managed to finish the line, and felt like killing himself. After the service, he fled the church, but the cardinal caught up to him in the small village cemetery. Surrounded by mossy tombstones under the shade of a pomegranate tree, they spoke, the man in his purple robe and the humiliated child in his tear-stained smock. "Music," the man said, "is the sign we give to ourselves of our faith. And sometimes music returns a sign to us."

"Y . . . y . . . yes," Giuseppe blubbered.

"Continue with your studies, musical and otherwise, and when you are ready—and you will know—you must send me a note to tell me what you have learned. And remember, words are signs, too."

So Giuseppe understood that all human harmonies were only a pale shadow of divine music, and that the beautiful words that had once come so naturally from his preadolescent mouth were there not merely for themselves, but to praise a being beyond comprehension, a being who, in His infinite wisdom, had given the child a voice and taken it away upon the advent of the wolf tone. Compelled to abandon singing as his voice changed, Giuseppe threw himself into his studies. Oh, perhaps he always felt a mild regret for one missed calling, but the passion he had invested in the reading of notes served him well when applied to the reading of texts.

Astonished by the lad's audience with the cardinal, the local school teachers subsequently succored him as a child with promise, a promise the inspired acolyte abundantly fulfilled. Upon ordination, he was invited to Rome to enter into an ecclesiastical career as the cardinal's own adjunct. He acted in this capacity until the opportunity came for his own advancement into the College of Cardinals, where he served for many years until he officiated at his mentor's funeral, and when the election for a new pope was held a year ago, Giuseppe's selection seemed obvious. On the first ballot, a stream of white smoke emerged from the Vatican flue. Half a century of service, and suddenly the newly christened Urban IX occupied the chair. It seemed as if he had been born there, at the age of sixty-eight, wearing a mantle instead of a caul.

John Paul II, the previous pope, had presided over a renewal of faith, especially in Eastern Europe, but also in Latin America. Even normally Islamic strongholds in Africa and Asia had recently provided fertile territory in which the church could extend its vast web of theological and political missions while dealing with secular authorities while maintaining the largest social welfare organization in the world. On a day-to-day basis, however, the job had been more or less ceremonial until now.

The main problem Urban faced was the Vatican doctor, who monitored him against his will and insisted on keeping him alive until his seventieth birthday, or at least until the next thousandth anniversary of their Lord's birth. But that very anniversary had opened the gates to a spate of millennial expectations that had begun to take the form of upsetting apparitions. In Georgia in the United States, a Mary cult drew twenty thousand spectators at weekly worship sessions, and in Xualtepeca, Mexico, a peasant boy was reported to receive messages from Jesus through the agency of a blinking Texaco sign. But those phenomena were easily discounted or taken under the church's own generous cloak, and none to reckon with had yet occurred in Rome's own capacious, continent-wide backyard. Perhaps such an event was inevitable, and Urban was lucky that the calm had lasted this long, but the message that had arrived at breakfast was, though minor, disconcerting. He agreed to listen further not because the story was so fearsome, but because, like the wolf tone, it might represent something larger than itself. He might even consider this silly, isolated incident inoculatory, a sample of the disease with which to vaccinate the body of faith.

Abruptly, the boys' choir ceased its music as their daily recital came to its ecstatic conclusion.

The Pope felt a nasty twinge in one of his back teeth—he needed to see the Vatican dentist—and said, "Send in Father Immaculato."

The aide nodded and left, already juggling the day's schedule in his head to compensate for lost time. He shut the nine-foot carved-walnut door behind him, and a moment later opened it again to allow a handsome young prelate to enter the papal chamber. Though tall, this newcomer was dwarfed by the gigantic jambs he stood between, waiting—perhaps a second too long—for the Pontiff to gesture to the chair opposite him at the intimate café table. But at least he waited at the far end of the room, saving his pride by not having to stand at Urban's heels before his existence was acknowledged. Finally summoned, his heels clicked on the strip of mineral between twin carpets that covered most of the stone floor. He was the only one who walked on the strip instead of the carpet, the clicking of his heels the only statement of personal presence he was allowed to make, and that only because of the pretense that it wasn't deliberate. He took the seat opposite the Pontiff and waited for another three long minutes.

They sat in silence while the Pope chewed the last remains of his treat and then turned to the matter at hand. "Tell me."

"The first call came from a village priest." Father Immaculato was all business.

The Pope folded his hands in front of his belly and nodded. He had already heard several fractured versions of the same tale, and had sent Immaculato to investigate. The young man reminded Urban IX a little of himself fifty years ago, smart and dedicated, but Immaculato would never be Pope, nor would he wear cardinal's red. He was too smart, too cutting; he had neither humility nor patience with fools, and the fools he had no patience with resented him precisely because they knew they deserved his disdain. Once, when a meeting between Cardinals O'Flaherty and Monzini and a group of Catholic Boy Scouts from America was described to Father Immaculato, he asked, "Weren't there any grown-ups?" He made too many enemies, and not least among them was the present occupant of the chair he coveted. Nonetheless, he was valuable. The Church was aware that the Church no longer automatically attracted the best minds of its generation, and therefore it treasured and rewarded those it did attract. At the age of twenty-five, Immaculato ran the Vatican press office; he might someday be in charge of the Jesuit educational system. With a less strong leader than Urban IX at the helm, he could become the power behind the throne, but this Pope was determined to keep him in his place, to serve primarily as the Church required.

Immaculato went on. "The Monsignor who took the call thought that Father Kepler had drunk a bit too much at the party and told him to watch the sauce. Apparently, the Father has been known to dip into the sacramental vats. It was a logical assumption."

Urban ignored the aspersion. He did not enjoy hearing of the foibles of his flock. He said, "But this is not a logical situation."

"No, not at all."

"Start at the beginning."

Three boys were singing in Kaltenhaven. Unlike the trained choir that soothed God's rock a thousand kilometers south, they were off key. Unlike the denatured voices in the Vatican, theirs cracked. Unlike the perfect white Egyptian-cotton robes with glittering golden threads worn under St. Peter's dome, these boys' robes were made of slick, stained polyester, and sneakers poked out from beneath their ragged hems. Nonetheless, they sang their hearts out for about forty people gathered about half a dozen redwood picnic tables set up on the lawn outside the chapel. In order to take advantage of the altogether unusual springlike weather, the ceremony was to be held out of doors, in a mating of ancient theology and modern ecology.

Aside from the choir, which aspired to a celestial vision, the rest of the participants in the scene were rustic. One young man wore an ill-fitting black suit, its collar chafing his carpenter's neck, a sun-ruddied slab unused to such formality, while the young woman beside him kept plucking nervously at her rented, beaded gown, which was just as unfamiliar to her as his suit was to her groom. Various guests attempted formality in their own fashion, here with a shiny-elbowed jacket that had been worn at every occasion for decades, there with an invariably too-small and painfully passé knockoff of a ludicrously passé dress. A priest in his vestments floated among the people, and most of the talk was still, a week after the fact, about the storm.

"Insurance company won't pay Hendrick for his lost cow. Says she might have wandered off anyhow."

"Cows don't wander off; this one swam off."

"You'n I know that, but the insurance company doesn't."

"Or pretends not to."

"Least the electricity's back."

"They're working on it."

Though not a fishing village, Kaltenhaven was close enough to the Baltic shore to feel the effects of the tempest that had sunk the *Farnhagen.* Basements were flooded, roads precarious, valuable livestock endangered if not destroyed. Most of the population of the village had taken refuge in the regional high school at Rostock, which had its own generator, stock of food, blankets, and medical supplies, until the government radio station gave the okay to return home.

Unfortunately, the homes people returned to were not as they left them. Without advance warning, a secondary—human—storm had swept through Kaltenhaven at some point after the last villagers fled. Fearless vandals, defying nature, apparently drove a van—or a convoy of vans, because the same thing had occurred in a score of villages—along slippery roads and through abandoned neighborhoods, parked in broad daylight, and removed every television set, VCR, CD player, computer, and jewelry box they could get their hands on.

"Least the insurance people can't say my satellite dish wandered off."

"Bastards!"

"You mean the insurance people or the thieves?"

"Take your choice."

"Too bad the *Farnhagen* isn't ready for them."

"But you know . . ."

"Yeah?"

"Gonna build a better one."

"That's true." There was one advantage to the situation. Kaltenhaven was a working-class village, most of whose men were carpenters and plumbers and masons who looked forward to much additional work in the next year rebuilding every structure that had been damaged for a hundred kilometers in either direction. In this way, the storm was a blessing, bound to bring prosperity in its calamitous wake.

"Just hope the Irish don't come."

Construction workers from the Emerald Isle were known to travel across the world, to take advantage of any opportunity. When Hurricane Andrew struck in Florida in '92, they were on the first plane to Miami, and in '95, when an earthquake broke up the freeways of Japan, they went there. And that was a distance from Dublin, as illegal workers on a tourist visa. Given Europe's internally open borders, catastrophe's green handmaidens were bound to rush to Germany.

"Vultures."

"There's enough work for everyone."

"Long as the storm's really over."

"Didn't think it would ever end."

And the conversationalists looked up.

"Who can tell?" The second man shrugged and held a palm to the empty and brilliant sky.

Even after the storm finally dissipated, there had been strange meteorological symptoms that the weather reporters couldn't interpret. Even after the storm, with not a cloud for two hundred kilometers, the barometer still bobbed up and down like a psychotic yo-yo.

"Least it won't stop the nuptials."

"No way."

"Not today."

So even though everything was damp and their houses were pillaged and their region a shambles, the people of Kaltenhaven assembled.

The priest signaled the beginning of the service. "We are gathered here today . . ."

Conversations died down, and for a moment the only sound was that of the three choirboys, who desperately attempted to fill the sudden hush that surrounded them. The boys' voices rose and fell and took weird, uncharted side trips, only occasionally coinciding in a semblance of melody. The priest listened for a while, alternately nodding his head and wincing until finally he gestured, with a single finger across his throat, for the three musicians to stop their caterwauling and scoot into the church kitchen to remove their robes and help prepare the wedding feast.

"To join this couple, Hans Wolf and Julia Schillinger, in holy matrimony."

"Don't they look lovely?" The bride's mother choked back a sob.

The priest ushered everyone closer together, into a tight circle around the awkward groom and horse-faced bride. Father Kepler had married most of the people in the square, had buried their parents and baptized their children, and was now marrying those children and fully expected to baptize Hans and Julia's children and bury their parents. "May God be with them." He opened a breviary and began a rapid recitation of the Latin text. "In the name of the Father, the Son, and the Holy Ghost . . ."

Before he could finish the sentence that would turn two into one under the auspices of the mystical Trinity, however, one of the three choirboys burst from the church door and screamed, "It's gone."

Father Immaculato pretended to be distracted by a cluster of tourists in the square fifteen meters below the open casement window. Of course the tourists appeared no larger and were no more significant to him than pigeons. But he knew how to tell a story and how to pause for effect. Also, defer as he would, he was determined to make the old man beside him squirm for information.

"What? What?" Urban prodded.

"Gone."

"I mean what was gone—the Madonna?"

"No?" Immaculato replied calmly.

"The chalice?"

"Noooo."

But Immaculato's sly game had gone too far. Urban's face turned red as he realized the position his eagerness to hear the conclusion of the story had put him in, and he spoke with a renewed authority that would brook no defiance. "Damn it, we're not playing twenty questions. Tell me."

"The food, Your Holiness. All the food for the marriage party was gone."

Unlike the Pontiff, the wedding guests immediately understood the smudge-faced lad who had delivered the bad news. Before Father Kepler could even respond, they abandoned him and Hans and Julia under the sky to gang up the steps of the church and pour into the pantry. There they confronted the other two boys and Herr Lindemann, the weeping grocer, who had been hired for the occasion.

"I left the food here, on this very table, all prepared, all delicious, I swear, nothing but the finest, a potato salad from my grandmother's secret recipe, I wouldn't sell that recipe for money."

"So, what happened?" insisted the bride's father, who had prepaid for the feast.

"I just stepped outside to see the party, to drink a glass of beer, to raise a toast to the beautiful young couple . . ."

"What happened, damn it?"

"When I came back . . . everything. Stolen."

It couldn't have been the monsters who had ransacked their homes. Surely there was no van in the neighborhood hiding a baked ham and aluminum trays of potato salad and coleslaw and bottles of white wine and several cases of beer.

And yet . . .

"Them," said Mrs. Koff, Hans's parents' wattle-chinned next-door neighbor, and everyone knew exactly who she meant. There had been rumors of strangers in the area. Three days earlier, a large man with a bullet-shaped head had been discovered sleeping in Theodor Knittel's garage in the middle of the afternoon. By the time help arrived, he was gone. Likewise, a pair of scrawny men had been loitering outside the village store. Herr Mannheimer peered out the window and they hurried away. "As if they had something to hide," he offered now.

"Half a dozen loaves of bread were taken from my shipment from the Breuhof Bakery yesterday—no, Friday," the grocer recalled. Every week the bakery truck deposited a sack of bread on his doorstep before the shop opened, and anyone could have taken them, but nobody ever had before.

Kaltenhaven was a safe place, one stop off the Nortbahn between Hamburg and Danzig, a way station only for those on the way to Wieland, which was even smaller and more remote than Kaltenhaven. The villagers knew every car and *Farnhagen*-bound paddy wagon that was likely to pass over their single main street.

More and more voices chimed in with recollections of the ominous strangers. They compared descriptions. Several had seen the bullet-headed giant, others a suspiciously dark and wiry young man. Soon, a few of the ladies from Julia's mother's bridge group remembered two elderly men suspiciously eyeing the cars at Knittel's garage. The same two who had been outside Mannheimer's store? With all the conflicting reports coming in now, it was difficult to determine how many of the strangers there really were, but it was beginning to feel like an invasion.

"I thought I heard voices in the woods earlier today," one of the choirboys piped up. "But I thought I was imagining them."

His mother turned on him. "What were you doing in those woods?" After an incident with one of the local girls, the lad had been strictly prohibited from entering the woods.

"Nothing." He hung his head, embarrassed by whatever inadvertent admission he had already made.

The girl blushed.

The boy's mother slapped at his forehead and knocked his hair askew.

"Don't blame the boy," a voice intoned.

The entire wedding party looked up to see a stranger in the doorway of the church. The light from outside cast a nimbus around His form.

.   .   .

"That was apparently His first message: Don't blame the boy," Father Immaculato said. He remained silent to allow the words to sink in.

"I would hardly define that as a message," Urban replied. "Whoever He was, or is, He was speaking quite literally. He was simply telling the mother not to vent her fears and frustrations on her son." The Pope described the motivations of the characters in the Kaltenhaven scene as if he had been there.

"Perhaps," Father Immaculato replied. "And perhaps that is the way the witnesses understood it at first, but by the end of the day the phrase had taken on a larger, emblematic significance."

"Do I really have to listen to this nonsense?" Inoculation be damned, Urban would rather listen to music.

"I believe so."

"Why?"

"Let me tell you."

"Go on. . . . But first explain what you mean by a nimbus."

At first, it wasn't an obviously holy glow that surrounded Ben Alef in the entry to the rural church. And a moment later, when twelve additional men crowded beside Him and blocked off the source of light, the doorway seemed to emit a murky aura.

"Who are you and what are you doing here?" Father Kepler demanded. Ignored in the rush to the empty kitchen, the broad, beefy-faced pastor strode through his parishioners to reassert his territorial prerogative before the phalanx of unkempt, ill-dressed men who entered the foodless church with suspiciously sated expressions on their faces.

"He is the Lord," Max Vetter said.

This brought another moment of silence.

"What?" Hans, the about-to-be newlywed, panted in exasperation.

"What did he say?" Julia asked.

The people of Kaltenhaven didn't believe they had heard right, but Father Kepler, though tipsy and disheveled, couldn't mistake the seriousness of Max Vetter's expression. The other strangers were not to be trusted, but Vetter, in thick wool and fishing cap, was clearly a native—a woefully misguided native, who had to be corrected. "Sacrilege," Father Kepler thundered.

"Only"—Snakes Hammurabi stepped forward from the group to clarify—"if he is wrong."

"What?" It was Father Kepler's turn to be baffled.

"Sacrilege," Snakes continued as simply as if he were giving a lecture, "is only sacrilege if it is false. When true, it must be alternatively defined as revelation."

These theological twists were too great for the pastor to comprehend, so he looked from Snakes back to Max Vetter for help. Sometimes it was easier to focus on the messenger than the message. "You from hereabouts?" he asked.

"By the coast."

"Bad storm."

But Max was not going to be sidetracked. "People still got to get married," he said, and looked pointedly at the two young people, who had been forgotten in the fuss.

Hans and Julia stood shyly.

"Life goes on," Dietrich Eisenheim said, smirking.

At the voice of the ancient criminal, Julia's right hand spontaneously clutched at Hans's left to protect her from the evil she could detect in the former *Farnhagen* resident's tone. Her fingers and Eisenheim's voice both trembled.

The high, hysterical voice of the old Nazi reminded Lindemann of the crime that had brought them into the church. "What about our food?" the grocer cried.

And the crowd of guests moved forward, and the criminals, who knew too well the power of righteousness, stepped backward, almost as one. Only Ben Alef stood His ground, alone now between the advancing victims and the retreating thieves.

"What about our food?" the pastor repeated, grateful to focus on the simple crime.

"Yes," Ben Alef murmured, thinking aloud to Himself rather than responding to a threat. "There must be food at a wedding feast."

"So where is it?"

Following His own logic, Ben Alef continued, "But the food comes after the ceremony."

"But where is it? You bas—" Hans's father stopped, afraid. There was a potency he couldn't admit.

"You couldn't have eaten all of it." Hans's mother joined her husband. "Just return what's left and leave us alone. Please."

Of course, the ravenous survivors of the prison could well have eaten all of it and more besides, but nobody was ready to acknowledge guilt.

"After the ceremony," Ben Alef declared. He had figured out the answer to His own, internal questions. "We'll need four poles. The poles represent the four corners of the earth . . . the east . . . the west . . ."

There were long pauses in His simple announcement of direction, and in those pauses Bruno rummaged through a janitorial closet and found two brooms, a mop, and a hockey stick that one of the choirboys had left there. Ben Alef accepted them as He concluded: ". . . the north, and the south."

There was a quiet authority to the stranger's voice that silenced the guests and Father Kepler, who stood in amazement as Hans and Julia nodded obediently.

"Now, there must be a cloth to represent the sky."

Franz Palitzsch approached Hans's mother. The woman gasped as he extended a prison-pale hand to request the shawl wrapped about her shoulders. She felt a chill, as if the shawl had already disappeared, and then, she couldn't have said why, she removed the real, palpable material, a lovely knit she had purchased during a vacation in the Black Forest, and suddenly felt warm. "Here."

"Here." Ben Alef turned to the couple.

No more capable of resistance than the groom's mother, Hans and Julia moved tentatively forward.

"You, too." He opened a palm to Hans's mother, and she, too, stepped out of the group.

"And you, sir." He brought Julia's father outward.

Ben Alef handed each of the in-laws one of the brooms, left the mop in Bruno's grasp, and summoned Anton to take hold of the final pole.

"Sure," Anton growled, crossed eyes twitching left and right. "It's an experience."

Then Ben Alef knotted the fringes from the four corners of the shawl to the broom and mop handles and the curved blade of the hockey stick.

. . .

"It was a Jewish wedding," Urban exclaimed.

"I don't think they knew that," Father Immaculato said.

"Usually done with a Hebrew tallith ornamented with blue, braided fringes."

A student of the faith that had given birth to his own Lord two thousand years earlier, Urban felt the same chill that had left Hans's mother run up and down his spine as Immaculato described the rest of the ceremony: the hushed guests adhering to the intruder's simple authority. "Even Father Kepler did not intervene. He was, by all accounts, paralyzed, maybe drunk."

"No," Urban said. "That's too easy."

"Yes, this is more difficult," Immaculato agreed, almost delighted to perturb his superior, and glad, for once, that this was not his dilemma to solve. He went on to describe the awkward rendering of the Jewish marriage, how Ben Alef directed the bride to circle the groom seven times, how the groom slipped a band of gold about the bride's finger and repeated the Hebrew words, "With this ring, I thee wed."

"At first," he said, "nobody could find any wine to fill the crystal goblet they found."

"Not the Eucharist cup? To smash underfoot according to the Hebrew tradition?"

"Unfortunately. But no wine. This damaged his credibility."

"You said, 'At first'?"

"A jug they thought contained water seemed to be filled with wine. . . . Of course, it was Kepler's secret supply."

"Of course." Urban IX looked out over St. Peter's Square, and thought he saw clouds coming from the north. The storm that had obliterated the Baltic coast was moving south, and he shied away from whatever omen this augured.

"I'm sure we can prove this."

"But what about the food?" Urban pleaded, hoping against hope that the fraud would be revealed here, yet enticed despite himself by the story.

"That was the worst of all," Immaculato said.

The second the ceremony concluded, the wineglass smashed into shards beneath Hans's steel-toed carpenter's boot, the people of Kaltenhaven were released from mass hypnosis. Once more, they demanded the food.

Once again, the convicts, except for Ben Alef, of course, and Bruno and Anton, who still held the north and east poles of the bridal canopy, retreated.

Awakened from his reverie, appalled at the rite he had allowed to be conducted upon the sacred premises entrusted to his keeping, Father Kepler regained, redoubled, his strength and harshly demanded, "Give us our bread."

Ben Alef smiled and said, "Step aside, children."

Hans and Julia immediately obeyed. Holding hands, they moved out from under the flimsy shawl, which fluttered in a breeze that must have slipped between the church's closed shutters.

"Yes?" Father Kepler insisted. Now, maybe, all would be put right.

"Yes," Ben Alef replied, and eight knees—Bruno's and Anton's and Hans's father's and Julia's mother's—sagged with a sudden, enormous weight from above. They tried to recover their balance, but the unexpected weight was too great. Bruno, Le Grand Blond, once upon a time contender for the title of mightiest man on earth, tipped forward first and then Hans's father and the broom and mop fell out of their hands and the shawl collapsed under the pressure of corn, "Yes, corn," Father Immaculato said, hundreds of ears of sweet yellow-and-white speckled corn that tumbled forth and rolled across the floor in a flood of silky green food.

"How many?"

"One per day, Your Holiness," answered the attendant, who had silently returned to remind Urban that his next appointment was waiting.

The Pontiff glanced up with a furrowed brow. He hadn't realized that he had speared, sliced, and dissected another treat while listening to the amazing story. Only when he popped the forbidden indulgence into his mouth and reached up to wipe the viscous, caramelized drippings from his chin did he understand what his aide was muttering about. "Tell the doctor he can go to . . . How many ears of corn, Immaculato?"

"Of course, there were folds in the shawl. This is the vulgarest form of stage trickery. Any amateur magician could do the same thing. Then set up a few card tricks for an encore. Pull a rabbit out of a hat. That sort of thing."

"How many?"

"Six hundred ears of corn, Your Holiness."

"Six hundred?"

"More or less. According to the best information we have. Most of it was eaten."

"Not six hundred and sixty-six?"

Immaculato paused to follow the ramifications of the suggestion. In as long as it took to hear the tale, Urban had already discerned one way of dealing with it. Perhaps the man deserved his chair. "Could be."

"Was it?" Urban insisted.

"I don't think we want to make demonological suggestions . . . yet."

"Yet?"

"But I'd better get hold of the cobs, to have the evidence in case we need it."

"All six hundred and sixty-six of them."

"Exactly." Immaculato wrote a memo to himself.

"To return to the story . . ."

"Well, these vaudevillians are good at what they do. They make elephants disappear. They saw women in half."

"Turn water into wine?"

"We do that."

"Yes, I know. . . ." The Pontiff deliberately paused before plucking another treat from the bowl on the inlaid table. He looked around the room, scanning a row of portraits of his deceased predecessors above the carved wainscoting. Other chambers in the papal quarters contained images of Jesus' life and passion and panoramic angelic assemblies, but Urban preferred this room and the company of his peers. There loomed John XXIII's benign countenance, Pius VI's pinched visage, and the two dozen other occupants of the papal chair going back centuries. Some were theologians, some politicians, some scoundrels, and some saints. Yet in a sense, all of them were magicians, because all of them participated in the transformation of mundanity into eternity.

Magic had been the church's stock-in-trade through the ages. The Eucharist and other rites provided almost a billion believers across the globe with the thrill of a more glorious reality than they knew in their daily lives. Every bejeweled altar and mosaicked dome and stained-glass window from the castle Urban occupied to the earth's far corners was physical manifestations of the Almighty's power on earth. And what could be more magical than that? Now some lunatic out there claimed to supersede the Church's magic in his flesh, and this was disturbing. It was dangerous. Urban immediately knew that he could not tolerate this usurpation. There was a word for it, and the word was heresy. Popes in the Middle Ages had had to deal with sacrilege all the time, but to Urban's knowledge, no one had faced such a difficulty since the evil days of the Enlightenment.

"Right now, it's a local phenomenon," Father Immaculato concluded. "Fortunately, newspapers haven't got hold of the story, yet."

Late and unshaven, Fritz Hofmann pulled up in front of the Kaltenhaven church with a squeal of the brakes of his beat-up Karmann Ghia convertible. He parked on the grass and attempted to hop over the lip of the door with effervescent je ne sais quoi. Unfortunately, the Hamburg University stringer for the *Frankfurter Zeitung* snagged his toe on the rearview mirror and tumbled into the nasturtiums at the feet of his family shucking corn on the steps of the church.

"Glad you could make it," his father said. "You only have one cousin."
"Deadline," Fritz muttered.
"Important, I'm sure."
"Damn team lost again, five to nothing. Beckler scored a hat trick."
"How'd Schultz do?"
"Um . . ." Fritz wasn't sure, since he hadn't actually been covering the game, but the scalpers outside—and didn't even rate a press pass into the stadium. "Oh, well," he muttered, "I should give Julia a kiss," and slipped on a cornhusk. "Damn," he said, scrambling upright to maintain his dignity, "doesn't anybody clean up around here?" Then he headed for the yard.

Ben Alef was standing between two enormous kettles of bubbling water set atop a heap of hot coals, the steam obscuring His face. Sprawled in a circle on the grass around Him were Fritz's cousin, Julia, her new husband, Hans, and the in-laws and friends, a bunch of children, chins dripping with melted butter, Father Kepler with an insipid smile on his face, and several elderly men who looked nothing like Kaltenhaven's town elders. Some were gnawing on their fourth or fifth or tenth ear of corn, and others were sipping a deep red wine from plastic cups.

Fritz looked at the scene and couldn't quite figure it out. The man at the center of the crowd exuded a weird kind of authority over the people of Kaltenhaven. That was obvious. They hung on His every word, but all

Fritz at a distance could hear Him say was a childish riddle, "Two men are going in opposite directions on a steep mountain. Where are they going that they should meet again?"

"Sideways!" Fritz called out.

Ben Alef beamed at the newcomer. "Truly, it is a wise man who approaches."

Something about the speaker struck Fritz as he walked forward. But even more striking was the attitude of the people of Kaltenhaven. They were tranquil, bucolic, their mild, silent picnic more like a herd of grazing cows than festive human beings.

"Fritzie!" Julia shrieked and leapt up to hug her cousin.

"Sorry I was late, kid. Looks like a good time is being had by all."

"Never a better in the entire history of the world."

"More corn," grocer Lindemann called from one of the kettles, pulling up ear after ear with a gigantic clasp.

"Hey, where'd the corn come from?" the young would-be reporter said, just to be chatty, just to make conversation.

"Fritz," his cousin Julia, suddenly serious and absolutely radiant, said, "You wouldn't believe it."

The corn was good; it was wonderful, and so was the wine, a rich, hearty cascade that gushed from Father Kepler's secret jug as abundantly as the springs that gave birth to the Rhine.

But the company! Dining al fresco, sharing the bounty with normal, honest citizens who accepted them entirely, *that* was heavenly.

It was the actual partaking of communal nourishment, more than the nourishment itself or the more profound events that preceded it, that finally fulfilled Max Vetter's dream and transformed the convicts into disciples. Nibbling an eighth or ninth cob, sipping an eighth or ninth glass of infinitely replenishable red, Anton Bartsch and Bruno Morgen and Blobel, Clauberg, Glucks, Kiehr, Langefeld, Palitzsch, and maybe even Nazzarian found peace. Of course, none of the disciples, drunk on sodality, was drunk enough to confess where exactly they came from, and sure, on a different occasion any one of them would have raped, robbed, or murdered his new friends, but this was different. That was then (and maybe later); this was now. Along with Ben Alef, they were the guests of honor and the respect, the belonging, the unpretentious affection, was dizzying. God may have convinced Snakes and Max Vetter and Dietrich Eisenheim who knew Him when, but God's good people convinced the rest.

"When I was your age . . ." Langefeld entertained the choirboys and even coaxed them to sing one more song, while Franz Palitzsch chatted amicably with Hans and Julia's mothers about their children's fine match. Clauberg stoked the fire under the kettle of boiling water, while Blobel and Herr Knittel discussed cars, though the mechanic noticed that his fellow auto fancier didn't seem to know any recent models and figured him for an antique buff.

The people of Kaltenhaven listened to the *Farnhagen*ers avidly, because as the latter envied the former their simple pleasures and uncon-flicted ease in their freedom, so the latter envied the former, formerly dross of the earth, their nearness to the being who brought both groups to-gether. The Kaltenhaveners might have witnessed a harvest of impossible corn appear out of the empty square of a cloth shawl, or the sky that shawl represented, but they didn't know what it was like to walk across the water.

"I swear that my feet weren't wet," Anton regaled a rapt, corn-stuffed audience while feeling the power of his testimony. "My ankles and my knees and thighs were soaked with splashing waves, my face was damp with spray, but the soles of my feet were as dry as a hundred-mark note."

Hans and Julia and their guests listened to the cop killer's description of that walk, and they believed. How could they not, given what else they knew? "It was, like, eternal," Walter, one of Hans's friends, later told a re-porter. Even Father Kepler had forgotten the bizarre impropriety of Ben Alef's intrusion, and sat cross-legged and entranced.

"It is, like, water," Ben Alef said.

Snakes explained: Life itself, rippling outward in opposing peaks and troughs of good and evil, structure and destruction, blessing and damna-tion, does have a point of origin, in the beginning, from a single pebble dropped in a pond—or a single deity dropped from heaven into *Farnhagen*.

Yet now that the number of witnesses had increased, something changed. Of course, the ring closest to that initial, wee splash felt pro-prietary. Max Vetter, the first person beyond the inner ring to behold the signs of the transfiguration, did not affect the dynamic. Max was more like a sand-crusted crab on the beach who had been granted the gifts of speech and faith than like an outsider. Besides, he *had* seen the walk across the water, at a distance, with his own eyes. Also, he had seen the raising of Eisenheim, twice. But these farmers and grocers and laborers at

Kaltenhaven, they were different. They were the first people who had not seen the miracle on the Baltic, and yet they had been vouchsafed their own wonder. And so a hierarchy—even here—developed, based on proximity to revelation.

The convicts were the first circle, and Max Vetter a privileged, attached observer; the guests were the second circle, closer than any of the hundreds of thousands of third-circle readers of the *Frankfurter Zeitung* or the millions of fourth-circlers who would soon hear about the Messiah via radio waves, television antennas, and e-mail, but secondary nonetheless. This meant that they knew, deep in their souls, that although Ben Alef belonged to them absolutely, He belonged more intimately to the misfits to whom He had first chosen to reveal his glory.

And the last arrival at the wedding reception didn't even know that, except by hearsay. That young man who wasted the entire, exquisitely sun-dappled afternoon taking feverish notes on a crumpled football scorecard, what was he about?

The men from the *Farnhagen* kept a chary distance from the young reporter, but none of the Kaltenhaven locals seemed bothered by Fritz. The buoyant goodwill of the occasion was too pervasive to hold one outsider's curious behavior against him. After Ben Alef, all outsiders were welcome in their community. Lindemann the grocer spoke to Fritz for ages, trying to describe his mother's top-secret potato salad recipe—first, boil the potatoes in dill-soaked stock—and Father Kepler just laughed when asked why he allowed the stranger to conduct the ceremony. Afterward, he couldn't have said why he laughed; it seemed funny. Much later, interrogated by Father Immaculato, he didn't find it funny in the least.

After all was said and done, however, the month was still December, and an appropriately wintry chill descended with an early dusk. The former *Farnhagen*ers were used to privation—freezing temperatures, sludge for supper, concrete racks, paper-thin linen—but the corn-becalmed residents of Kaltenhaven missed their cozy cottages. Hans winked at Julia; a loft over his father's woodshop, prepared by the two mothers-in-law in an act of prenuptial familiarity, awaited them, complete with feather quilt and down-filled pillows.

Suddenly it was obvious to everyone that the remarkable day was over. So although Fritz's cousins and their friends believed in its splendor as empirically as they believed that the sun came up in the east—as it now began to sink into the westerly marsh grass—they were not going to follow Ben Alef. Such was not their appointed role in the grand drama to come. Already they looked upon Him as a ghost, a memory, as fading yet forceful as a recollection of infantile bliss.

He stood.

The company left Fritz behind, scrambling for a telephone, and escorted the thirteen men—Ben Alef, the disciples, and Max Vetter—to the boundary of their domain. There, at a timber post that demarcated Kaltenhaven from the next township, Father Kepler spoke for the community. He did not take the opportunity to orate from a tiny hummock in the slanting, diminishing sunlight, but simply wished the "visitor" well, and gave blessed thanks for their glorious encounter.

"No," Ben Alef said. "Not mine to give. Yours to receive."

"If," Snakes reminded them, "you will."

Book III
Pilgrimage

Chapter Seven

Frankfurter Zeitung, *December 2, 1999, p. 26,*
bottom righthand corner:

Feed Them and They Will Follow

Kaltenhaven. A curious event occurred last Sunday at the wedding of Hans and Julia Wolf in this tiny village east of Hamburg, near the Baltic coast devastated by last week's tremendous storm. Minutes before the ceremony was scheduled to begin, an anonymous stranger entered the church and spontaneously conducted the nuptials, much to the surprise of all present. Why he was allowed to do this and whether the marriage is legal are both unclear. Afterward, the villagers claimed that the stranger "magically" provided a dinner consisting of out-of-season corn and red wine. The magician modestly said he had done nothing unusual, but the guests were impressed. At the end of the party, they followed the stranger westward in a procession in the direction of the sunset, witnessed by a reporter for the *Zeitung.* Whither? Stay tuned.

MORE A COLUMN of refugees than a messianic procession, the thirteen men—or was it twelve men and a god?—inched forward at the pace of the slowest and oldest among them. The sun had set during Father Kepler's farewell, and a pale quarter-moon cast faint gleams into the fields beside the empty highway. Snakes Hammurabi once more recalled the path to the River Lyons, but that had been a march and this was a simple walk with abundant time to stop and watch the supple marsh grass rippling in a breeze from the shockingly benign Baltic fifteen kilometers away.

Occasionally a car sped past, its occupant squirming around in his seat to canvass the unusual parade.

"Wouldn't think of giving us a ride," Omar complained.

"Would you give us a ride?" Kiehr replied.

"Besides," Bruno informed them both, "there isn't room for all of us in one car."

"Who cares?" Omar said.

"He does," Max said.

"This is nice," Bruno sighed. Impetuously, he flung his heavy right arm across Anton's shoulder.

Anton shrugged, but allowed the tree trunk of a limb to remain, and the cross-eyed, mean-tempered former leader of the band didn't shove it off when they settled down to rest beside a fire that Clauberg conjured out of construction refuse in an abandoned truck-weighing station. The situation was conducive to reflection in a way Anton's years of communal solitude had never been. Maybe if he had had a second's peace a decade earlier, he might have recognized the Son of Man slumbering in the bunk underneath him, or maybe they all just had to await the necessary hour. Even Anton felt the same comfort that Bruno did. And like Le Grand Blond, he felt utter confidence that everything that was wrong with the world might conceivably be rectified. Nor was he alone. The prisoners tried to discuss this among themselves after Ben Alef drifted off to sleep. To their knowledge, He hadn't slept during His entire stay in Cell #306—and none of them could recall how long that was; estimates ranged from days to decades with equal assurance—but He was the only one able to sleep after the events in the Kaltenhaven churchyard.

"Fuck this," Nazzarian suddenly announced. "I'll go from party to party with Ben Alef, hail the conqueror, and all that, it's a gas, but I'm not walking back into prison with Him. The party's over."

Clauberg prodded at the embers with a long stick and a few sparks rose lazily on the updraft until they blinked out in the sky. He found an untouched ear of corn wrapped in tinfoil and nudged it to the edge of the pit.

"Oh," Bruno said, "it will be fine."

Nazzarian sneered. "Fine for who?"

"What's bugging you, Turk?" Anton said.

"I'm not a Turk."

"Yeah, yeah, you're the Shah of Iran."

"Don't you yeah, yeah me, you cross-eyed son-of-a-bitch. We're out now and I don't have to take your racist bullshit anymore. Besides, you just don't understand. It's dandy that we had such nice food, but with all those people and that reporter there, man, it's only a matter of time. They're going to find out who we are."

Anton understood immediately, but Bruno said, "Huh?"

"Forgot already, Blond? Allow me to refresh your memory. *Farnhagen*. Cell Number 306."

"But with what we've been through . . ."

"Oh, so you're suggesting that maybe this time the police will just let bygones be bygones? Or at worst, they'll fine us when the truth comes out, which it will? Let's see, a hundred marks per murder. That means you'd only owe a hundred, Bruno, because you are such a good boy. You can earn that in one night in the arena, but what about Kiehr—they stopped counting the bodies in his basement when the stench grew too great. And forget about poor Eisenheim. He'd have to live another eighty, no, eighty thousand, years to work off his debt, hard labor. Remember, my comrade, we're guilty."

The Obersturmbannführer nodded modestly at this recognition of his accomplishment.

Anton glanced sideways and asked Omar, "What did you have in mind?"

Omar returned to his previous desire to leave. "There's a road. I have feet. If they can walk on water, they can walk on pavement. I'm thinking about traveling east. I hear that Russia is wide open for anyone with brains and guts."

"So why are you telling us?"

"I don't know. I just think this is going to end up . . . not fine."

Bruno insisted, "But Snakes says . . ."

"And that's another thing: since when does Hammurabi speak for me? How come he gets this special pride of place?"

"Don't forget Eisenheim," Glucks reminded him. At the church and on the road, Ben Alef was flanked by Snakes, his spokesman, on the right, and Eisenheim, His murderer, on the left, and some of the remaining ten disciples were envious. Now they were back in the land of backbiting and jealousy they knew best. These were the men who would kill for a *Farn-hagen* pillow.

"They were the first to recognize Him," Bruno explained. "We needed greater proof."

Nazzarian ignored this comment. "Dietrich doesn't give a shit, and Snakes has the least to lose. Remember what he was in for: peeing. Then the goddamn prison nearly drowns us. You really think the same government that practically killed a guy by mistake is going to put him back in stir for peeing? They'll make a deal that he won't sue the Fed for negligence, and then they'll say he served his time."

"Yaw!" Anton laughed. "They're the ones peeing . . . in their pants."

"Screw that, think of us. The rest of us. Subtract ten years, twenty years, fifty years from a life sentence, and what's left?"

Anton knew the math well. "Life."

"Yeah. That's why I'm splitting. You can sit here, but as soon as a real sheriff appears, you're going back to jail." Omar stood up to let his logic sink in.

Back to the fire for a second, he wondered why he needed these others to leave with him. It was sheer weakness. Or was there strength in numbers? Or was there significance in particular numbers, like the twelve followers of the man who would surely doom them? Or was there magic in the the six-digit number inked into Ben Alef's forearm, 108016, the secret the twelve men had not released in Kaltenhaven, because they knew they could not yet bring it to the world's attention?

"He's right. This is crazy."

Glucks took up the discussion in an offhand manner. "Well, here we are. What do we do next?"

Palitzsch agreed. "I mean, the dinner was lovely, but . . ."

"But what?" Snakes turned on the elderly killer of elderly ladies.

"But this is crazy."

"He's right," Langefeld agreed. "I mean we can't exactly believe what's happening."

Despite their rescue, and despite the satisfying human warmth of the feast, doubt was seeping back into the ex-convicts' hardened souls. Blobel and Kiehr inched toward Langefeld and Palitzsch, while Clauberg stopped staring into the campfire long enough to nod.

"Why not?" Max asked, afraid that, food digested, the disciples were relapsing into their previous discontent. Throughout the churchyard meal, the fisherman had been almost as silent as Ben Alef. Like the young journalist, he squatted on the periphery of the circle and inscribed page after page of a sheaf of lined paper, adrift in his own solitary world of thought. "Just look at what you've been through. I only saw it and I believe. You lived it, so if you don't believe this, then you can't believe anything."

"Possible." Omar smirked.

"How about you, Kommandant?" Anton asked the most unregenerate one of the bunch. "Do you believe?"

Without aligning himself either way, Eisenheim only asked his own question. "Does He care if we believe? Remember what He said—the gift is ours to receive. What if we don't want it?"

"But we have to. We . . . we . . ." Snakes stammered. So eloquent when conveying Ben Alef's meaning, he struggled to express himself, until he finally discovered yet another truth in the midst of Eisenheim's bleak inquiry. "Right," he declared. "That's the point, exactly. He doesn't have to care. *We* have to care."

Bruno, of course, understood implicitly. "If He is our God, we must follow Him."

"And teach others about Him," Glucks, the schoolteacher, added.

"By example?" Omar was the only one who was still suspicious, but he, too, was softening. His question implied the genuine desire for an answer.

"We must follow Him," Bruno repeated. He didn't need to know more.

"And protect Him."

"From what?"

"Ourselves, maybe."

"As He protects us from ourselves?" Anton suggested.

"Does He?" Omar replied. "Does He protect us or endanger us? Does He save us or doom us? Does He heal us or wound us? What does He actually do?"

Anton stared at Nazzarian, on his right, from his left eye. Suffering cruel childhood mockery for his abnormal gaze, Anton had turned vindictive early, and only in the society of outlaws and outcasts had he ever felt at ease. If anyone looked at him wrong, he looked back at them wrong and forced them to regret the encounter. But just now, the notion that he could escape the burden he had born since birth was astounding. Examining Eisenheim, on his left, from his right eye—the Nazi was gnawing on a bone, healthy as a crow, silent as a stone—Anton wondered if a simple retinal adjustment might be just as possible as a resurrection. He didn't dare mention his dream out loud—his vulnerability might be misconstrued, or, worse, understood—but to himself Anton thought, "Can He heal me?" Instead, he said, "Erich is right. This is crazy." And then he laughed.

"Crazy as a crackpot," a tipsy Blobel added.

"Cracked as a crazypot," Clauberg added.

"You're the ones who are crazy," Nazzarian said.

"Crazy he calls me," Langefeld sang a snatch of an old favorite song.

"Crazy." Kiehr giggled.

Crazily, the entire crew exploded in a fit of laughter that shook the night and hardly ceased until dawn, each one laughing himself to sleep and laughing as he dreamed, believing at last, because it was crazy and nothing else made sense.

By the time the thirteen crazy wanderers set off again in the morning, news of their existence preceded them. Laughing under a skyward streak of telephone lines, they couldn't imagine that those lines out of Kaltenhaven had been abuzz from the moment Hans and Julia's wedding party guests returned to their homes. Local calls were placed to friends in adjacent villages, while long-distance calls informed Aunt Irma in Munich and grocer Lindemann's old acquaintances in Weimar of the good news. Even Father Kepler had been on the phone from his rectory to Ulm's Father Zollinger, with whom he had attended seminary. "Am I glad I reached you, Rudolph. Pour yourself a tall glass of schnapps," Father Kepler said. "I know I have."

"So what's new, Jonas?"

"I'm serious, Rudy. I have never had a day like today, and I doubt I ever shall again. I don't know what I've seen."

"Why don't you try and tell me?"

After the conversation, Rudolph Zollinger did indeed open his liquor cabinet, and he sat for an hour mulling over his friend's story. He knew that the spiritual leader of Kaltenhaven was not necessarily a reliable narrator, but there was something in Kepler's voice that demanded to be taken seriously. Tippling Jonas might not have known what he saw, but he definitely believed that he saw it, and the appearance of authenticity was as serious as the authentic itself.

The hour was late when Zollinger padded to his rectory's kitchen to rinse out the glass he had been sipping from, but he returned to his desk and cautiously dialed the Monsignor of the See, who, roused and grumpy, nonetheless listened to the bizarre bedtime story and tossed restlessly until the next morning when he made yet another call, which finally led to the office of Vatican City's resident theological troubleshooter, Father Immaculato.

Much later, one further call was issued from a solitary phone booth beside the weighing station. Late at night, after the soon-to-be-deemed disciples drifted off to sleep, Snakes Hammurabi dropped a coin into the Deutsche Telefunken slot and punched in the digits he knew as well as his name.

"Hello!" a voice answered over a background of pounding disco music.

"Leon! This is Snakes. Is he in?"

"Hey, S-man, where you been?"

Snakes paused, and refrained from replying, "Where the fuck do you think?" It was inconceivable that everyone at the Kastrasse didn't know that he had been arrested. Unless this information wasn't made public. Old suspicions crept into his head and old attitudes prepared to burst out, but his newfound serenity kept him in check. "No time to chat, Leon. I need to talk to the Peddler."

Miffed at his caller's lack of congeniality, Leon huffed, "If that's the way you feel," and put Snakes on hold until a familiar deep voice jumped onto the line. "Herr Hammurabi, how good to hear your voice. I've been so terribly worried."

Where, Snakes wondered, had he heard that distinctive Slavic accent before? "Yeah?"

"My lawyer was working on your release two weeks ago."

"I was in for three weeks."

The Peddler ignored the gentle accusation and kept talking over the throbbing music. "When the boat went down we thought you were a goner."

"And you were never in hot water?"

The Peddler chuckled. "Could be. But how'd you get out?"

Snakes laughed. "No matter, I'm fine."

"Best news I've heard today. We lost three kilos in transit."

"Actually, I wasn't calling on business."

Glasses clinked in the background. "Everything's business, boychik."

Was this the Peddler's sideways manner of explaining Snakes's long imprisonment—that he'd been too busy to bother to pull a string and help his protégé out of hell? But Snakes never did have a clear reading of his mentor's motives. That was how the Peddler operated. Keep everyone guessing, both friends in the rackets and enemies in the police—and also enemies in the rackets and friends in the police. Whatever the truth behind his mysterious origins or ambiguous intentions, he was undeniably successful. The Peddler had been involved in North Coast crime since before Snakes was born, and hadn't done time yet, not that Snakes knew of.

But Snakes wasn't—or didn't think he was—just any moon orbiting the Peddler's strange planet, where today's ally became tomorrow's antagonist. No, he was the prize student of and presumptive heir to the fatherless, friendless Peddler's empire, and what sort of king lets his prince rot? Perhaps he was teaching Snakes a lesson—something about maintaining strength in adversity or trusting no one. But Snakes had learned a greater lesson, because a greater king had intervened. And now it was up to him to teach his former master. "No." He laughed.

"Something funny?"

"No." He couldn't stop laughing. "Everything is not business."

"For example?"

"For example . . ." Suddenly serious, ignoring a reluctance he couldn't define, Snakes surrendered to the same desire felt by Father Kepler and the Kaltenhaveners, to relay his extraordinary story. From his first perception of the one quiet soul in Cell #306, through the storm, from the waves, onto the shore, he described the events of the previous month as he hadn't—even to himself—until now, and the Peddler didn't say a word. By the time Snakes concluded the narrative with the wedding scene, he realized there was absolute silence on the other end of the line. The Peddler must have left the dance floor of the Kastrasse and gone to his private office which nobody, absolutely nobody else, not even Snakes, ever entered. "You there?"

"Hmm."

More silence. The Peddler was thinking.

Snakes knew the mode. The Peddler had taught him: when a deal is presented, you should never answer until you were sure of your response. Whether you let the dealer in on it or not was your decision to make.

"Where are you calling from?"

"The road."

"Anything else?"

"No. I mean yes." He had left out the most important part of the story. One small fact: a number, the number on Ben Alef's arm. He was just about to mention this when some instinct made him shut up, like a cop with a decisive piece of evidence that only the culprit can identify. And then, again, he heard himself say, "No." He wasn't tempted to laugh. Nothing was funny anymore.

"Curious."

Snakes knew when he wasn't being believed. Moreover, he knew when he shouldn't be believed—like when he lied, like when he said he had drugs under a table and really had a gun. But this was different. At this moment, he was as straight as he had ever been. His rational self understood the impediments to belief of this story, but nonetheless it was true. There was evidence (corn); there were witnesses, ten others, then eleven, then dozens. He was about to call them to the imaginary stand to testify, but halted. The word alone must speak for itself. "Yes, curious."

"At the least." The Peddler's brain was working hard, and Snakes could imagine the logic it must necessarily follow.

First question: Was this story possible?

First answer: No.

So Snakes was deluded. But the Peddler took one step further, and that was another secret of his success.

Second question: If Snakes Hammurabi, as skeptical a mind as any the Peddler had ever met—that was why he loved Snakes as much as anyone he had ever met, as much as he, irredeemably flawed, was capable of loving anyone—believed, wouldn't others, too?

Second answer: Yes.

And suddenly Snakes wished he had kept his revelation to himself, even if the purpose he received it for was to transmit it to the world. But not this way. Suddenly, he feared the consequences of his confession, and tried to figure out how to backtrack, too late.

Rapidfire, now. Third question: What could one do with this?

Third answer: Not so obvious.

Fourth question: Could one do something?

Fourth answer:

A second too late, Snakes arrived at the same conclusion as the Peddler. The answer to the fourth question was "Yes."

Oh, word was percolating swiftly, and the Peddler was bound to hear it in due time, but ought not to hear it a minute earlier. Advance information was everything. Snakes had to shut the door he had inadvertently opened through his desperate need to speak. "I hope you enjoyed my little fairy tale."

"Much, boychik, very much." There was that tone again, a voice from another world.

So Snakes would pretend he had lied, and the Peddler would pretend he believed Snakes had lied, but neither believed the other and they each knew that another element was now in play. "Good-bye," Snakes said.

"Hey, boychik?"

"Yes."

"We miss you. Take that road home."

Chapter Eight

WORD ABOUT THE MANGY BAND of men and their strange leader rippled outward from primary to secondary sources and beyond, from witnesses to neighbors to cousins to friends to friends of friends as the yearning to convey the news spread. By the time time Ben Alef and company reached the village of Warnemünde a committee had been organized to greet them, house them, and—another, perhaps greater miracle, if anyone had thought to define it as such—feed them. After all, when was the last time a community of stolid German bourgeois poured into the streets, offering food and wine to a ragged and vicious criminal gang?

Clauberg and Blobel halted abruptly as they rounded the corner of Warnemünde's tiny town square. Their combined first thought was not of celebration, but of apprehension, and they were ready to flee.

Too late. The enthusiastic crowd surged forward and swept the confused disciples into a joyous uproar. A few of the laggards—Glucks, Eisenheim, Bruno, Anton, and Franz Palitzsch—were thrust into chairs dragged out of the local café and hoisted above the tumultuous sea of celebrants. Bobbing up and down like campaign placards at a convention, the disciples glanced at each other across the heads of citizens, Anton's eyes twitching nervously. Bruno was the only one for whom the sensation was even vaguely familiar. He could remember the day when, as Le Grand Blond, he won the heavyweight divisional title and was carried through the Bonn Arena amid a similar multitude.

Omar Nazzarian picked a pocket.

Only Ben Alef was untouched. The crowd parted as He walked forward in a circle of silence that closed after Him on the way to the village center.

Snakes followed immediately behind, like a savvy motorist plowing through a traffic jam in the wake of a fire engine. He didn't know exactly what was going on, but he, who had made a career of giving the public what it wanted, knew more than any of the others—except for Ben Alef, of course, who knew everything.

"Greetings. I say, Greetings!" a rotund little man standing on a makeshift platform called into a microphone propped on a lectern borrowed from the town hall. Tapping the head of the microphone, creating thumping sounds like the heartbeat of a gigantic beast, raising his hands for attention, he repeated again, "Greetings!" until the crowd gradually hushed. "My fellow citizens. Honored guests. And . . ." He paused for a moment. ". . . others . . ."

The others included Fritz Hofmann, with the first bona fide press card of his young life laminated in a clear plastic sheath dangling from a silver chain around his neck, and a tall, beaky man who alit with obvious distaste from a late-model sedan with white VC plates. The man's shoes were as fine an Italian leather as anything Snakes had ever dreamed of back in his dandy days, but unlike Snakes's shoes in *Farnhagen*, Father Immaculato's loafers sidestepped the Warnemünde gutter. "Wait here," he said curtly to the driver, who had cruised through the night while the Pope's representative alternately napped and contemplated his destination.

"What a significant honor for our small burg," the mayor continued from his platform.

The audience cheered.

The mayor extemporized, as the chairs bearing the first of the refugees were set beside him. "Here, in a little town that not many, indeed all too few, people know is the source of the finest broccoli in Europe . . ."

The rest of the gang was ushered onto additional chairs on the platform.

"Here, in a little town that brought forth the secondary school champions of the German Youth Football League in 1963 and, I say *and* 1964 . . ."

"Which one is He?" the mayor's aides whispered to Eisenheim.

"Here, in a little town proud to be voted one of the most pleasant places in Germany to live by *Stern* magazine in 1975 . . ."

"The dead one," Eisenheim smirked, and pointed to Ben Alef down below, still in an empty circle, the only one not yet ascended to the platform, until Snakes guided the Messiah up the rickety steps.

Having finished listing the town's multiple claims to fame, the mayor sighed, "Here," and wasn't sure what else to say. He had been in a tizzy since an early-morning call from his secretary, Anna, informed him that the Messiah was coming.

"Thank you for sharing," he said, and hung up.

The phone rang again and Anna clarified: "Today, Herr Schmidt."

"Oh, fine, then I'll see it on the news tomorrow."

"You don't understand, He's coming here, to Warnemünde."

"Is this on the calendar?"

The good secretary continued, "In a few hours. I have a reporter from the *Frankfurter Zeitung* in the office, sir."

"Who?" he muttered.

"Apparently his name is Ben Alef."

"The reporter?"

"No, sir, this Messiah. Yesterday he made . . . pardon me . . . corn appear at a wedding in Kaltenhaven."

"Whatever sort of practical joke this is, it is not funny."

"I told my sister the same thing last night when she called with the news. She heard it from her mechanic in Brotmanburg, who heard it from the mechanic in Kaltenhaven. People are already gathering in the square, and Herr Hofmann would like to interview you."

Rubbing his eyes, beginning to remember that Anna, a rock-stolid civil service bureaucrat who essentially ran the two-room city hall from administration to administration, never told a joke, he asked, "Have you checked his credentials?"

"I have the press card in front of me, sir, and I already called the *Zeitung* for confirmation of identity and assignment."

"This is so stupid I can't believe it, but I'll come in after breakfast."

"Please make it sixty-second oatmeal, sir. The office is getting rather busy."

From the second he lifted his heavy feet off the mattress, Herr Schmidt wanted to collapse back into bed and pull the comforter over his head. Until now, the most complicated issue he'd had to reckon with during his three successive four-year terms was the regional sewer bond. Otherwise, his time was occupied with zoning variances, local service contracts for snow removal, and a ceremonial appearance at the kickoff of the annual broccoli festival. Redemption and resurrection were not on the average week's mayoral docket.

But if indeed the entire population was gathering—and a quick call to the chief of police unfortunately confirmed that Anna had not slipped a cog, at least not the obvious one—he simply *had* to attend and convene. But what sort of nonsense was this? How had the entire staid citizenry—Warnemünde was a town of Annas—turned into mushminds overnight?

Okay, so be it, the same mushminds had been wise enough to elect Schmidt three times, and another election was coming up in a year. It was good to remind the electorate that he was their leader whenever the opportunity presented itself. Who knew if Schebeck, that snot on the school board, didn't covet Schmidt's seat, wasn't contemplating a run on a "new blood" ticket?

Three coffees later, Schmidt decided not to go on the record with his usual draft and delivery of a proclamation, but he also chose not to leave town on an unspecified emergency. The apparently spontaneous enthusiasm of the people of Warnemünde, who had begun gathering shortly after sunrise, could not be denied by any politician. Thus weary and wary, Mayor Schmidt arrived at Libenhauser Square, a grassy quadrangle centered on a monument to the (unspecified) War Dead, and began shaking hands, waving to familiar and unfamiliar faces in the distance, and pretending to supervise the construction of the platform.

A carnival air pervaded the square as cars backed up blocks away and parked on lawns, their occupants streaming inward, past the local merchants who quickly set up sidewalk booths on sawhorses to sell food and drinks, sausages and hot chocolate proving especially popular even at a price that inflated when supplies dwindled. Children peed in the bushes, mothers called to the children to stay nearby, and a group of girls in tie-dyed smocks held hands and sang "Michael, Row the Boat Ashore."

Well, Mayor Schmidt thought resignedly, it's too late to do anything but welcome the fellow in the name of the great little village of Warnemünde, and it couldn't hurt to have their photograph taken together. Or could it? A grainy black-and-white print half a century old had destroyed the political career of the last Minister of Justice; then again, the future Minister had been in uniform, and the surroundings were unsavory. Maybe Schmidt would avoid the photographer. The worst that could happen then was that if—or rather, when; he was enough of a realist to say "when"—the world discovered what a fraud this so-called Messiah was,

Schmidt would cry that he, too, like a true man of the people, had been duped.

It wasn't an ideal scenario, and Schmidt feared the appearance of absurdity more than fear itself, but he was roped in by circumstance. Anyway, everything ought to be be okay today, as long as this Mr. Ben Alef didn't try to pull any sneaky tricks. There had to be some law against miracles, maybe disturbing the peace, but the crowd was in no mood to have their fun curtailed. What alternative did Schmidt have? As for his statement, well, the mayor frequently recalled his predecessor's sage advice: "Speak loudly and say nothing."

The crowd was uncommonly peaceful—no beer-hall songs, no unpleasant placards denouncing Auslanders—and the troupe the so-called Messiah brought along with Him—a little rough around the edges, not exactly the kind of men Herr Schmidt hoped his daughter would marry—didn't seem too bad, either. For all their shabby attire and motley appearance, one cross-eyed, another a giant, several wizened ancients with hippielike hair down past their shoulders, they radiated a strangely mild cumulative effect. So Warnemünde would throw a party, similar to the broccoli festival. Schmidt finished his litany of the town's virtues and concluded with a resounding "So here we are!"

Fritz Hofmann jotted notes on a lined pad with a coiled metal spine at the top, purchased to solemnize the occasion of his first official assignment. Fritz was proud of himself. After his first filing from Kaltenhaven ran on page 26 and the human interest story of the wandering disciples seemed to arouse curiosity, the *Zeitung* was set to send a seasoned reporter to follow it, but Fritz had argued for the right to pursue Ben Alef himself. He had the inside track. He had connections among the witnesses. He had the spirit. The Messiah was his intellectual property. "Fine, kid, go for it," the editor said with a laugh. But the editor could not have imagined this response in Warnemünde. Fritz could see the next day's headline in his head as he moved above the fold.

Scribbling busily, he nearly missed the scene of the afternoon, when a portly middle-aged man dashed out of the crowd in such a rush that his toupee slipped askew. The man was clutching a machine-gun sized box under his arm.

The crowd cried out as the man thrust his hand into the box. For a second, they had visions of assassination. Before anybody could wrestle him to the ground, however, the man, owner of a local clothing store, removed a bathrobe from the box, gray silk with a silver lining, and draped it over his Lord. It was December. "You must be cold," he said.

"No," Ben Alef replied kindly, "it's warm."

"What did he say? What did he say?" Fritz repeated as he shoved his own way toward the action, desperately fearful of missing the quote of the day.

Luckily for the cub reporter, he asked this question of the one person capable of answering him. Snakes Hammurabi, who was already wondering why he alone had not felt the sharp thrill of fear when the clothing store owner jumped at Ben Alef, replied, "He said, it *was* cold, but now it is warm. We are all coming in from the cold, into the fold, to the warmth, to the comfort, to the light. Where is there warmth? Where there is light. Where is there light? Where the Redeemer lives. Where does the Redeemer live? He lives among us."

Where did this knowledge and the language with which to convey it come from? Wasn't the Peddler right to suspect that Snakes had lost his sanity? He looked at the crowd, already so fervent in its adoration—or did they adore their own ardor more than its object? The Kaltenhaveners had been given a spontaneous gift, but the Volk of Warnemünde, what did they know? Or had the Peddler orchestrated this? And if he did, and if these people were just looking for an excuse to have a good time, did that make a difference? Since when did a crowd's opinion make a difference to Snakes Hammurabi? As long as he believed Ben Alef was real and true and good, that was sufficient.

No, it was happening too quickly. But how else would revelation occur? One moment you live in a normative world, and the next moment everything is different. Maybe it's because of something you see—call it a miracle—or maybe it's because of something you feel—call *that* a miracle—but the end result is the same. Like lightning striking, or love! This sort of knowing was not the outcome of slow accretion, like technological advances. Even them, weren't they, wasn't everything worthwhile, the effect of transformation rather than development? The tinder may be present all along, but the kindling is a different matter entirely. Think of Edison. He knew that an electric bulb was feasible, but he tried thousands of filaments and none of them worked. Then he tried tungsten. Twisted the little wires into place. Threw the switch. Let there be light.

But before Snakes could figure out what he had said, Mayor Schmidt was already pouring glasses of celebratory champagne, Schebeck and other local dignitaries were milling onto the platform, cameras were flashing, and Ben Alef's three single-syllable words were all the crowd was destined to hear.

That didn't matter. They had seen the Man, heard His Voice. One of the besmocked teenage girls swooned. The rest eagerly plowed into the dark bread and smoked salmon they had forgotten that they themselves provided.

Thus, garbled in Fritz Hofmann's hastily written copy, Snakes's words were placed in Ben Alef's mouth, and in the eyes of the world the spokesman became the speaker.

Frankfurter Zeitung, *December 4, 1999, p. 8,*
upper righthand corner:

The Messiah Moves On

Warnemünde. The strange saga of Ben Alef, the so-called Messiah, continues. Mr. Alef, along with twelve unknown men, appeared at a wedding party in the sleepy northern village of Kaltenhaven several days ago. According to witnesses, Mr. Alef conducted the ceremony and presented the party with a mysterious feast of corn on the cob "from the sky," and yet more remarkable, unverified miracles have been attributed to him.

Yesterday, the band of believers reappeared in the nearby village of Warnemünde, where Herr Arthur Schmidt, Mayor of Warnemünde, population 140, claimed that over 200 people from as far away as Rostock were there to greet Mr. Alef. The so-called Messiah produced no miracles but claimed, "I am the warmth. I am the light. I am the Redeemer."

Asked if he thought that Mr. Ben Alef was the savior we have been waiting for, Mayor Schmidt replied, "No comment."

Chapter Nine

Dear Frieda,

Ten days, and the fifty-seven years before them that I've breathed upon this earth mean nothing.

Ten days, and all that was unknown is known and all that was known is forgotten.

But this should be easy arithmetic. He created the world in seven days—He, or His Father, or a Force between them; the theology is unclear.

Some of the disciples with Papist backgrounds are already placing Him within the context of their church, while others have adopted a more deist (I think that's the term) interpretation. As for me, I don't care. He is here and His gifts are manifold.

I should have realized that on that first day back in Wieland, with the new sea spread to the horizon in directions where land used to be. The world around me was different, and the world inside was about to change. But I was selfish. I thought that the vision was given to me because I was unique. Now, I realize that the vision was given to me because I was not unique.

I wish that I could avoid the word "I" in this letter, because the brother you knew, the little boy who wheeled you around the bumpy yard in a red wagon while you screamed with delight, the teenager whose fishing rod might have been his third arm, the adult sibling who joined you to bury our parents, is no more. "I," Max, have been subsumed into a greater whole. Everything is "we." Everything is in Him.

This sounds awkward, because my language is inadequate. Snakes speaks very well, indeed, but I just follow, and feel happy as a tiny particle in Ben Alef's single, purposeful unity.

The gift was not *mine*. How egotistical! I would feel ashamed if—another gift—He did not teach me that shame, like pride, was human, and the human was false, because we are all part of His divinity. He was too generous to give this single flawed vessel named Max a gift. Instead, He gives to all *through* some, who are blessed *because* we are the conduit of His wisdom.

You should have seen the people in Kaltenhaven, in Warnemünde, in every village we pass as we go . . . somewhere. Where? That question will surely be answered in time—and, we, like everyone else, cannot help but be aware of the calendar, twenty-eight days and counting. But maybe that's a false, human construction. Maybe the question will be answered out of time, because time has lost its meaning. For now, the passage is everything. We are like the sun, which illuminates each line of longitude in its daily journey across the sky, lightness behind, darkness ahead, darkness which shall turn to light.

Every day brings new light that has never existed before.

He understands that people need a reason to believe—even if we shouldn't. He gives unto them as He gave unto us on the Wieland shore, as required. You've heard of the corn, sweet as peppermint candy, and I told you about His walk and the raising of Eisenheim, but there is more, much more to come. There is a secret—an incredible secret—about His history that is not for me to reveal, but for Him to determine the time and the place, which He shall. He shall. This is a world without secrets.

Only the future is mysterious. Whither we go, for what purpose. Patience abides. We follow, and we are in heaven.

Your loving brother,

Max

Believing, disbelieving, suspicious or swept up in the enthusiasm of the moment, the crowd in Warnemünde could no more stop themselves from following Ben Alef than their ancestors in Hamelin could from trailing a more musical leader. But unlike that first German master who led his acolytes to the watery brink, Ben Alef emerged from the purifying destructiveness of the deep. Still digging out from under the wreckage of the storm that destroyed their homes and livelihoods, the sea folk found relief in His appearance. In each town the Messiah passed through, His very presence offered an intuition of something beyond the brutalities of nature and the shabby day-to-day accommodations of life. No matter what domestic, national, professional or cosmic dissatisfactions they felt, Ben Alef was there to rectify all. He almost never spoke, but He was the blank slate upon which each individual could write the recipe for his or her own redemption. After Kaltenhaven, after Warnemünde, there He was in Ostseebad, Rerik, and Dassow, and everywhere He went they hailed, "Hallelujah!"

At each stage, Father Immaculato and the experts expected the crowds to shrink in number. They assumed that Ben Alef would not be met so enthusiastically inland since most of the shore folk who followed Him with tents on their backs had lost their homes or livelihoods in the "storm of the century" and appeared to derive comfort from nearness to this man, or god, or whatever he was—this . . . personage—who had endured the same blast.

But they were wrong. In Dirche, a prosperous cement factory's whistle blew for lunch just as the motley procession passed outside, and it seemed as if the whistle blew to announce Ben Alef's arrival. Scores of workers in heavy boots and flannel coats poured through the plant's gates to share their lunch pails with the ragged and hungry.

Like a geyser's low rumble turning to a roar before the spout, the underground buzz of rumor grew in volume, and the *Frankfurter Zeitung* realized that the item its young stringer had sent in might become more than merely human interest, but suprahuman interest, or even news, before this strange episode came to its own conclusion. Newspapers were in the business of selling pages per day, cults from Switzerland to California were a hot topic, and there Ben Alef was, ripe for the plucking in their own backyard. Here was a story that had lain dormant for centuries—chanted millions of times a day from Mount Athos to Tierra del Fuego to Malaysia by believers with utter faith and fervency, but not as a living record of the chanters' own world—suddenly awoken like Sleeping Beauty after the Prince's kiss or a resurrected Nazi Obersturmbannführer.

But where the *Zeitung* blazed the trail, others were bound to follow, and several were already sniffing around. A reporter and accompanying photographer from the *Berlinspiegel* caught up with the procession a few kilometers west of Ostseebad while the German correspondent for *Le Monde* perused the wire reports and contemplated his own next move. It was time for the city desk to take its own copy seriously.

On the phone to Frankfurt, Fritz Hofmann was informed that he was to turn over all his notes to a senior staffer.

"It's my story!" Fritz cried.

"We're sending another reporter," the editor replied, no longer charmed by the cub's sense of property, and then tossed him a bone: "But if you want to tag along, you can."

The stuff that journalistic legend was made of evaporated. Fritz saw a vision—as clear as any disciple's—of his scoop moving up in the paper, toward the front, toward the top, and knew that his name would now be in italics at the bottom of the article, "with assistance from . . ."

Enter Richard Federman, a chunky middle-aged pro who had covered everything from dog shows to civic politics over two decades at half a dozen papers. Richard strolled into Fritz's room at the Nortbahn Ramada, poured himself a shot of schnapps from a dented flask, and demanded, "What's the deal: feature or leader?"

The question the senior reporter was really asking was not whether Mr. Ben Alef was the Messiah or just a local crackpot who provided an illustration of the desire for faith in our time, but whether the Alefites—as Ben Alef's followers were already calling themselves—genuinely believed. If they were out for a ride, he'd catch a lift and enjoy himself and write the story in his sleep, but if they were likely to beget a real and properly conclusive drama, then he might have an aisle seat on the next Waco.

"Front page," Fritz answered cockily. "At least as far as these people are concerned."

"The people don't make that decision. We do." Federman condescendingly patted Fritz on the back. "And you know how we make that decision? Timing," he said. "Timing is everything. And I'll grant you one thing: the timing of this story is very, very good." A drunk and a rascal,

Federman immediately understood Mr. Ben Alef and his companions' connection to the most potent angle of all, itself a story of timing, the calendar. For the past year, magazines had been filled with millennium pieces and papers were already counting down the days until the turn of the chronometer, and this might be the perfect hook onto the big fish. "So, where's the show?"

"I . . . I can't say for sure. I don't think they really know themselves, but they're moving in the direction of Hamburg."

Federman whistled. "Won't be so easy for them there." He explained that until now Ben Alef had only encountered rubes—economically middle-class maybe, but uneducated. When the naive rural tribe finally arrived in Hamburg—port, financial center, pornographer's paradise, original site of Beatlemania—surely the sophisticates would sniff out a sham or hoot at their sentimental spiritual message. "These folks are going to wake up in a city that never sleeps. It's the acid test."

"Does this mean anything?"

"Sure. It either means that they're really confident or they're really stupid. Care to lay any bets?"

"I . . ."

"Let's get to work." Federman unpacked a laptop computer, plugged it in, humming.

"What are you doing?"

"Taking the next step."

When a soccer team captures the World Cup or a movie becomes a hit, reporters who are not on the sports or cinema page search out a hook to latch on to. Not the winning goal or the Oscar—that's someone else's beat—but the player's diet for the food section, or the movie star's summer house for a real estate page. And what about the little people in the big man's life, the football striker's mother or the movie star's dissolute younger brother? The first obvious take on the Messiah Beat was to find out where the disciples came from, what *their* story was.

Actually, this was not only the logical, but the only possible take, since no record anywhere provided any information about Ben Alef. In fact, neither reporters nor the first tentative followers had yet figured out that "Ben" was not a first name.

Early fact checkers for Fritz's first dispatches had scratched their heads at the utter lack of references—no birth certificate, credit record, driver's registration, nothing. As far as the data banks were concerned, Ben Alef was a nonperson. And as far as the faithful were concerned, that was good. In fact, it was vital that He simply emerged from the ether onto the ocean. That, the Alefites knew, because Max Vetter had told them, but he never answered the obvious next question, because nobody asked it: What the hell were Ben Alef and the disciples doing out on the Baltic during the storm?

And they didn't say.

The first assumption was that Ben Alef and company were a group of North Coast natives whose brains had been scrambled by the storm along with their villages. "You watch . . ." Federman said as he shepherded Fritz through the forking paths of cyberspace on his Internet hookup. "We're going to end up finding the butcher, the baker, and the candlestick maker. Give me one of their names."

Fritz flipped through his notes and came up with his major source.

"Funny name," Richard said as he typed it in.

"Funny guy," Fritz replied, watching the screen jump to Richard's command.

At first, however, Snakes was as elusive as Ben Alef—no phone listing, no address, no bank account—although there was a tantalizing story that had run in the paper two decades earlier, about the death by snakebite on a NATO base of a couple named Hammurabi.

"Do you think there's a connection, I mean Snakes and snakes?" Fritz suggested.

"No, I think there's a coincidence," the experienced reporter scoffed, and continued to pursue his quarry deep into the caverns of modern identity.

No residence, no telephone number, no vehicle, no tax return, until, on a hunch, he tried for a criminal record. Where there wasn't an answering machine, one often discovered a conviction. The machine beeped and blipped, and six listings appeared on the screen.

"Bingo!" Richard cried as they scrolled down from "9/88, juvenile delinquency, sentenced to time served," to "1/90, assault, guilty, sentenced to thirty days in Potsdam Penitentiary, released after time served," to, as the suspect grew more professional and hired better lawyers, "5/94, narcotics, case dismissed due to lack of evidence," to "3/97, narcotics, guilty, reversed on appeal," and "3/97, promoting prostitution and possession of a firearm, case dismissed, witness unavailable," and finally arrived at "10/99, public nuisance, guilty, remanded to *Farnhagen.*"

"Wasn't that . . . ?" Federman said.

"The prison barge that sank a few weeks ago with four hundred and twenty-four prisoners."

"Or four hundred and twenty-three."

"Or"—Fritz did a quick calculation—"four hundred and eleven."

"Wait, wait, do you think . . . ?"

"Try another name. Bruno Morgen."

At home in the criminal database, the two reporters hot on the scent of the next development in the Messiah Saga went down the list of disciples, and sure enough all but Max Vetter shared the same last address, which went a long way to explaining why they didn't appear elsewhere on the roles of burgherdom.

"What does it mean?"

"They escaped before the barge went down."

Ahead of the pack, the *Zeitung* held effective copyright on a story suddenly bound to move straight up to the front of the Metro section with the next dispatch. No more cute, cosmic maundering. This was what a real reporter was in the game for. "Start writing," Federman commanded Fritz as he pondered their subjects' and, more especially, their rivals' next move once the late city edition hit the streets.

He chuckled to contemplate the consternation in other journalistic circles, which were undoubtedly debating whether to give any ink at all to the *Zeitung*'s loony serial. He could imagine his ex-boss at the *Düsseldorf Freiheit* waving his fortieth Camel of the day and snap-judging, "Naaah, just another jerk." But now the story had steam, and Düsseldorf would shit. He could see the headline: "Cons Come Home." From here on in, this was going to be fun.

"Now if we can prove that there's any connection between their escape and the disaster, we'll fry those suckers and have front-row seats at the barbecue."

The image was a little strong for any German to stomach, but they were citizens of the latter portion of the century, and this time justice was on their side. The two men looked at each other while the computer continued to hum and crackle as if frying the information within before frying the culprits without. Fritz felt mildly queasy.

. . .

"I don't like this," His Holiness said the second Father Immaculato entered the papal chamber. The minor investigation was beginning to feel like a major headache. Every morning there had been a message from the North Coast. Forty people in Kaltenhaven, two hundred in Warnemünde, three hundred in Rerike. And some who came never left, but followed Ben Alef and the convicts to the next station.

"I—"

"I don't care what you think. I don't like this, this *mockery.*" Beyond their obscene theological implications, the messages from Immaculato interfered with Urban's enjoyment of music. Knowing that good people, and more of them daily, were singing "Amen" to a false Messiah made it impossible for him to appreciate the choir.

"I—"

"Walking on water, corn from the sky—this isn't the Middle Ages! I want to know who these people are and what they think they're doing."

"I—"

"Stop talking about yourself, Immaculato, and give me the answer to a simple question. What is happening here?" He had canceled a goodwill trip to Africa because of this business.

"It is still small, Your Holiness."

"You call this small?" the Pope cried, and waved a column titled "Millennial Madness" from *Le Monde.*

"Hmm." Father Immaculato had seen the piece already and rather hoped that the Vatican Press Office hadn't picked it up, but the clipping service was apparently on alert. He pretended to skim the column lest he be castigated for not including it in his dispatch. "But they treat this as a joke."

"Not a funny one. I am a man who understands humor. Humor is a leaven that God gives us to make life bearable. I respect humor. I admire humor. But this is not humor; it's not humorous at all. This is sacrilege."

"There is good news, however. Look." Father Immaculato waved his own bit of press at the Pontiff. It was Fritz Hofmann and Richard Federman's piece from that day's *Zeitung,* hot off the presses.

The Pope perused the clipping, and nodded contentedly. "Criminals?"

"Apparently so. They admit it, especially the Arab who appears to be their spokesman, Hammurabi. No shame, no morals. He was in jail for urinating in a church. And the others are not much better."

"Hmm." The Pope read. "Thieves, arsonists, kidnappers, murderers. A delightful bunch."

"Once the reporter confronted them, they told him a bizarre story about lightning striking the barge. But that is in doubt, and when the barge is found—which it shall be; divers are searching for it now; the location is fairly certain—the truth will come out."

"And after the lightning?"

"That's where their story shifts to the water, but obviously they are lying, lying or demented because they really were struck by lightning, a miracle that . . ."

Father Immaculato was about to allow himself a small joke, but apparently it, too, wasn't funny and did not meet the stringent standards of the man who understood humor. The Pope humphed.

Father Immaculato continued, "The barge did slip its moorings, it did float to sea, and it did sink, and everyone but the twelve men from Cell Number 306 did drown. There the facts end. The rest is conjecture. The twelve must have found a sandbar, hence the alleged walk across the water. The process of rational explanation is under way. And the best news is that when they get to Hamburg, at the pace they are moving we expect tomorrow, they will be taken into custody."

"Why not today?"

"Well . . ."

"Spit it out."

"The local police chief in Tristau refused."

"Refused to carry out the law? A German policeman? On what grounds?"

"But they're going to Hamburg."

"So what?"

"As soon as I leave this room, I'll catch a plane and speak to the authorities there. The moment Ben Alef crosses the city line he and the rest of his crew will be apprehended."

Urban nodded with grim satisfaction, but he knew that his question was being avoided. "That police chief, the one who refused to obey the law. On what grounds?"

Father Immaculato took a deep breath and exhaled. "He said that his daughter, a nine-year-old child, she had been hit by a car several years ago and was paralyzed. . . ."

Ten minutes after the *Zeitung* hit the stands, Luther Huber, Hamburg Generalstaatsanwalt with larger aspirations, was awakened at his mistress's country house when a number to be dialed only in an emergency rang, and ten minutes later he was en route, siren clamped to the roof of his car, screaming, to the Municipal Courthouse and Jail Complex, thinking, thinking.

Unfortunately, he had more time than he desired, because Bette lived fifty kilometers outside the city. Of course, this had to hit the fan just when he had allowed himself the luxury of a two-day midweek vacation. He had told his wife that he had to attend a judicial conference in Mannheim.

During the agonizingly long two-hour ride in rush-hour traffic, speeding on the shoulders, blitzing through the tolls, Huber reviewed the situation. "Escaped prisoners. Messianic delusions. Cult following." Worse, the press was on top of this one, which always meant delicacy. It was a pity that a reporter had beaten the police to a major breakthrough involving the sinking of a state prison, but so be it, what was done was done. He had damage control ahead there—nothing he hadn't done before—but his focus was ahead as he nearly sideswiped a pedestrian crossing Bellstraße, oh!, at the green. There was also no doubt that the damage could get much worse if the combination of cult and criminals ignited. Hardly mentioned, but festering like a tiny, unnatural cancer in an embarrassing orifice was the history of previous occasions in which similar mania had led to fiasco: Jonestown, Waco, and far too many medieval antecedents that occurred within hailing distance of the current events' situs. Huber had seen careers go down the tubes when a situation like this was not handled properly. On the other hand, this was also how national reputations were made. If only he had time to think.

By the time he arrived at the complex at ten, the lobby was a madhouse like the Generalstaatsanwalt hadn't witnessed since he served as a legal intern in Munich in 1973. "No comment. No comment," he said, flicking off the reporters while an aide handed him a telephone book–size stack of files forwarded from the National Prison Authority in Berlin.

Worst of all, the delicacy of the situation was compounded by public concern. Upstairs, as the elevator opened on five, the executive floor, the local-affairs liaison handed him a batch of messages, faxes, and telegrams, some by morally outraged voters who wanted the felons apprehended, but many more by an uncharacteristically charitable populace that urged the state to give Ben Alef and his men a break. Striding down the hall, flipping through the messages, the General thought that if he saw the phrase "paid their debt to society" one more time, he'd puke.

To add to his worries, Huber's private secretary informed him of a request for an interview with a representative of Vatican City.

"Vatican City, what does Vatican City want?" he muttered, until, with an awful intuition, he knew. "Look, Grete, tell him I contributed to the Easter Fund. Tell him anything. Put him off."

"I can't, sir."

"Why not."

"He's already inside."

Huber was about to chew out the secretary when he saw her lids flutter as she crossed her rather abundant chest with a swift, practiced motion. "Fine, fine," he muttered, entered the office, threw the furled umbrella he carried rain or shine into its designated receptacle like a javelin, and shook Father Immaculato's cool, pale hand with transparently feigned politeness.

Fortunately, Immaculato was not in a mood for small talk, either. The father stated that, in the eyes of Rome, the events of the North Coast in the last few weeks were pure blasphemy, and that it ought to be stopped.

"Blasphemy is not a crime in the Federal Republic."

"But murder is, and these men are guilty of it."

"Not all of them."

"Most of them. Arrest them."

"We did, once."

"Are you suggesting that escape is a justification for pardon?"

"No, but there are extenuating circumstances." As chief lawyer for the government, the Generalstaatsanwalt oversaw both prosecution of criminals and representation of the state in civil actions—everything from national employment questions to defending the FR against an old lady who slipped on the waxed hallway of a courthouse. There were substantial liability issues regarding the *Farnhagen* disaster, and a class-action suit had already been filed on behalf of the drowned guards. Huber explained that the twelve men could be witnesses to the act of God and thus save Berlin many millions of marks.

Secular coffers were not Father Immaculato's concern. He interrupted the attorney's fine calculus with "They are already claiming to witness too many acts of God."

"Prisons are breeding grounds for religion. You yourself have sent emissaries—or should I call them missionaries?—into the penal system. For all we know it was a priest who gave these men their ideas."

"Since their ideas are at variance with every tenet of the church, I doubt that, but even if true, this is irrelevant. They must be arrested."

Huber sighed. "And they shall be. The law is clear."

"Good."

Huber did not, however, feel a burning need to add that although the law was clear, its dispensation was not. Call it weakness or call it largesse, but it was the state's prerogative to decide how vigorously to execute its statutes. A sign from Heaven was not easy for Hamburg to ignore. Nor was the voice of the public. Yes, the authorities said they would arrest the *Farnhagen* survivors, and they would, but there was no guarantee that they would be incarcerated. There would be an investigation, first.

For now, though, the General's statement was sufficient. Father Immaculato repeated, "The law is clear. Amen."

"Checkpoint Charlie," Federman whispered to Fritz.

Here, at the farthest city line of the metropolis, the procession moved toward its rendezvous. But it no longer included only Ben Alef and the twelve. The group had increased daily since Kaltenhaven as a multitude of so-called Alefites followed. Anna, town secretary of Warnemünde, and a few dozen solid citizens from each stop who just couldn't bear to see the last of Ben Alef had given spontaneous notice to their landlords, employers, and families to cast their lot with the disciples. Some walked, two boys from Tristau rode bicycles, and one couple with hair as long as Ben Alef's pushed a stroller. Each evening they sang songs and shared corn to recall the first public miracle.

As for the article that appeared in the *Zeitung* complete with mug shots, it created a flurry of excitement, but, strangely, no repercussions. Oh, a few more reporters attached themselves to the group like barnacles to the *Farnhagen*'s hull, but the upright Volk who met the messianic band in town after town didn't seem to care where they had come from or what their past was as long as Ben Alef and Snakes and the eleven killers and Max Vetter hallowed their ground by pausing to rest there. In every town, a small shrine arose where they stayed, and already those shrines had attained a ritual shape, a heap of stones covered with cornhusks and flowers, and rumor spread that the cut flowers spread over the stones never wilted, never shriveled, never died.

In fact, several of the convicts found it a relief to have nothing to hide. From the gavel of their conviction till the lightning of their liberation, they had been free to be murderers, but the pressure of public saintliness in Kaltenhaven and Warnemünde had almost been too much to maintain. They couldn't be themselves while Ben Alef floated onto yet another hastily erected platform to bless another crowd, but now they no longer had a choice.

"The law is clear," Omar Nazzarian said bitterly. Since his crisis, Omar had been quiet, worried but quiet, while the rest worried aloud. At some moment, almost every one of them considered fleeing, but each one finally remained. Partially, this was a matter of practicality.

"Where could we go?" Franz Palitzsch asked. Forget about post-office walls; their pictures were in the newspaper on a daily basis, and people followed their progress like a comic strip.

"There's nowhere to go," Langefeld said, sighing, so they strode forward to meet their fate. Down a last stretch of highway the bizarre train walked, past a line of dingy row houses with gaily strung Christmas decorations and fiberglass reindeer prancing atop their roofs. It still hadn't snowed yet that season, but the weather had turned fierce, and their prison rags were inadequate protection from the elements. Shivering, they marched until they saw the glimmering glass skyscrapers of downtown Hamburg from afar, like Oz, and their welcoming committee poised at an inconspicuous corner where the city legally began.

Fritz remembered the wise hack's statement back in the Ramada about how the cynical urban population would prove a tougher nut for the Messiah to crack than the bucolic country folk had.

But the wise hack was wrong. Here, at the farthest boundary of the metropolis, five hundred men and women awaited, some of them holding babies. There were also a heck of a lot more press vehicles. And, of course, a row of police cars and a van.

Suddenly, the macadam underneath the procession changed from black to gray, because the county had repaved while the city could not afford the expenditure. Ben Alef stepped over the line, and the reporters surged forward. "Mr. Alef. Mr. Alef, would you care to comment on this report?"

"Ever been in jail, Mr. Alef?"

"Over here, Mr. Alef," the photographers cried, holding their cameras over the heads of the reporters, hoping for one good shot for the morning edition, while the reporters continued to elbow each other and shove their microphones toward Ben Alef's wan face.

Hamburg was pandemonium. No one had expected anything like this—the crowd, the cameras, the sheer excitement that filled the air as densely as water filled the ocean bed.

"Critical mass," Richard Federman explained to Fritz Hofmann, who watched in amazement. "There's a high school science experiment in which a glass of water is saturated with salt, and then a branch is placed in the solution and immediately, voilà! it all adheres and gigantic crystals form before your eyes. One moment the salt is invisible and the next it blossoms. You and I have been the invisible salt, mein Herr, and now it's reached critical mass. Voilà! If this was America you could tuck the Pulitzer in your back pocket."

"But this is not America."

"Who cares. You're on staff at the *Zeitung* now."

"What?"

"I told you this was going to be fun. Let's watch."

"Mr. Alef! Mr. Alef!" they cried until a squat police captain with a badge on his breast stepped in front of everyone.

"Herr Ben Alef?" he said.

"I am that I am."

The captain did not catch the biblical reference and called out the roster of disciples in alphabetical order—"Anton Bartsch, Karl Blobel, Martin Clauberg, Dietrich Eisenheim, Herbert Glucks, Snakes Hammurabi, Georg Kiehr, Erich Langefeld, Bruno Morgen, Omar Nazzarian, Franz Palitzsch"—except for the one who would have been last, Max Vetter, who had done nothing wrong his entire life.

One by one they nodded their heads.

"In the name of the people of the Federal Republic of Germany, I arrest you."

"Shame!" cried out a woman waving a homemade placard reading "Haven't they suffered enough?"

The policemen linked arms to keep the crowd in its place in the convenience store parking lot.

"Do you understand?" the captain asked.

"I understand," Ben Alef said.

"He understands," Snakes repeated.

"He understands," a man in the crowd echoed. "He understands everything."

At that moment, three black limousines dispatched from the city center pulled up to the periphery of the crowd and three drivers in livery as grand as a Prussian field marshal's hopped out of their front doors and opened the sedans' back doors. Two were empty, but in one of them a familiar silhouette stood out against the bar light. Snakes wanted to say, "Excuse me, but I think my ride is here," except, of course, a different ride in a paddy wagon awaited. The Peddler nodded his head and shut the door.

"This way, please," the captain said, extending an open hand toward the paddy wagon as if inviting the men to a reception in their honor.

Cameras clicked like mad.

"Get them in the van," the captain ordered, and then he touched Ben Alef.

Snakes cringed, but there were no fireworks, no lightning, this time. All that happened was that the robe Ben Alef wore draped about his shoulders—the gray-and-silver garment presented to Him by the merchant of Warnemünde—slipped askew and His left arm was exposed.

"Look," a rookie cop declared, and his finger froze on the trigger and he repeated, "Look."

Police, protesters, and followers all looked and saw what the disciples had first seen on the safe beach of the new world.

"Holy Christ," the police department press representative gasped.

"Precisely," Fritz Hofmann replied.

"I don't get it," the police chief muttered, but that was untrue; he knew very well what the image meant. There were not many such tattoos in this country, but the image was indelible in their minds. It was the one symbol of their century they could never erase.

The thin blue numbers glowed on the thin man's flesh as if lit from within: 108016.

"Are you . . . ?" the reporter from Cologne could hardly ask the question.

And then Ben Alef delivered the longest speech he had given since

Kaltenhaven, the four short words destined to flash across the news wires of the world. In a voice as clear as the six numbers on his arm, he said, "I am a Jew."

One girl fainted, while a photographer fell to his knees, together with the rookie policeman.

The captain shrank back, but it was too late to avoid his duty. In the hush of half a thousand silent witnesses, the armed German authority marched the unarmed Jew off to jail.

Book IV
Grace

Chapter Ten

"JUDEN!"

NO OTHER WORD in the German lexicon was as terrifying. Despite the nation's large, secular publishing houses and its international electronics conglomerates, despite the frugal Volkswagens and luxurious Porsches its factories, filled with well-treated, unionized workers, produced, despite the voice of humane amity its ambassador advocated in the United Nations, despite its Nobel Prize winners in literature and science, despite its medical advances and excellent school system, despite its freely and endlessly acknowledged guilt and remorse and the billions of dollars of reparations payments the National Bank had issued over the last half-century, all it took was the single "J" word to rip off the dress of culture and civilization and reattire every German man, woman, and child in black leather boots and a brown shirt emblazoned with the sign of the twisted cross. The "J" word propelled modern *Homo germanicus* back to the twelve-year reign of the Thousand-Year Reich and its single defining moment of apotheosis, to the time when the entire nation bonded together in a vast national project to eliminate and incinerate another people, because . . .

Because why? Because the Jews were poor or because they were rich. Because they were clannish and isolated or because they wore top hats and attended the opera. Because they drank the blood of Christian children.

Because their tailors and seamstresses were spiritual, unworldly wraiths or because their bankers and journalists insidiously plotted to dominate the world from within the corridors of power. Because they did not believe in the common deity or because they did believe in their own tribal God. Because, like Everest, they were there. Because.

Every time the "J" word was mentioned it was as if a pick hit a tremendous cavity in the communal German maw. And yet the gigantic German tongue could not keep itself from probing that cavity every few minutes to remind itself of the pulsing rot beneath its cultured enamel. Of a second, Fritz Hofmann's headline, inexorably bound now for twenty-point type, wrote itself: "Juden."

And the secret was out.

Across Germany, people turned first now to the news from the Hamburg courthouse. The Messiah was one thing, but a Jewish Messiah was entirely another in this country where the few remaining Jews had attained the status of talismanic objects. Suddenly the curious, archaic story took on the resonance, the echoes, that the truest fiction requires. Suddenly, it was debated. Was He or wasn't he?

Ben Alef said no more for the present, but Eisenheim, the oldest, most degenerate disciple, calmly explained the situation to the mass of journalists who descended upon his new home in the Hamburg jail. "Yes, I killed Him. Strange things happened in Belsen. People think otherwise, but really, most of the Jews refused to die. Some were shot and crawled up the sides of the pit like cockroaches, others breathed in the gas and breathed out oxygen. All I know is that however many left the camp, as many more arrived and they looked the same and acted the same, so they must have been the same."

"Are you suggesting that the Holocaust is a myth?" asked one stupefied representative of the press, while the police chief, aware that Germany was the only nation in the world in which denial was a crime, prepared for a new indictment.

"It was an era of bright shining life; He was the only one I could kill."

"*You* killed him?"

"Of course, what do *you* think I was in jail for?"

"How?"

"However." Eisenheim smirked. "It didn't make a difference, gold-capped bullet or silver dagger, a little rap of the mallet to the side of the head or a shot of phenol in the heart." He mimed a hypodermic with a thumb plunging between the V of his first two fingers and laughed and the reporters cringed, but Eisenheim continued. "Or more mass methods: machine gun, rat-a-tat-tat, or Zyklon B, hisssss. I told you, it didn't make a difference, they were all effective, because He was the only one who really wanted to die."

That was the point when they knew he had gone over the line from evil to mad and left him ranting.

"The other Jews," Eisenheim insisted to a diminishing audience, "they weren't happy in the lager and that's why they're all over the place today. Don't you get it? Ben Alef was glad to die, and that's why I'd kill him again. Say, do you have a gun? A knife? A toothpick?"

Eighty million people lived in Germany, fifty thousand of them Jews. A minority! An endangered species! Like pandas in a New York zoo or a single nest of condors discovered in a Bavarian forest! The state strove to protect them and make their environment as hospitable as possible, to assist them to breed and thrive. But despite the renovated synagogues, the subsidized Yiddish-language newsletters, the klezmer concerts, the generously endowed libraries and centers for Jewish culture—the Federal government did everything but artificially inseminate buxom farm maidens with Jewish sperm to aid the growth of the tribe—the native stock of Jews refused to be fruitful and multiply in the boiled-ham-, butter-cookie-, and blood-scented air of the Fatherland. They were old and decrepit and their children tended not to marry, not to have children of their own, and most definitely not to wear the quaint, tourism-boosting and morality-enhancing costume of their ancestors. For some incomprehensible reason, they preferred other identities.

And now here was this . . . this . . . this throwback claiming proudly to have killed the one Jew who ever returned willingly.

Even the most rabid right-wing apologist was so embarrassed he had to leave and follow the rest over to Max Vetter, cornered in the courthouse phone booth from which he was frantically trying to arrange bail. It was Max who described the moment on shore when Ben Alef brought the dead Kommandant back to life.

The phenomenon that began with the miracles at Kaltenhaven was easy to dismiss. "Parlor tricks," skeptics said, laughing at the gullibility of the sea folk. "Any sixteen-year-old with a mail-order magic manual can hide half a granary in a square of cloth." When confronted with the walk across the Baltic, the same skeptics patiently explained the science of sandbars and tried to get the fisherman who knew that harbor to admit that it was possible.

"Anything is possible," Max replied calmly. "I know that now."

For now the claims of merely physical marvels had grown into primal mystery. Until now Fritz hadn't reported on Eisenheim's alleged revival; it was far too weird. Forget about the corn or walking on water; he couldn't go on record in a responsible publication, even presenting the story as an "unsubstantiated rumor," about raising the dead. But now there were no secrets.

Resurrection, first Eisenheim's and then, as the story spooled backward, Ben Alef's, was no parlor trick, no nautical anomaly. Plenty of strange things happened on this planet. Life itself germinated from some elemental stew and, if that wasn't sufficient, fish splashed up onshore and developed lungs and opposable thumbs. Hairy hominids figured out how to use a rough stone; what were the odds against that? Every day a new wonder, and almost no telling what the next day would bring. The lords of empires lost their heads, and paupers rose to fame and fortune. Incomprehensibly, crude venal men wrote sensitive, searing poems and functional morons made brilliant scientific breakthroughs. Look at language, look at love—miracles all! Every day, the odds against something, from a tone-deaf child hitting a perfect high C to an impoverished hod carrier winning the Irish Sweepstakes, shattered. There was almost no telling—almost, only almost, because—no matter what—there was always one single, absolute verity.

"I've seen a million dead fish," Max Vetter said, "and more dead men than I'd prefer."

"Were you in the war, sir?"

No need to say which war. In German—and Jewish—history there was only one.

"I was born in 1942, and my first memory is of a bomb and my brother tossed like a rag doll. Hit the ceiling, fell to the floor. Not a mark on him, but the air was gone from his lungs. I've seen men drowned and friends with cancer and kids in cars upside down in ditches with the wheels still spinning, volunteer fire department. I'm telling you, that soldier on the beach, that man walking next to Our Lord, that man telling you stories, he was dead."

Better nutrition and medical advances raised the average life span from thirty-seven in 1700 to seventy-three in 1950 and eighty-three in 1990. Looking forward, scientists assumed that improved care for and multiple part replacement of the human machine implied that there was no reason in principle why people could not theoretically live forever—the graph of existence no longer a rise and fall, but a rise and plateau—but no one had ever imagined traveling in reverse through the barrier from death back to life. Life might be reproducible in a test tube, but once that bulb flickered out, kaput. Resurrection was the ultimate proof of divinity.

Now, one man had confessed that he had killed another, who was in jail rather than underground, and a second man, a credible witness in all other respects, said he saw a dead man spark.

"You can forget about the corn," Max offered, "and you can explain away the walk on the Baltic, which I personally found convincing," he insisted. "I won't even mention that little girl in Tristau. . . . But show me anyone besides the Messiah who can raise the dead. Now, if you gentlemen will excuse me . . ." He unfolded the piece of paper that Snakes had slipped him in the midst of the scene at the border. "I have phone calls to make."

Outside, in the parking lot, Anna from Warnemünde turned to her friend Gertrude, who, along with a butcher named Hossler from Kaltenhaven and several others, had accompanied Ben Alef in from the coast. They were settled around a fire set in a municipal garbage can dragged from the perimeter of the property and filled with newspapers and cardboard. A dozen similar fires glowed from other spots on the parking lot. "We should never have let Him go."

"What could we have done?"

They looked up at the nine-story jail, its rows of wired windows like a hundred chessboards against a blank concrete table, the *Farnhagen* turned vertical and floating on land.

"I worked for the government. I should have known." Anna sobbed. "They'll never let Him go."

"They will, because they'll have to."

"Who's going to make them, you? You and me and those teenagers and that insurance adjuster from Rerike with pleurisy?"

A voice came from the perimeter of the circle. "Don't forget faith."

"Hello?"

A woman stepped into the flickering light and introduced herself: "My name is Margot." She spoke in a cheery, high-pitched voice that was more youthful than the creases at the corners of her mouth and the webbing across her forehead suggested. And then she just stood there, waiting. Every hour new arrivals wandered onto the parking lot, but this woman seemed childlike in a way that neither Anna nor butcher Hossler had at nineteen or nine or ever. She had the disconcertingly forward manner of a three-year-old approaching a stranger in a train station. As if she didn't realize that she was the stranger in this situation. "Hi," she said.

Well, it wasn't a formal occasion. Anna had never thought she'd be sleeping in public like a vagabond, but here she was, and how shocked Mayor Schmidt would be to see her. Served him right, the stuffy old coot, who couldn't believe she'd ever do anything on her own. "Hello."

"My name is Margot."

Poor thing, she was probably visiting someone else in jail and just happened onto the scene—although which prisoner she could comfort, whose imprisonment she could ease, Anna couldn't imagine. "Yes, you already introduced yourself. My name is Anna and this is Walter. We come from the Mecklenburg district."

"Then you shouldn't forget faith," Margot said, repeating her opening line, "unless you're a dunderhead," and she giggled.

The Warnemünde town secretary had entered onto her journey with high seriousness, and she automatically recoiled from Margot's silliness, but the ethos of the parking lot was to welcome everyone who joined. Ben Alef had made that clear, so, for lack of better conversation, she asked, "Are you lost?"

"No."

"Where are you staying?"

"Here, I guess." Margot shrugged. There was something weird about her. She wore a dingy white-and-gray peasant sweater embroidered with blue thread, daringly if fetchingly low-cut and tucked into a long skirt made of orange and yellow patches quilted together and cut dirndl style, tight at the waist and pleated at the hem. It was a fashion that Anna recognized but couldn't place and didn't trust. Likewise, Margot's long gray hair hung down her back in a thick braid that bespoke a frivolous adolescence instead of sobriety. That was it. The mature woman, fifty if she was a day, was dressed like a hippie. Indeed, she spoke like one, too, and said, "This is cool."

"Where are you from?"

"Actually, Paris."

"France?"

Margot smiled, "It's the only Paris I know."

"And what brings you here?"

"He does." Margot turned to gaze up the prison block.

At last, Anna understood, and her heart melted. No matter the chasm that separated the bustle-bound German bureaucrat from the dizzy French dame, they were connected in a deeper spirit. "You came all the way from Paris for Him?"

"Yes, I read an article and I don't know why, but I knew that I should be here. I saw His photograph in the paper and I felt that I had known Him all my life."

"I feel the same way," Anna replied, forgetting the odd forwardness and flighty impropriety of the stranger. "Walter, listen to this lady. All the way from Paris."

"Don't forget faith," Margot repeated.

And Anna recalled the worries she had voiced before Margot appeared out of thin air. "I know. I believe," Anna said. "I believe," she attempted to convince herself. "I believe," she said, but each time she said it her voice grew fainter, and between each "I believe" a choked-off sob grew stronger.

"Cool," Margot said, oblivious to everything but the light from the prison while Anna's lament passed from the Warnemünde corner to a group from Rerike who banded together beside their own fire. They, too, believed, but they, too, worried.

Anna's fears were contagious. It had been a gloomy march after the police van through the bitter cold, and everyone in the parking lot had made sacrifices to be here. Now, with Ben Alef and all the disciples except for Max Vetter in jail, it was hard to reconcile themselves to the end of the dream, and perhaps harder yet to believe that this wasn't the end. Each Alefite in his or her own way said the same thing: "Yes, yes, it's true. He is risen and He is here and we are saved. But this time I thought it would be different."

The sorrow traveled from cluster to cluster until the entire parking lot was an undulating, wailing sea of sorrow. Prisoners looked out of the windows to watch the flickering fires and the groaning multitude beneath them, and the guards turned up their radios to drown out the sound, which penetrated the prison like wind.

"Alas, for we have failed Him," cried the butcher, spitting out the saddest word he knew: "Again!"

"Again!" the dirge echoed from across the lot.

"Again," Margot said quite brightly, and this time Anna and the butcher looked at her and realized that she was an idiot.

Then, tortured because his faith was not as strong as it might have been, thinking of pain made palpable, maybe—not merely the intangible anguish of the soul, but the authentic suffering of the flesh—thinking perhaps of Ben Alef's forearm, the butcher thrust a hammy fist into the flame.

"Herr Hossler!" Anna cried, but he gritted his teeth and kept his hand in place. The tiny hairs on his wrist singed and the acrid scent of burning hair spread, but the butcher knew the smell of raw meat well and was not fazed by its flaring. He gritted his teeth and held his arm steady.

"Cool," Margot said.

"Walter, what are you doing? Walter!" Anna screamed, and the scent suffused the atmosphere.

Finally, when the pain was too great, and Walter was about to yank his fist out of the flame in defeat, Anna thrust her own red, mottled, thick-fingered, beringed right hand to cover his and hold it as they both charred and crackled, and she fainted.

From eight floors up, Snakes Hammurabi at the window watched the dozen glowing orange circles below, first one and then all of them blocked by the silhouettes of hands, fingers curling and twisting. He remembered a similarly shaped barrel, and he knew the consequences to come. These people were doomed. He turned on Ben Alef. "Do you know what they're doing?"

"What?"

"They're burning themselves."

"What?" Ben Alef repeated himself.

"My God!" Glucks, the schoolteacher, addressed or exclaimed. "They're turning medieval."

"Burning themselves," Snakes repeated with an unusual harshness. The Alefites could quit their jobs, leave their homes, abandon their once-loved ones, turn their entire lives upside down to follow Ben Alef, but that meant nothing as far as Snakes was concerned, because those jobs and homes and wives and children meant nothing. And Snakes, like any career criminal, was by nature at peace with a certain degree of personal and social disruption that his acts might cause—but this was different. For the first time, real human beings were being hurt as a direct result of their faith. From thirty meters up, Snakes could see the grimaces of the mass of people circled about each fire with their multiple hands thrust into the flames like so many puffy white marshmallows on thin armlike sticks. He could hear the half-stifled shrieks, and feel the agony of pure pain inflicted without reason, yet the greatest pain of all was inside him. It was a pain he had not felt since the afternoon when his lungs nearly burst under the water of the River Lyons. Water, fire, no difference.

"No."

"They're not burning themselves? Pardon me if I'm mistaken. Then what is that smell?"

"The odor of faith." Ben Alef inhaled deeply.

"But why should faith . . ."

Ben Alef turned now, His own eyes ablaze.

Snakes looked down at his ruined shoes, afraid that as the butcher's and secretary's fingers were shriveling, so he would be immolated if he stared into the inferno of his Lord's gaze. How could He remain silent?

"Samuel," Ben Alef said, and fixed his foremost disciple to the spot. "Samuel, I call thee," he said, christening Snakes with a new name.

"Samuel," Blobel whispered to Clauberg, pointing out this remarkable blessing.

But Clauberg, the arsonist, was rapt, and noticed nothing but the enticing pirouettes of flame. Aside from the too well-controlled campfires of the last ten days, he hadn't seen real fire since being incarcerated a quarter of a century earlier.

"Samuel," Ben Alef said, "you must understand. They are turning themselves into Jews."

And Snakes did understand, absolutely and immediately. Fifty years earlier a male Jew could be identified simply by dropping his pants, but the sign of the covenant had changed. Circumcisions were now common procedures in modern hospitals. In the new dispensation, a new sign was necessary, a sign not of the blade, but of the brand. The people down below, whether they knew it or not, were converting.

It all made a horrific sense, and Snakes struggled to accept it, but this time he could not. All he could do was ask himself again, "How can He remain silent?"

"Samuel," Ben Alef said softly.

"My name is Snakes."

. . .

Followers became penitents, but what the fuck were they atoning for? Thirty meters above sea level, the multimurderous crew of disciples watched in astonishment as down below the Alefites lit themselves like festive Roman candles for their sins: jaywalking, littering, lust in their hearts or must in their hearts, those desiccated organs that beat in name only from the day they were born until the day they were reborn. The parking lot replete with sinners who had run stop signs and neglected to call their parents on their birthdays did as did butcher Hossler who had occasionally misweighed a rump roast in his favor. They pushed their way to the fiercest part of the fire, and their sleeves exploded in flame.

The weakest sinners only singed their fingertips from afar, but the strongest retained pride of place at the red-hot rim of the barrels, gagging on the fumes of the fire and burnt flesh until the signs of their remorse on the shells of their souls were evident for all to behold. Finally, satisfactorily mortified, they raised arms aloft toward Ben Alef to display garish streaks of charring and places where their skin had split to reveal the liquefied pulp and shafts of exposed blackened bone and blood vessels that had burst and cauterized in the same moment. Everyone at the circles of fire was covered with soot and spattered pus and eccentric human fluid. Blistered and begrimed, they prayed.

"Familiar," Eisenheim wheezed.

"Strangest thing I've ever seen," Clauberg agreed.

"Except in your dreams," Kiehr commented.

"Maybe not even there. Hey, look at that one." Clauberg pointed toward the edge of the lot, where a woman whose hair had caught on fire danced amid a circle of clapping sinners.

Snakes was the only one in the cell, besides Ben Alef, who was not engrossed by the spectacle in the parking lot. Unlike the Messiah, however, who sat on the floor in contemplative silence, his blessed one, Samuel Hammurabi, paced back and forth, shook but failed to rattle the bars that encased him with their familiar geometry, and only every ten laps peeked down at the delirium so explicitly displayed for his theological delectation. He looked at the people and then at Ben Alef and then—as if a light were blinking on above his head—he noticed the light above his head; it wasn't *just* a light, but a beacon to the multitude.

Despite the frenzy on the macadam, every so often, about as frequently as Snakes glanced out, he saw someone glancing up, arms aflame, seeking affirmation, recognition.

So while Clauberg, Kiehr, Blobel, Palitzsch, Langefeld, and the rest pressed against the window the way those below pressed toward the glowing barrels, Snakes hunkered down into a squat and then propelled himself as high as he could. With fingers extended rigidly upright in salute, like the once-dead Kommandant on the beach, he shot toward the ceiling and smashed the light, and collapsed into a suddenly dark cell, together with a shower of shattered glass.

"Hey, what gives?" Anton shouted.

"There, that's what gives," Snakes answered, certain before he could brush the shards of glass from his shoulders, let alone get to the window to confirm it, that his statement was true.

Yes, the signal worked. As immediately as the hysteria down below had erupted, it ended. The spigot that regulated the Alefites' dementia shut. One black square in a façade filled with illumination was enough to stop the pandemonium in the parking lot. "Look!" the sinners cried.

"Shunned." Anna totally misread Snakes Hammurabi's intended absolution. "Though I believe, I am shunned." She sobbed.

Apparently the Alefites' self-immolation was too meager a payment for their sins. The verdict arrived with a clap of darkness that meant, "Insufficient!" And immediately, more imaginative penitents began to cast about for more fearful instruments with which to assail themselves: stakes from municipal rose bushes and staves from the benches that had not yet been burned and chains that cordoned off official police department vehicles and perhaps the vehicles themselves, liberated from the secular lot and put to spiritual good use.

But before they could employ any of these implements, a crushing rumor spread that, rather than too deficient, their payment was maybe too abundant for their iniquities. Across the charcoal-specked lot, people suddenly felt that a palpable scourging to satisfy an incorporeal yearning might be a gross violation of the order of things, the prideful atonement itself a greater offense than the offense presumably atoned for.

Insufficient. Overabundant. Too little, too late; too much, too soon; who knew? In either case, unsatisfactory. The blank window spoke with silent eloquence.

Alas, the penitents' wounds also spoke in their own mute, sensory language. Its idiom was composed of rent, shriveled, and flaking skin, its vernacular one of oozing, throbbing flesh, and together they shrieked of suffering and the desperate need for justification for that self-inflicted, other-directed pain.

And it was not forthcoming.

Butcher Hossler's scorched right palm still glowed with the embers of its ignited innards as he lifted it up for Ben Alef to see, but Snakes had shut the light, and Hossler felt humiliation atop agony, a pain of the soul to parallel the pain of the body. Now that the sole chance for relief was gone, only pain and grief remained.

But if there was no solace from above, an unexpected comfort reached out from a more human source standing next to the butcher. Margot clasped his exposed palm between her gaudily ringed fingers and, before he knew what she was doing, she kissed it, the cooling moisture of her lips sizzling on the simmering flesh.

Hossler sighed and Margot carried his disfigured limb to her heart, leaving a smudgy black streak across the embroidered white cloth. Then, from her heart, she slipped the thick, broiled fingers under the edge of her blouse to caress her unencumbered breast.

Again, a message circulated throughout the lot with the speed of spreading fire. This time, however, it was not a message of fire, but of flesh and desire. Minutes after the passion for destruction came to the halt dictated by Snakes Hammurabi's unilateral blackout, passion itself overwhelmed the multitude. Margot and the butcher, oblivious to the company, sank to the pavement, her long, quilted skirt riding up over calves, knees, and thighs.

Not everyone participated at first. Even as teenage Alefites eagerly shed their clothes to seek a deeper warmth within each other's bodies than the fire from the barrels had been able to excite on the outside, and couples who already knew each other familiarly *knew* each other in an unfamiliar venue, Anna from Warnemünde whispered fearfully, "Herr Hossler? Herr Hossler, excuse me, but Herr Hossler, what are you doing?"

Although the answer ought to have been obvious, the good German butcher did not hold Anna's obtuseness against her. He was too involved. Grunting under the swaying torso of the half-century-old hippie chick who had climbed astride him—which enthusiastic occupation by no means inhibited her from reaching out to undo the belt buckle of a postman from Rerike—Hossler replied to Anna with nonverbal generosity. He extended five charred emissaries out from under Margot's exotic clothing and entwined them with Anna's burnt and trembling fingers to invite her to join the fun and redemption.

"All is allowed."

"Cool," someone said, and Hossler wasn't sure if it was braless Margot or the bustled Anna.

Gradually, the literal flames of the parking lot faded to crackling cinders while newly kindled and stoked human flames intensified. First, one could hear subtle unbuttoning, unclasping, and unzipping sounds of garments being removed. This was followed by gasps and audible shivers in the cold, which sent the goosebumped Alefites directly toward the nearest supply of hot and vital fluids, like thirst-crazed Saharan wanderers stumbling upon an oasis.

Murmuring welcomes and avid embraces swiftly turned to the wet sounds of mouths and multiple openings engaged—wed—in the flexible apportionment of the imminent millennium. Even the neutral reporters, whose job it was to stand aside and record, were drawn to participate. Tempted by the earlier flames, Fritz Hofmann had abstained, but tempted by orgy, he dove in with youthful joie de vivre, while Richard Federman sighed, "Like Berlin in the thirties," before he, too, dropped his trousers and entered the fray.

Some modest souls hastened into makeshift tents, which shook with their ardor, while most acted in public, on the pavement, draped over police cars amid the rising aromas of fecundity that replaced the charred scent of the site. As the prescient list maker from the *Herald Tribune* might have noted, "Omnisexuality."

Wind ripped through the lot, carrying stray newspapers and empty paper cups aloft in a heaven-bound spiral, but the zealous, earthbound Alefites hardly noticed the climate. They pursued their temporal mission to gasps and yelps without a pause. Their previous moaning had changed in tone, from anguish to ecstasy, as those who had sought to ravage themselves rewarded themselves instead, because Ben Alef could not. By the flickering shadows cast by the dying garbage fires, they fucked, one in all, and all in one.

Where everything is allowed, everything is required.

"I can't believe it." Langefeld sighed.

For most, the scene of ghostly white figures cavorting like mad amid the constellations of embers burning through a dozen metal garbage cans was a dream image that did not begin to echo the world they once knew.

"Damn, isn't that the cop from Tristau?"

"How can you tell?"

"He's wearing his hat."

"What is the world coming to?" Eisenheim asked of nobody in particular.

That was the moment when the disciples' curious glee turned sad, for even less than their own debauched society did the field of writhing figures express the new world the men thought they had occupied for their single precious week in transit from one cell to another. These were dangerous incorrigibles who had been incarcerated for stabbing, poisoning, shooting, or elsewise killing other people for their own small profit or momentary pleasure or various demented ends. And they were caught, and they understood that their punishment was just, because they were guilty, not of sins of the soul, but the corpus. Nobody minded what they thought as long as they acted like civilized people; which they hadn't. And the twentieth century wasn't the Middle Ages. Basically, the law's attitude was "We don't care if you hate your mother as long as you don't kill her, we don't care if you envy your neighbor's Mercedes as long as you don't steal it, we don't care if you lust after teenagers as long as you don't rape them, and we don't care what your feelings about churches are as long as you don't pee on the pulpit."

But a week earlier, the ethereal world of thought had become as real as a stony beach, and their own thoughts had undergone a transformation. The procession from the Baltic along the shore had had an entirely unbodily sense that changed the convicts. Not only did they believe that their erstwhile colleague in shackles was the Messiah, the very One humanity had being awaiting for, lo, these thousands of rotations around the sun, but that He had redeemed them and would do the same for everyone on earth, every forsaken sucker and weakling they had once preyed upon with all the compunction of a barracuda cruising for cuttlefish. Now, as Snakes had told an audience in Rerik, they were all fish together in the grand, oceanic deep.

Ben Alef had led them to a holy, unworldly place where the soul was more veritable than the body—where they *had* souls. Suspicious at first, then reluctant, even they had ultimately converted, and perhaps it was their conversion more than any of Ben Alef's other miracles that had in turn convinced butcher Hossler from Kaltenhaven and Anna from Warnemünde and the rest of the Alefites. If Ben Alef could change these creatures, He was real. Who else but the Messiah could do that?

Nor was it a sham. These arsonists, rapists, kidnappers, killers, and con men believed in their new, true selves, a giving, sustaining, loving community of peers, a beatitude of saints. They cherished the wash of pleasure that came over them as they walked the scrub routes parallel to the Nortbahn to speak to and save another crowd, to add the chosen to their troupe and move on. Oh, they might relapse occasionally—Kiehr might have the same frank, ferocious desires as before—but then Ben Alef made that sick girl walk, or they might just catch a glimpse of themselves in a mirror, and once again all would be well. Until now.

Now the flock of elderly widows Palitzsch had smiled at, the gaggle of innocent tenth-grade girls whom Glucks had befriended, the band of boys whom Langefeld had met, met one another and assembled in every arrangement imaginable. It was appalling.

The disciples watched the ceremony they had unwittingly ushered, shocked as any reformed sinner to witness what they had once been.

Even Snakes Hammurabi, who had most recently known his own version of such high life at the Kastrasse, not a kilometer distant from the Hamburg Municipal Jail, stared at the abandon. Unlike Bruno and Anton and Glucks and Kiehr and the rest, however, he felt an emotion dissimilar to their saintly repugnance. To the contrary, for the first time since the story had begun, he felt a longing to return to the life he had once known. Shabby and shallow as it was, he yearned for the peace of the unblessed. Snakes was jealous. Then, even though the light in the cell was still dead, it was resurrected inside Snakes's own head.

Despite the vulgarity of his every waking moment of the last decade, Snakes had always been chaste in language. No matter what the desperateness or appropriateness of the occasion, he seldom cursed, but now he muttered every obscene description of the incidents occurring below he could think of, all those four-letter words connoting orifices and appendages and every combination thereof. Now that he had experienced firsthand the eunuchly glory of the clouds, he craved the erect, inflamed organs of pure mortal Eden. Maddened, he tiptoed to the far corner of the cell while the others stood mesmerized at the window, unzipped his stained and torn lime-green pants, and masturbated.

Ben Alef slept.

Chapter Eleven

CALL THEM REMARKABLE or call them miraculous, call them human or call them divine, a series of events happened. Eleven men witnessed all of them. A twelfth man witnessed most of them. Forty men, women, and children witnessed one of them. And then, those people themselves were witnessed by the newspapers, which led to the police, which seemed to have led to . . . what?

So Snakes Hammurabi thought to himself when he woke to the scent of smoldering fires. He also thought of his father, the seeker whose search had killed him and Snakes's mother. Snakes—or was it Samuel?—didn't remember much. Hamad Hammurabi was always busy, with his work or with his private spiritual quest. Trying to summon his father's image from the well of the past, all Snakes could bring forth was a thin, well-groomed mustache and a pair of soft, pliant hands that pushed a boy named Samad under the water and brought forth one named Stephan.

Then another name came to mind—Esteban—and another image: a craggy mountain in moonlight, a large structure with a pitched tile roof, a heavy gate with enormous iron hinges, another procession vaguely resembling the march of the Alefites. Suddenly the image was washed away by more water.

Where the hell had water been when those stupid wretches outside started immolating themselves? They could have used one of Ben Alef's famous showers.

Snakes looked at the sleeping Messiah. It was as if His insomnia in the *Farnhagen* had been debited from some grand ledger that had to be balanced, rectified, now! Or perhaps it wasn't until He was fully exposed, at large, in the world, that He *could* sleep.

All the men in the cell were sleeping. Only Snakes's cot was empty, except for the coarse blanket and thin pillow that also reminded him of the *Farnhagen*. Regulation prison linen. The Ministry in charge of these things probably bought them from the Chancellor's brother-in-law by the hundred thousand. How easy it would be to place that lousy pillow over Ben Alef's face and hold it there. See if He could resurrect Himself.

Snakes smiled. When he smashed the light and shifted the Alefites' attention from self-destruction to sex, he had turned the effects of Ben Alef's silence upside down, and was delighted with the voluptuous frenzy that ensued. That was the gross, physical world he knew and felt comfortable with. He just hadn't known he was happy to share.

Of all the changes occuring inside him, Snakes's newfound compassion for others was the strangest, most difficult for him to accept. Two months ago he would have gladly ripped off those folks sleeping below for every pfennig they were worth. And now he was their protector. He had smashed the beacon that misled them toward the rocks of their crazed mortification when their Messiah refused, because, as Ben Alef said, they were converting.

What the hell did that mean? Snakes had been the first to notice the number on Ben Alef's arm, but he hadn't dwelt on it. The Messiah was the Messiah, and maybe it was obvious that He had to be Jewish, but this Jewish stuff mystified Snakes. Yes, he knew about the War. He was sick and tired of hearing about it. Every season brought forth new books, movies, memorial services as his German neighbors wallowed in their own castigation. Maybe it was the same impulse that had led the Alefites to burn themselves when they discovered that Ben Alef was a Jew.

But the Peddler was Jewish, too, and he didn't wear funny clothes or eat any weird food. He ate anything, anytime. Maybe this was what Jewish psychiatrists called a love-hate relationship. The Peddler was what he was, and maybe it had shaped him, but Snakes didn't think psychologically. What about the Peddler?

That brought up the second question, the simpler one. If Snakes couldn't yet figure out, what was happening inside himself, he could focus on the outside world, which would surely play a larger role in this drama than any of the actors suspected. Besides the Peddler—call him commerce—whom Snakes had unwisely brought into the equation with his ill-advised phone call, there was also the press, also the police, and neither of those institutions was going to leave this alone.

Thoughts Snakes—or Samuel or Stephan or Esteban or Samad or whatever his name was—could only tentatively recognize as "religious" swept through him as he gazed over the charred wreckage from the night before. Although he had acted to counter Ben Alef's unconscienable silence, he still felt as if the sleeping figure had filled a void in his life. Of course, he had never known about the void until it was filled, but now he felt the belated terror of a man who strolls across a meadow to read a sign with small print that says, "Warning: Land Mines."

The sheer presence of Ben Alef was a relief and yet a fright. Snakes was not alone and the world was not meaningless. What it meant, he still couldn't say, but *that* it meant was sufficient. He could distrust the Lord and believe in Him at the same time. What Snakes didn't know was how extraordinarily "Jewish" this was.

Was he the only one awake in the whole universe?

In fact, in less cosmic, more mundane terms, Snakes was not alone. Several floors beneath him, one other person looked out a window of the Hamburg Municipal Jail, scanning the field of the previous night's hysteria.

Generalstaatsanwalt Luther Huber had been awake half the night, half inclined to arrest everyone in the parking lot, half tempted to join them. But no, he was the responsible one who had to mop the cage after the animals. Sometimes he thought that all he was was a garbage man with a fancy title, cleaning up every nasty human mess on the North Shore, especially those left by the likes of his upstairs guests. And what gratitude did he receive? Every time the phone rang, he jumped; he spent most of his life on the phone with his various assistants and department heads who were unable to decide whether to put on their left shoe or their right shoe first unless he told them. And now, all the shoes were dropping. One piece of bad news followed another throughout the early morning, until he couldn't take it any longer and decided to sneak out for a quarter-pound of tasteless beef drowned in mayonnaise and a cup of fries; but he should have known better.

A score of reporters from every major German and European and international publication, some just arrived in Hamburg, were drinking coffee on the courthouse steps and teasing Fritz Hofmann and Richard Federman about the night before.

Fritz blushed, but Richard said, "Sometimes a reporter must really get to know his subject."

"And from what I hear, you got to know most of them," said one of his old friends from the *Freiheit* with a laugh.

"What do you mean 'most'?" Richard replied. "Who'd I miss?" He surveyed the field of exhausted Alefites, covered now with the blankets an emergency medical crew had delivered along with powdered eggs and the coffee the journalists were scarfing down and the treatment some of the most burnt and lacerated required after their sexual urges were spent.

"Look, here comes Herr Huber. Herr Huber, a word please." They pushed toward the Generalstaatsanwalt, who couldn't avoid the gauntlet.

"Sorry, guys, no comment."

"What about the orgy that took place here last night?"

"Unsubstantiated rumors."

"Far as I hear, it was substantiated by about a hundred witnesses. Every prisoner in the city had a front-row seat."

"Unfortunately, these are not reliable witnesses." Huber tried to speak with a straight face.

"What about the police on duty?"

"They were inside the jail and had no business with whatever was going on outside."

"Nothing happened, huh?"

"Whenever there is a large crowd, some rowdy elements may get out of control. We are looking into it."

"Don't look too hard or you might find it, sir."

"No further questions." Huber stormed back inside without his daily ration of mayonnaise, muttering to his aide, "Get those jackals out of here."

"I don't think they'll leave until the Messiah is released, sir."

"Who?"

"The escaped prisoner."

"Well, let them wait."

"And what about the journalists, sir?"

The General looked at the gray and lowering sky as if he expected a new storm. "Keep 'em from drinking the city's coffee and let 'em freeze." As far as he was concerned everything was under control at that moment, and the escapees would be on their way back to prison within the hour. But by the time he got back upstairs, the phone was ringing again.

"What the piss fucking shit is going on there?" shrieked the mellifluous voice of Jürgen Grabner, elected leader of the German Republic.

"Well—"

"Shut up, Huber. If I want to hear your cocksucking, cunt-lapping excuses I'll ask for them."

"Yes, sir."

"So, tell me already, you asshole. A fucking freak show you're running? What is this, the fucking 1960s?"

"Felt like it for a second out there, sir." Huber was prepared for verbal abuse, but he was no clerk and didn't have to take it. A civil servant, the top-ranking lawman in the north owed nothing to Berlin except cooperation. In fact, he secretly coveted the Chancellor's office and thought he might have a decent chance in some future parliamentary election.

"What about the press?" Of course, that was the Chancellor's real question.

"Full force gale. But we didn't give them too much of a show, besides taking God into custody, I mean." Huber sighed. No way around this. It was miserable, and the only pleasure he could find was in passing along some of his torment to the Chancellor, who still didn't know the really bad news.

"They still there?"

"Who?"

"The press, goddammit." But then, before he could receive an answer, perturbed by Huber's question, he demanded, "Who else might I be referring to?"

"I thought you might have been referring to the prisoners, sir."

"Well, where the hell else would they be?"

There was no use hiding the result of his last hour's other calls. The Chancellor would surely hear about it himself within fifteen minutes. Huber softly spoke one word into the receiver only to hear it echo back like thunder.

"*Bail?* What the fucking hell do you mean bail?" the Chancellor screamed across several hundred kilometers of airspace at the Generalstaatsanwalt in Hamburg.

Huber replied mildly, "Do I have to explain the word?"

"How the hell did they get bail?"

"According to a little document called the Constitution, all prisoners are entitled to bail. The judge set an amount and it came in."

"What, some night court bozo thought this was a speeding ticket here? I want to know who's responsible," the Chancellor ranted.

"Actually, it was Judge Uhlenbrock."

"Asshole."

"I believe he prefers the epithet 'defender of civil liberties.' Besides, I don't think any other judge wanted to touch this case."

"Can't blame them. I don't exactly like this pile of shit on my desk either."

"Be that as it may, the prisoners made bail."

"Who provided it?"

"A well-known criminal lawyer."

"Is that a lawyer for criminals or a criminal slash lawyer?"

"Take your pick."

The Chancellor hardly had to guess. Even in Berlin, the dean of the northern legal establishment received press. "Otto Loritz."

"Precisely."

The Chancellor had already been briefed on the scene at the border by the arresting officers, and had been assured that everything would go smoothly from here on in. Unfortunately, the senior partner of Loritz, Jambor, and Eicke was not the Chancellor's idea of smooth; he was familiar at the courthouse as the attorney of record for high-powered mobsters and white-collar embezzlers, not individual nut cases.

"Everything *was* under control; we had cordoned off the parking lot and were considering arresting the entire band of Alefites—trespassing, public indecency, you name it—and the escapees would be on their way back to a real prison by now but . . ."

"Yeah, yeah, so what happened?"

"At first Loritz only wanted the Messiah."

"Let's get our terms right, Huber."

Touché. The General had made the same mistake as the aide he had chewed out earlier. "So-called Messiah."

"How about 'escaped prisoner.' "

"Fine."

"Wait a fucking second. This is no indictment. Bail is not a function of all arrest, only arrest prior to trial and conviction. There's not going to be any trial here. These men had their day in court."

Huber sighed. "Frankly, I agree, but Uhlenbrock accepted Loritz's argument that because of the *Farnhagen* disaster there were now questions of double jeopardy involved. He also pointed out that these men have not attempted to escape. Just the opposite. They came to the police."

"They did that for the fucking press!" the Chancellor wailed.

Huber refrained from pointing out that the Chancellor would put on tap shoes and dance on a toy drum in return for half an inch in the same press. "You know that and I know that, but it doesn't make a difference. The important thing is to avoid making a martyr of this guy."

There was silence across the wires. Huber could feel his superior wince. In the current context, the word "martyr" was especially potent. Finally, the Chancellor asked, "So how did it go down?"

When Loritz, whose briefcase would have cost a civil servant a month's pay, arrived at the Hamburg jail, he cut to the chase—"I've been retained to represent the defendant Ben Alef"—and asked to see his client privately.

Standing on the other side of the bars, with a semicircle of disciples arced behind him, Ben Alef asked, "Why?"

"I have been retained on your behalf, sir, and bail has been arranged. Please come with me."

"But what about them?" Ben Alef gestured toward the eleven remaining ex-convicts.

Loritz shrugged. "I have only been retained on your individual behalf, sir. I'm sure these men will find adequate legal counsel."

If the bars hadn't stood between them, Snakes, tapping his toe at an increasing beat and simmering with fury, might have jumped the attorney and cut his clean-shaven throat. Loritz was *his* lawyer, dammit, and if Hammurabi remembered correctly there was a small matter of his own, apparently meaningless retainer. First, Loritz couldn't handle the minor misdemeanor charge that had put the public urinator in this position, and now he wouldn't even deign to recognize his former client.

Ben Alef repeated, "These men are with me."

"Yes, I understand, but . . ."

"Unless they leave, I cannot."

Frustrated by Ben Alef's silence the night before, Snakes—perhaps Samuel—now had the pleasure of interpreting his Lord's words. "You heard Him, shyster."

"Ah, Mr. Hammurabi," Loritz said, as if he noticed the speaker for the first time. "I wasn't informed that you were one of the chosen."

"I've always felt chosen, shyster. Now you do as your first client suggested or you can scram. Together we stand."

The consternation this provided Loritz was of deep satisfaction to Huber, but the attorney immediately returned to Uhlenbrock, gritted his teeth, and cut checks for the eleven other men. It was like a mystery the General had once read, in which the killer plants a bomb aboard an airplane in order to kill one of the passengers. Loritz had his orders to get Ben Alef released and would empty the rest of the jail if he had to do so to accomplish his goal. The checks were duly processed and, by noon, the disciples walked out the front door of the Hamburg jail, where the scene looked as if Germany had won the World Cup, the square overflowing with banners and placards hailing the Messiah and damning the state. Loritz hustled the twelve men into the same three oversized limousines with rental plates that had appeared at the border.

With Alefites and press confined to the far side of a police line, the only one standing on the steps was Max Vetter. It was Max who had phoned the man who phoned Loritz, and Max who then waited as meekly as a shadow. He said, "I hope I did well."

Ben Alef smiled and said, "Yes, you did well. You did not betray me today."

"When?" Omar asked.

Book V
Incorporation

Chapter Twelve

"ABOMINATION!" declaimed the preacher on the television set mounted over the bar. "Truly, this is the age of abomination. Look at the early signals. Abortion on demand, murder of the precious, vital fetuses floating at ease inside the motherly womb, r-r-ripped out—" He pantomimed his part of a tug-of-war. "And flushed down the toilet."

Sweating profusely, the preacher rolled up his white sleeves and looked straight into the camera, which zoomed in on his face. "And it gets worse, much worse. Abortion on demand is a code, I tell you, a code for abortion on command. From the 'right.' "—he used the word with disdain—"to kill the produce of one's own flesh, this will lead down the slippery slope to the state's absolute requirement of abortion. . . .

"And abortion isn't the only vehicle on that awful road to perdition. Nope. Drugs, pornography, fornication, the deterioration of all moral standards, that's the world your children—if you're lucky enough that the state lets you have children—will live in, unless you act now to stop that world from demolishing ours."

The speaker paused for a moment to wipe his brow with a monogrammed handkerchief.

"Now here's the pitch," the man standing under the television said as he fiddled with the sound.

"Now, you people know that you can buy your Bibles right here in the lobby, but the folks at home can do just as well by calling the number coming up on the bottom of your screen right now. We'll wait a second for you to get yourselves a pencil and write that number down, or, better yet, don't wait, grab a phone and call right now, trained operators are waiting for your call—"

Click. The television went dark.

"Hey, is that something or is that something?" said the man underneath the empty screen. "I'm telling you, the guy's a genius, rakes in forty million a year, tax deductible. But you know what, we can do better."

None of the thirteen men watching responded until Georg Kiehr finally drawled, "Good reception."

"Cable," their host replied. "Best thing since onion rye. We receive two hundred channels here from all over the world. There's a huge dish on the roof that gives us the best reception in Germany. Football games from South America, opera from China, the diamond database from South Africa, and this crap from the States."

They sat in a long room without any windows, a cavern with black leather banquettes curled into alcoves along the perimeter and a winding staircase up to a mezzanine with yet more tables that could, as the permit framed on the wall authorized, seat two hundred and twenty-five people according to local fire code regulations. The room was located inside a two-story warehouse in the St. Pauli district, where the three limousines seen earlier at the border had sped as soon as they left the courthouse.

Anton turned to Snakes and said, "So this is the place."

It was a dumb question, because a strip of pink neon script reflected in the mirror over the bar read "Kastrasse."

"Yep," Snakes replied, "all forty foreign beers and two hundred channels. You want to watch some opera from China?"

The man beside the television leaned across the bar. He was pudgy, balding, elderly—everybody's favorite uncle—and rolled an unlit cigarette between his thumb and forefinger. "Now, Snakes, surely you are not resentful?"

"Moi?"

"Toi."

"What do I have to be resentful about?"

"Nothing. You're free and you're home."

"Not much thanks to Attorney Loritz."

"Oh, that. Otto was going to get around to you."

"Sooner or later?"

"Sure."

"Which one?"

"Oh, come on, have a drink for old times' sake. Ilsa!" he called to the far end of the bar, where a woman in a pink leotard and short black skirt was painting her nails. "Get our friend his usual."

Snakes reached out and plucked the cigarette from the man's fingers. "No, thanks, Peddler. I don't want what you're selling anymore."

"And do you think you know what I'm selling anymore?"

Snakes swiveled on his bar stool and looked pointedly at Ilsa and up to the mezzanine where an angle-featured, olive-skinned man sat with a leather satchel on the table in front of him. "I think I have an idea."

"No, my friend, you have no idea. Oh, all the usual minor investments go on apace, and I will have to attend to Mr. Andropoulos momentarily, but there's a new game in town, the biggest, the best of all. Who knows, it may even make me legitimate."

Snakes lifted both hands into the air by his ears, and rolled his eyes in mock horror. "What is the world coming to?" he gasped.

"What indeed? That was precisely what I was hoping to ask you."

"And why should I answer?"

"In case you're feeling unappreciative, just remember that I did get you fellows released from jail. Think of me as a guardian angel."

Ben Alef's eyes lit up, like those of a tourist hearing his native tongue in a foreign locale.

The Peddler thought he saw the glimmer of a like mind and decided to delay the proposal he was about to make. "Hey, Snakes, make your associates comfortable. You, sir!"—he addressed Anton—"I'm sure you would enjoy a tour of the operation. Or even"—now he spoke directly to Ben Alef, who was squinting into the dark recesses of the establishment—"even you." Before he could receive an answer, the Peddler said, "Ilsa, take the gentlemen around and show them everything."

Snakes was about to speak for Ben Alef one more time when the bewildered Messiah stood up and nodded His unexpected approval.

"Splendid." The host clapped his hands.

"Everything?" Snakes confirmed.

"Sure. I will join you in the private lounge in, say, half an hour."

And so, before Snakes could caution Ben Alef or the disciples that the Kastrasse was nothing like the Kingdom of Heaven, they were trooping toward the back of the bar like a line of tourists entering Goofy's House at Disneyland.

"On your left," Ilsa announced, "the showroom," and she waved her glistening fingers toward a ratty alcove that contained what appeared to be a large green felt pool table without pockets set among twenty small round café tables beneath a low ceiling from which a mirrored disco ball reflected a thousand fragmented images of the visitors.

"What show?" Glucks asked.

"Well, you know," Ilsa said. "Girls."

"Girls?"

"Girls," she repeated, and rotated her hips to illustrate. "Oh, for God's sake, come here." She opened a padded black door off the show-room. "He did say to show you everything. Look . . . girls."

Behind the door several not-so-young women sat in various states of undress in front of a row of bulb-circled makeup mirrors. The mirrors provided a touch of bygone glamour, but the rest of the room was dingy and not one of the women so much as glanced at the visitors.

"Burlesque?" Blobel asked.

"That's what they used to call it, Pops."

"First, they dance," Snakes explained. "Then they lure the customers upstairs. Then they take their money. But because the club is 'private'—for members only—the police can't intervene. You guys can understand that, can't you?"

"And you were a part of this?" Karl Blobel asked Snakes with new-found admiration in his voice.

"Continue the tour, Ilsa. Remember, we're supposed to show these men ev-er-y-thing."

And the excursion continued, through the secretarial and accounting offices where receipts from the Peddler's various operations besides girlie shows and prostitution were tabulated. A bank counting machine riffled and automatically banded a stack of fifty-mark notes.

"Here is the bookmaking desk," Snakes said, "and over there is loan-sharking. Sometimes a client has to borrow from one to pay the other, that's nice."

"What, no drug dealing?"

"Hey, we may be small, but we're multiservice. Take us there, Ilsa."

"Are you . . . I know, I know"—she shrugged—"ev-er-y-thing."

The pack traipsed through a steel door, up a concrete ramp, past an armed guard who looked a lot tougher than the paunchy civil servants on the *Farnhagen*, into an adjacent building, again past various functionaries at desks.

"Come on, Ilsa, what about the processing center?" Snakes taunted their reluctant guide.

"Take a peek." She gestured to an observation window set into a wall, into a room where another table as long as the green felt downstairs sat under a bank of fluorescent bulbs not so flattering to the room's occupants' complexions as spotlights. Four naked women sat at the table. Each had a stack of glassine envelopes, a tin of white powder, and a small scale in front of her.

"They're naked"—Snakes took the invisible microphone from Ilsa to explain—"so they can't even think of smuggling anything out."

"Then what happens?" Omar was fascinated.

"The various partners receive their cut." Snakes allowed himself a little inside joke. "Perhaps you noticed the gentleman waiting for the boss back in the bar; that's a good example. Finally, the profits are laundered through the local Deutsche Bank branch, and then invested by our own Herr Loritz, Esquire, in various legitimate businesses."

Unnoticed by the tourists, the Peddler had returned. He nodded approvingly. "Liquor distribution, cigarette vending machines," he listed the organization's multiple holdings. "Really, not so different from cocaine."

"The only difference is that one is illegal," Snakes pointed out.

"It never bothered you before."

"Who says it does now? I was only comparing and contrasting."

"With your usual fine discrimination. Yes, legality is the *only* difference," the Peddler agreed. "By all means, compare booze and drugs. Both satisfy a physical longing through a chemical substance. Or compare my girls to the glamour girls of Hollywood; Marilyn Monroe, Elizabeth Taylor, whatever the name of the hottest tootsie on the block today, they've been selling their tits for decades; they just don't give the final satisfaction. We do. What's wrong with that? Ilsa?"

"Nothing."

The Peddler grinned. "Yet drugs and prostitution are considered weak and shameful, whereas a gin-and-tonic or a big-budget motion picture, oh, that's just a part of international culture. Personally, I think we're more frank. I think that people should be able to do whatever they wish as long as it doesn't hurt anyone else."

Snakes had heard this before. He could repeat the argument verbatim. "My friend is a ferocious advocate of freedom," he told his new friends, "except that whenever an ordinance comes up that might plausibly lead in

that direction—legalizing drugs, for instance, or regulating sex for sale—
he channels funds to various honorable groups to fight it, because it's much
more profitable illegal."

The Peddler scoffed, "Victimless crimes."

"Except when someone fails to make a payment."

"And when the bank takes your house or repossesses your car for the
same reason, is that any better? A loan is a loan is a loan is a contract which
requires responsible behavior on the part of the debtor. And if that debtor
acts irresponsibly . . . You, sir." He addressed Omar Nazzarian. "My
sources inform me that you were engaged in a similar line of work for one
of my esteemed competitors, alas."

Since his own moment of doubt, Omar had followed Ben Alef's train
with a strange passivity that baffled Snakes. In any other circumstances,
Snakes would have assumed that Omar's silent assent to every next move
from their march to their arrest to the Kastrasse was a ploy, but the Persian's obedience had the distinct scent of faith. Either that or he was hypnotized, but he glided along with the unquestioning belief Snakes
recognized from the Muslim masses he had seen on television. Though
Omar's faith occurred in the West, out of a Western model, he was still a
creature of the East. "Alas?" he said.

"Yes . . ." The Peddler continued. "I remember the fellow quite well.
He met with an unfortunate accident some while ago."

Omar nodded, and the Peddler continued.

"Yes, it seems he was packing his underwear into a suitcase when the
lid slipped and chopped off his head. The suitcase with the head was later
found in a locker in the train station. Maybe the feet walked it there and
the hands checked it in."

Snakes waited for the old, quick-tempered Omar to jump to the bait.
He didn't really trust any of the disciples except for Max Vetter. He saw the
changes in himself, but didn't believe that they were occurring in others.

But all Omar did was nod.

Snakes said, "I never heard this."

"Contrary to popular opinion, Herr Hammurabi," the Peddler said,
"you do not know everything."

Just then, a side door into the packaging room opened and two
men walked in. The first had the heavyset, too-much-starch-in-the-diet
physique of a Kastrasse employee. He wore a baggy suit jacket over un-
matched pants, and sported an ill-fitting toupee and looked bored. His

companion, however, a lithe, dark-haired man, trembled with excitement. The second man said something, but the observation window was sound-proof.

"That's the guy who was up on the balcony," Palitzsch noted.

The Peddler beamed and explained, "Mr. Andropoulos, a friend, asked a small favor we are about to grant."

Suddenly, one of the four girls jumped from her seat, knocking over several tins of the white powder, which crashed soundlessly to the floor in four simultaneous puffs of white while a thousand translucent envelopes fluttered down like autumn leaves. For a moment she stood, naked and narrow-hipped, with unwashed light brown hair that barely covered her small breasts. She faced the window with lips twisted into a wild, feral expression and then she rushed to the window and pounded on it, her fists landing soundlessly.

The heavyset man reached a thick hand around her waist and lifted her off the ground and carried her out like a sack of potatoes, while her tiny fists punched helplessly at his shoulders.

"What's happening?" Bruno asked.

"The child was just offered a promotion. Apparently she doesn't want it . . . yet."

"Out of the sorting room and into the bedroom," Snakes said.

The Peddler just looked at Hammurabi and said, "If I didn't love you like a son, you might get in trouble."

"The last time I was loved like a son I did get into trouble."

"Why don't you gentlemen come downstairs and have a drink with me?"

It was only six o'clock, but the bar was filling up with men from the financial district, in for an after-work quickie of one sort or another. Two waitresses in skimpy outfits circulated while a bartendress leaned over the mahogany to offer newcomers a drink along with a peek of cleavage.

"The mezzanine will be quieter," the Peddler said, lifting the velvet rope that blocked off a curving deco-style staircase illuminated by a strip of pink neon that ran under a brass banister in a serpentine glow. "We can have it to ourselves."

"VIP room?" Anton asked.

"Only the best for my guests," the Peddler replied.

"Very Important Pricks," Snakes added.

The Peddler gestured for the rest of the men to ascend the staircase. "After you."

The lounge on the balcony was decorated in the same glossy black and carmine surfaces as the cavern below, and it had its own bar with its own large television suspended in the corner. The only difference between the two spaces was that instead of a sexy waitress a striking young man in a tight black outfit waited to serve the upstairs customers. "To each their own," the Peddler always said.

Erich Langefeld stared at the young man. "Heinrich?" he whispered. Was it really twenty years ago that he had known a young man who also wore his hair marcelled with the same glossy bear's grease? He hadn't seen hair like that since the police tore him sobbing from Heinrich's body, the blood from thirty-six puncture wounds soaking into the bed beside the black smear from the handsome boy's curls. "Gay Lovers' Quarrel!" the papers shrieked. Heinrich had promised the older Erich fidelity. Heinrich had lied, and he had to pay the price. But the judge had not understood, and had sentenced Langefeld to one year for each puncture.

"Mostly we run sporting events," the Peddler said, noting the blank television screen, "but, for now, why don't we see what's on the news?"

Nobody seemed particularly interested, but the Peddler wasn't about to be dissuaded. He switched among the stations until he came up with the image of a reporter standing in front of a building that everyone in the bar knew too well, the Hamburg Municipal Jail. "Ah, CNN. Great stuff. Nowadays there is global reach," the Peddler said, and turned up the volume.

"Last seen on the road to Damascus, a familiar figure has supposedly reappeared as the two-thousandth anniversary of his birth approaches," the reporter intoned with a smirk playing at the corner of his mouth. "For these people"—the camera panned across the parking lot and lawn, where a tent city had sprung up, its population doubled from the night before as word spread of Ben Alef and the interesting high jinks of the Alefites— "have come here to Hamburg to announce the resurrection of Jesus, the Messiah, in our time. Throughout history there have been eruptions of messianism, but not really in the modern age. Yet these people believe that a sequence of—perhaps?—miraculous events that took place in the villages of north central Germany last week prove that a man named Ben Alef is indeed here to announce the end of history and usher in an age of peace and goodwill.

"Hamburg may seem like a curious place for such an announcement, but it makes sense when you hear about the career of this contemporary incarnation of a recurring archetype. For what does it mean that Mr. Ben Alef, a former prisoner about whom little is known, claims to be reborn out of the ashes of a concentration camp? Is this one more instance of the millennial fever gripping the world, or is it a sign of the enduring trauma of the Holocaust, or is it possible that these men and women know something that we don't? What does it all mean?"

"Yes." The Peddler turned to Ben Alef. "What does it mean?"

For a moment, the reporter perked up his head like a dog to listen to his earphones. "More later on the alleged orgy that occurred here last night, but first we have a remote coming in from Israel, where a rabbinical council has convened to discuss this same matter. On to you, John."

Again, the Peddler switched among the channels until another familiar scene appeared. "Oh, look, he's still at it."

The preacher they had seen on the bar TV stood against a painted backdrop of a mountain with a gigantic cross lit at its crest. "Friends, this is the battle we've been waging, lo these many years, since I started preaching back in Bayswater. And you've been with me. You heeded the call when we built the Boise Tabernacle. You raised funds for our Guatemalan mission. You know the rewards of doing God's work. And until now you thought you knew the enemy, the Washington abortionists and the Los Angeles pornographers and the New York journalists. But I tell you, friends, that the call is more urgent now than it has ever been in all of recorded human history. You see, there are recent developments. You know what I'm referring to. You've seen the newspapers. You've heard the ba-a-ad news. Even as I speak there is a man, a man I tell you, on the European continent who—yes, friends, I say this with sorrow—claims that he is the Christ." He shook his head and nodded into the camera.

"Word spreads quickly," the Peddler commented, and lit his cigarette.

Suddenly Snakes understood why the Peddler had appeared at the border and why he had been so determined to "rescue" Ben Alef from jail. "Now here's the pitch," he said.

The Peddler clicked off the television. "You fellows are at the center of a very big story. First the newspapers, now television. They can't get enough of it. And this is just the start."

He was about to go further when Ben Alef spoke his first words since the tour began. "What do you want?"

"That's the attitude. I like a Messiah I can negotiate with. Let me lay my cards on the table. I'm tired of all this." He gestured to encompass the shabby criminal empire that surrounded them. "I want to go straight, but I can't without the right connections. I think you can provide those, and in return I can provide certain managerial expertise for your enterprise. I'll tell you honestly, Benny—can I call you Benny?—this is genius, here."

"Genius," Anton echoed.

"I think of my miserable little nickel bags, the rotten tricks my girls turn one at a time. Sometimes I'm ashamed of myself."

"Not often."

The Peddler glared at Snakes. "But this, this is big. We're talking the franchise of the century, make Bugs Bunny into rabbit stew, make Mickey Mouse look like a rodent. Even Coca-Cola, Microsoft, they've got to produce their product before they sell it. But salvation, wow! The only product that the consumer sells himself. Look at that guy with the choir. I've done research. I wanted you to see him. Did I mention that he collects forty million dollars a year for his congregation, which fits inside a studio? And that's nothing; he's a preacher and you're a god. Managed properly, you can make a killing."

"What do you want?"

"Fifteen percent, and, of course, salvation."

"You're ridiculous," Snakes took it upon himself to reply. "We don't care if you cough up all the bail and provide all the expertise in the world."

"I didn't ask you, my erstwhile friend."

"One condition," Ben Alef said.

Immediately, the disciples turned with varying degrees of bewilderment. Was He really the fraud that the Peddler cynically assumed? And was He going to admit it here, in this nest of venality, vulgarity, and sin? There was silence.

"Name it."

"The girl."

The Peddler appeared confused. "What girl? I mean, what about the girl? I mean, what about which girl?"

"The girl in the room."

The Peddler allowed a sly smile to play at the corners of his mouth but he refrained from slapping Ben Alef on the back and laughingly saying, "You dog." Instead, he agreed. "You want her, she's yours."

"Bring her."

"Your wish is my command." The Peddler lifted a phone behind the bar, gave instructions, and returned to the table. "Here's how we'll do it. You sign an exclusive representation contract, a fair contract for a fair portion of all monies received, and everything will be taken care of."

"First, the girl."

"Fine. First, the girl." The Peddler pointed to the stairway and sang out, "Here she comes."

Standing in a waist-length muskrat coat with a full frontal zipper that led to the belt of a short black patent-leather skirt, she seemed more vulnerable than when she had been carried screaming, naked, half an hour earlier by the thug who now held her arm with the air of a gentleman escort. If anything, her legs looked thinner beneath the skirt than they had before. And the feral twist of her lip now revealed itself as a harelip, the only thing that marred a glowing beauty. But all the emotion was drained from her face, and a dull, glazed expression coated her eyes. Snakes immediately knew how the thug had pacified her. He recognized the signs of heroin.

"What is your name, my child?" Ben Alef asked gently.

"Celia."

Snakes leaned over to see if Celia had a tattoo on her ring finger, the Peddler's mark of possession, a single searing dot with a blue nimbus, because the Peddler insisted that excess dye be plunged in so deeply that it could never be expunged.

Ben Alef asked, "And what are you doing here, my child?"

"I give blow jobs."

The girl's simple description was so blunt that even Snakes cringed. He thought of the wild sexual frenzy that had seized hold of the Alefites the night before, and how this child's indifference to her predicament was as disturbing as Ben Alef's detachment in the Hamburg jail.

But now Ben Alef seemed aroused, if not sexually then morally, if not morally then as one arouses from sleep. For the first time, His own blank eyes attained a glittering clarity, and Snakes gave thanks, because he knew that Ben Alef was finally going to act. Then the Messiah leaned forward and pressed His lips to the girl's.

It was the kiss of an inexperienced adolescent, an awkward pressing of the flesh more than a passionate engagement, but it was so loathsome that Snakes almost jumped on his Lord.

Then the kiss was over. Ben Alef stepped back from Celia.

"Look!" Bruno cried.

The girl's upper lip, its flesh knotted in a deforming hitch a moment earlier, was straight.

"Amazing," the Peddler murmured, while the thug who had brought the girl upstairs turned her body toward the bar's mirror. "Look," he said.

Still blank despite the kiss of presumptive divinity, her own eyes lit when they discerned the truth of the mirror. "I'm . . . I'm . . . pretty."

"Yes," Ben Alef agreed.

A second later the girl's reconfigured face bore the same expression of stark terror the men had seen once before. "No!" she screamed.

"Yes," Ben Alef said gently.

"No! More pretty, more men." She stared at the disciples, wild-eyed and savage again despite her perfected lips.

Snakes was the only one who understood, because he knew how the system worked. The prettier Celia was the more customers she received, the more money she made the more valuable she was, the more she was worth the less likely she was ever was to see the light of freedom. He watched her finger with the single blue dot caress the smooth surface of her lip.

Thick-tongued and unaccustomed to her mouth's new formation, the girl tried to explain the cycle, but the more she said the less she felt herself understood, and she jabbered, "More men. More men!" with a frenzy bordering on hysteria.

"There, there." Ben Alef reached out a hand to soothe her.

Eisenheim knew the touch and shrieked, "Beware the Jew!" but it was too late.

A yellowish froth accumulated at the edge of her beautiful lips. Her limbs twitched and she fell to the floor, arms jerking as if jolted by a series of electric shocks, her head slamming left and right.

Nazzarian, who had been quiet throughout the afternoon, explained the obvious. "Epilepsy. The girl has the fits. She's no good."

The Peddler would have been glad to exchange his damaged merchandise for better quality, and was ready to call downstairs for the entire supply of Kastrasse pulchritude to be marched in front of the Messiah, to choose from as He wished.

But Ben Alef knew His mind. "Her." He bent down, sat, cradled the girl's spastic head in His lap, and said, "I want her."

"Fine," the Peddler replied. "In return for sole rights, that's a deal I can live with. Now, here's what we're going to do. The first thing is to set up a limited liability partnership. I mean, hey, we can't tell the world about divine incorporation without incorporation. Hey, there's our name: Inc., Inc."

Chapter Thirteen

"**W**HAT ARE YOU WRITING?"
Before the words were fully out of Snakes Hammurabi's mouth, Max Vetter snatched a ragged sheaf of pages off the café table in front of him.
"Sorry." Snakes raised his palms.
"No, I should not have reacted so strongly."
Actually, Snakes thought, the fisherman should have reacted more strongly, because Snakes only asked the question after he knew the answer. He had seen a good half-page of cramped, blue ink commencing "Dear Frieda . . ."
Fully understanding that this was a private letter, Snakes froze, motionless as one of his namesakes, reading the entire first paragraph. . . .

We were so innocent and I didn't know it until I saw real depravity. Can Hamburg be only a hundred k. from Wieland? It is another world here composed of every evil you've ever feared. A world of flesh utterly devoid of spirit. The pastor, when he cautioned us, those sermons we laughed at, was correct. But how could he have known? Hamburg is a fever dream. Hamburg is a nightmare. I cannot sleep and when I wake the things I see on all sides make me shut my eyes. The very thought that the fish I caught and the sweat of my labor ultimately came to this sewer makes me retch. Makes me want to return to the drowned town I knew and was safe in. We were so innocent in Wieland by the sea, our life of ropes and nets and boating caulk and maybe a nip of wine, until the beast came. But

Ben Alef was in that beast, and that is why He must return to this evil city which is merely *Farnhagen* writ large.

Yet Hamburg was Snakes Hammurabi's home, and he was responsible for bringing his Lord and His disciples here. He couldn't precisely recall how they chose a southwestward path out of "innocent" Wieland, but how else could they have arrived in just this spot, unless Snakes's own internal compass directed them? Every day, he regretted the phone call he had made from an abandoned weighing station.

Yes, the Peddler kept his side of the bargain. The rooms upstairs, which had once hosted a body an hour were scoured of gallons of bar girls' fluids and their clients' semen; brand-new sheets were laid upon the much-used mattresses. Still, Snakes felt uneasy sleeping on them, though he had never minded in the past. Max called Hamburg a nightmare, but Snakes had nightmares of his own in which filament-thin gray fingers extended between the pores of the mattress to wrap about his limbs and pull him under until he woke sweating.

Then, when he padded downstairs to knock back a medicinal slug of vodka or join in some early-morning-extended-from-the-night-before bull session at the bar, he felt like he had left one dream only to enter another. The perennially dim corners of the Kastrasse were brightly illuminated with banks of newly installed schoolhouse globes, and Irish carpenters were further sledging a hole in the exterior wall to let the sun in. Instead of moribund degenerates sunk into their drinks and half-clad women enticing them to order a superfluous one for the road, the disciples rushed back and forth on urgent assignments, while the Peddler sat at his usual table on the mezzanine, poring over plans both architectural and strategic.

"You see," the Peddler crowed. "Now we really spread the gospel. Now, we've got a gospel to spread. Guilt. Contrition. Absolution. Salvation." He listed these as if they were the secret ingredients in Coca-Cola. "Now, Benny"—he thrust a batch of documents at his divine companion—"sign here, please, and here, and here, and . . ."

The entire situation smelled. Prosperity was not the vision Snakes had seen shimmering on the beach at Wieland, nor was it the virtue the band represented in the villages on the trek from the *Farnhagen*, and, besides, it was as bogus as a three-mark bill. The deal Ben Alef had cut with the Peddler to save Celia had the same cloying scent as baby powder substituted for cocaine. And Snakes knew that when one party got burnt, there was hell to pay.

Hammurabi, whose family was presumably surnamed at some point in the dusty pre-Christian era for the giver of the first written laws, looked upon the commercial juggernaut of Inc., Inc., with cynical apprehension, but there was no denying the improvement in outlook since they had taken shelter under the Kastrasse umbrella. Despite—or because of—the Peddler's evident self-interest, he managed well. So neatly oiled was the mechanism that it was able to shift gears without missing a beat. Within days of the contract's signing, every gun on the premises was traded in for a cell phone, and the the sleazy dive that no mayor could padlock was transformed into a juice bar. Instead of furtive, raincoat-clad men bringing shame and notoriety to the district, the Kastrasse ("Keep the name, it's got a recognition factor") was full of curiosity seekers who lined up at the door and practically drove the Hard Rock Café down the block out of business. The bar's huge kitchen (the place had been a garment workers' cafeteria back in the twenties), which had been used for baking enormous bloody hams for the "free" buffet that gave the customers the stamina to follow the girls upstairs, now boiled truckloads of corn, which the three limousines ferried to the jail parking lot. Instead of shedding their clothes, the former dancers shucked corn, and journalists ate it up with a series of articles headlined some variation of "From Porn to Corn."

Still, Snakes didn't like it. He had always subscribed to the notion that you know who you are by the company you keep, and the Peddler, for all his cheerful conversion, was perennially the Peddler. No offense intended, but dammit, he was a Jew. Then again, so was Ben Alef.

Snakes looked around him, at the Peddler and the busy legal and accounting departments, at the newspaper reporters who hovered like flies, and beyond in directions he could hardly discern let alone define. Everywhere he looked, he sensed danger.

Unfortunately, Snakes could not convey his unease. He tried once or twice to voice his qualms to Ben Alef, but He who knew everything only smiled and offered Snakes an ear of corn. His poor oblivious Lord! Refusing to sleep on a bed because the Alefites in the parking lot didn't have beds. Refusing to eat more than absolutely necessary, because somewhere someone was hungry. Refusing to protect Himself, because His own Father would do that for Him.

This left just one other person whom Snakes might confide in: Max

Vetter. Snakes caught sight of Max, alone, at a café table beside the pocket-less pool table in the old show room, scheduled for renovation into a visitor reception area. Until their arrival at the Kastrasse, Max had acted as the group's aide, guide, and manservant; he cooked their food, scouted out their sleeping grounds. But now the organization executed those tasks. Abruptly left without a mission, the former fisherman retreated into the scroll of pages he carried everywhere.

"Hey there."

"Hello, Samuel."

Oh, yes, Snakes had almost forgotten his own rechristening. "Taking notes?"

"Sort of a diary."

"Some place, huh?" Snakes gestured around him.

"I've never seen anyplace like it."

"You should have seen it in the old days."

"Somehow I think that it's not all that different."

Snakes looked at Max and wondered: Was this the first hint of irony or judgment? Then he decided to take a risk. "Disgusting, isn't it?"

Slowly, Max took a pipe out of the pocket of his worn woolen vest.

Snakes couldn't restrain himself. He blurted, "What have I done?"

Max lit his pipe with a long wooden match. "What have any of us done?"

"You've done nothing. I mean you've done everything you could. But I brought Him here. I brought us into this . . . sewer." He inadvertently used a word from Max's letter. The fisherman blinked, but Snakes continued, "I brought all of . . . them." He pointed toward wherever the Alefites were encamped beyond the back door opened by a delivery man hauling in a new set of office furniture.

Max stopped him. "No. You are falling into the trap of pride when you say something like that. You are not responsible. Ben Alef has His own purpose, His own reason."

"Which is . . . ?"

"Samuel . . ." Max blew out an aromatic plume of smoke. "Of all of us, you know best that we must wait for revelation. You were the one who showed us that *we* must have faith. As hard as it is, His will is not for us to question."

"Hey." Snakes tried to lighten the moment. "We all have our sins. Mine isn't pride; it's doubt."

But Max would not relinquish his high seriousness. "Just remember, He came because *He* wanted to."

"And them?"

"They came because they wanted to. Because they need Him."

And they came in ever-increasing numbers now that word was spread by the army of reporters who followed Fritz Hofmann's lead. Whatever Ben Alef's claims, or his disciples' claims for him, there was nothing like an actual arrest to grab attention. Even before the first evening's insanity, the fourth estate's juices were flowing—and the burning and fucking were too great to believe.

Nor did the Alefites stop. Now calling themselves Neue Juden, those who bore scars from the Night of the Flesh, as initially the press and then the immolants/jubilants themselves named it, celebrated an ongoing holiday in the parking lot—not quite so frenetic as during the initial exhilaration of liberation from all mores except Heaven's, but fervent enough to satisfy even the horniest high school junior. Chancellor Grabner was right. Outside the courthouse, it did rather feel like the 1960s, complete with tents and festive banners. All the scene needed to be complete was Jimi Hendrix. Fires served now only to cook pots of vegetable mush and brown rice and corn. Music played, and some people danced while others huddled together in prayer, heads covered with yarmulkes and shoulders draped with tallesim they back-ordered from the only Judaica supply house in Germany, inspired perhaps by the hippie outfits of the woman named Margot whose style echoed the Jewish fringe. In the span of less than a month from the sinking of the *Farnhagen*, biblical awareness exploded in the general populace. Necklaces with six-pointed stars ("JEWelry!" a chic shop on the Pamplatz proclaimed) were all the rage, while Testaments Old and New moved out of bookstores like the latest Hollywood roman à clef, and not merely as a vicarious expedition into ancient history, but more as how-to books for people struggling to make their peace with the apparent, alleged, amazing transformation taking shape around them. They were dressed to the Hebrew nines, waiting for the Messiah, whose return had been rumored since he left.

Jesus first and Ben Alef now. But while the Galilean only had to ransom the sins of a primitive culture that might have invented prophecy and philosophy but was barely advanced beyond hunting and gathering, his successor had the vaster task of redeeming modern iniquity. More than fifty percent of all the people ever born were still living in the year 1999, and modern science had given each one of them a greater capacity for sin than any Roman emperor. Jesus forgave arrows and battering rams; Ben Alef had to contend with gas chambers and hydrogen bombs.

Also, the territorial stakes were raised beyond the individual souls of the Mediterranean basin to a global soul that circumscribed the earth, so as Jesus had failed upon the Temple grounds and thereafter through the Stations of the Cross en route to Golgotha, Ben Alef *had* to succeed upon His own chosen field; so the disciples and their followers were determined.

So they waited.

But the living, breathing key to their redemption was a mystery, a cipher. Sometimes Ben Alef appeared a cunning con man, at other times a guileless simpleton led wherever police or criminals took him like a dog on a leash. Go as He would on those occasions, He did not necessarily speak as His handlers desired—or speak at all—yet His silences were eagerly parsed for layers of meaning and complexity, and thereafter revealed to be as full of substance as His listeners imagined.

Only in the Kastrasse was there anxiety, because the Peddler, alone of little faith, worried that the believers might prove fickle. He begged Ben Alef to make a statement, "any statement, just to let them know you're alive."

But as He had been silent on the Night of the Flesh, and as He spurned Snakes's warnings, so the Messiah turned a deaf ear to His partner's entreaty. Instead, He offered the Peddler an ear of corn, and said, "They're waiting. I'm waiting."

"For what?"

Ben Alef shrugged.

Finally, out of frustration and a desperate need to maintain the Kastrasse's hold on the Alefites' imagination, the Peddler asked Snakes to go out and address the crowd.

"Why should I?" Snakes demanded.

The Peddler shrugged.

Why he agreed, Snakes didn't know, but as he had spoken for Ben Alef before, it seemed natural to speak again. Stepping up the courthouse steps under Luther Huber's window, he didn't even know what he was going to say until he found his voice and began, "God . . ."

"God!" the Alefites chanted.

"God, I thought, was the problem." Not knowing what else to say, Snakes chronicled his entire dissolute career. He told the people, and the eavesdropping police, about the boy who fled the NATO base and stumbled into crime. The hell with the Peddler; he told them about drug dealing and prostitution and the rackets and the more he confessed the better he felt, cleansed by the confession as he had never been cleansed by the water he detested, until he arrived at the gloriously inevitable conclusion, "What I never understood was: God is the solution."

Then, as if woken from a trance, he looked down, appalled at his admissions, expecting the crowd to engulf him.

Instead, the Alefites gave him a standing ovation.

And the Peddler realized that he had not one, but twelve potential emissaries. Swiftly acting to remedy its earlier blunder, Inc., Inc., signed the rest of the disciples to their own contracts and the CEO regretted the lack of foresight in his original intention to bail Ben Alef alone out of jail: "I'm sorry. I didn't see the opportunity."

Well, if that passed for an apology it would have to suffice. But Snakes knew that confession of innocence was harder for the Peddler to make than the confessions of guilt that Snakes and the disciples and their disciples had in abundance.

Everyone had something to confess.

One by one the disciples—whose stories had already been rehashed in the tabloids—appeared to avow their guilt and receive absolution at the parking lot. Each time one of the twelve arrived on the site in a limousine dispatched from the Kastrasse, the crowd hushed as an obliging press contact set up a mike—which incidentally provided a direct feed to his network—for Langefeld to howl with remorse for Heinrich's punctured chest, or Kiehr to expound on his guilt and salvation and bask in the rays of public forgiveness.

Each had a remarkable tale to tell, complete with novelistically gripping detail. What it felt like to watch Kiehr's garrotte form a tourniquet on his victim's carotids. What it felt like to drink Palitzsch's everyday tea and say to his victim, "Ah, but you must try this special blend." What it felt like to watch a building burning with Clauberg and feel the burning in his soul. Oh, the pain of the violator of social norms and taboos! Discovering in themselves a capacity for parable, the killer ex-cons were an ad hoc lecture bureau, spreading the good word that one could do *anything* and find peace.

And the people loved them. Especially the people closest to their victims. Schoolgirls swooned at each appearance of Herbert Glucks, whose Humbertian adoration of Lorna Kirtchner led to her demise. The night after Gluck's class returned from their field trip to Amsterdam, Lorna, a responsible girl, was doing her laundry when she came across the stained stockings her teacher had removed from her chunky thighs. Until that moment, Lorna had been destined for a life of hausfrau-ly laundry and lard-fried schnitzel, but the sight of the stocking was too much for her. She sneaked out of her family's flat and into her school and hoisted herself onto the flagpole that jutted out the window over the front door of the school like a penis, and tied the stocking around her neck and . . .

Now girls thrust stockings at Glucks to autograph. Likewise, Langefeld was popular in the waterfront taverns that catered to the gay community, while old ladies tittered and raised a cup of tea at each mention of Franz Palitzsch's name. Pinkies properly extended from their precious Meissen, the widows of the world drank a toast of the same tepid liquid he had used to poison their peers, and each time they didn't die, they were reborn in his name and gave blessings.

Martin Clauberg became the patron saint of firemen, whereas both Anton Bartsch and Karl Blobel were identified in the public mind with the banking industry, as though each time a customer made a withdrawal from an ATM it was the precedent of the disciples' earlier withdrawals that made the thing work, although Anton's cross-eyed stare was also taped to the grimy walls in more than a few police locker rooms. Ancient wrestling magazines with a photograph of Bruno Morgen pumping iron sold at a premium in used-book stores.

"I confess," they cried, and the crowd cried with them.

The people of Germany were crazed with a rage for forgiveness, and the Generalstaatsanwalt was under enormous pressure to give the people what they wanted, not justice, but mercy.

The Peddler sent them out in different combinations, like a baseball manager tinkering with his batting order to see who worked best with whom. But all of them worked well. All except Omar Nazzarian, who remained mired in an unbridgeable sulk, and Max Vetter. Indeed, Max was the only disciple whose story failed to resonate. His ritual recitation before the assembly was distinctly different from theirs; it lacked the essential elements of sin that made their stories so satisfyingly provocative.

The fisherman was not a crowd pleaser. Yes, he had seen the light, but not from the depths of darkness. There was no contrast, no drama. His listeners applauded politely and then sat on the edge of their seats for Karl Blobel's description of the texture of the goose-down pillow he had pressed down on the lips of the chief executive officer of the Bank of Bonn, just in case the airless trunk of his car had left a breath at the bottom of his victim's lungs. "And then I slept on the pillow and what dreams I had," Karl ended his talk, and his audience dreamed with him. Now *there* was a speaker.

Nor had Max enjoyed the euphoria of messianic success. Simple Max avoided the mercantile hubbub at the Kastrasse and quietly sneaked away to the Hamburg fish market to gaze longingly at the sleek mounds of herring he himself might once have provided. He recalled his solitary days out on the Baltic in a seven-meter dory named *Dory*—the only witty thing he had every done—before those waves brought Ben Alef ashore and changed his life.

There was the key. Max Vetter's life had changed, but not his being. If the kidnappers, rapists, and killers of the North Coast suddenly discovered good in the world, Max, the first outside witness to the Truth, *was* good. Grizzled from the rugged labors of the sea, he never donned the robes that all the other disciples—except for Snakes, in pear-colored trousers and matching socks—had taken to wearing, and instead of a yarmulke he still wore a visored cap bleached by the sun.

As Max failed on the stump precisely because he had not failed in life, the others returned for encore after encore. The crowd listened to each man raptly, marveling, and then added its own testimony, aloud or in silent communion. It was an orgy of forgiveness, and Snakes Hammurabi was the undisputed master of the divine narrative, which moved always in the same direction: you sin and you are saved.

Even Eisenheim was hauled up on the platform to squint and squirm and murmur obscenities taken for recognition. The Obersturmbannführer was a national hero, and those who had advocated his pardon through the decades felt vindicated by his honored place beside the King of the Jews. Only the few born Jews of Germany looked suspiciously at the disciple who, according to the dominant illogic of the moment, ought to have been their natural pet. No matter his resurrection at Ben Alef's fingertip, Dietrich Eisenheim was tainted.

But that was considered grudging. Understandable, given the circumstances, but the time had come to put an end to ill-feeling. In fact, the witnesses were there to testify that the end of time had come.

Eventually, however, the crowds began to feel that the substitutes were lacking. For all their newly learned oratorical skills, the disciples were merely men, whereas the Neue Juden craved the deep satisfaction of deity.

"Two thousand years we've waited," read a banner strung between two lampposts over the crowd.

Still they waited.

For the moment, this had to satisfy the Peddler. You didn't handle a messiah the same way you did a lounge singer. To appease some of the crowd's yearning, he sent them pamphlets of Ben Alef's sayings on the walk to Hamburg and T-shirts with an eerie silver hologram of Ben Alef's face silk-screened onto the black background by the women in the newly reconfigured production facilities of the Kastrasse complex.

"The product is moving nicely," Leon said.

"The hell with product!" the Peddler scoffed. "Product is not where it's at. Product is just more of what we've been selling for ages. Now we've got to deliver, well, deliverance. But how to package it?" he asked himself and paced the mezzanine, while Ben Alef braided Celia's hair into twin pigtails that sat on her shoulder blades like epaulets. The time had come to deliver, but all the Peddler could do was wait for his main man to determine the hour. And that was tricky.

"Maybe you're right," he said to Ben Alef. "It's not time to make a definitive statement, yet. Yeah, you've got to let the wave swell and appear at the peak. At this moment, your momentum is building on its own. That's a delicate mechanism. Touch it and you can destroy it. Look at Elmer Kleiner."

"Who?"

"Ya see! . . . Hey, lighten up, it's a joke. The point is that right now you have nothing to gain."

"I have nothing to gain," Ben Alef echoed.

"Precisely," the Peddler agreed as he scanned a chart listing the various disciples' engagements that took up one wall of the former lounge that he had begun to refer to as the Salvation Room. That day, Thursday, December 16, Bruno, hand held by one of Inc., Inc.'s staff, was meeting with representatives from an international sporting goods company interested in attaining his endorsement for their sneakers, while Glucks addressed a group of schoolchildren in the Hamburg Gymnasium and Kiehr was being interviewed by a Wall Street firm about establishing a postmillennium investment fund. They were a team.

Snakes sat in an armchair, sedated from an hour in a tub and a trip to the Cosmo Boutique, where he had bought three pairs of silk trousers, peach, plum, and lemon, together with matching socks, and a dozen white shirts that hugged his chest as tightly as a leotard. He was now cleaned and changed, a new man, his fingernails clipped as finely as Hoffritz's top-of-the-line could shear them, shuffling a deck of cards. "Nevertheless," he said, "the message must be delivered."

"Got any bright ideas?"

"Maybe we need a delivery boy."

"A delivery boy?"

"Or why," Snakes asked as if speaking to himself, "does it have to be a boy?"

"Who else, a frog?"

"What about a girl?" Snakes laid the cards down for a game of solitaire.

Celia's eyes darted to Ben Alef as the Peddler examined her like a bolt of yard goods and then returned to Snakes. "Helping, all of a sudden?"

Snakes set a queen atop a king, but didn't say anything more.

"Yes, yes," the Peddler murmured, "they're getting a bit tired of boys. We need a new face, a new gimmick. A girl of deliverance."

Celia's shoulders hunched as if the temperature had instantly dropped thirty degrees, and ripples of nervous energy twitched down her arms to her fingertips, which curled in toward and clenched her palms. She hadn't had a fit since the scene in the production room, but seemed ready for another one right now.

Of course, the Peddler saw Celia's appearance as his first crack at the female media market, and he was already envisioning *Oprah* and the cover of *Paris Match* and a book of recipes.

"Go," Ben Alef said, and her fingers relaxed.

"But what shall I say?" Celia asked plaintively in the plush comfort of the chauffeured limousine that drove her and Snakes and Omar, who had been delegated to accompany her on her first expedition out into the world, on the familiar route to the assembly point.

"Just tell the truth," Snakes said.

"Right, and then you'll change it around and tell the people what you want them to hear," Omar added.

"Or what He wants them to hear," Snakes clarified. "Don't worry," he told Celia. "I will repeat what you say. I will translate it."

Snakes watched Omar gaze out the tinted windows of the car.

They arrived at the site and Celia nervously climbed the platform for her introduction as the latest evidence of Ben Alef's presence.

"Hello," she said shyly.

"Sholom aleichem," butcher Hossler, who had been reading up on Hebrew culture in the off-hours between orgasms, called out.

Snakes whispered the proper response to Celia, who awkwardly repeated, "Ah-lay-kem So-lem," and then described the path of her own degradation, ending in a kiss. "And the split in my lip cleaved."

"He kissed her," Snakes Hammurabi began his extemporaneous commentary when the applause died down, "and the split in her soul cleaved, and was whole. But look, look, my friends, at the events that preceded this . . ." He almost said "cleavage."

"Yes?" Omar, at the side, asked with an innocent expression.

"This change . . ." And the word "change" gave Snakes an inspiration. "You see, Celia, when I first saw Celia, she was involved in the drug trade. Yes, I say that in front of police headquarters, because she is changed. In fact, she was at a table covered with drugs, and with nearly superhuman strength this wee, slight slip of a girl overturned that table, and you know what that reminded me of?"

Snakes was chagrined at how, in his expressions, in his manner, he aped the bombastic American preachers he had been listening to on the evangelical station the Peddler left on in the Kastrasse for the disciples' instruction. He sweated up a storm and wiped his brows to dramatic effect, tempted to toss his wet handkerchief into the crowd like a rock star, but he went on. "It reminded me of the Bible, of the episode of Jesus and the moneylenders."

If there was one literature Snakes knew, it was that of faith. Hamad had pored over it in the Hammurabis' various living rooms over the years. "And here is the key. For Jesus himself had to fight against evil. This time, He has not come to do it for us, because that did not work. That led to thousands of years of pain. This time, we do it ourselves. This time, not only He walks across the water, but We do, too."

For all Ben Alef's divinity, Snakes spoke about humanity. "This time, it is not He who wreaks havoc inside the temples of commerce, but She, We. This time it is humanity triumphant. This time We become the gods. This time, We are divine!"

"Now, this has got to stop," the Pope said to Father Immaculato.

Summoned back to Rome from his watch in Hamburg, the young troubleshooter had entered the papal chamber without his usual castanet-rap footsteps. Instead, he shuffled along the carpet in shame. What had started as a strictly local phenomenon that he had felt oh-so-clever in bringing to the Pope's attention, and ought to have quashed with the ease of a Paraguayan bishop breaking a tin mine strike between appetizer and apéritif, had spiraled out of control. Father Immaculato continued to send reports about the mass thronging back to the Vatican, but they were no longer as informative as the front page of the *Osservatore Romano.* And now came the dictum. This had to stop. And Immaculato was at a loss. The only response he could manage was "How?"

"How?" Urban imitated his protégé's whine. He slapped the marble table. "How come I have to tell you how?" He glared at Immaculato, and expected an answer.

Immaculato knew the answer and despised it. "Because you are Il Papa."

Indeed, everyone from the other cardinals to this youngster thought they had what it took, but they were wrong. There was a divine spirit vouchsafed to one in a generation. Look at the heavenly clock. Galaxies as gears. Quasars as quartz. Surely, Aquinas's celestial maker kept that time so that the planets orbited the sun in their proper sequence so that this millennium would arrive when Urban IX was here, overlooking this square with those pilgrims who had not yet been tainted by Ben Alef.

Urban felt like making an appearance and might have stood out on the balcony to give the tourists a thrill. Destiny was at work, overtime, to bring the right man to the right place at the right time. And in this era, the right man was not some interloping Jew with those hoodlums and that hooker parading around declaring His consecration. Until now Urban had refrained from responding to the irksome questions of the press regarding the Messiah of the North. Perhaps the time had come.

"Will you speak out?" the younger man asked, humbled at the potential power of the chair when it made an official statement. For all Immaculato's awareness of his own shrewdness and his superior's flaws, he was, first and foremost, a believer, awestruck at the majesty of the position he sometimes took for granted. When the elderly white-haired man in front of him played chess badly, complained about the diet his doctor enforced, or spoke as Giuseppe Caldino, he was all too human and pathetic, but when he spoke as Urban IX, Vicar of God, mountains trembled.

"Of course not," the Pontiff replied. He, too, knew the might of the robe and would not squander it. To address Ben Alef directly was to grant the usurper a credibility he did not deserve. "We shall use the most effective surrogate for this ticklish situation, someone who knows the world of the pretender."

"You mean . . . ?"

"Yes, a Jew."

"But which Jew?"

"Pick one, any one. Do you think they appreciate this any more than we do? I have received calls from Israel, from Brooklyn, from my many ecumenical friends. They despise this. We need only decide who shall speak for the church, from the synagogue."

"Yes, surely a lot of Jews have been frothing for the media in Israel and Brooklyn, bu-u-ut . . ." Immaculato suggested, "there is one man who might be possible, who *would* be better."

"Tell me."

"Most of these commentators are buffoons. Perhaps photogenic, and delighted to get more press, but not serious, not eminent, Your Eminence. The person I was thinking of is . . ." He mentioned a name.

"Yes, that's it!" Urban's eyes flickered with the fierce intelligence that had brought him to the purple throne. "Speak to him," the Pope commanded and rang the bell for his adjunct to bring in the silver implements reserved for special occasions, and turned dreamy. "Why do they believe, Immaculato?"

"I'm not sure, Your Holiness. Why do we believe?"

"A good question. Some people, some people whom we both know well"—his eyes veered in the direction of the Cardinals' Chamber—"do not believe. They consider Jesus to be an exigent fraud, unlike this extra-ordinarily inexigent fraud in Germany." This reminded Urban of the situation that had brought them together; his eyes shrank to a small black pin point. "We are not here to ask questions; we are here to provide answers."

Immaculato was dismissed, and had started for the door when Urban called him back. "Wait a minute."

"Yes, Your Holiness."

"He has a beard?"

"Excuse me, Your Holiness?"

"Does he have a beard?"

"Ben Alef? A rather scraggly, goatish growth."

"Not him. You know who."

Immaculato smiled and put his left hand horizontally to his chest. "Down to here."

Elsewhere on the continent, in a room less beautiful than the Pope's, a group of men more used to dealing with questions of taxation, military expenditures, and foreign relations also wrested with the sticky problems raised by the presence of Ben Alef. As Germans, they were also frequently called upon to ponder painful moral issues raised by their ancestors' ghosts when Nazi booty was discovered in Swiss banks and benign Thuringian shoe salesmen turned out to be mass murderers. Allegations and proof of atrocity smeared the conference table's surface as often as mayonnaise, but the incense of theology left an unfamiliar scent in the room, and no one in attendance felt comfortable with Ben Alef.

"I don't like this," the Chancellor's legal adviser said. "There are laws, structures. We can't just ignore them."

Officially, they were meeting to discuss the issues of double jeopardy and prison conditions brought up by the case of the escaped convicts. But everyone knew that was secondary to the real issue created by the reams of unpleasant publicity that made the German government look alternately cruel and incompetent.

"Screw the laws!" The Chancellor slammed his fist down on a curling stack of faxes. "Three hundred and forty-seven!" he said. "And if I go out to my secretary there will be a dozen more by now. And do you know how each one of them begins? Not 'Dear Herr Grabner,' no. Not 'To Whom It May Concern,' no. Almost every one begins with the same three words: 'How dare you!' Except for those that cannot be quoted in a family environment. 'How dare you torture these poor souls?' How dare I? Tell me, geniuses, how the fuck do I dare do what? How the fuck—"

But before the Chancellor could get any further, a large man standing by the window, hands clasped behind his back, smoking a cigar without removing it from his mouth, interrupted, "That's not the point."

"Yeah?" the Chancellor said.

"Yeah." Gerhard Schwarz spun around in a small cloud of smoke as an inch of ash fell to the carpet. That was okay with him; he treated the Chancellor's offices the way he did his own atop the Schwarz Tower, like a pigsty. Schwarz had been the Chancellor's most trusted adviser since their puppy days in Munich, when Grabner was just a junior councillor and Schwarz a small-time developer. The fact that their careers had ascended simultaneously, as the former became lord of the public domain, while the latter built sewage plants, airport extensions, and most of that domain's largest-scale construction projects, was neither disagreeable nor accidental. Schwarz subsidized Grabner's early campaigns; then Grabner slid government contracts in the direction of his old friend. Now Schwarz occupied a position without portfolio in Grabner's inner circle, and his opinion meant more than that of any mere cabinet member. "We've got a hot potato here." He addressed the legal adviser. "The thing to do is get rid of it."

"Amen," Grabner said. As far as the Chancellor was concerned, he would have granted blanket amnesty to all survivors of the *Farnhagen* if they promised to march to Jerusalem and never darken his bailiwick again.

"I agree," the Foreign Minister said. "My office has been under pressure from the embassies and consulates. People want this taken care of."

"Which people?" Schwarz asked.

"To start with, the ambassadors of every country in which Alefite movements are starting. Even the legate from the Vatican."

"Does he vote?" Schwarz asked, and that subject was closed.

"So what do we do?" Grabner moaned.

"Easy. We do the same as we did with the tax surcharge. Study the issues. Delay. Waffle. Obfuscate."

"Why?"

"Everyone is forgetting that this mess is entirely a function of coincidence. To paraphrase the Haggadahs that idiots are reading on every street corner and subway: what makes this nut case different from all others?"

"These people believe in him?" the Chancellor ventured.

"No, the followers always believe in the leaders. That's their purpose in life. The reason this Messiah is different from all others is the calendar. Timing, Jürgen. Never underestimate timing. The only one involved in this mess who understands timing is, well, an old buddy of mine in Hamburg—but forget that. Timing is why Ben Alef got so big so quick, and that's why he'll shrink to the size of a pea three weeks from now. The timing has worked for him so far, because Joe Blow is expecting *the Change* at the stroke of midnight, 2000. But when Joe wakes up on January first and his fat wife is still on the other side of the bed, and his miserable job is still waiting for him, and when he gets home that night and his jerky teenage son curses at him and the mortgage payment is due assuming we've solved that mingy little computer problem and everything in his life is the exact same shit it's always been, he's going to ask himself, 'What did the Messiah do for me?' That's when you can call off the SWAT team and send my aunt Hilda to take the punk into custody. So take a vacation, lose some paperwork, lie low, wait till after New Year's . . . and then put the son-of-a-bitch Son of God away for good. In the meantime, keep an eye on him."

Heads across the conference table nodded in agreement, but the Chancellor himself just shook his head and muttered, "I still don't understand the attraction. What does He have that I don't?"

"Spirituality," Schwarz said with a laugh. "Shall we take a look? They're broadcasting live from Hamburg."

He tuned in to the news just in time to catch Snakes Hammurabi's latest appearance. Although Snakes's shabby misdemeanor was less dramatic than the other disciples' felonies, his crime contained theological ramifications that brought the whole assembly's flaws home to them. "God," Snakes began, as always, "was the problem," and continued until he concluded, "God is the solution."

"Or," Eisenheim muttered offstage, "the re-solution."

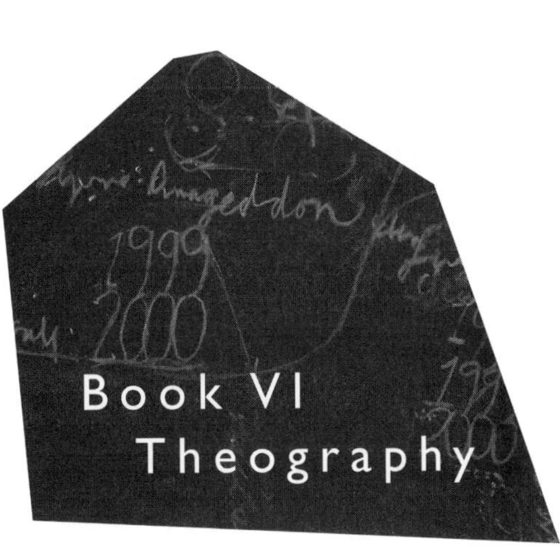

Book VI
Theography

Chapter Fourteen

L ET PEDANTS POINT OUT that December 31, 2000 actually marked the earth's two thousandth orbit around the sun since Jesus of Nazareth was presumably born, because the retroactively designated year number one commenced three hundred and sixty-five days into the millennium. That begged the import of numbers for people without any special horological ax to grind. No, the nice round date with three zeros was the moment in time that popular attention imbued with transhuman significance, and the countdown toward it induced a feverish intensity.

Even children dismissed from school for their midwinter vacation waved and chirped gaily, "See you next millennium."

And Ben Alef was suddenly poster boy for the calendar.

Less than a fortnight to go until the second, minute, and hour hands on the clock turned in sync with the year, decade, century, and magical millennial digits on the longer-term docket of time, three weeks after eleven drowning prisoners were saved by Him, two weeks after the seafolk of the Baltic witnessed Him, one week after the Alefites followed Him, a day after the Germans discovered Him, the morning after they burnt themselves and fucked each other for Him, everyone had the same questions:

Was He or wasn't he?

And what about His precursor?

What about His ancestors?

What about His people?

Three basic theories regarding Ben Alef were advanced by the thinking class once He became the kind of phenomenon that required professional reflecters to have an opinion. According to the experts, He was either (A) a fraud; (B) deluded; or (C) a really nice guy whom some honest people mistook for God in their search for meaning.

No one in the op-ed columns or on the TV panel shows opining any of these three suppositions in either pure or hybrid form disputed the faith of the Alefites, although they did emit a great deal of intellectual gas attempting to explain that faith. It was a field day for analysis, which blossomed into a wild profusion of theories ranging from psychological (triumph of the id vs. revenge of the super ego) to political (left-wing communitarianism vs. right-wing conspiracy) to scientific (relativity vs. chaos theory) to multiple metaphysical and anthropological perspectives. Deconstructionists took apart the "messianic narrative" like Lego blocks, and soon there were as many sociologists with notepads and mini–cassette machines as there were true believers at the "assemblies," which occurred daily at noon in front of the courthouse.

For the first time in memory, theologians from divinity schools were in demand by the media; professionally somber, they were sandwiched between actors hawking their latest movies and politicians treading a high-wire balance between outcry and sympathy over "the events" in Hamburg. Scholars, moralists, and commentators spent afternoons pontificating in front of the cameras or behind computer screens, the experience proving as deliriously orgasmic for the thinking class as nights in the parking lot were for the believers.

On only one thought were all the savants agreed: Ben Alef should keep better company. If He was the blank slate upon which each member of the mass could write his or her own prescription for salvation, the disciples, at least the first eleven of them, were far too fouled by the graffiti of their personal histories.

As for Snakes Hammurabi, okay, his "crime" was different, but he was still an obvious if unconvicted career criminal. Of course, Max Vetter, the honest fisherman, really was another question, so the skeptics tended to separate him from the first disciples and categorize him together with the believers on the mainland.

But neither the press that promoted this particular Messiah nor the political and religious authorities who fretted about Him and His influence could quite grasp how swiftly the expansion of the story might occur. Since the era of Judea's donkey-driven gossip mill, the mechanism for transmission of information had attained a rocket-ship pace; rumor evolved and mutated into extravagant fantasy. Not only did half the papers in the world pick up the Reuters reports from Hamburg, but a geologist in Indonesia posted a notice on the Internet asserting that aliens had landed in Brussels—"Yeah, and I'm a sprout!" a teenager in Brooklyn flamed him back—while a newsletter emanating from Wyoming added that a black helicopter was seen in the vicinity.

Fulminators raged, eggheads scratched their shell-like skulls, and most everyone whose immediate territory was not threatened by Ben Alef enjoyed the show. But only one reporter ventured further afield.

The city of night bustled as much by starglow as sun. Trawlers from the North Sea, barges carrying the slag of the Saar, tugboats and cutters on errands cluttered the old harbor while several hundred meters farther down the Elbe a modern facility hummed with the labor of Eiffel Tower–like cranes loading and unloading railroad cars from container vessels as easily as if they were a child's building blocks. And every bulb on ship and shore was reflected in the inky darkness of the water, creating the wavering image of a mirror civilization welling up from beneath.

Most of the industry operated according to law, but custom allowed a tithe from each shipment to slip off its skid into trucks waiting with engines running. In grubby offices just beyond the gates of the port, money was loaned out and payments on outstanding loans came in, while down the block that same money changed hands again in an informal betting parlor behind an Armenian restaurant. The Peddler might have retired from illicit enterprise, but not everyone in Hamburg was saved yet.

Despite the new chastity at the Kastrasse, a half-dozen blocks inland toward the city center, prostitutes pursued their trade along the harbor district side streets, although their business was down significantly since Ben Alef's arrival in town.

"To what do you attribute this, um, trend?" Fritz Hofmann asked. Since the scene at the jail had hit the big time, there was such a tangle of reporters following all-too-little news that by now they were reduced to the metajournalistic enterprise of interviewing each other and reporting on the reportage.

As breaker of the story, Fritz was the subject of great interest from his elders. Initially he basked in this interest, and saved the clips about him besides those by him, until he realized how ephemeral newsprint fame was. When the thrill wore off, he complained to Richard Federman: "This is ridiculous. All of them chasing each other, and nothing from on top."

"Unfortunately, we can't call Heaven for a confirmation." The Solon of the city desk shrugged and tapped the bar where Fritz had tracked him down. Federman had no burning desire to seek out new stories. In fact, he had no problem whatsoever with his practically permanent stool at this local watering hole, which he had featured in one of his articles in return for a generous tab. "Thank God, even if the Kastrasse has turned holy, this place is still in business."

Then Fritz had a brainstorm. Rather than stick out another night of the high jinks in the parking lot, which so vastly entertained every new press card in town, he set out to find a story, although what story he wasn't yet sure. He wandered into the night, exploring the city in search of his next scoop, and felt himself drawn to the harbor, where the same water that had carried Ben Alef to shore lapped against the wharves and connected with the Atlantic Ocean, the Mediterranean Sea, and, ultimately, through underground channels, the Sea of Galilee.

Briefly, he contemplated an interview with a longshoreman or one of the loiterers by the Armenian restaurant, until he caught a glimpse of a woman in a black satin raincoat dashing out of a doorway into an idling Mercedes. Perfect. On the spot, Fritz decided to speak to a prostitute for the whore's-eye view of the millennium—front page, second section. By now he had a small discretionary budget from the *Zeitung* to spend on sources as he saw fit, so he went shopping, cruising the red-light alleys, re-coiling from the mottled crones who must have occupied those same alleys since the Wehrmacht was in town and the few specimens with a hint of five o'clock shadow and suspicious bulges under their miniskirts, until he espied a young woman only begun on the path of her inevitable descent.

She was thinner than Fritz preferred his women, but a sweet, almost embarrassed smile flitted across her pale features when he lingered and lit a cigarette in her vicinity. "Hello," she said.

"Hello."

"Looking for company?"

"In a way." Fritz began to explain his desire for conversation, "just conversation," but he could see that she didn't believe it, so he cut to the chase. "How much for half an hour."

She gauged his pocket with a professional eye, and said, "Fifty marks."

Fritz extracted five bills from his wallet and steered her to a shabby longshoremen's café with beer-stained tables. There they talked, at first generally, until he brought Ben Alef into the conversation. From there he moved to the ongoing orgy at the jail and then shifted to business. Perhaps he was leading the witness, but he knew what story he wanted to tell and how he wanted her to tell it—even if he had to provide the dots for her to connect. "To what do you attribute this, um, excitement?"

"Free sex," the girl said blithely. She was more attractive in the dim light of the café than on the street corner—and Fritz was sufficiently self-aware to realize that he had chosen her instead of one of her hard-bitten peers for that reason. Not for a moment believing the john's "I'm a reporter" line, the hooker generously assumed that he wanted more than talk and merely needed encouragement. "There's a hotel down the block," she said, and, right there in the open, hoisted her skirt, way above the knees.

But Fritz was professional, and considered a byline more erotically satisfying than intercourse.

Above the thigh.

He was tempted, and mentally calculated the money left in his expense account. "Um . . ."

Higher yet the cheap polyester skirt rose, to reveal a thin thatch of black hair and a delicate blue ankh at the joint between her leg and groin.

"Yes!" he shouted, and ran from the café, leaving the girl to shake her head in wonder and wink at the bartender.

Fritz suddenly knew where he had to go now to connect his own dots. The whore's story was good for a sidebar, but suddenly he had a scoop. No longer a cub, the senior man on the God beat had the genius, the intuition that others followed. He blazed the path, and he knew where it led. He looked around, saw the huge cranes of the loading docks in one direction, the skyscrapers of the financial district in the other. He was probably within five blocks of his destination, but how to find it? How to find it? His brain whirred. The answer was simple: the telephone directory.

In one of the last corner phone booths remaining from a previous era, he found the book he had been seeking hanging from a chain attached to a small metal ledge where he placed a stack of coins. "Let's see," he murmured out loud as he hastily flipped the pages. "Storage. Television. Back a bit. Telescopes. Telephones. Tailors. Other direction." Moving page by page now, fingers burning with excitement, he passed Tanning Salons and Tapestries, hit Tax Returns, backed up again, and there it was: Tattooing.

There were four listings: Big Jake Tattooing, Inkorama, the Lotus Studio, and the Sin on Skin Shoppe.

Luckily, Sin on Skin and Big Jake were within hailing distance, but Inkorama was in the suburbs and the Lotus Studio in midtown, probably a loft in one of the forgotten nineteenth-century buildings between the high-rises. Fritz ripped the page out of the phone book and hit the streets again, as he had earlier in the evening, but now with a specific goal in mind.

Big Jake's was a dank, dark, miserable place, still open at this hour. Fritz entered under a stoop to the basement where, obviously, Big Jake himself sat behind a battered wooden office desk amid dust balls, grease, and the particular odor of aggrieved flesh. Samples of Big Jake's work lined the walls, glossy, enlarged photographs of biceps, breasts, chests, and other intimate anatomy emblazoned with snakes, Hawaiian hula girls, art deco curlicues, Chinese symbols, and more. Scattered across the desk were magazines catering to the shop's special clientele. The phrase "the flesh trade" popped into Fritz's head as he glanced at the covers of the magazines.

Big Jake reached across the desk and picked up one issue of *Tattoo Digest* and flung it toward Fritz. "Page fourteen," he said. "That Tweety Bird is mine."

Fritz opened the magazine to a full page of a dewy-eyed cartoon creature with fangs that would make Dracula sit up and kick a hole in his coffin. "Nice."

"So what do you want?"

"Information."

"You from the Health Department?"

"Newspaper," Fritz answered, passing his press card across the table in the opposite direction from the carnivorous canary.

"Oh, Christ," Big Jake grumbled. "You think I've got nothing better to do than sit here and gab."

"I'll pay."

"What the hell, I've got nothing better to do."

"How long have you been in business?"

"Forever, give or take a few years."

"How many tattoos have you worked on?"

"A lot more than the times you've been laid."

Fritz blushed and recalled the girl he had left in the café. "Do you keep records of your tattoos?"

"What do you mean records? You didn't say you were from the Tax Department."

"I told you, I'm from the press." Glancing around the room, Fritz noticed a camera hanging from a nail on the wall and had an inspiration. "Photographs?"

Big Jake nodded toward several leatherette-covered folios stacked on his desk. "Polaroids. I take pride in my work."

"Can I see them?"

"Sorry, they're private."

Fritz opened his wallet.

"Not that private." Big Jake pushed the books across the desk.

For the next forty minutes Fritz gaped at body parts and entire anatomies covered with the distinctive red, blue, and green inks of the trade. There were real and mythological animals and ornamentation ranging from a set of Corinthian columns to rocket ships blasting off above one client's penis.

"Very proud of that one," Big Jake commented occasionally as Fritz turned the pages of the photo album.

But finally Fritz reached the last page and he still hadn't seen what he had been looking for. "Is that all?"

"Well I only started with the Polaroid six, seven years ago. So why don't you tell me what you're looking for?"

"A number."

"What do you mean, a number?"

"One oh eight oh one six, on the left arm, you know, like . . ."

"That's disgusting!" Big Jake spat on the floor.

"Be that as it may . . ."

"Say, does this have anything to do with that guy I've been reading about down at the jail? What a scene. Been thinking of heading over one night myself."

"So you'd remember if you'd done anything like that, could be anywhere up to . . ." Fritz paused to do a mental calculation of Ben Alef's age and the time the Messiah had spent in the *Farnhagen*. "Possibly twenty years ago."

"Yeah." Big Jake turned dreamy. "I'd remember."

Still doing calculations, Fritz tried to figure out how old Big Jake himself was, and if he could have done such a tattoo, say, fifty-five years earlier. But Jake wasn't nearly that old. "What about your competitors?" Fritz unfolded the page he had ripped out of the phone book.

"Yeah, I know them all. Inkorama's a jerk, specializes in superheroes, Batman-on-the-butt kind of thing, no artistry, just started two, three years ago. Sin on Skin's possible. Ask for Bella. What the fuck, tell her I sent you. Give her my regards. As for the Chink, who knows? He's a weird one. Does nice work, though."

So Inkorama was out, and an hour later Sin on Skin was, too. It was nearly two o'clock in the morning, but these places seemed to keep late hours, waiting for some drunk high school kid to get some dumb phrase like "Born to Fail" permanently etched into his shoulder on a dare. Fritz found out that Bella and Big Jake had lived together, which might have made for a nice feature, except that Fritz was after bigger game. He jotted the idea into his notebook and left, two strikes behind him, one to go.

The Lotus Studio was, as Fritz suspected, a third-floor walk-up above a Chinese restaurant and a nail salon, in an old three-story building squeezed between competing office colossi. But instead of a dingy repeat of Big Jake's or Sin on Skin, Fritz was met by a series of inlaid Oriental screens that gave the impression of hills receding into the distance. Only gradually did he perceive a faint music that sounded like distant wind chimes, and a scent of incense that reminded him of the parking lot.

A curtain of bamboo fringe hung in the doorway instead of a door; it clattered gently as he entered. "Hello?" He stepped forward toward a low table, also inlaid with several different dark woods and mother-of-pearl, and not a copy of *Tattoo Digest* in sight. "Hello?"

"Please sit," a voice whispered into his ear.

Fritz nearly jumped. A young woman, perhaps Fritz's age, perhaps younger, stood beside him, holding a tray with two small ceramic cups and a matching teapot.

"Where did you come from?"

"The kitchen."

"I meant . . . Are you the proprietor?"

"Ah, no." She giggled. "But my father will be very glad to see you. Please sit."

He felt as if he were the first person to enter the place in decades, but he sat, with difficulty.

Then an old man in a crimson robe, with silver hair down to his shoulders, appeared, just as the girl had appeared, from nowhere, just as Fritz realized that while he was working his long, failed-football-player legs under the table, she had disappeared. "Hello?" he repeated, beginning to feel rather stupid.

"I have been expecting you."

Did he say that to everybody, or had Big Jake called ahead, because the fraternity of tattooists—no matter their different styles—was an intimate one?

"I must tell you that I'm not here to get a tattoo."

"Tea?"

Fritz thought he had been staring at the old man, but he hadn't noticed him sit across the table or lift up the ceramic pot. "Yes, thank you."

And the cup was filled with a steaming green liquid and it was in Fritz's hands, though he couldn't recall picking it up. He felt as if he were in some time-lapse photography film, catching only one out of every ten frames. The cup was empty. His stomach was warm.

"Very curious, indeed," the old man said. "I urged him to consider something more personal, but some people know their minds."

"I'm sorry," Fritz said, his mind cloudy. Perhaps the tea was drugged. Perhaps the air was drugged. "What were we talking about?"

"One zero eight zero one six."

"I didn't think I—"

"Over here." The old man pointed to his extended left arm.

Fritz gaped at the skin, wrinkled as a paper clipping kept in a wallet for, say . . .

"Sixteen years ago," the old man said. "A night very much like this one. A quiet night. No students. No sailors. Yes, I do my share of anchors and 'Sweet Louise's. And, of course, chinoiserie: dragons, pagodas, kites to fly across your upper back. You are sure that you don't want . . . ? No, no, of course. I am sorry. More tea?"

Fritz shook his head, unable to speak.

"A strange customer, in both senses of the word. I do love European languages. An angry night, not a night for kite flying; forgive my little joke."

Fritz waved his hand to dismiss the apology.

"He was a quiet, determined young man. Tall, very thin, not very much flesh on his bones. It is more difficult to draw on such a canvas. One must anticipate the subject's future weight and muscle tone, so that the image may retain its consistency. It is a question of how deeply to insert the dyes, how much to insert."

Idly, Fritz wondered if Big Jake gave such thought to his artistry, or considered the enterprise of his miserable basement artistry at all.

"But he knew, the idea of the numbers, the specific numbers, the shape of the numbers, the shade of the ink. Alas, I did what he said."

"Alas?"

"It was a task that I did not enjoy."

"But you did it?" Fritz regained his voice.

"The child must eat." The old man referred to the girl, who now appeared once more and removed the empty cups.

"You did it?" Fritz insisted.

"Yes," the old man declared. He was an excellent source.

"Bingo." Time returned to its regular pacing. "Tell me the procedure and His words exactly, as well as you can remember, and I'll call the desk and have a photographer here in the morning."

"Don't bother."

"Why not?"

"I don't wake up until the afternoon."

Back at the Kastrasse, the Peddler sat at the downstairs bar while a train of mendicants, applicants, and suppliants stood in a line that led from the mezzanine, down the deco staircase, out the front door, and around the block. It was three o'clock in the morning and the line was longer than it had been at three in the afternoon, when word that Ben Alef was "receiving" percolated out from the former strip joint to the streets.

At the top of the stairs, the Messiah sat behind a round café table together with a rotating accompaniment of disciples. It reminded Bruno of a tag team match. Clauberg and Blobel sat on either side of Ben Alef until they were exhausted by the sheer plentitude of human misery that crept up the stairs to confess, complain, or simply reveal itself in the presence of the Lord. Eventually, after hearing one too many elderly men with shingles, one too many young women with cheating husbands, one too many adolescents boggled and agonized by the idea of infinity ("But I don't understand. If the universe comes to an end, what's on the other side, but how can't it come to an end?") they passed their chairs over to Palitzsch and Kiehr, who passed them along to Glucks and Anton.

"And what about time? In the beginning, there has to be something, because something can't come from nothing," another distraught teenager moaned.

To which Ben Alef replied, "Good question."

To which the teenager smiled and said, "Yes, it is, isn't it?" and left contented.

Ben Alef was inexhaustible, seeing all, speaking to all, not precisely curing all, but giving them the hope they needed. Sometimes He uttered a word or two, sometimes He nodded, sometimes He smiled.

The Alefites waited silently for hours to speak their piece during a three-minute audience, and then they left with beatific smiles. A train of zombies departed into the night, which chugged on toward dawn.

"Happy?" Snakes said.

"What?" The Peddler bestirred himself from a moment of private reverie. "Oh, you. No, I can't exactly say I am."

"Maybe you should wait in line, domini, domini, excelsior, pax vobiscum." Snakes waved his hand in front of the Peddler's glazed eyes. "It's late. Maybe you should get some sleep."

"Why? He doesn't sleep." The Peddler waved his own pudgy fingers upstairs. "I've always been able to outlast anyone in my club; that's why I'm the boss."

"I always wondered about that."

"That's why I took you in, Snakes. You're the only one I ever met who genuinely doesn't give a shit."

Snakes ignored the presumptive compliment. "Maybe you're not the boss any longer. Maybe that's why you're not happy."

"I just have the feeling that something bad is coming down the pipeline."

"Are we talking mystical vision here?"

"Shut up and try and take this seriously for a second. There's a pattern to events and they don't deviate. We've been riding this pretty well—word of mouth to international attention, produce, revenue, a franchise the envy of McFuckingDonald's—but after you reach the top of the mountain there's a slope. The trick is not to try and stay at the top, because nobody does. Presidents of the United States, boxing and box office champions, they all have to give way to new blood. And there are enough people out there who dislike this enough to give us a tiny, helpful shove off the peak. You just wait, they're coming. I can hear the hoofbeats."

"So?"

"So the only way to go is *over* the top, into a realm where the normative sequence of development and decay can't touch you. It's hard to make that leap, but Ben Alef's got a shot, and I'm trying to figure out what to do about it."

"And?" Snakes knew the Peddler either had something in mind or would soon.

"Everything to date has built beautifully, but I think we should skip the next logical steps. Do Not Pass Go. Do Not Collect $200. Go Directly to Salvation. If Ben Alef stops messing around with individual souls and saves the world—or at least a goodly portion of the world believes that it's been saved—that's good enough. Then, man, we cruise. Automatic pilot from here to Heaven. Guarantee."

"But how does He save the world?"

The Peddler tapped the cover of a thick volume that Snakes hadn't noticed sitting on the bar. "Follow the blueprint. Read the good book." Snakes looked over the balcony to where Max Vetter was reading, or writing, his own book.

Dear Frieda,

I am sorry. I was interrupted by Snakes before I could even tell you the latest fantastic things that have happened since I last wrote. Snakes is restive. I cannot say that I know him well, or no more than any of the others, but he is different. Of course, they all must fit into the plan, but Snakes has a special role. Ben Alef calls him Samuel.

I think that something happened when they were in the jail without me, but no one will speak about it, and I can't ask anyone anything—except maybe myself—or maybe you.

By now, of course, you have heard. Ben Alef is Jewish. Ben Alef is a Jew. I don't think I ever saw one before. That wretched people, they have born the brunt of our fathers', *our* father's— yes, I guess I learned grammar—baby Frieda's daddy who art in heaven, *his* evil impulses, so this too makes sense. If there was one lesson the schools drummed into us, besides grammar and the math necessary to weigh a catch, it was that we as a people sinned terribly when we as a people slaughtered the chosen people.

108016, branded into my brain. That number makes me remember the cottage by the sea, and our brother tossed against the ceiling like one of your rag dolls and lifeless as a rag doll when he came down. Where did you get those dolls, Frieda? An endless succession of dolls—you had more of them than any other little girl. Father brought them for you. From work.

For years I thought Father worked in a doll factory. It was just down the road, beyond the wire fence that separated Ben Alef from us. HE was there, too, in the factory with Father and Eisenheim. But it wasn't a doll factory; it was a death factory.

Father worked there the way the drowned men of Wieland worked in the *Farnhagen*, a job, just a job. He and Mother never said it, because they couldn't mention it, but that was the lie that every minute of our lives in that small village by the sea was intended to make us believe—a job, just a job. It was a lie, just a lie, and we were no finer people than the pimps and prostitutes—excuse me, *former* pimps and prostitutes—and former drug dealers of Hamburg. In fact, we were worse.

But Father drowned, too, just like the unredeemed souls aboard the *Farnhagen*. It was a slow drowning that took decades of schnapps to accomplish.

And yet Ben Alef didn't drown—or burn. He didn't let it destroy Him. Instead it destroyed us. Fifty years later, we, the nation, we are prosperous, yes—except for our village, of course, where the dead men went to work in the *Farnhagen*. But we do not have the spirit that we had during the years of their first employment, the marches, the parades, the radio, the passion that we cannot admit now, but that led us here. Of course, He had to come in our dirtiest moment. That *would* be the time of His arrival, wouldn't it? That was when we needed Him.

Surely, He is necessary here. Without him, they will burn, although because of Him they burn themselves. There is much that I do not understand. But it is not for a mere fisherman who only really understands knots and tackle and the habits of herring to ask questions. It is sufficient to know that He comes to save these people, one by one. We have been joined by a girl from the center of the fire. Very frail. Very sick. She was wounded, and He healed her.

Another miracle. Miracles bind our days. Ben Alef holds us together, though the rest of the followers—I cannot call us what others do, disciples, preposterous—sometimes act strangely.

Why do we believe? Is it because we need to think that God is with us, in the sky and now on earth, in Hamburg, this dirty, industrial city? How I miss the village, the shore, the fishing nets I once knew as well as my thrice-darned socks. They seem as distant as childhood. As innocent. But I must remain here among the, pardon my language, scum of the earth. Why, sister? Is it because of the moral lesson that Ben Alef and Snakes speak so well, a lesson that tells us that we are better—make that *potentially* better—than experience has shown us? All those sins, the shabby ones and the serious ones. We lie as frequently as we tell the truth; we cheat as often as we are honest; the disciples kill as easily as they breathe; and He stands there, with that number on His arm, and it glows, and people weep, and, you've heard, they burn themselves from sorrow and concord.

I see so many question marks in this letter. I have been asking myself questions when these reporters, like flies on a week-old flounder, are not asking me questions. I cannot answer them as they wish. They wish to hear something else. They do not hear a word I say. But it is a comfort for me to know that you are in Munich and that you receive this.

But now I know why we believe. I don't know if it is a good reason or a bad reason, but it is *the* reason. We believe because of the miracles. The walk, the resurrection, the policeman's daughter, and the girl who now travels with us, the one on the cover of *Stern*. Ben Alef knows that this should not be necessary, but that we are weak and that we require proof, and so He gives it to His children. The miracles are His gift to us, because they allow us to see the light behind them. And then, the true miracle, we see the light.

I am bathed in illumination. Every day I wake up wondering at the beauty of what I shall behold, and even the brick prison, the concrete yard, the polluted sky over the filthy harbor, produces in me the feeling that all is new, and that all is good. I have always been contented, but now I am happy.

Now Ben Alef comes. He is the only one who can relieve us of our guilt and our shame and restore us to eternal life. Here in this hellhole of Hamburg, He turns darkness into Light.

With love in God,

Your brother, Max

Chapter Fifteen

"MESSIAH"?

Complete with quotation marks connoting and a question mark affirming suspicion, the word appeared on the front page of December 22's *Frankfurter Zeitung,* and the day after that the real story of Ben Alef's tattoo reappeared in almost every newspaper in the world, together with AP photos of a somewhat baffled Mr. Lee and a perennially baffled and still misdesignated Mr. Alef. "Fraud Revealed!" blared the *Daily Mail* of London. "Brand X!" cried the *New York Post.* "Ink Stink," "Holocaust Hoax." Headline writers fell over themselves to take the cheapest shot they could.

If the journalistic corps that dogged Ben Alef and the disciples' every move had once been inclined to good-humored tolerance, neutral fascination, or mild sympathy—even if it couldn't overcome a natural cynicism sufficiently to believe—now, well, hell hath no fury like a reporter duped—and, with the exception of Fritz Hofmann, scooped. Overnight, stories changed in tenor from "a funny thing happened on the way to the millennium" to a tone of vituperation that aimed to bring Ben Alef down to earth, or, better yet, six feet under. The pack fed.

But it didn't make a difference. Despite all the howls of outrage from the editorial pages, the "Now we know . . ." pieces from the thinking set, the believers refused to listen to reason.

"What is wrong with those people?" Urban IX lamented to the speaker phone sitting on his inlaid table beside the crystal bowl. The Pope was sitting in his formerly favorite chamber, overlooking what he feared might be a diminishing number of tourists in St. Peter's Square, comparing the marble-decked scene at hand to the macadam-bound one Father

Immaculato witnessed outside the Hamburg Municipal Jail. "Look at them and tell me what you see."

After the first flush of excitement when the *Zeitung* hit the stands, the young papal representative had sent an e-mail to Urban's private site stating that he thought their problem was solved. "The press has done its job," he wrote, uncomfortably aware that he'd thought the press had done its job once before, when the disciples' histories were revealed. Now, again, he was awkwardly backpedaling. "I don't understand," he whimpered.

"I didn't ask you to understand," the Pontiff snapped. "I asked you to describe. Look out the window and tell me what you see."

Reluctantly obedient, Father Immaculato answered, "People." He was sitting in an office in the jail loaned him by an accommodating administration that had its own reasons for preferring the show ended, the curtain dropped.

"How many people?"

Immaculato sighed. "A lot." And that was an understatement. Rather than ebb with scandal, the crowd outside the prison expanded as yet more seekers flowed inward from the areas surrounding Hamburg and farther afield. Tents were folded, not to depart, but to make room. Every inch of the parking lot and an adjacent park was filled with milling humanity. Some held sheets of yellow paper that turned out to be a sheaf of Ben Alef's collected wisdom, while others were clustered in organized prayer sessions. That very morning, two mobile kitchens had pulled up to the perimeter of the site to disgorge huge helpings of brown rice and beans and powdered scrambled eggs and juice—and, of course, corn—to the pilgrims. Rumor had it that the vans were funded by a reclusive pharmaceuticals tycoon who, perusing the newspaper one fine morning, recognized Dietrich Eisenheim as his old comrade in brown-shirted arms. But that was just a rumor, and the crowd peacefully accepted the offering, as all expiatory offerings were accepted, be they of food or the money that flowed into the Kastrasse's counting room or the flesh singed at the evening fires as foreplay before each midnight's acts of ritual love.

"How many?"

"I can't quite estimate, but I would say that there are not so many as fill St. Peter's Square on Easter."

The Pope snorted. "Small comfort."

"But they seem to find comfort."

"Yes, that is the problem."

"So what should we do?"

"Bring in the Jew," Urban said, and hung up the phone. He listened for a moment to the choir in the background, but music had not been the same for him since this delirium started. Those boys whose voices had always seemed part of an angelic choir were suddenly just boys, and Urban could not bear their human fallibility. He picked up the phone again and commanded whichever one of the church's staff had the bad luck to answer, "Stop that racket."

Likewise, the failure of Ben Alef's followers to renounce their faith in response to reports of their Lord's fraud dismayed the various government officers who had to deal with similar eruptions at other major jails across the country. People in Berlin and Cologne and Munich who could not travel to Hamburg spontaneously gathered in front of their own cities' prisons to stare up at the barred windows and pray to the men and women behind bars, each one of whom wore a presumptive halo above his or her striped uniform. It was an epidemic of faith.

And like the Pope, the German Chancellor called his man at the pebble point to scream, "What the fuck is wrong with these people? He's a total fake."

Luther Huber twirled his umbrella and smiled to himself, delighted with Grabner's consternation and transparent hypocrisy. So what if Ben Alef wasn't the son of God? What politician, present company included, wasn't self-constructed? The only difference between successful and struggling politicians was that the former presented as authentic an image that the latter could not help but reveal as artificial. Perhaps Ben Alef was simply a better pol than Grabner. Both were taking a beating in the press, but Ben Alef overcame it while Grabner was drowning. His desperation told in his hysteria. There was no way the Chancellor could avoid the taint of this episode. When it was over—and it would be, of that Huber had no doubt—the hard-liners would hold it against Grabner that he hadn't been able to contain the public frenzy, while the followers, embarrassed by their gullibility, would shun anyone who reminded them of their moment of weakness. Huber planned to sit tight, keep out of the papers, and then, when the moment of genuine opportunity arrived, step in, strong, competent, trustworthy, electable. "At least they're well-behaved," he said, not the first to point out that the mass of Alefites—who could easily have degenerated into a mob—caused less trouble than the spectators at a football match or a matinee performance of *Tannhäuser*. So what if they screwed like rabid bunnies every night? At least they were clean. "Remember last summer's demonstration by the Greens on behalf of the recycling legislation; what a mess they made. It took a week of municipal overtime to clean up."

"Forget about the fucking Greens," Grabner huffed. "I'm concerned about today. Your sheep in Hamburg may be well-behaved," Grabner raged, "but what about the border?"

"What about the border?"

The news was just coming in, but Grabner explained that a near riot had broken out in the south as a horde of foreign workers from the former Yugoslavia chanted, "We want Messiah! We want Messiah!" and "You cannot keep us from the Lord." The gates that separated Germany from the rest of the world were crumbling.

"Afraid that's not my problem, sir," Huber said, thinking to himself: Until I'm in your chair, and then I'll deal with it, you wimp.

As if he could read the Generalstaatsanwalt's thoughts, Grabner slammed down the phone.

Huber listened to the silence with deep content.

Certain stories echo. "Why" is a mystery; "what" is a fact. Newspapers and television stations toss a thousand items a day into the public domain, and the computer networks of the world add untold more, yet only a few stick around after their initial inches, seconds, or bytes. Then, of course, those same media play up those same stories with reams and hours and discloads of attention. It's never the first blast of twenty-point type that defines the real news; it's the echoes.

Despite the journalistic establishment's universal condemnation, Ben Alef echoed so loudly that the true believers simply couldn't hear what the echoes were saying. They saw His face, and they stopped their ears. Which meant that every subsequent news report was compelled to admit, against the gritting of the reporter's teeth, "Despite recent information disproving the claims of Ben Alef, so-called Messiah of the New Jews, Mr. Alef's followers keep the vigil in Hamburg, Germany, now referred to by this throng as the Land of Promises. Whether these promises will be kept remains to be seen, but the police estimate that approximately five thousand people have gathered. Estimates from the Alefite headquarters at a former sex bar range considerably higher."

Even the police numbers jumped higher when a press release issued from the Kastrasse announced that Ben Alef was going to speak on the following morning. For twenty hours, there was no stopping the inflow. Soon, the patches of macadam or grass visible to observers from the jail itself were impossible to make out among the crush. The few shelters that had been erected over the previous week were trampled as the crowd surged forward against the human chain of Kastrasse thugs—arms linked, eyes raised in common purpose—who protected the steps that served as a stage until the usual train of enormous black Cadillacs, antennae festooned with fluttering cornsilk, arrived.

"You have one more chance," the Peddler begged his companion in the backseat. "Please. Have you ever heard me say 'please'? Ignore this. We can let the others go on, but you don't have to leave the car."

For a week the Peddler had been pleading with Ben Alef to reveal himself. For a week he had been spinning tortuous, face-saving Talmudic the-time's-not-ripe justifications for Ben Alef's refusal. But now that the time was as ripe as a rotten tomato and the Peddler didn't want Ben Alef to appear in public, He insisted.

Snakes Hammurabi, squeezed into the huge vehicle's opposite seat together with Bruno—who could have occupied it by himself—Eisenheim, Max Vetter, and Celia, smiled. The irony was delicious, though the situation worried him, too. Although Snakes, alone of the disciples, could not shed the lingering doubts that hovered over him like a pall, he still maintained utter fidelity in public. Why, he didn't know, but kept returning to one incantatory phrase: ich kann nicht anders, I cannot do otherwise. But what about the Messiah?

If all Ben Alef had up His sleeve was the spurious tattoo, what could He do but confess His own lie? Maybe such a confession, like those of the disciples, would rebound higher than ever, but they were the saved; He was supposed to be the savior. The Peddler, used to calculations of risk and reward, said, "The gamble is too great."

Ben Alef reached toward the door.

Unable to stop the inevitable, the Peddler ordered Snakes, "Go with Him."

Snakes looked at his mentor and wondered what was going on behind that mild avuncular countenance. The Peddler appeared—there was no other word for it—stricken, and not merely by the potential for disaster. He looked the way he looked when he came out of the private office only he was allowed to enter. But just as the faraway expression he bore the moment he left the mysterious office disappeared when he took in the dance floor, so it disappeared now. If the ever-resilient Peddler had to retool by tossing a few proven favorites into the hopper to dilute the false Messiah's deleterious effect, he would, and quickly added Bruno to the bill. "You first," he said, "Then . . . Samuel."

"Come," Ben Alef invited Eisenheim, too.

A visible twitch broke through the Peddler's fixed grin. For all his hail-fellow happy mingling with the disciples and his tolerance of multiple forms of homicide, he always kept his distance from the local Obersturmbannführer. Whenever Eisenheim stepped up to the Kastrasse bar, the Peddler silently retreated into his ultra-private domain.

But Ben Alef insisted, and the Peddler gave up. "You're the boss."

So the bill was set, and the moment arrived. Onstage again, with a star turn at the finale.

First, Bruno took the mike. Hesitant and awkward a week ago, he, like all the disciples except Max Vetter, had grown adept at public speaking. Perhaps the strength of his faith would ameliorate Ben Alef's display. "I thought I was strong," Bruno began, and the crowd that had once thought itself strong sighed. "I thought I was the strongest man on earth"—Bruno himself sighed—"Le Grand Blond, meeting all comers." He raised twin tree trunks of arms upright and continued. "Headlocks, hammerlocks, half nelsons: I knew all the techniques to crush my opponents. I crushed all my opponents. I crushed Dom, the Düsseldorf Bulldozer; I crushed Maurice, the Monster from Marseilles; I crushed Ivan Nagy, the Crazed Hungarian; I even crushed Mack the Truck Smith, heavyweight champion of the United States of America."

The crowd, proud of its native talent, cheered.

But Bruno was not proud. Bruno was penitent. He lowered his arms and whispered so faintly that he would not have been audible if not for amplification, "And then I really crushed Lewis Edgar, the contender from Prussia. I crushed Lewis—first a backflip and then a full nelson. He was squirming. I was on top of him. Then a headlock, his ears between my hands. These hands . . ." He held them outward, palms open. "These hands"—Bruno was sobbing—"they squeezed Lewis Edgar's skull until I heard it crack. . . ."

Some members of the crowd, terrified of the next sentence, placed their hands on their own ears.

"Blood poured from the ears, from the wound deep inside the brain of Lewis Edgar. I crushed him, and I paid the price. I went to prison, to live with my guilt for five years, and I would have lived with my guilt for the rest of my life if I had not met Ben Alef: my blessed Ben Alef; *your* blessed Ben Alef." Bruno smiled. "Our Lord, our King, who forgave me and showed me the path to righteousness. In the kingdom to come I will meet Lewis Edgar, and I will fall to my knees"—he fell to his knees—"to beg him to forgive me, and he will, and we will reside together for all eternity. Hallelujah!"

"Hallelujah!" repeated thousands of voices, and if there had been room between them they, too, would have collapsed.

Next, as Bruno, shaken anew each time he gave his testimony, tottered off the podium, came Eisenheim, who stood silently, too silently for too long, until the crowd was uncomfortable, and then he was at ease. The other disciples' recitations had become as ritualized as prayers, but he was the wild card—always acknowledging guilt, never reneging on the pact to admit, but never in the same way. Today, for his most major address, Eisenheim chose a rhetorical mode. "What is guilt?" he asked.

"You are!" cried a voice from the crowd.

"What is guilt," Eisenheim repeated, ignoring his audience, "but the result of action? And what is action, but the attempt to make the world better? Everything that everyone does every day is done with one single aim: to make the world better. The only difference lies in our ideas of what 'better' means." His voice was high and screechy, but he maintained the posture of Hegelian aplomb, and proceeded to follow his logic through to its necessary conclusion. "When you go to work in the morning you may not think it is so much fun, but consider the alternative. You have decided— even if you are not aware of the decision-making process—that the world will be better if you earn enough money to buy food and clothes and a new car than it would be if you were poor and homeless and hungry. When you rape a woman, you have decided—even if you are not aware of the decision-making process—that the world will be better if you were satisfied. And when you—or I—or we—kill most of the Jewish citizens of Europe you—even if you are not aware of the decision-making process—have decided that the world will be better as a result of your actions than it was before."

Responding differently now than it had to Bruno's confession, the German crowd of New Jews cringed backward from Eisenheim's lecture, and a crescent of pavement at the front of the parking lot grew visible.

"Guilt"—Eisenheim plowed relentlessly ahead—"is only how other people define your actions, which were aimed for the better, because they think something else, responsible labor or the safety of women or the existence of the Jews, is better . . ."

Suddenly the Peddler snorted, "I've had enough," and slammed the car door shut.

Snakes and Max and Celia were alone now, beside the podium. Then Max, leaning on the car, looked up at the Kommandant and muttered, "Why is he here? I mean, maybe he's right—I don't mean about Jews," he stammered. "but about why we do the things we do, but why does he have to say it?"

Snakes shrugged and gave the answer that Max would have given if Snakes had asked the question. "Ben Alef thought it would be better." Then he turned back to hear the rest of Eisenheim's talk, but the old man was already leaving the mike.

"That's it?" Snakes asked.

"That's it." Eisenheim laughed. "Food for thought. Hey, it's your turn. You better hurry up—as long as you think it's better, haw!"

Snakes had begun the trek from the coast to acclaim with better-honed communication skills than his peers, and he had grown more adept at using those skills than he was at the beginning of his journey. Sometimes, these days, he felt like a press secretary, interpreting Ben Alef's elliptical parables for digest, re-reciting the same worn phrases for one interviewer after another as he hopped from Fritz Hofmann, always the first, to a portable radio broadcast unit to a sumptuously appointed network trailer, spreading the word.

Now, he stood before the familiar crowd, and couldn't get Eisenheim's ideas out of his head. "I guess I don't know what guilt is," he said, more impromptu than he had been since the early days. "If my . . ." He paused to find the correct word. ". . . colleague . . . is correct, it may be the basic state of human affairs. But if Ben Alef is right, or "—his voice grew stronger—"*because* Ben Alef is right, it may be just . . . just . . . just false. In Ben Alef we have discovered our better, our *truly* better selves, and that is a gift, a gift we dare not deny, because it is our only chance to fulfill that better, that truly better nature. . . ."

And he wondered if all of this was *truly* coming out of his mouth. For during the last week Snakes—or Samuel—had doubted more than ever. When the disciples were alone with their Lord on the beach, nothing but sand and salt and Max Vetter for miles, he had felt exalted, enlightened, content as a seagull gliding on the wind, and had further been happy to spread the word along the shore communities. But then . . . in the blink of an eye, a miracle: acceptance. Oh, not from the declaimers on the pulpits and in the parliaments, but from the butchers, the schoolteachers, the people whom Snakes had preyed upon in his previous career. Even the Peddler, in his own greedy way, believed.

Perhaps that was the root of Snakes Hammurabi's dissatisfaction. What did salvation mean if it occurred amid such society? Having fled the world of material self-interest, he suddenly found himself joined in the land of enlightenment by the exact same people he thought he had left behind. Yet wasn't that prideful of him? Did he selfishly wish to keep Ben Alef for himself?

For the last two nights, unable to sleep, Snakes had wandered down by the inky Hamburg harbor along the same alleys as Fritz Hofmann. Nervous yet strangely compelled by the sight of the water—almost, almost itching to jump—he watched a ferry and several tankers slowly come in, faint moonlit ripples spreading from their prows hardly suggesting motion, just massively advancing bulk, like an iceberg. Only when the sky turned a shade lighter than the water did he return to the Kastrasse, where he nodded fitfully for an hour or two on a banquette, too exhausted to ascend beyond the balcony to the sleeping quarters upstairs. But really, wasn't that only a way of separating himself even from the small band of early initiates?

Pride, sloth, doubt: how many of the seven cardinal sins did he personify? Was he missing any? Was he the last sinner? He looked over to Max for comfort, but suddenly found it no easier to come by here than he had at the edge of a splintery, oil-soaked wharf that overlooked a world of water. Snakes did the best he could to convince the crowd that he believed, but he lied. Nobody had mentioned the fact that they were there to refute. What about that tattoo?

"Our truly better selves?" Eisenheim repeated Snakes's last spoken words from the edge of the steps. Whether he was gently reminding his "colleague" to go on, or mocking him, or reading his mind was unclear.

"Um, yes," Snakes said, jolted back into the moment. "The selves we can be, and with the Lord's help will be. Men and women of faith, here is . . ." He paused again, shocked at how simple the word he was about to utter was, and then uttering it: "God."

Ben Alef stood patiently until Snakes left him alone on the stage, while the wash of adulation poured forth from the crowd. Like the water in the harbor, it came in waves. And he stood, silent and permanent as a stone statue on Easter Island.

But as the roar of the crowd finally began to ebb, a smaller, more vocal set of humanity was finally heard: the press.

"Mr. Ben Alef! Mr. Ben Alef, over here, please," they called to draw his attention, thrusting microphones on poles over their competitors' heads to catch any murmur to emerge from the still, stark Son of Man.

"What do you think of the story in the *Zeitung*, sir?"

"Could you show us your tattoo?"

"Have you ever been to the Lotus Studio?"

"Look at what you've done."

Ben Alef didn't understand. His eyes jumped from one inquisitor to another until they came to rest on the cause of this latest to-do: Fritz Hofmann.

The young reporter blanched beneath Ben Alef's gaze and felt the first twinges of queasiness since he had started on his exuberant professional pursuit. Until now, it had been a game, and now that he had won the game it suddenly seemed shabby. He realized that he had helped to create a movement in Kaltenhaven; was he destroying it in Hamburg?

"Here," Richard Federman grandstanded. "Behold!"

Following his clever associate's lead, the drunkard with the sharpest journalistic instincts in Germany had not spent all his free time leaning up against a brass rail. To the contrary, while Fritz basked in his most recent scoop, Federman tracked down a boy, perhaps twelve, whose parents had been among Ben Alef's earliest adherents and were currently among the few to heed the implications of the week's headlines. Before their disillusionment, however, Irma and Konrad Wilk had taken their son, Willy, to the tattoo studio closest to their home, the one Fritz hadn't bothered with, Inkorama. As a sign of faith, the mother had held little Willy's hand while the father gripped his shoulder and the acned teenage tattooist on duty, a younger version of Big Jake, took out his inks to transcribe the weirdly requested number, 108017.

Now the Wilks regretted their haste, and Federman dragged a teary Willy onto the stage to thrust his slight, recriminatory limb in the face of the man who had inspired its disfigurement.

Ben Alef could claim that His own tattoo belonged, whether it had been etched into His skin five or fifteen or fifty-five years ago, but the innocent child's was another matter. For the first time at this rally, the mood of the crowd was not in the Messiah's favor. It was fearful, anticipatory. If the united press of the world could not break their trust, the image of a single child bearing the evil burden on his flesh was almost too much to bear.

Ben Alef said one word: "Water."

"Going to take a shower?" Eisenheim said.

"Please, get me some water," Ben Alef requested.

There was silence in the crowd as a large pot that had been used for boiling corn on the cob was passed from hand to hand onto the stage.

Max turned to Snakes and whispered, "Watch."

Ben Alef took the boy's arm from the reporter and stroked it. "Don't be afraid," He said, and escorted Willy toward the pot.

"Wait!" Federman cried. He could see the next move a moment ahead of time.

"Yes?" Ben Alef was patient.

"An examination first, if you don't mind."

"I don't mind," Ben Alef replied, the soul of obligingness, relinquishing His hold on young Willy so that a swiftly convened group of police, reporters, and several neutral witnesses could examine the tattoo.

Willy cowered while they peered at his scarred and mottled flesh, and started crying when one of the journalists roughly rubbed a mustard-stained napkin against his skin.

"Leave the child alone." Celia grabbed Willy from the harsh investigation and cradled him in her own scrawny arms. "Can't you people see . . . anything?"

"Enough?" Ben Alef asked.

"Enough," Federman declared.

Cooing words of encouragement, Celia passed the child back to Ben Alef, who inserted his arm into the pot of cool liquid. He placed His own hand in next, palm to Willy's elbow, and stroked once, down toward the wrist. A moment later, He removed the boy's hand from the water. And it was clean.

"Hallelujah!" yelled a lady in the front row, and the cry swept toward the back of the enormous square, where people who couldn't see the miracle understood precisely what had occurred.

It was as if the whole crowd had been holding its collective breath, released now in a delirious exhalation. People hugged each other and the boys on the tops of the food trucks whooped and swung their hats around their heads. Circles of dancing formed spontaneously, and the entire square became an ecstatic arena, while authorities feared that the wild sexuality unleashed at night might occur right there in full view of the cameras, and that the square would ignite the entire city into one endless orgiastic hullabaloo.

Yet it wasn't over, not by a long shot. Two further miracles remained for that afternoon, the first of which Bruno Morgen noticed. Bruno stood gaping at a round metal container on the stage while the crowd celebrated and the journalists rushed for the phones. "Look," Bruno said, trying to get people to notice. "Look." He tugged at their elbows like a small boy. "Look," he practically begged until the boy Willy responded to his plaintive cry.

And only because Willy himself was the focus of so much attention did people look in the direction his dripping finger pointed, back toward the forgotten pot full of water, where the number 108017 floatcd lazily on the surface.

Chapter Sixteen

W AS IT THE ACCUMULATED emotional weight of Ben Alef's sojourn on shore, or the ecstasy of the crowd, or the single image of a six-digit number drifting as clearly in a pot of water as if its ink had been pressed onto a page by Mr. Gutenberg's wonderful device that suddenly jolted the memory of one person in the crowd? In any case, she was thrust in an instant from Hamburg, 1999, back to Paris, 1968.

"Liberation!" she could almost hear the students of the twentieth arrondissement cry from the barricade of uprooted cobblestones and overturned automobiles they had erected to keep the police from entering the so-called Free City of Montparnasse. So infectious was it that even a twenty-four-year-old resident of the Benevolent Sisters Convent felt the tug of her generation for the first time in her life.

Away from the only home she had ever known, the Little Sister could not help but linger among the colorful throng of students gathered by the Ecole de Sans Serif. She was used to expeditions out of the convent, a massive stone structure on a side street that backed onto the Seine, but until now her laced-up black jumper and cap had protected her from contact with the world. The shopkeepers she knew smiled at her, but nobody else, no strangers, had ever addressed her, nor she them.

Until a year earlier she had been able to recognize students by their button-down shirts and priests by their clerical collars and soldiers by their uniforms and Gypsies by their coats of many colors and convent girls by their heavily laced jumpers. But by the time dull, black coats went back into storage after the winter of '67/'68, everything had changed. Paisley shirts appeared next to miniskirts and polka-dotted pants in the student district surrounding the convent, while a wild proliferation of fantastic outfits and every out-of-date fashion that had moldered in used-clothing shops for decades showed up on the streets and in the discos. Teenagers dressed as mock duchesses or the king's hussars in frayed military tunics, complete with epaulets and braids. Even the serious radical fringe outfitted themselves in buckskin and U.S. Army khaki. Every day was Halloween. So, for the first time since the Little Sister had been allowed to venture beyond the convent gates, when she was fourteen, her churchly garb failed to define her—or, worse, it read as a sly and sexy comment on outmoded religion.

"Excuse me, excuse me," she apologized as she attempted to make her way against the stream of students on their way to some demonstration or other precisely as they had gone to classes a week earlier. But a week earlier the Little Sister might have held a string bag full of peaches while the students held their papers, and now the students were freed of their academic burden while she carried a heavy stack of pages against her chest like a dissertation. She was on an errand to fetch three reams of mimeo paper for the convent newsletter, which printed the hours for matins, vespers, and meditation on the prayer of the day on a hand-cranked press in the basement. Jostled left and right, she felt the pages sliding apart, and clutched them more tightly until a young man wearing jeans and a black vest and wire-framed glasses bumped into her and the entire stack went flying.

"No!" she cried, and bent down to gather the pages, but some were immediately soiled underfoot the festive army. "Please, no, please," the Little Sister sobbed as she picked up page after page, but she lost hold of one as she picked up another.

"Damn!" cursed a voice next to her on the pavement. It was the boy. "All my fault. Here. Here." He handed her a smudged portion of the stack that he had managed to scoop up. "Hey, these are empty."

Aside from a limited circle of shopkeepers' sons, the Little Sister had never spoken to a boy. He had deep, glittering green eyes, enlarged by his lenses. She nodded.

"You're in the wrong place," he said, but she knew that. "*Liberation News* is the next block over."

"What?"

"You must be the delivery everyone's waiting for. We need this now for a new release. Hurry." And before the Little Sister could explain, before she could refuse, the boy took her hand—his was warm—and the next thing she knew they were bounding down the block, past a café, a clothing store with an array of American college T-shirts, and a bookstore with a red fist stenciled onto the glass.

"Cops!" screamed another boy with a blazing mop of hair that haloed around his head like a red fist, as a stone shattered the glass. And the students who had been stomping ignorantly on the paper the convent needed came tearing down the side street like bulls, heedless of what lay in their path. The Little Sister had never known fear, and the sense of threat was galvanizing. She felt a tingling under her smock where the boy's hand held her elbow. But then again, she had never known much of any emotion—not want, not anxiety, not affection. Until that moment, the only reality in her life had been the convent routine and, beyond matins, vespers, and occasional errands, the purpose for that routine: endless devotion to God.

"C'mon," the first boy called, and they were flying too, holding hands, hair streaming, laughing, a thousand-plus sheets of white gusting to the winds.

The Little Sister couldn't remember ever laughing so hard. Joy wasn't forbidden in the convent, but was channeled into a spirituality that would have deemed outright mirth frivolous. But this was plain funny, the more so because the danger behind them was real. For the first time in her twenty-four years, life was real.

Despite the pounding at their heels, the Little Sister howled with delight until her stomach hurt from the exertion of the getaway and the laughter itself, but instead of slowing her down the laughter fueled the Little Sister in her flight, and she knew that she could run forever as long as the boy's hand touched hers. In fact, she realized that she had never run before, never broken the convent's sober rhythm, never played tag with the neighborhood children she had envied throughout her nonexistent childhood.

They ran through a sequence of twisting alleys until they arrived at an arched wooden door sunk into a damp brick façade. Pausing briefly to make sure that no police were in sight, the boy knocked.

"Who is it?"

"Me, Alain," he said, and the door swung open.

Inside was a low-ceilinged room dense with smoke and the chemical smell of a mimeograph machine that sat on a table together with a bulky black Royal manual typewriter and a sleek electric Smith-Corona. "It's a madhouse out there," Alain huffed, and collapsed onto a torn velvet couch the editors of *Liberation News* had dragged in from the trash several weeks earlier.

"Should we stop the presses?" a girl wearing black leotards and a dull green T-shirt with a red fist stenciled across her chest said in greeting as she took a drag off a cigarette dangling from her long fingers.

"But we—" Suddenly Alain recalled his errand. "We lost the paper."

There was a flushing from behind a narrow door, and another boy, emerged, tall, gangly, wearing faded corduroys and a stained sweatshirt. "I heard that," he said, and took up his position behind the mimeo, which he switched on and nonchalantly began to crank. The machine purred as page after page slid between twin rollers to come down into a waiting tray. "Jean brought the paper hours ago."

"But I assumed . . ." Alain was confused, and turned to the Little Sister.

"Oh, no"—she giggled—"that was the convent's paper."

"The convent's?" he repeated stupidly, and stared at her outfit, which had ceased to be an ironic statement.

The girl in the leotards laughed bitterly and described the situation to everyone: "I do believe you've brought us a nun."

"Yes, but a beautiful one!" the wonderful boy said, unaware that he was still staring. "Hey, my name is Alain."

"I'm Margot."

While she sat beside the Hamburg courthouse, under the watchful eye of a different country's police force, memories from the rest of that day and that season came back to her. Into the evening they sat in the cellar, talking while music unlike anything she had ever heard before played and Pierre the Mimeo Monster, as Alain introduced his comrade, worked his press. Mostly it was Alain, a refugee from the philosophy department, who held forth on everything from imperialism to structuralism, but every once in a while he'd break off in the middle of a disquisition on Levi-Strauss to ask about Margot's strange history. "You say you've lived in the convent your whole life?"

"The sisters are my family."

"But how were you born?"

"I'm sure it happened the usual way," the other girl, Tasha, sulking in the corner and listening to every word, interrupted.

Margot giggled, because she had never learned what the usual way was. "My parents were poor and put me up at the convent during the war. But they didn't come back."

Something about the vagueness of her reply compelled Alain to examine his new friend more carefully. Margot had large, dark, liquid eyes set in a wide, Slavic plane of bookish white skin under a canopy of wavy brown hair, and Alain knew, even if she didn't, why her parents had never returned to claim her, and where they must have gone. But his thoughts disappeared in a cloud of the marijuana they had begun smoking with as little ceremony as the bourgeoisie might pour a glass of dinner wine.

From the moment Margot tried to keep breathing in from the tight cigarette he handed her the world grew wonderfully woozy, and indeed it still was. Nevertheless, she recalled the impassioned way Alain had spoken of the group's plans to either topple the Eiffel Tower or paint over the *Mona Lisa* with Day-Glo until she felt a stitch in her side, touched her black jumper, and held up her hand. "Look, it's red."

An evil crimson blossom the size of a championship rose bloomed from a small tear in the side of Margot's innocent white blouse. Had she been knifed by a policeman in their chase, or had she snagged herself on a strip of barbed wire behind some shops that might have set up protective coils? Whatever its cause, the wound had bled copiously, but had already begun to heal. A rim of brick crust surrounded a blackened hole no larger than a sou. "This is the price we must pay for the sake of the movement," Alain said. "The world as we know it is coming to an end."

"But isn't it fun?" Margot replied, so happy to gaze at this young man with the warm hands and the passion in his voice.

And while the Alefites chanted, she remembered Alain's oratory, continued after he had escorted her upstairs to rest in a room with two bare mattresses under a Japanese lantern that cast orange shadows across a poster of Che Guevara.

"Imagine something like a comet, but more mystical," he began. "A primeval ball of flame, somewhere in the higher spheres, hurtling through the ether toward earth at incredible speed. If it collided, man, wipeout! But this is not a destructive comet. There's an explosion, all right; it happens just before the comet is about to change everything. Up in the air, a missile from the Pentagon intercepts the comet, and the ball is fragmented into ten million cinders dispersed throughout the globe. Every kid who's listening to The Who on a transistor radio in Tashkent is a cinder. Every kid with a Peter Max poster glued to his ceiling in Buenos Aires is a cinder. Every kid smoking pot in Sydney is a cinder."

"Or Paris?"

"They're all sparks and they're all blazing. Every kid who lights a joint is lighting a tiny spark from the eternal flame. Where was I?"

"Eternal sparks."

"Yeah, the thing is that all of the sparks are separated. Some begin to get together in New York at Columbia University, in London. The different colors on the spectrum are the different parts of the flame—say yellow is political action and orange is rock 'n' roll. They're all good. They're all part of the same original ball of flame. So they seek each other. But . . . the same people who sent up the missile to intercept the ball want to stamp it all out before the sparks unite here on earth to fulfill their cosmic mission."

"You mean . . . ?"

"The Pentagon, the Vatican, the Kremlin, the Sorbonne, they're all in it together. They're firefighters who don't want the world transformed by the healing heat of the stars."

"What can we do?"

Alain was a comet blazing with enthusiasm. "We've got to bring as many sparks together as we can and fan them, make that fire hotter and hotter until it explodes." He stopped abruptly and gazed deeply into her eyes. "We've got to . . ." he said with an earnestness that was almost painful. "We've got to. The whole world depends on it. "We've got to . . ."

"To what?"

For the first time since he had begun his cosmological rant, Alain came to a full stop. Then he said, "To come together," and smiled.

Margot's first thought the next morning was: "The sisters." On second thought, however, there were other sisters to take her place, and she had a new place—here—and a new time divorced from eternity—now. She saw her old jumper wadded up and bloodstained on the floor beside the mattress. Kicking it aside, she rummaged through a battered dresser and donned a pair of jeans and a T-shirt with a silk screen of a purple flower.

Alain was nowhere in sight, nor was he downstairs when Margot walked into the press room, but there was another boy she hadn't seen before, taller and more masculine than Alain, but also intellectual, reading the morning's *Le Monde*.

"Hey," she said to introduce herself.

"Hey, you," he replied, and ten minutes after she had put on her new clothes, she removed them.

Thus a pattern was set for the next five months, from the revolutionary spring into the sweaty summer. Margot helped put out a semi-daily broadsheet of the cadre's activities and wheat-paste it onto walls and post boxes in the shadow of the convent that had once been her home. She helped build a barricade when the police threatened to evict students occupying the buildings of the university. She stayed up late and went out in a daze of drugs and a blazing commitment to change the world. It was a time of passionate liberation and personal love: with Alain, with David, with Pierre, with a bearded drummer, with a freckled painter, with a shy professor, with an undercover cop (but she didn't know that), with several beautiful young men she couldn't recall a day later, even with Tasha one wild night after the paper had been put to bed.

There was only one problem. Ignorant of the body but not the flesh, Margot failed to mention to any of her many mates the frequent bouts of queasiness that began to assault her by July. Nor did she understand why her stomach, despite a pauper's diet of brown rice and vegetable mash, grew bigger and bigger through the summer of '68.

It was Tasha who suddenly realized one evening in September, "Jeepers, you're preggers."

"What?"

"I forgot that you really don't know anything. Honey, we've got to have a little talk."

In midwinter, with the cadre's revolutionary ardor cooled by the snow that blanketed the streets of Paris and formed a tiny drift on the inside sill of a cracked window in a crummy attic, Margot screamed louder than she ever had on the barricades, and gave birth.

"Voilà!" Tasha cried as she lifted up the child, and snipped the cord with a pair of rusty scissors.

Delighted, the cadre tried to take communal care of the baby boy, but their attachments to the cause and each other were already fraying, so come the following summer Margot packed him into a cloth sling on her hip and set off on her own farther journey. Like a human spark floating on the winds, she drifted south from France through Spain to Morocco, and east past the pyramids for a sojourn in India, seeking wisdom, and back west to accompany a touring musician she had met in Madras to . . . she couldn't remember.

Nor could she particularly remember when the child disappeared. Had she inadvertently left him by the side of the road while hitchhiking through northern California? Was he taken by a court-appointed foster parent after a run-in with the law in Stockholm? Or, like her own parents, did she deposit him in a wicker basket at the iron-knockered front door of a benevolent convent back in Paris? She didn't know, and didn't think about it as she continued to wander, until, compelled by obscure necessity, she arrived in Hamburg thirty-some years after being reborn on the Rue de Flores. Only one memory stayed with her: the infant bathing in a corrugated metal washbasin, laughing and splashing amid the uncanny—at the time she had assumed hallucinatory—vision of numbers on the water.

Thus, the third miracle of the day.

From out of the crowd of followers, Margot pushed her way to the front, gazed into the bowl glittering with the reflected light of a hundred flash bulbs, turned to Ben Alef, and cried, "My son!"

Book VII
Devotion

Chapter Seventeen

THE WORD "REBORN" has been adopted by so many nullity-fearing, serenity-seeking groups with clouds on and in their minds that it has lost its connection to a brutishly individual biological event. At the very least, the metaphorical usage ought to connote something more literal, say a fierce and disorienting passage from warm, dark anchorage into a state of blindingly illuminated freedom—like a toboggan at night shooting out of its tunnel onto a floodlit plain. Here I am! I breathe! I see! Me!

Everyone knows that other people must have been born, too, but only one's self experiences birth. Yet every one of the people standing in front of the Hamburg jail instantly felt the pure and shocking realization and comprehension of another birth. Everyone present for Margot's statement immediately knew that even if they were not reborn, Ben Alef was, and He was their son, too. And each one felt the spontaneous—biologists would claim Darwinian—adoration of the begetter for the begotten. Suddenly the endless wine at Kaltenhaven, the endless corn in the parking lot (actually provided by the large but limited kitchen of the Kastrasse) made sense: they were baby gifts, but the difference between them and a flannel nightie or a fuzzy bear was that these gifts were presented by the divine child to those who by their faith made Him.

Only then, through the entirely human process of empathy, did they reexperience their own birth. They gazed raptly stageward to a sacred bucket made of ridged alloy that might just as well have risen to the sky and sprinkled each of them with its soothing, baptismal fluids. And the news of the Day of Three Miracles effected the same transformation in previous nonbelievers across the globe.

No matter the logic of the intellectuals, every piece of evidence for Ben Alef's humanity assured the faithful of his divinity.

"We know where he received the tattoo," the agnostics cried.

"Amen," the believers said, drowning them out, and turned the street in front of the Lotus Studio into a shrine, its sidewalk covered with husks of holy corn.

"We know that he had a mother," the scientists said.

"But she knows not the father," the believers prayed at Margot's feet.

"A slut!"

"A virgin!"

"A tramp!"

"A saint!"

At each point, the irrational triumphed. If hundreds had followed Ben Alef and the disciples into Hamburg, and thousands had joined them in the square beneath the jail, as sympathetic rallies mustered in Lagos, Kyoto, Barcelona, Prague, and Los Angeles, now untold numbers worldwide packed their bags and prepared to meet Him.

"This story doesn't have legs," Richard Federman marveled. "It has wings."

Every plane to Germany was jammed with pilgrims to the new promised land—and for those without resources, well, their no less holy meeting would occur in the spirit, for the end of days.

Confusion reigned in the corridors of power. The Pope and the Chancellor, who had been monitoring events since the beginning, conferred with their peers in foreign capitals whose populations ceased to attend earthly laws and customs. What difference did a paycheck or political affiliation make when the end was nigh? Assembly lines at automobile factories emptied, but what difference did that make? Nobody was buying cars. Likewise, new motion pictures went unseen, new software untested, news itself, except for that pertaining to Ben Alef, unread. Bank reserves were depleted as depositors rushed to withdraw and give away their money, hindered only by the reluctance of anyone else to take it. Mundane business affairs ground to a halt, and the stock market teetered on the verge of total collapse.

Only the churches were full, and also mosques and Buddhist temples, and, most of all, synagogues. But this gave no satisfaction to religious leaders, because it wasn't their traditional verities the congregants demanded; it was the Messiah.

In some places, services grew so raucous with spontaneous hosannas of "Hail! Hallelujah!" they had to be suspended, lest the frothing faithful act as their antecedents did in the now infamous parking lot, where a popular T-shirt read "Fuck for God."

A meeting was called, not a meeting to determine the agenda for a committee to propose to investigate the problem, but a real meeting of the real powers that shaped the real world. Only the top level of international shapers and their most intimate advisers were invited, and they knew who they were: Chancellor Grabner; the American Under Secretary of State; the Russian Commissioner for Internal Affairs; a scattering of ambassadors; and a senior partner from one of Wall Street's largest firms, to speak for the business community.

That was where the guest list might have concluded for a routine crisis, such as a comet about to crash into the earth, but the Alef situation required experts from its own abstract realm. Therefore several additional men were included, and no politician considered their status less substantial than his own. Father Immaculato represented the Vatican, and a dark, hawk-nosed man (tacitly understood to be the Mossad's head of covert operations), flew in from Jerusalem on behalf of the Chief Rabbi while a Saudi imam stood for the third monotheistic faith. Last of all, another Jew came. He had no title and occupied no office but his own book-lined study, but wore his portfolio on his lower left arm, and unlike the others in their private jets, he arrived on a late train from Paris.

In mundane circumstances, involving, for example, a few thousand daily deaths, the choice of venue for the summit could have taken months of diplomatic negotiations to determine, but the calendar set its own date. Playing for time was no longer an option as the intensity of public response mounted. The meeting *had* to occur immediately. Locations considered included Camp David, Downing Street, and the Vatican, but each involved logistical problems as well as those of pride. For a moment, the various social secretaries of the principals considered a special Internet hookup, but fear of eavesdropping made a face-to-face encounter necessary. That being the case, where? One logic indicated removing the meeting as far as possible from the insanity in Hamburg, but proximity was finally felt to be more of an asset than a detriment. Germany was the epicenter of this nasty little episode, and Germany was where it had to be resolved.

Official government quarters were out, because the media had mounted a twenty-four-hour surveillance of the Reichstag, so the Chancellor's aides frantically scouted for a practical alternative, eliminating one after the other until Axel Kahn, a sly, chinless sublunary in the Facilities Administration, suggested an abandoned, all but forgotten, state-owned villa in a secluded Berlin suburb.

The place had all of the advantages of access, comfort, and privacy, so, without due historical diligence, the proposal was okayed. Thus, a runway was cleared at the Berlin Airport, a fleet of Mercedeses met the jets bearing various national insignia, and eighteen of the most powerful figures on earth convened at Wannsee.

Only one of them realized that the villa had been the site for a meeting that aimed to solve another problem nearly sixty years earlier.

"We all know why we are gathered here, so let's not beat about the bush," Grabner said, convening the gathering. He stood at the head of a dark walnut conference table under the dusty chandelier that had looked down on the German high command in the early days of World War II against England, France, and the rest of Allied Europe, before the secret war they were about to declare commenced. It was at the Wannsee Conference of 1942 that Hitler gave the unrecorded nod to Heydrich and Himmler to proceed with their generation's final solution.

"Anybody want anything to drink?"

"Vodka," the Russian said.

"I meant coffee or tea or soda."

"Vodka."

Orders were taken by a squadron of waiters, and participants settled into the leather swivel chairs delivered only hours earlier. The American and Russian secretaries flanked Herr Grabner just as they were used to sitting beside their respective superiors, who awaited phone calls from the special lines channeled in overnight by the German KRP. Likewise other power factions distributed themselves: the Chinese and Japanese ministers opposite each other, ditto the Israeli and Saudi, straight on down the burl to the foot of the table, where the single, unaffiliated Jew sat, odd man out, as far from Grabner as the polished walnut would allow.

"We are used to the disruptions of, well, disruptive forces," Grabner continued. "We are used to racial and national hatreds; we are used to the dispersal of plutonium or biological weaponry into the hands of terrorists"—he blinked at the Russian—"and we are accustomed to establishing international regulations and accords for the good of all."

"You don't need to make a speech," the banker said. "There's no press here."

Grabner, determined to remain in control, said straight out, "If word of this is leaked, it will be denied."

Future autobiographies might or might not mention the Second Wannsee Concordance, depending on what ultimately resulted from its deliberations and what the authors' personal or national agendas were at the moment of publication of their memoirs, but everyone in the room knew that the pens of posterity were poised.

"Understood."

"Gerhard." Grabner nodded to his mouthpiece.

As always, Schwarz was all business. "Less than a month ago, after the *Farnhagen* disaster, Ben Alef washed up on the North Coast of the German Federal Republic. Twenty-some days later, there are approximately one hundred thousand Alefites in Hamburg alone; there are chapters of the New Jewish Church in every major city in Germany; and you have joined us because this is not just a German problem. Am I correct?"

The man from America nodded.

"Da."

"We had hoped to ride this out on the assumption that once the calendar turned and nothing changed it would all look silly, but events have escalated beyond control so that even January first may not bring surcease. It may bring worse upheaval, precisely because of the discontent. We cannot wait. We must stop it now. . . . Nor is this a merely secular problem for the nation-states of the world. Am I correct?"

Father Immaculato agreed, "That's why we're here."

"So, if the New Jewish Church is a threat to the established church and the established state, we, the representatives of the established church and the established state, have an obligation, a moral imperative, to protect ourselves and our people. We must obliterate it in the name of . . . of . . ."

"God and Country." The man from England sighed.

"Precisely."

"You know . . ." The Russian minister took the floor. "This may not be so easy. We, I don't mean the current democratically elected representatives of the Russian people, but the Communists who ruled over us with an iron fist for eighty years . . ."

"Blah, blah, blah," the ambassador from China said.

The Russian glowered and continued, "The Communists tried to obliterate the churches in 1917. The doors were padlocked, the buildings converted to youth centers and cultural centers and administrative facilities. Nobody went to a church for eighty years; people forgot the prayers, the customs, and the meanings beneath the prayers and customs. Then, come glasnost, the doors were opened, and maybe we could have guessed that a minor, antiquarian interest would develop. But no, from the day of release, a century's pent-up demand surged out. Post-perestroika, the churches are full, and they are getting fuller."

"What are you saying?"

"I am saying that it is difficult to control the will of the people. There was a meeting of Alefites in Kremlin Square—"

"They call them assemblies in Mecca," the Saudi representative said, correcting the Russian's vocabulary.

"What the fuck," the Russian said, like Grabner. "The point is that more people came than used to go to the military parades. Herr Grabner is correct. This is an explosive situation."

"Are you suggesting anything in particular, Ivan?"

"Caution," the large man said, and sat.

There was much muttering around the table, and a few more short speeches—for the record—to establish the parties' distance from the action they knew they were about to pursue off the record, before Grabner took the floor again and said, "As we see it, there are only two possible alternatives, the secular and the spiritual."

"By 'secular,' you mean . . . ?"

"Discreet," the Chief Rabbi's "adviser" explained.

"Be direct," the Under Secretary of State said. "There is no time for diplomacy and this is no moment for euphemism."

"Gentlemen, we are facing the most disruptive possible force in the world today. This is a virus—the way it arrives, as an outsider into the system; the way it spreads; the way it breaks down the host from within. In response to this virus, we must use an epidemiological model."

"You mean?"

"Eradication." Grabner took back the floor, standing now, beside the picture window overlooking the overgrown grounds at Wannsee, which hadn't been tended for more than half a century.

"But isn't there a risk of martyrdom?" the cautious ambassador from Japan asked, perhaps unwilling to be dragged into one more vortex with his good friends from Mitteleuropa.

"It must be acknowledged."

"Risk-to-gain," Gerhard Schwarz declared.

Father Immaculato had been listening silently, but the moment he felt Urban's invisible signal, he spoke. "With all due respect, we have been observing this . . . ahem . . . virus for longer than anybody in this room, and we, the church, have had greater experience with similar situations through the years than anybody in this room. We have also considered the path of eradication, but believe that we should first attempt one subtler path."

"Which is?"

Fingers in a cathedral shape in front of his chin and lower lip, Father Immaculato continued, "To extend the Chancellor's elegant viral model, I propose, not eradication, not yet, but immunization. You deliberately infect a portion of the body with a sample from the disease to protect the entire system." He went silent and allowed his intertwined fingers to fold in upon themselves.

"Thank you for the elegant allegory," the impatient banker said. "But what, specifically, do you have in mind?"

"I say that rather than look to the kinds of solutions we, the infected, can offer, we look instead to the source of the infection, and try to use that source itself to to allay its effects."

"The source being . . . ?"

Immaculato looked around the room, at the men in their three-piece suits, doodling on yellow legal pads with their Waterman pens. He glanced up at the chandelier, a cloud of teardrop crystals that refracted dozens of tiny, teardrop-shaped rainbows across the ornately molded ceiling. Alas, it did not hold the beeswax candles that might have betokened an older period of human endeavor during which he would have been not merely one among equals here, but paramount. What had happened to the church since the days of the previous Urbans? It was sad, but it was true, and the representative of Rome dealt, first and foremost, with the truth. And certain truths remained absolute. There was a God, and the Church perceived Him. "The source being," he answered, "Judaism."

Silence in the chamber.

If Grabner had dared mention the "J" word, the meeting might have adjourned from sheer historical chagrin, but the Pope's man, the man of this Pope in particular, a figure of consummate ecumenicism, was the only one who dared speak.

"We have invited a rabbi to the table," Grabner said.

The man from Israel grunted.

"And we have considered using a rabbi," Immaculato replied. "But, with due respect, this is too big for *a* rabbi; this requires a statesman of the highest order from the innermost circle of Zion. Fortunately, we have such a person in this room. That is why we requested he attend this meeting."

Every eye focused on the man at the end of the table. He was short, squat, rather like the Peddler—not quite as heavily bearded as Father Immaculato had told Urban—unremarkable in every physical way, yet he was the embodiment of the particular experience that vexed the men in Wannsee.

"The Holocaust," Immaculato declared, "has been a cancer in the Western soul since 1945. It lay dormant for a number of years, but starting in the 1960s one issue after another has brought it forward, from the Eichmann trial until now. Recently it seems as if these flare-ups come to wide public attention on a two-year cycle. Some are specific contretemps, others more abstract, and, of course, some are more vicious than others. A museum opened in Washington in 1993 and it was international news. Two years ago, there was that fuss about Swiss gold."

The banker nodded and shook like a wet dog, remembering the recent multibillion-dollar settlement.

"Now we have . . ." Father Immaculato skimmed an eight-by-ten color photograph into the center of the conference table. It was a life-size image of an arm from slightly above the elbow to slightly below the wrist. "This."

Nobody reached forth to touch the photograph, and it sat like an amputated limb on the dense wood grain.

Father Immaculato explained, "Ben Alef has drawn his water from two wells. The first well, the one that concerns us, is the well of messianic consciousness. That source of nourishment anticipates the future and is indeed the well that his followers yearn to drink from. That is the well that is poison to both the sacred and secular world. That is the well that we are concerned about. Yet that well gains its . . . its . . ." He rubbed his thumb and forefinger together in search of the correct word. ". . . its pressure from its connection to the second well, which is the well of the past. This false Messiah can only justify his future by his past, by that"—he paused dramatically and pointed down at the photograph on the table—"thing on his left arm.

"We suggest that only a person with absolutely impeccable credentials, with an intact passport from the past—in short, a person with a number on his arm, a person who has essentially become the number on his arm—be the one to destroy Ben Alef." And then, ignoring everyone else in the room, the representatives of most of the power on earth, he turned to his only peer on the spiritual plane, and asked, "Are you ready?"

Asher Rose stroked back the halo of silver hair that fringed his bald head and looked out at the room. He was accustomed to such environs, but they hardly came naturally to a man of his background. That was part of his charm.

Born in the tiny Polish Jewish village, or shtetl, of Proszowice, Moshe and Sarah's youngest child could hardly have imagined a trip to Cracow, twenty kilometers to the west, let alone Warsaw, Jerusalem, or New York. Yet he had been in all those places, and Tokyo and Buenos Aires and Johannesburg, too. And even if his parochial adolescent mind, filled with the lore of the sages, could have encompassed foreign travel, the notion that he might be lauded, applauded, and virtually beatified precisely because of his origins would have been simply inconceivable.

But in between a shtetl infancy and international glory the doors of human possibility had opened further than Asher or his father or any of the other Jews of Proszowice could have dreamed. The doors were slatted, splintered planks on a cattle car, and they led Asher's family, after four days' transit among their starving, shitting, and dying coreligionists, to a whistlestop named Oświęcim or, as the thick German tongue called it, Auschwitz.

Weaned on tales of ancient woe, mourning the destruction of the Holy Temple in A.D. 76 as if it had been yesterday, lamenting the Spanish

Inquisition and the Crusades, close enough to Czarist pogroms to smell the manure on the Cossack's horses' hooves, here they were—in the fulfillment of every Jewish fear.

The scent of burning flesh suffused the air, but who could breathe deep the odor of theology when German soldiers were shrieking "Raus! Raus!" and brandishing whips to herd the human cattle from their cars straight to the crematoria?

"You, this way," a young, wispy-bearded SS man called Asher out of the line.

"Me?"

"You, and"—he paused to allow Asher's father and mother to pass before his pale, silvery eyes—"you," he said, summoning a few other young men, a handful out of three hundred deemed fit to work before dying.

"Go!" Moshe commanded his son, and continued his own march to the pillar of fire.

Asher went. Ten minutes later, his forearm bore the same tattoo as Ben Alef's, and he was assigned to a labor brigade. Along with the other boys from Proszowice and several score more from other shtetls, they carried forty-kilo bags of cement five kilometers toward an electrical plant under construction on the outskirts of the main camp, and the forty-kilo bodies of those who died en route back to the camp for "disposal."

By the end of the war, Asher Rose was all that was left of Proszowice; he *was* Proszowice, skeleton-thin, soul-seared with everything he had seen. But Asher was different from most of the fifty thousand–odd survivors of the camps who flooded Europe in the strange interregnum before their eventual dispersal to the United States and Palestine and the rest of the twentieth-century diaspora. While they scrambled to mate and make new lives for themselves, Asher couldn't let go of the evil he had witnessed.

Of course, none of the survivors really let go, but they looked toward the future; Asher could not escape the past. He sat on a barrel in the DP camp at Feldafing, watching the rest of the survivors' attempts to organize exit visas, barely able to summon the strength to line up for the food the Allies provided for the pathetic remnants of the Jewish world. Just sitting without imminent threat of execution was an astonishing luxury, and it so faintly recalled a time only a few years earlier, when he had sat in the Proszowice shul beside his large, strong father, reciting the prayers of medieval mystics and contemplating the benevolence of God, that he found himself sobbing.

Perhaps it was Asher Rose's ability to cry that really separated him from the rest of the survivors. Their tear ducts, long since drained and dried, were as arid as the Sinai through which their ancestors had marched out of Egypt millennia before there was such a concept as a millennium. But Asher sobbed, and then—as great a miracle as his survival—he understood why he had been spared. He borrowed a small black notebook from a representative of the Joint Distribution Committee, and started writing, "In the beginning . . ."

Compelled by the enormity he had experienced, the preternaturally aged young man hunched over his notebook, scribbling in a fever, for six months, so diligently transcribing from life into what he did not know was art that the other inmates of Feldafing laughed and called him Der Schreiber.

Whether his nickname was sarcastic or honorific he neither knew nor cared. For six months he was able to forget the last six years and dwell at peace back in the Proszowice that no longer existed. He recalled anecdotes of that sleepy village lost in time and braided them together like his mother lacing strands of dough into a challah bread for her family's Shabbos dinner. And yet, despite the apparent benignity of those stories, any sane reader could not help but be aware of the shadow that overcast that world, and what future lay in store for every single one of the characters except for the nameless twelve-year-old boy who narrated it. The effect—and Der Schreiber had had no particular literary effect in mind— was simultaneously sweet and sorrowful. Only when it came time for him to title the collection did he realize what he had done, and how far he had come, so, contrary to all autobiographical intent, he called it *Mythology*.

Befriended by a French essayist who had written a series of dispatches on the chaos in Europe, Asher was convinced to send his precious notebook to a publisher. In truth, he had not thought of what might happen to his work once it was concluded, but he agreed, and was neither thrilled nor surprised when he received notification that *Mythology* had been duly accepted for publication. That seemed only natural, although payment (he had never seen a check before) and an invitation to Paris were still beyond his ken.

Knowledge, however, arrived swiftly for Asher Rose. A year later, when the book, translated from the Yiddish, came out, the shy, reclusive former cheder bocher was instantly hailed as a "voice from the ashes," a voice, moreover, much in demand for his sorrow and insight. Nor did the

flood of attention abate, as Asher went from strength to strength, suc-
ceeding and exceeding his initial strike with book after book that belatedly
traced the painful and exotic path of his life through the eyes of the same
nameless narrator. *Mythology* was followed by *Archaeology* and *Paleontology*,
as he worked his way backward in title though forward in the fictionalized
chronology of his own experience, until he hardly knew whether he was
flesh or fossil.

Each book found additional readers, as the world proved insatiable
for every last detail of the horror of the era. Readers alone would have been
sufficient as heaven for most writers, yet more than readership and financial rewards were in store for Asher. To begin with, there was respect. For
two decades starting in the mid-1950s he became a professor. But such was
his particular combination of mournful lamentation and high moral distinction that he was slowly but inevitably transformed from an individual
victim of atrocity to the authoritative chronicler of that atrocity to the emblematic figure of the Holocaust. He continued to produce books, but
long before the turn of the century he had become more of a statesman
than a writer, and was frequently called upon to lend his gravitas to multiple issues of international tragedy, be they Jewish, Rwandan, Tibetan,
or whatnot. Asher Rose, the avatar of catastrophe and resurrection, spoke,
and people listened. As a result, he was the only one at the meeting in
Wannsee—the ironic significance of which he was the only one in the
room to get—who could speak to the allegedly resurrected Messiah as an
equal.

Thus Chancellor Grabner looked around the room and said, "Are we
agreed?"

Everyone nodded, and Father Immaculato gave his blessing on behalf
of the Pope.

Only the businessman who had never known spirituality remained
uncertain and said out loud what they were all wondering: "And if this
doesn't work?"

"Plan B," Grabner announced, and turned to Asher Rose. "You have
twenty-four hours."

Chapter Eighteen

Silent night,
Holy night

CHRISTMAS EVE always made Rose nervous. Despite the secular life he had led for most of his years, Christmas was the one day in the calendar that made him feel as if he were still wearing a yellow star. The moment evergreens started appearing for sale on street corners late each November, Asher tended to stay inside. And when strands of celebratory lights festooned window frames in his neighborhood, he shut the blinds. He went into the kind of hiding his family had not been prescient or fortunate enough to find in Proszowice in 1942. And although he had given speeches and participated in ceremonies and symposia in hundreds of churches in the name of ecumenicism, he always felt a tremor beneath the sign of the cross.

All is still
All is bright.

The sounds of caroling wafted through the streets like smoke as a gigantic parade traversed Hamburg. Starting at the municipal line where Ben Alef had first entered the city, the parade alit briefly at each of the stations of the Messiah's passage, from the Municipal jail to the bright yellow (the pink had been replaced) awning in front of the Kastrasse to the alley outside the Lotus Studio, and at each stop it was joined by more and more of the Alefites.

Many were dressed in loose white robes despite a cold front that had come down from the Arctic to chill the air and create miniature ice floes in the harbor. Police, those who hadn't gone over to the Alefites, hoped that the weather might keep attendance down, but no such luck. The bitter gusts that set them shivering pleased the most dedicated of the believers, who had billed this sacred evening as "A Night of Contrition." Contrite, they marched and sang and bore the cold as a welcome test from God and some of them availed themselves of the service offered by freelance tattooists who set up booths at major intersections to assist those who required a sign on the flesh.

Professional parlors also did a land-office business, working around the clock to meet the demand. Mr. Lee, of course, but also Inkorama, Sin on Skin, and Big Jake were booked solid. And these were easy jobs, since they only used one color, aniline blue. Big Jake jokingly put up a sign at his door that read, "Pick a Number. Any Number."

Some groups of Alefites broke off from the main procession to follow individual acolytes or prominent adherents, as Anton Bartsch led three score to the site of his crime, and the Wilks hosted all comers at their small semidetached house in the Winkler district. As penitence for their moment of doubt, the family of the boy who had precipitated the second miracle of the three-miracle day by complaining about his tattoo removed every single pot and pan from their house, filled them with water, and displayed the holy vessels on their front yard beneath multiple loops and strands of the gaudiest holiday lights they could afford.

From which they all trouped off, singing "O Tannenbaum" and "Gloria in Excelsius Dee-eea-o." These tunes clashed with those of other roving bands singing other carols and psalms, as the entire city appeared to be on the march, freezing their toes off and singing their hearts out, prior to midnight services in the old Wandsbekstrasse Synagogue, where Ben Alef was set to deliver a birthday address and the entire clan of Alefites would gather.

Even Asher Rose had requested a few moments for—Snakes, main organizer of the grand event, assumed—the most compelling public affirmation of Ben Alef's identity yet. Once Mr. Rose, keeper of the Holocaust legacy, acknowledged Ben Alef as Messiah, it would surely signal the conversion of the last Jews, and, following that notoriously stiff-necked tribe, less than one week later, at the last tick of the millennial clock, the entire world.

. . .

The acoustics were splendid in the vast nineteenth-century structure, built in a Byzantine style with groined arches and lesser domes leading to one central dome. So the evening hours went, from music to testimony, as the Wandsbekstrasse Synagogue, which could theoretically seat a thousand on the ground and five hundred more in a three-sided balcony, seemed to expand to accommodate any number who wished to enter. The synagogue was a hive, with people wandering in and out, the aisles abuzz with people waving to friends, comparing their respective moments of illumination— "Where were you when the lights went on?"

Young interns from the Kastrasse, led by Celia, who reported to the Peddler, hopped about behind the scenes with clipboards and walkie-talkies, helping the many journalists find their stories and telling the various speakers when they were scheduled to go on or where they should sit, smoothing over the logistical difficulties that invariably attended such an occasion.

"Pretty impressive," Richard Federman said to Fritz Hofmann.

"All is possible," Fritz replied.

Federman peered at the young man who had come so far in the last month. From gawky university stringer to hotshot ace reporter, Fritz had grown since November, and now he had grown again, this time disconcertingly. "All is possible, huh?"

"Yeah," Fritz declared, eyes shining, because those three words had become the mantra of the Alefites, and there wasn't an ounce of cynicism in his usage. Oddly, his very discovery of the Lotus Studio warranted Fritz's faith rather than destroying it. A mystery unsolved was merely a mystery waiting to be solved, but here the answer to a mystery had proved the irrelevance of worldly answers. "Yeah," Fritz repeated, what about it?"

"Just asking," Federman replied, holding up his palms.

All things may have been possible, but few were necessary on Wandsbekstrasse on Christmas Eve. There was such an abundance of goodwill in the synagogue and the surrounding streets that everything that could have gone wrong just magically went right. The sound system worked, the lines to the bathrooms were orderly, and even the wild cards acted straight. Margot and Dietrich Eisenheim sat next to each other on the side of the dais as if they were exhibits in a wax museum.

Asher Rose looked carefully at the Mother of God as he was led past her by one of the Kastrasse usherettes to await his opportunity to testify. Something about Margot fascinated him, but, of course, that was only reasonable; she was fascinating. Why else was her face on the cover of that week's *Ladies' Home Journal* and *Bundt* and half the women's magazines in the world? A profile of Margot in *Oggi* said it best: "Every mom thinks her son is God, but only one can be right."

Then Asher Rose caught a glimpse of Dietrich Eisenheim, and just as suddenly as the years had evaporated for Margot back in the parking lot, so they disappeared for Rose. The Jew's and the German's eyes met, and whether they had ever literally occupied the same damned patch of earth was irrelevant; they knew each other.

Eisenheim smiled and tipped an imaginary hat to the success of the survivor.

Asher Rose found his seat and crossed his legs and gazed out on the crowd.

Instead of a traditional religious service, the scene resembled a political convention. Some Alefites prayed and some held hands and danced in a broken ring around the sanctuary and others held up placards that bore a confused amalgam of religious symbolism ranging from six-pointed stars to Muslim crescents as the procession was joined by a horde of Eurasian immigrants who had hiked over the Alps several days earlier. One follower dragged a gigantic cross made of two-by-fours up the aisle to deposit his offering, the meaning of which he couldn't comprehend, at Ben Alef's feet.

Asher Rose shivered in his three-piece suit. He knew that his mission was to bring down this house—like Samson bringing down the Philistine temple—with the might of his moral stature, but . . . For the first time he asked himself, why? He had agreed because he was appalled at the despicable hoax being perpetrated in the name of the martyrs of his people, worse than the deniers', but now he wondered why.

Because it was bad? Well, these people's lives had been composed of daily privation until now, and now they knew glory. But since glory itself was neutral, the moral question ought to be: "Where did glory lead them?" The Alefites were gratified, satisfied, saved, and redeemed according to the truth they witnessed. But how did they act? They gave up their jobs and fucked in the parks. Did that make them any less fine human beings than the world leaders at Wannsee with their expensive clothing and the excellent pastries passed around the elegant table and their belief in the superior nature of the nation-states that had led to World War II? How had the little Jew found himself the defender of the status quo?

So then, as Bruno Morgen stood up to recite his testimony for the hundredth time, Asher Rose looked for another reason to destroy the faith rampant in Wandsbekstrasse . . . Because it was false? Asher believed that dogs heard sounds too high for the human ear to perceive, so maybe these people, with their tongue-wagging, canine enthusiasm, saw light too bright for him to see. Maybe.

So if the Alefites' faith was not bad, and if it was not false—and that took care of both the "He's a fraud" and the "He's deluded" camps—what was left as the final truth? Asher felt the itch of an idea at the back of his neck. He tried to rub it away, but the itch was insistent, and rubbing only aggravated it. "Ludicrous," he muttered.

"What's that?" the woman next to Eisenheim asked. She wore several loops of chains and beads, which clattered with an odd melody that took him back in time.

Yes, undoubtedly the notion that teased at the periphery of his mind was ludicrous, and Asher Rose knew that as well as he knew the words of the Torah sages of his childhood or the philosophy he had later read at the Sorbonne. Arrived in Paris and lionized for *Mythology*, he was nonetheless insecure in his renown, so he matriculated at the Sorbonne as a special student and then taught in the Department of Judaic Studies until his prominence spun out of the literary-academic orbit into the stratosphere.

"Say, haven't we met before?" the cheerful woman persisted.

Unable to stop the rush of images, Asher remembered his days as a special student. No older than the other students, but white-haired, he learned to drink wine in a large studio over a used-book store. He remembered his own and his fellows' fervor for ideas during the 1950s—a fervor that, when he was a teacher, a decade later, turned into a political passion that nearly tore the school apart. Sympathetic to the rebels at first, canceling his classes, Professor Rose, however, grew uneasy with the anarchy of the 1960s, which he feared could lead straight back to fascism. And so, without knowing how, he became a voice of worried conservatism in a time that had no patience for logic.

So irrational and emotional was the moment that all of Paris was at sixes and sevens. One day the transit workers were striking in solidarity with the students; the next day those same workers were bashing those students over the head. One day, trapped between a demonstration of would-be revolutionary rabble and a line of mounted police who reminded him of Cossacks, Asher Rose took refuge in the only place he could by pushing through an ancient, arched door inadvertently left ajar.

The door led to a small office dominated by a printing press. He had always loved the smell of ink and paper, and instantly felt at home in the dim, low-ceiling room. But a strange, flowery perfume wafted about the premises. The scent was so extremely vivid that he smelled it now on the platform of the Wandsbekstrasse Synagogue as he had thirty-two years ago at the *Liberation News.*

Then, as now, a flood of public rhetoric and private ecstasy gushed over the land, and then, as now, the depth of the passion was impressive. The movements were equivalent; only the vocabulary was different. Just substitute the word "sin" for "injustice," or "redemption" for "liberation," and the arrival of the Messiah might have been foreshadowed in the troubles of the sixties. It was no accident that middle-aged flower children as well as steel-booted skinheads flocked to the Alefite tent. Then, as now, the language and actions of salvation and redemption hailed the end of all things awful and the advent of universal delight. Yet now, as then, Asher Rose knew that the fever of idealism would lead only to doom. He looked at Ben Alef.

Surely he had never seen the youngish man, yet he knew Him as well as he knew himself. But suddenly he didn't know himself at all.

Wavering visibly on the grand stage, sweating from the lights of a dozen cameras, his small, tight mouth blocked from view by a forest of microphones, and rubbing the back of his neck, Asher Rose cleared his throat.

Father Immaculato, incognito in the crowd, didn't know why, but he, too, had a bad feeling at the back of his neck. The Voice of the Holocaust was standing there, with the world expecting to hear that he believed in redemption—when the Voice had secretly agreed to declare that he didn't—and now . . . something had changed from yesterday to today, as if Rose didn't know which world to satisfy, the one above, or the one below. A man of equal parts moral weight and realpolitik wisdom, he was clearly torn.

"At first . . ." Rose's voice boomed through the rows and aisles of the synagogue, implying through its initial phrase an opposition to come. "At first, when I heard about the man we are here to recognize, I did not know what to think." The professional speaker modulated his voice to give people time to find seats, settle in, and make themselves comfortable.

But the speaker himself was far from comfortable. He squinted up toward the beams and out through the orange and yellow stained-glass windows and everywhere but next to him, where the presumed subject of his address sat.

"At first I was doubtful. How could I not be? And weren't you all?"

"Yes," Snakes Hammurabi whispered to himself.

"What do we think when we hear the word 'God'?" Rose reverted to a professorial manner. "Some idea of God is as old as the human race. The ziggurats of Babylon, the pyramids of Egypt, the temples of Angkor Wat— they were all built as a sign of human faith in the numinous, whether it was defined in natural or supernatural terms. Was it a true faith, or is it sufficient that people have always been truly faithful, be their belief in thunder or a divine elephant or a prophet or the all-seeing, all-knowing, all-embracing God of my forefathers?

"I say 'my' not because I am proprietary, but because it is the simple— or complicated—historical truth that the Hebrews of Israel were the first to perceive—although the word 'perception' is flawed in this case—the presence of the single unearthly force that has shaped world culture.

"In what way has that shaping occurred? As Jews through the ages have tried to adhere to the moral strictures of God, so others have interpreted that same God's mandate to convert the Jews, and, if that was impossible, to destroy us . . ." Asher Rose continued, and as he worked his way through the devastations of the Islamic conquest of the Middle East and Christian domination of Europe, his voice grew stronger, more like thunder or a divine elephant trumpeting his grief. By the time he arrived at the current century, he was half shouting, half sobbing, and the mostly German audience was sobbing with him.

"A genius," the Peddler, behind the scenes, said to no one in particular. Here was a prime example of how to convince the public. Compared with Rose, the preacher on the Kastrasse TV was an amateur. Der Schreiber held the room in his hand, outstretched now with dramatic effect. He could do with them as he pleased.

"And so," he said, "when we are told that God has chosen to appear at the end of this awful century, what are we to think, to feel, to perceive? At first, we are skeptical: we have heard this before; we have been fooled and betrayed before. But then good people tell us that miracles contrary to the law of nature, explicable only by the law of God, have occurred, and we are hesitant, fascinated, fearful. And then . . . we see, we meet, we breathe in the same room as the messenger, we . . ."

The entire room was waiting for him to say "believe," but Rose veered at the last second.

"Patience," Immaculato tried to soothe himself as he moved along the south wall of the synagogue toward the stage, but he was unsure, because Rose himself was unsure. The Father had sat in enough confessionals to recognize the moment of hesitation before the blurt that might just as well be truth or lie and either way would come as a genuine surprise to the person who said it.

"We . . . know . . . the . . ." It was excruciating, with more time between words than the words themselves took to utter, as Rose crept toward some resolution. "Man," he said.

"There!" Immaculato slapped the wall, as the audience in the synagogue gasped and the Peddler's eyes darted to the podium.

"Or . . ." Rose added.

"Or what, damn it?" Immaculato muttered, as surely the men from Wannsee were muttering as they watched the speech unfold via network television.

"Or . . ." For the first time, the eyes of Asher Rose alit on the being in the center of the stage. "Or son . . . of . . ." He stopped.

Everyone on Wandsbekstrasse and worldwide knew that that phrase "Son of Man" was the Bible's description of Jesus, but the single, short word—the article "a"—as in "son of *a* man"—would undercut that entirely.

But Asher just gazed at Ben Alef and tears glistened in both sets of enormous eyes.

In those tears, Father Immaculato saw the final truth. Somehow Rose had been converted; he was an Alefite. "Damn!" he said, and meant it.

"Say it!" the Peddler urged from an adjacent niche, and his eyes met Immaculato's.

But if the plotters with opposite aims in their heads whisked through possibilities with laser speed, the calculus was not yet complete in the head of Asher Rose. His mind whirred with all sorts of absolute contradictions that were all absolutely, impossibly true. Yet what else is the nature of God?

His first feeling was undoubtedly the same one that the rest of the Alefites felt: pure ecstasy. The roof of the synagogue might have peeled open to reveal the undimmed light of heaven. There was a God, and He was here. Life was real; life was sane; life was good. History mattered. To everything there was a purpose.

The niggling locus of Roses's own experience—that blot on the face of the earth, named Auschwitz—shrank to insignificance, or expanded to truly glorious significance as the pillars of flame that shot from 1944's crematoria turned into fingers pointing to this time and place and the return.

In this moment, Asher Rose, whose grief had become his identity, overcame both grief and identity itself. His pain was transformed into joy and his very self was subsumed in the euphoric group soul that made the Wandsbekstrasse Synagogue as large as the universe. All doubts of Ben Alef's bona fides were dispelled in the transcendent magnitude of the occasion.

But . . . but . . . Rose's mind struggled to maintain order and follow the path of his revelation. So he would betray the world leaders. Big deal. So everything he thought he had known about life was an illusion. Big deal. So his decades of suffering and success were meaningless. Big deal. Which mortal, truly believing that deity incarnate had come to redeem him and herald the age of God, could not consider the politicians' concerns suddenly, irreparably, immediately irrelevant? The ground rules of life on earth no longer applied. The Messiah was here.

And that was the problem. For all the Alefites' love and worship of Ben Alef, they had really been thinking about themselves—precisely as those at Wannsee were thinking about themselves. Asher Rose was the first to ask what the frenzy of 1999 meant for Ben Alef. Look at the Messiah, sitting there, radiating holiness in His shabby gown and sunken eyes. Rose was a writer, so he wondered: where did the narrative go now? Deny Him, and it's back to jail, to obscurity, to a footnote in the theological chronicle of the age. Confirm Him, however, and what happens?

In a purposeful world the Messiah does not merely appear. He has a role to play in a prewritten script that leads from the opening scene on the Baltic to a climax . . . where? Here? When? Now? Most vitally, what?

"Lord!" Asher Rose moaned, for just as the specific maple-planked stage he stood upon had expanded to encompass the entire world, so time collapsed into the hour in which he stood on that stage, and he could see the future as clearly as he saw the watch on his wrist ticking. The Messiah was not subject to the fits of circumstance; He had a destiny, and Asher Rose saw it all. "Lord!" he cried, because he knew as deeply as he had ever known anything in his minor span on earth, as deeply as he knew that Ben Alef was the Messiah, that the Messiah was here to be killed.

And the only reason Asher Rose could see the future was because he was the only one—besides Margot, the Mother of God—to understand that as Ben Alef *was* the Son of Man, he was also the son of *a* man. And in that instant, Asher, a man, decided to do all he could to thwart destiny, because that was the only future he could not abide.

Perhaps events had already gone too far, perhaps the end was inevitable, but as Asher had rebelled against the inevitability of his own fate in 1944, so he would do everything he possibly could to save the One who had come to save him. Like any father, Asher Rose would lie to protect his son.

For Ben Alef's sake, Rose turned and pointed his own finger. "You!" he cried as loud as he could, voice rolling through the aisles, echoing in the rafters, and everyone in the room knew that here was the moment they were waiting for. For all Asher's preliminaries, for all his strange, half-articulated internal dialogue, the prophet had reached a decision.

The fourteen men from Wannsee and innumerable more men and women across the planet leaned toward their television sets.

"You may be good. You may speak the truth. You, with your recent tattoo and your miracles or magic tricks or whatever they are . . ."

"What is he saying?" the people in the synagogue whispered to each other.

"You may even be a Jew," Asher Rose declared, looking Ben Alef straight in the eyes, communicating silently and privately while putting on the performance of his life. *"But . . ."*

"Yes, he's going to do it." Father Immaculato sighed.

"Why?" the Peddler asked.

Neither of them could conceive of a father who would deny his son precisely in order to save him.

"But you do not speak for the Jews. *You* are no God!"

. . .

Dear Frieda,

I am writing this letter on my knee in the back of the synagogue—such a beautiful structure, I have never been in a synagogue before—rather than, as I do most of my missives, at
leisure late at night when the hurly-burly settles down. So forgive the scrawl. But I am in agony. I've left the stage—I never
feel comfortable on the stage, but Snakes insists that we maintain a presence, that Ben Alef needs us there as we need Him
here.

It is the eve of the anniversary of His first birth that first
brought the gift of forgiveness into the world. We thought that
tonight was to become the night of the second, and final, re-
birth, to ring in an age when all was good and forgiveness no
longer necessary. First mercy, then redemption. Psalms more
glorious than any I ever heard in the Wieland church rose to the
roof of this structure. Why do we imagine psalms or prayers rising? Why not, say, rolling? Like waves? Anyway, all the disciples
and all the Alefites joined together, and Asher Rose—you've
heard of him—was to be the keystone in the arch that sealed the
whole portal together, and we would all pass through it into
the new age. Alas, the Jew was still a Jew, and now the gate is
collapsed.

You can read about it in the newspaper, you can see it on
the television, but I could not bear it, and ran—immediately, the
way you run to the bathroom when you have to vomit. I am in
pain, worse than a kidney stone, worse than I've ever felt in my
entire life. Something went wrong. I could see it in Asher Rose's
eyes. He knew that Ben Alef was the Christ, and still he denied
Him. Why? Not from blindness, but some other motivation
that I do not hesitate to call evil.

But perhaps the divine plan is to tarry till the next millennium, and because time is so compressed now, that will occur in
six days. What shall happen in those days, I don't know. Nor do
I have any inkling of what shall happen when the clock runs out.
The thought of a week of calm after the pace of this last month
soothes me. Everyone needs time to relax and prepare for the
end. We have waited so long. . . .

I must hurry. There is much noise from the front. I hear anger. Probably the Jew himself has been denied.

No, I must be charitable. As Ben Alef surely does not hold his betrayal against Mr. Rose, I must be charitable. I must strive to understand.

Struggling, in God,

Your brother, Max

"Liar!" Celia broke the silence.

Like the bell at a boxing ring, like the gun at a race, Celia's accusation set off the crowd, which surged forward, knocked over seats, and rushed the stage.

Prayers turned into howls, which turned into prayers as the trampled pled for mercy.

"Liar!" Celia shrieked so loudly that the microphones in front of Asher Rose picked up her voice and amplified her complaint to the sky. "He saved me."

And the rest of the disciples also called out their faith. Grown used to mockery and denial over the last month—from the press, from the police, from the unenlightened public—Kiehr and Blobel and Langefeld sang as one, "He saved me!" while Bartsch and Palitzsch took up Celia's lament, "Liar! Liar!"

The back of the synagogue was empty now, the entire assembly jammed up front.

If the structure had been a ship, it would have tilted and gone full fathom five just like the *Farnhagen,* as the multitude echoed the chants and created a round of its own, alternating "Liar!" "He saved me!" "Liar!" "He saved me!" and drowned out all other sounds.

Alone as a leper in the center of the stage, Asher Rose turned pale while the charges lashed against him like whip points. "Liar?" he repeated against the beat. "Who are the liars? Every one of these men." His arm swept wide to include the disciples. "Every one of them pled not guilty in court, and every one of them was found guilty and every one of them is guilty." He turned on his accusers, strong as a Warsaw teenager facing a

Panzer tank with a Molotov cocktail, and shouted, "How dare you accuse me?" forgetting that he, too, had lied with every ounce of his authorial imagination.

And the more he lied, the more furious and tongue-tied his antagonists become. Only Eisenheim crowed with delight, "Yes, yes, I knew the Jew would tell the truth."

"No," Celia insisted. "He couldn't tell the truth. He is a liar from the day he was born. Look at me, hey you, mister, I'm talking," she raved, and tore off her jacket as if to roll up the sleeves of the lacy blouse she had taken to wearing and call Rose outside. Pushing her sparrow chest toward the recoiling speaker, she demanded an answer. "Am I a liar?"

And the sight of her frailty, brazenly thrust, demolished him. Asher Rose had seen chests as diminished as this one before—by starvation rather than addiction, but that wasn't the point—and arms as scrawny, and faith as great. Those broken people knew they were doomed, yet rather than deny their religion, they walked toward the gas chambers chanting Ani Ma'amin: "I believe with perfect faith in the coming of the Messiah. Even though he may tarry, despite this I believe." Rose could not deny the authenticity of Celia's faith. Finally, to protect a girl he had never seen before, as indeed Ben Alef had once protected that same girl, he admitted the truth. "No"—he sighed—"you are not a liar."

But it was too late.

Bubbles collected at the corner of Celia's mouth. "You wouldn't know the truth from . . . from . . ."

At first nobody noticed the girl swooning as the first of the spectators climbed onto the platform, but her right foot beat the stage with rhythmic intensity and compelled attention.

"Make room!" Margot shouted, and knelt at the girl's side.

"You're responsible for this," Herbert Glucks hissed at Rose, then turned his attention to the prostrate child. He took a deep breath, remembered Lorna Kirtchner hanging in front of her school, and pressed his lips to Celia's to try to revive her.

"Of course." Rose shrugged.

"Bruno," Anton commanded.

"Yes."

"Get him."

"With pleasure." And the yellow-haired giant stepped forward and pinned Rose's arms to his side, although the speaker had no intentions of escaping. He had escaped once, was old now, and never intended to flee again.

"Apologize," Erich Langefeld demanded.

"Never."

Langefeld slapped Rose. "You . . ."

"What?"

"You bastard."

Rose laughed. "That's not me; that's Him," and he jerked his head in the direction of Ben Alef, all but forgotten in the furor, the only one in the entire hall remaining silent.

"He saved me! He saved me!" the believers cried, trooping up the aisles, storming the stage, and the Messiah gazed out on the swelling mass as if He were contemplating the Baltic Sea.

"Get him out of here!" the Peddler shouted. He was the only one besides Asher Rose who knew how uncontrollable a crowd could become.

Bruno, baffled, didn't know whether to hold on to Rose or tuck Ben Alef under his arm like a valise and whisk him to safety.

"Get him out of here!" the Peddler shouted again as his eyes met Asher Rose's and a communication that might have been interrupted decades earlier was completed.

Langefeld slapped Rose again, and Blobel poked a desiccated finger at Rose's eye, missed, and scratched his cheek. Worse, Snakes Hammurabi, official spokesman for the Alefite movement, yanked the microphone away from the bleeding renegade.

"Wait," Ben Alef said in a tone so low and mild it went entirely unnoticed, as Palitzsch and Clauberg tried to guide Him from the stage.

The disciples were organized now, several attending their Lord, several holding and several more belaboring His betrayer, Snakes at the podium trying to call for order and a doctor for Celia.

The groups formed a triptych: the Peddler looking at Asher Rose gripped by Bruno Morgen in the left tableau; Ben Alef turning toward Rose from between disciples hastening him offstage right; Snakes in the center. The synagogue's wooden ark was the picture's dominant vertical element and Celia the horizontal. From right to left, Ben Alef called out one last statement: "Let the man be. He's suffered enough."

But the plea for mercy from the God of mercy went awry. Snakes simply echoed, "He's suffered enough," and the logical assumption was that the pronoun referred to Ben Alef.

"He's suffered enough!" clamored the angry mob, and Bruno hoisted Rose's arm up behind his back until he heard the sound of bone cracking, and repeated, "He's suffered enough."

Asher's body slumped in Bruno's arms, as the crowd angled the cross one of them had brought from the floor to the stage and started ascending.

"Forgive them, Father," Ben Alef mouthed to Rose across the un-bridgeable expanse that separated them.

"Forgive me, Son," Asher Rose moaned in response, "I know exactly what I do."

And they fell upon him.

Chapter Nineteen

ASHER ROSE paid for his blasphemy, but it was only a down payment on the greater sum the rest of his tribe was fated to pay for its greater denial. All the collectors required was a sign, a nod, or a wink—and Dietrich Eisenheim gave it to them. The oldest, most unregenerate disciple reached toward Snakes Hammurabi and grabbed the microphone Rose had used to broadcast his abomination. He held it for a second and then, rather than speak into the tainted instrument, he reared back and, with a strength no one could have expected from his wizened carcass, flung it through the air.

The black-bulbed object streaked above the Alefites' heads like a comet, trailing electrical wire like a vicious black tail. It flew straight into the Wandsbekstrasse Synagogue's massive stained-glass window bearing an ivory replica of the Ten Commandments.

The glass exploded on impact and tiny shards inlaid with text—odd splinters bearing single words like "Thou" or "Shall" or "Not"—cascaded upon the multitude.

With every injunction obliterated, those of four thousand years ago and those that had so diligently been inculcated into the local population for the last fifty years, native German and right-thinking foreign New Jews alike swept through the synagogue like a plague. Every intact window on the premises was broken, every pew upended and turned into a battering ram wielded by enthusiastic teams to smash down doors and pummel holes in the brick walls. Wild groups organized themselves into acrobatic pyramids, enabling one delegate at the peak to grab hold of a hanging chandelier and swing, screaming, "He saved me!" until the fixture tugged loose from its plaster casing and crashed.

The Wandsbekstrasse Synagogue had been devastated once before, in 1937. It remained a shell for decades until the guilt-ridden postwar government spent millions to reconstruct it for the dozens who remained. No expense had been spared, as virtually none of the original congregants had been spared. The chandeliers, now blasted into bits on the floor, leaving sparking wires dangling from the ceiling, were Murano glass; the pews, now demolished, were Black Forest cherry; the newel posts of the grand stairway to the balcony, now toppled, were hand-carved; and the brass ornaments, now defaced, once glowed. Only the ark, holy receptacle for a painstakingly recreated simulacrum of the sixteenth-century Torah it once housed, commissioned from a famous local artisan who constructed it out of weathered planks from the barracks of the Belsen concentration camp, was still untouched.

A group of Alefites stood before the ark, hesitant to touch it, as if, like electrified barbed wires at the lager its wooden facing came from, the thing might be lethal.

Something was missing, some deep and perfect connection between the wooden box containing the paper scroll that first named the monotheistic god and the raging congregation howling, sobbing, smashing the furniture, and climbing the walls. In the midst of the turmoil, the few disciples who hadn't hustled Ben Alef and Celia from the premises met the first Alefites who had scaled the stage.

Without his microphone, Snakes Hammurabi felt naked and helpless while the demented Alefites acted like animals. Yet just as he didn't mind their actions in the parking lot that first night in jail, neither did he now. Doubt Ben Alef then and still, he still despised any who refused the Lord, and stood by silently at the slaughter of Asher Rose. He watched as the Neue Juden ripped Rose's hair from his head and chin, gouged his eyes from their sockets, and tore his tongue from his intemperate mouth as if seeking relics for future contemplation, and Snakes understood less than ever, but the one truth he did grasp was that he was an animal, too.

Killing Asher Rose was not sufficient as long as the ark stood, silently delivering its own eternal condemnation of everything the Alefites found sacred. Here was the enemy.

Snakes recalled the last time he had been inside a house of worship, and immediately knew what he had to do. He stepped forward and slid the twin doors to the ark sideways into their cleverly designed pockets and unveiled the velvet-covered, gold-embroidered, silver-crowned, and breast-plated beast. Now what? He could throw it to the floor; he could rip it to shreds, but the Torah would still retain a majesty even in its destruction. After all, this very Torah had been burned once, and here it was again. No, Snakes Hammurabi had to degrade it, so that nobody would respect it ever again. Only then could the reign of Ben Alef truly begin.

Snakes slowly unzipped his pants, exposed himself, and aimed at a forty-five-degree angle. A moment later, he let loose a fountain into the receptacle, where the urine spattered against the inscribed plate, stained the noble dressing, and dripped down to form a yellow puddle of hatred and disdain.

And that was only the beginning.

If the vigil in front of the Hamburg jail had really taken off when the Alefites began mortifying their own flesh in sympathy with their imprisoned Lord, and if more painfully tattooed arms were now roaming around Hamburg than had been liberated from nearby Belsen fifty-four years earlier, the noisy and unholy events of Christmas Eve were a dizzyingly liberating gift that demonstrated that—at last!—the people had suffered enough. There was no longer any need to chastise their own bodies, for they were cleansed, redeemed, and saved. Ben Alef was here, and Asher Rose, the Anti-Alef, was slain and dispatched to the hellish reward he had once eluded. Now, it was time to chastise—no matter how brutally necessary—and, through chastisement, cleanse, redeem, and save the rest of the world, starting with the Jews.

Until now, the Alefites had been content to look inward and lament their own guilt, but suddenly they beheld a guilty universe to punish as deserved. Eisenheim's comet and Snakes Hammurabi's jet of urine were the first strikes in the Alefites' motion outward. By using a common talent in the uncommon way that had initially propelled him to *Farnhagen*, Snakes became the leader of the new authority, which others were swift to adopt. Martin Clauberg, for one.

Clauberg, arrested and incarcerated for the minor arson of an abandoned hospital that had, due to an unexpected gust of wind, led to a major blaze in an adjacent apartment complex that temporarily filled another hospital and permanently filled fourteen graves of tenants and three of firemen back in 1973, had, despite therapy, never overcome his love of fire. For the duration of his sentence, he had imagined fires in the fireproof cell, but now he was free—and now, like Snakes with micturating tool, he knew that the one element lacking in his salvation was precisely the indulgence he craved. Now arson was more than okay; now it was sanctified; now it was necessary. Earlier, backstage, he had stumbled over a can of paint thinner and cursed his clumsiness, but now he knew that his inadvertent misstep was a sign, and he sought out that can, and a few other cans of flammable liquids carefully stored away by the synagogue handyman.

Dancing gleefully behind the scenes, imbued with the spirit of a deity who demanded sacrifice, Clauberg splashed generous helpings of thinner along the floorboards leading to the lath–constructed walls, leading to the beams. He climbed a convenient ladder and doused the curtains that flanked the stage filled with hollering Alefites, and crawled along a catwalk used to change bulbs in the recently collapsed chandeliers that had hung from the towering peak of the structure. And everywhere he went he left a wiggling line of liquid that would soon turn to the splendid gas of flame. He knew the patterns fires follow because, prior to lighting up the old hospital just for fun, he had been an arsonist for hire by small businessmen more interested in insurance than sales.

There. The streaks of iridescent petroleum-based products looked beautiful. And there was even greater beauty to come. Clauberg shook a cigarette out of a packet and took an elegant box of matches that bore the old, pink sinner's emblem of the Kastrasse out of his pocket. He removed a match, put a fingernail to the tip, and was about to strike when he saw the pipes.

Set into the wall above the ark at the far end of the catwalk was an enormous organ composed of two dozen gleaming wooden pipes varying in length from two to six meters and in thickness from ten to thirty centimeters. It had never been used, but, in the name of punctiliousness, the German authority that rebuilt the synagogue from its original plans also rebuilt the musical tower that had accompanied services through the latter decades of the nineteenth century for the assimilated congregation that first built the structure so as to echo its neighbors in tone as well as architecture.

A student of the art of arson, Clauberg knew that the effect of an explosion in a contained space was even more thrilling than the random pyrotechnics he had intended. He crawled along the catwalk toward the organ, carrying two remaining cans of solvent in each hand. There he ensconced himself on a dusty bench in front of the impressive triple pile of ivory keys, ebony knobs, levers, and pedals. And for a moment he was torn, because in addition to the skill that had led him into the penitentiary, Clauberg had once played the piano.

He set down the cans and fingered the keys. No sound emerged, but he played around with the controls until he found the switch on a gigantic mechanical bellows that pumped air into the pipes according to the musician's instructions. Faint gusts of artificial wind blew through the twenty-four mouth-shaped orifices at the base of the pipes. Then, just as he felt the reservoir of compressed air building up enough to enable specific notes to fly through the intricate channeling system of the instrument, he heard further cries from below: "Saved!"

Music was only the handmaiden of divinity, and Clauberg had his work set out for him. He stripped off his shirt and stuffed the material into one of the mouths. Then he stood on the bench, balanced one foot on the topmost level of the organ, and carefully decanted the liquids, can by can, into the tallest, thickest pipe he could reach, until the solvents filled the cavity and overflowed. Already the cotton sleeve extending from the mouthpiece was soaked through and, seeping out, a miniature waterfall descended from level to level of keys down to the bench.

He sat and contemplated his work for a moment, and saw that it was good. Now, he lit the match.

A jet of fire shot upward from the pipe, blasted a hole in the ceiling of the synagogue, and exploded in the Christmas sky so gloriously that people two kilometers away thought it was a comet.

Inside the synagogue, a rain of fire poured down to catch further on the catwalk, and the curtains, and the floorboards Clauberg had so diligently saturated. He was surrounded by fire, immersed in fire, reborn in fire, and so delighted that he didn't even realize that the very bench he sat on was in flames.

It must have been seconds, but it felt like an eternity of bliss before shrieks from below finally attracted Clauberg's attention; by then, however, it was too late for the master to escape his monster. It breathed and roared and raced across the catwalk, which turned into a bridge of cinders and cut off any possibility of joining the fleeing Alefites below. No matter; the disciple was fulfilled. He did the only thing left to do; he stretched out his fingers and began to play the one song he remembered from a pageant of his youth: an opera, by Handel.

Outward, outward, outward, the waves of flame and mania spread, fed by torches ignited from the Wandsbekstrasse font and the knowledge that at least one disciple had sacrificed himself to bring down the old temple, so that the new, pure and perfected Temple could take its place. Bathed in the flickering light and the ashes that rose up and fluttered down across the city, the Alefites took their message to the streets.

The message was redemption. Absolved of all sins, the New Jews no longer had to mortify their own flesh. Instead, they struck outward, and the old Jews, that stubborn, stiff-necked people who refused to accede to the right world order, were the first to feel the sting of the lash of salvation. The butcher from Warnemünde who had followed the track of the Messiah from the beginning took up one blazing timber and threw it through the plate-glass window of a nearby butcher shop that bore the legend, in three Hebrew letters, "Kosher."

"Now it's kosher," he shouted to Anna the secretary as they warmed their hands and inhaled the scent of burnt steaks and burnt chops and burnt kidneys of cows and the family named Bloom who lived in the flat above the shop.

Windows were smashed and fires were lit elsewhere in the city, wherever a store front had the gall or ill-fate to bear a Jewish surname. Thus Goldstein's Yard Goods and Stern's Used Books (with its illuminated manuscript of the medieval "Tale of a Kite") and Rosenbaum's Stationery lost their identities and fused together in one great, charred pyre of Yiddish business and lore.

Thus the Night of Contrition turned into the Night of Conflagration.

Jingling all the way, Herbert Glucks led a band of girls with voices like angels from St. Teresa's Convent into the Yeshiva of Hamburg, which mostly served a community of recent immigrants from the former Soviet Union, trapping and laying waste to a flock of tiny earlocked boys cowering in the basement, while Franz Palitzsch ravaged the Home for Yiddish Elders and Erich Langefeld and two friends searched high and low for their own Jew to torment. They found him in a café, and knew him from the pasty complexion of intellectual isolation he wore as evidently as a yellow star.

"Komm her," Erich commanded, but he might have said, "Raus!"

Resigned, or spineless, the Jew set a bookmark at the page he would never finish, and followed.

Anton Bartsch, crooked eyes keen as a hawk's, went after the cash he had always found alluring and elusive. From a dealer, he purchased a handgun that fit perfectly into the palm of his hand; then he inserted the first bullet from a package of forty—"It's cheaper in bulk," said the dealer—spun the chamber, and aimed it between the dealer's eyes. Was he Jewish? Who knew anymore? Giddy with delight, Anton distributed the stolen cash to strangers roaming by in front of the gun shop, then robbed the liquor store next door, and took some schnapps, too.

Even Omar Nazzarian found an outlet for decades of repressed anger as he joined a group of Muslim Alefites—they pronounced themselves "Allahfites"—and led them in a charge on the Israeli consulate, bearing down on the blue-and-white flag with a scimitar liberated from a looted pawnbroker's down the block from the Lotus Studio, which Mr. Lee and his daughter guarded from further rampaging mobs.

Sirens blared as the unconverted remains of the Hamburg police and fire departments desperately attempted to cope with a city gone mad. But there was no restraining the ecstasy of the people. Those who burned and some who were mistakenly burnt out surged through the downtown, hard by the Helsedink section where a few Jews were known to reside, seeking out the unconvinced and convincing them by any means necessary that the end of days had come.

Georg Kiehr, always the dreamiest of the disciples, figured out a way to secure a length of greasy tow rope around a group of Hasidic Jews he found playing gin in a shipping agent's office, looping it through their legs, curling it behind their heads, cinching their waists, bow-knotting the heavy length beneath their gabardine tails. He herded them in a shuffling mass to the edge of the dock, lit the rope with an excellent Zippo lighter, and cast the flaming bundle into the water, where the flames caught on the iridescent rainbow-slicked surface before the flailing—now praying—minyan sank like a hissing stone.

Across the city, specific targets went up in smoke. The Commodities Exchange, meant to expedite trading of the goods that flowed through the port, was lit and burned to the ground, and the jail itself, Ben Alef's first roof since the *Farnhagen*, was "liberated" like the Bastille at the end of a different era, before the Revolution spiraled out of control.

But fire knew no Lord, and the combustion spread from Jewish locales to their neighbors, and the city was filled with small and large fires that the fire department, impeded by spontaneously erected roadblocks, could not reach before they burnt themselves to ashes. In some places, the firemen themselves lit the fires and paraded around the blazing structures, safe and secure for the first time in their professional lives.

Casualties mounted as the moon rose and dispassionately watched the passion of its planet—but the dying also knew that they were sacrificed in the name of the Lord, who would resurrect them soon, so soon. A few victims wheeled into hospital emergency rooms refused treatment, hesitant to question the shape of their revelation as made manifest to them by the multitude of prophets of God wielding pikes, knives, staffs, bludgeons, and the ever-present flames of eternity. Five days till the millennium.

Hamburg was the epicenter, but it wasn't the only center. Smaller but no less violent riots broke out in large cities in Europe and at the holy sites of prominent or esoteric denominations abroad. Besieging shrines from Seville to Kiev, formerly Catholic or Greek Orthodox New Jews tore martyrs' relics from catacombs and monasteries to march with and maraud freely, while in India, the Ganges overflowed with cinnamon-skinned former Hindus chanting Ben Alef's name as they belabored and burned their neighbors who hadn't seen His light. With only a handful of old Jews, people made do with substitutes. Every scene of murder for God in the last two millennia witnessed murder for God once again, as former Catholics and former Protestants in Belfast tore at each other in a night of gunfire and flame.

Christmas Eve, and evangelical missionaries in Jerusalem massed beside the Wailing Wall, although unlike their more successful peers in Europe they were dispersed by the rubber bullets of Israeli army soldiers, to regroup at the Church of the Holy Sepulcher, mourning because here, only here, they could not triumph. Nonetheless they would try, because the conversion of the Jews was imperative, the last sign, the last wonder, before the final advent. Undeterred, they marched on the Jewish quarter, joining throngs of delighted Arabs. Everywhere, fire.

In China, the respectful citizens of Beijing ransacked an ancient pagoda in the name of a Messiah they had never heard of before this month. In Hong Kong, just recently returned to Chinese dominion, the most precious thoroughbreds at the Kowloon Racetrack were ridden by drunken jockeys into the lobby of the Intercontinental Hotel, where two of them tried to leap over a fountain and broke their mounts' million-dollar legs.

At tabernacles throughout the American West, the faithful gathered for mass prayer sessions that turned into tornadoes of destructive fury. And not only the Alefites danced in the streets and destroyed the citadels. Previously modest citizens of no particular spiritual bent felt the lure of anarchy justified by God; it gave them a power different from and superior to the power that had been denied them since their ancestors dropped from the trees and took up cave dwelling; it set them loose in intemperate delirium. There was so much catching up to do, and much confusion. Some who had not reached the state of enlightenment of those closest to the Messiah fell into the earlier patterns of sexual fever and self-abasement.

Not every one of the globe's six billion temporary residents indulged. The majority watched their televisions with trepidation and curiosity. There it was Christmas Eve, and the networks had dispensed with the usual seasonal stories of Salvation Army Santa Clauses to endlessly replay the gruesome scene of Asher Rose's public murder, only breaking for further dispatches of hysteria and chaos from far-flung correspondents. Yet it was the viewers' silence that terrified elected officials and intellectuals, more so than the Alefite heresy. They were cautious, but they were interested. They couldn't help but wonder, "What if?"

Order was old; freedom was now, freedom from fear and restraint and the antiquated rule of law. Freedom from the Sinaitic "Thou shall not." All the systems gradually constructed over measured time dissolved in the sheer, animal delight of Heaven on earth, because earth now meant Heaven, which meant whatever the hell one desired.

All this came into the Chancellor's war room via softly treading aides bearing the latest "news." Grabner looked at the efficient blond intern who handed him a bulletin announcing that a mob in Munich was marching on Dachau, and wondered if he saw fire in the young man's blue eyes. Then he made a call.

Urban IX answered in the midst of a coughing fit.

"Are you okay?" Grabner asked.

"Is the world okay?" the Pope answered after he managed to clear his elderly throat. "They believe the end has come."

"Well, I guess we're here to prove them wrong."

Apparent to both men was the ultimate truth that all "lay-clerisy" differences were inconsequential in the face of the uncommon threat they faced. No matter their different notions of order, they shared the faith that the world ought to be an orderly place, and they both knew for a dead certainty that they were the force of order, which was being undermined in a hundred city squares and a thousand village bonfires even as they spoke.

"What are you saying?"

"That we're right and they're wrong. Fu—" The Chancellor halted his natural profanity and continued, "Whether there is a God or not, I don't know; that's your turf. But there is work, and there is hunger, and they are connected, because you can't eat God. If the people don't work they are going to be hungry, and their children will be hungry. If they burn down their fu— their homes they'll be cold and their children will be cold. But what these idiots haven't figured out is that they're going to have to live with each other once this is over."

"With each other, yes. And us."

"Right."

"So when will it be over?"

The storm would pass, they told themselves. All storms pass. This one had a maximum of six days' duration—six brutal days to come, December 26 till the stroke of midnight on the thirty-first—because then, when the world did not end, the frenzy would disappear into a bad memory. Like Germans in 1945, like Africans in 1996, like Dutch merchants after the tulip mania, like all people swept up in a grand passion that fails and leaves multitudes trampled by the tracks, like lemmings at the bottom of a cliff, like bulls sweating in the ring at Pamplona, like swallows at Capistrano, they would shake their heads and wonder how they got there. Maybe.

There was silence on the line as both men pondered whether time would cure this ill, because wherever authorities tamped down brush or building fires new ones sparked up under their feet, frequently abetted by the authorities sent to quell them. And nowhere did they burn hotter than Hamburg, the grubby industrial city on the Baltic where He had first showed Himself.

This was more than an embarrassment; it was a stain that had to be expunged, as cleanly—or, if necessary, as dirtily—as possible, as long as it was expunged as swiftly as possible.

Plan A had been a good idea.

Enlisting Asher Rose was brilliant.

But one Jew couldn't kill another.

And Rose was a Jew.

And so was Ben Alef.

Rose had spoken the words that Wannsee wanted, but he had spoken them to save rather than destroy Ben Alef. In the process, he destroyed himself, yet accomplished his real goal. Grabner looked back on the logic. They were right to look to the past, but they should have brought in an expert.

Once before, half a century ago, there also had been silence on the line from Berlin to Rome. Urban and Grabner were descendants of the occupants of their seats, but either Urban or Grabner had to make a choice. One of them had to talk, for the sake of order. They had to act.

Finally, Grabner asked, "Your man is on site?"

"Yes. And yours?"

"He doesn't know he's my man yet, but in five minutes he will, and he'll do what he has to."

"As do we." Urban sighed.

"Right."

"But, Chancellor . . . ?"

"Yes, Your Holiness."

"After this is over, I pray that I will never have to speak to you again."

Plan B.

Book VIII
Rapture

Chapter Twenty

"THERE ARE TWO POSSIBILITIES."

"Yes, I know."

Neither of the sleepless men hastily convened in the public park at three o'clock in the morning named names. Each stood in the thin dusting of snow with hands in pockets, buttoned up to the neck, breathing out clouds of mist, and each had a car with a driver waiting at a different entrance to the park.

Orders received, they only had to make a decision. "One, of course, is likely to be more competent."

Strategy determined from above, tactics must be enacted from below. "Yes, but the other is surely going to be more enthusiastic."

"Both competence and enthusiasm are values."

"Of course, they both have extensive experience."

"And motivation."

The men spoke abstractly, because they knew that what they were doing was as deeply wrong—each according to his own principles—as anything they had ever done in their lives.

"That's what makes it tricky."

"So tell me," the taller, darker, more angular man in the finer garment finally asked, "which one do we offer silver?"

"Aren't both of them Judases?"

"Aren't all of them?"

The shorter man, bundled in his civil service overcoat with a furled umbrella tucked beneath his arm, snorted. "An abundance of riches."

A fire engine screamed on the periphery of the quiet park. The two men stood still until the siren faded, and then one of them removed his bare hand from its pocket and wrote two sets of initials on the snow-covered bench beside which they were standing. Now their respective superiors had been served. Now the proposal was real.

The second one pointed.

The first one nodded.

The second one started to erase the names, and the first one leaned over to help him. Now the plan was real. They were in this together, God help them.

"From darkness we come; to darkness we go," sang out Dietrich Eisenheim. He stood at the edge of the flat tar rooftop of the Kastrasse, watching flames sear the sky in a dozen corners of the city like reverse lightning, jumping up from earth to blast the firmament. Eisenheim was so excited that he could hardly restrain himself whenever a flame skipped to an adjacent structure or a distant gas tank exploded with a muffled roar. "Isn't it lovely?"

"Clauberg's dead," Bruno said. He and a few of the others who had returned from the pandemonium sat at a pair of café tables dragged up an emergency ladder to simulate a sultry Mediterranean terrace on the industrial surface overlooking the frigid Elbe. It was cold and a slight hesitant snow drifted down, but the view of the burning city was irresistible.

"I haven't seen anything this lovely since '45."

"I said that Clauberg is dead," Bruno repeated and hugged his brand new nylon athletic jacket tight to his thick body.

"Yes, I heard."

"I thought that maybe since you lived with him for the last twenty-five years you might care."

"Of course I care, and I am jealous."

"What do you mean?"

"Well, just look at the language we use. Look at the grammar, mein Bruder. Clauberg *is* dead. Is. Present tense. We are accustomed to thinking of being as present, but actually being will be past soon enough, whereas nonbeing or deadness is universally current. Death is the natural state."

Lost in theory, Bruno simply repeated, "Clauberg is dead."

"So is Palitzsch," the head of Kiehr announced as the serial killer climbed through the hatch with the latest information from below.

"What?"

"Poisoned, apparently."

"Appropriately." Eisenheim laughed.

"What happened?"

"He was having a party, but it wasn't his usual tea and crumpets. There were drugs, and he overdosed. There is a suspicion of tampering, because his fellow partiers, two old ladies from Altona, are also in the hospital."

"Not my merchandise, that's ninety-nine point four percent pure," the Peddler said, leaning back on his chair and trying as hard as he could to concentrate on anything else besides what he had seen. Perhaps he'd establish a rooftop restaurant next summer. He'd need to lay down a better surface to protect the membrane, maybe tile, and install some lattice for shade, and maybe a small, recirculating fountain. Of course, a new staircase would be necessary, and a dumbwaiter to facilitate deliveries from the kitchen, and a chute to dispose of waste. How much horrible waste there was in the world! No, the restaurant, focus solely on the restaurant. What sort of food should it serve? Italian? French? Anything but German. The more he thought of the restaurant, the calmer he felt. Maybe he'd name it Rose's.

The Peddler had always been one step ahead of the pack, but the way the impresario of the entire Alefite movement sat, staring toward Wandsbekstrasse, murmuring, "No, no, the plumbing has to go through the joists," was strange. He ought to be regrouping rather than retreating. Instead, he sounded . . . defeated. Still, the disciples thought only of their own.

Bruno did the highest math he understood—"Two of the twelve, gone." only to learn soon enough that by the time his calculations had been executed they were also wrong. Blobel had been run over by a speeding taxi that bounced him through the plate-glass window of the main Deutsche Bank branch downtown and sped off without stopping.

"Doesn't anything strike any of you?" Nazzarian asked. He had been standing apart from the discussion, mulling over each additional item of bad news from the world they had helped create.

"It's sad?" Bruno answered.

"It's wild," Anton offered, eyes crossing, the right one on Nazzarian to the left, the left one rightward upon an especially brilliant fire where an oil-soaked pier caught by the shore.

Nazzarian felt the cold brush his spine. It caressed the spot at the base of the neck that his ice pick had once sought in his victims. Despite Omar's acclimation to European manners and morals, the weather, like the food, always remained foreign, and he hated northern winters. But this cold, which no goose-down-filled parka could alleviate, was not a consequence of the temperature; it came from within and frightened him. He was just as cold indoors, sitting on a radiator, as he was outside. "It's more than wild," he said.

Anton and Bruno waited for him to elaborate, and Nazzarian grew aware of an irony here. Of course, he was smarter than Bruno—so was a toadstool—but he also knew more than Anton and all of his Teutonic ancestors put together, yet Herr Bartsch had been undisputed master of Cell #306, while Omar was just an ancillary power. Now the pecking order was inverted, and Anton awaited the Persian wise man's declaration with two steamy cones emerging from his nostrils.

"What is it?" Anton begged.

"It's a plot."

The blunt word hung in the air and Bruno grunted, "Huh?"

Nazzarian explained, "They're killing us. One by one, they're killing us."

"That's ridiculous," Kiehr scoffed. "A thousand people are going to die in this city tonight."

"Ten thousand," Eisenheim hooted, as if raising the bet and tossing a pile of chips into the center of a green felt poker table, but they ignored him.

"Heart attacks," Kiehr continued, "car crashes, the fires, dammit. Clauberg was an accident."

"A hundred thousand."

"There is no such thing as an accident." Nazzarian said. "Not anymore."

"A million!"

"You seem sure."

"The door to Clauberg's chamber in the organ room in the synagogue was locked. From the outside."

"How do you know?"

Omar shrugged and answered elusively, "A criminal without sources in the police is a prisoner. But that doesn't make a difference. What makes a difference is that unless we do something, we're dead meat." He may never have liked Western food, but Nazzarian's time in the mob had given him a taste for Western vernacular.

"Six million!" Eisenheim sighed.

As far as the Peddler was concerned, the dream was over. Oh, he had killed when he'd had to, but never for fun, and never for an idea. Maybe that was why he was out of sync with the movement he had helped to create. But the movement had outgrown its origins and was rushing headlong down the path to self-destruction or, if he wished to use its own vocabulary, damnation. Major retooling was necessary, barring a miracle, and after tonight the Peddler no longer believed in miracles.

"Look at it this way," Nazzarian said, following out his logic. "The arsonist dies by fire, the poisoner by poison, and Blobel, with that banker in the trunk of his car until the smell gave him away, is hit by a car, where, but into a bank. You call that coincidental?"

"Where is everyone?" Bruno whimpered.

"Gone to ashes, every one," Eisenheim sang.

"Shut up, already," Anton exploded. "Shut up or I'll throw you off the fucking roof."

"Wouldn't make a difference. I'd just fly back." Eisenheim flapped his arms like wings.

"Ignore him, he's crazy," Kiehr told Anton. "The important thing is, whether Omar is right and we're in danger, or not, we should stick together. I saw Herbert and Erich downstairs by the bar."

"Maybe we should call them up here." Anton felt himself yearning for the security of Cell #306.

"I don't think they'd want to come. The two sex maniacs were having a drink and comparing exploits."

Eisenheim broke in: "Ah, yes, the boys have been in good hands. Good hands." He mimed masturbation. If there was one thing the ancient unregenerate enjoyed as much as death, it was sex.

Anton, protective of his mates, said, "As long as they're together, they should be okay."

"Or . . ." Nazzarian suggested, "maybe they, and we, should split up."

"You wanted to bail out on the road to Hamburg."

"Maybe I should have."

"The eternal debate," Kiehr said. He was the most sophisticated of the disciples and the only one capable of standing outside himself.

Bruno whimpered, "I don't like this. I'm getting a very bad feeling if we're getting dead."

"Nonsense," Eisenheim said, returning from his own reverie. "Don't you get it? Death is the only truth there is. An eternity stretches on either side of this moment of breathing; it's life that's an aberration. Maybe it's *His* fault. But that's okay, you see, if we come from and return to darkness, then the best use we can put our threescore and ten—I've been given a few extra for bad behavior—is to bring darkness to earth."

Anton grabbed at Eisenheim's lapel. "Shut up, you psycho!"

"Hey, I'm only telling the truth. And stop twitching those eyes. If you can't take it, maybe you should go back to the *Farnhagen*, glug, glug, glug." He raised his right palm in salute and held his nose with his left thumb and forefinger, and pretended to sink.

"That's appalling," Kiehr murmured as he tapped a cigarette from a pack plucked from between the gaping shards of the window of a looted tobacconist. "Sobranie?"

"Don't you pretend anything is appalling." Eisenheim glugged from an imaginary six feet under. "Look at what you've done. Didn't you enjoy eating those people? Of course you did, ingesting the stuff of life. Everyone would do it if they dared, but they're cowards. And they've persuaded you that there are these qualities called good and evil. Nonsense. There's life and death, and death is infinitely stronger, so the strong ally themselves with the strong. Screw the weak. That's what Glucks and Langfeld do. Eat the weak. That's what you did tonight, wasn't it?"

Kiehr licked his lips and blew out a plume of dark, scented smoke. "Maybe I was carried away."

"Don't be ashamed. Shame is a meager emotion. I've never known it in my life. And neither have you, so don't pretend otherwise, you faker."

"And because you've killed more people than me, you think you're that much better?"

"Glug, glug, glug."

"Stop it, all of you," Bruno moaned. "You're all forgetting why we're here. You're forgetting Ben Alef. Whatever is happening, He will save us. He will. He will. I know He will."

But Bruno's agony only stimulated Eisenheim. "Right," the Kommandant sneered. "You really think that the creator of the universe gives a flying fuck about you? You've got this deity, stars colliding, galaxies being born, and even here on earth you've got eighty gazillion tons of ocean sloshing back and forth, mountains grinding against each other, species evolving, and all you can think to say is 'Oh, God, please let me eat some strudel and kiss Helga's tits and I'll be happy and good forever. I'll do whatever you say.' As if He's sitting around, sweating, and mops His brow. 'Whew!' As if you had the maker of the entire world nervous there. No, God sets it in motion and then when He gets bored with the little spinning top, He puts out his big fat unopposable thumb and stops it. He has two functions: brings it in, takes it out. God is present at birth and death, especially the latter. The only thing about us that's interesting to God is our torment, so He ladles it on. The more the better. Every individual reckoning with pain and decease, that's what gets Him licking His chops, and then, on a minimally grander scale, slaughter satisfies. God was behind the Crusades, the Inquisition, God's in Bangladesh and Bosnia and Rwanda, and the one time in recent history when He really got a hard-on, God was at Auschwitz."

Just as at the synagogue, the "A" word stopped everything cold. Nobody said anything for a long minute, until the Peddler addressed Eisenheim, "You sound like the late Asher Rose."

"We had a lot in common. But where was I when you interrupted?"

"Auschwitz."

"Right. That was where God came when He came down from the clouds. That's where He showed His divine nature. That's how you know who He is."

"But—"

"Oh, sure," Eisenheim answered the Peddler, who shrank further and more uncharacteristically beneath each word. "He speaks. He speaks and you listen. Why? Because you are cowards, because none of you have the intensity, the integrity, the courage of your convictions. To kill. They"—he gestured outward—"whoever killed Martin and Karl and Franz, whoever's going to kill us, they know. And they're the ones who are doing *His* bidding. Because Ben Alef is not the master of life, but of death. That's what makes Him a God."

"He will save us."

"Todt."

"He will."

"*Tod. Tod. Tod.*" Eisenheim drowned Bruno out, until the miserable giant's diminishing statements turned into pleas turned into a piercing wail like a muezzin calling the faithful to prayer.

"Sob away, bubeleh, you only killed once and can only be killed once, it's a zero-sum game. But me—what are they going to do, kill me six million times?" Eisenheim laughed triumphantly. He was ahead of the game forever.

And Anton couldn't take it any longer. Not because he had any great love for the Jewish people—though, like all German schoolchildren of the latter part of the century, he had been inculcated with intense postwar regret for the mistakes of the 1940s—but because of his own terror he leapt upon Eisenheim, grabbed him by the hair, and started smashing the ancient soldier's head into the rooftop's parapet wall.

"Isn't this where I came in?" Snakes Hammurabi popped up through the hatch.

"You're lucky I didn't shoot your head off," the Peddler told Snakes, revesting a revolver that none of them knew he carried.

"Moi?"

"Don't be coy, boychik," the Peddler said. "You shouldn't sneak up on people like that. For all I knew you could have been some nutty arsonist like that Clauberg."

"May he rest in peace," Eisenheim croaked as Anton dropped his head in disgust.

"I mean it," the Peddler went on. The restaurant in his head already open for business—he had survived worse than this—he declared, "If you think I'm going to allow some bozos to burn this place down, forget about it. Never again. This place is all I have left. Man, if you had told me what was going to happen, I would have shorted insurance company stocks. Do you know how much those suckers are going to have to pay out? Damage in the hundreds of millions, already, the telly says."

"Rising hourly." Snakes brushed past him.

"The whole city's gone cuckoo. And what does this mean about Inc.,

Inc.? Jeez, I've got to figure this out." The Peddler was tired of theology and wanted to bring the conversation back to something he understood, the only thing he understood, money.

"You'll never figure it out," Snakes said, and turned for confirmation to Margot and Max Vetter, who rose after him from the hatchway. But Margot, maternal instincts aroused, had already hastened to dab her blouse against Eisenheim's bleeding forehead and Max was as silent as Ben Alef, who emerged last. He arrived with a doleful expression, peering beyond His disciples into the starlight and the orange flickering of approaching flames.

"Speak of the Devil." Eisenheim laughed.

"Where is the fire department when you need it?" The Peddler cursed and rushed past Margot on his way down the ladder to marshal his own men and equip them with extinguishers in a worst-case scenario. If all of Hamburg burned, he was determined that his club would be the last standing structure.

Kiehr was the first to observe that Snakes's new clothes were ruined, torn and black. "Where have you been?"

"Yeah," Anton said, further noting that Snakes's face and hands were discolored by a fine gray powder. "You look like Omar."

Nazzarian glowered.

"Where, indeed?" Snakes looked at Max Vetter, but the fisherman was already sitting apart on the parapet wall scribbling furiously in the notebook he had taken to carrying everywhere, as if he were a journalist.

Snakes thought for a moment, and then figured that there was no reason not to tell them what had occurred, or most of it—at least the portion he hoped Max wasn't writing about.

Unfazed by the general chaos on Wandsbekstrasse, Snakes only worried about Ben Alef Himself. In fact, Hammurabi's heart was still hammering because the Messiah had gone unaccounted for for a good hour after the synagogue caught fire, separated from his guards and lost in the pell-mell rush to escape the burning building. Only when Snakes saw Max Vetter out on the street, gesturing frantically to the police who had first failed and then entirely abdicated their responsibility to keep order, did he realize that Ben Alef was gone.

"Where is He?"

"I thought maybe you had Him."

"When was He last seen?" Snakes tried to ask logical questions.

"On the stage."

"Which way did He go?"

"Out . . . I hope."

The hundred-and-fifty-year-old roof of the synagogue collapsed amid a cloud of sparks and cinders and flaming rubble.

"I'm going back in."

"Don't." Max clutched at Snakes's sleeve. "He wouldn't want you to. He's safe, I know it." But the terror in his voice belied his statement.

Into the burning edifice, Snakes plunged, with as little regard for the danger as a person diving into a suburban swimming pool. All around him the pews that hadn't been upended were smoking, and the stained-glass scenes of biblical revelation that hadn't been shattered were melting into smeary pools of pigment. Eerie organ music accompanied the roar of the flames.

Bent low to the ground, with a puce handkerchief pressed against his mouth and nostrils, Snakes stepped over bodies until he came to the stage where the gigantic cross the Alefites had left behind led to the mutilated corpse of Asher Rose, and he heard a faint sobbing.

Could dead men weep?

For a second, Snakes was truly frightened, but he pulled himself together and shook his mind clear of the fumes. The sound couldn't be coming from Rose, but there was nobody else onstage and nothing nearby, except for the toppled ark Snakes had peed into only half an hour earlier. Then he saw two blackened scrolls of the discarded Torah, which meant that the casket itself was empty. He opened the door and discovered a cringing little boy stuffed inside, knees wedged under his chin like a contortionist's, smoke-stained tears dripping down his cheeks. The boy gasped out one word: "Water."

Snakes immediately recognized Willy Wilk, the child who had questioned the miracle of the tattoo, whose own tattoo had been cleansed by Ben Alef. Forgotten in the burning building, he had sought refuge in the only place the flames did not seem to go, but where they surely would in minutes.

Snakes lifted Willy out of the box like a rabbi extracting the Torah whose cinders now writhed and curled like serpents on the stage floor, and ran for the exit. Walls were starting to crumble and the organ music from the rafters had ceased. Snakes zigzagged between insurmountable heaps of fallen roofing material and gaping holes that led to the flaming pit of a cellar.

But somewhere nearer the door than the stage he either tripped or his lungs gave out from the heat and the smoke, and, Willy still tucked beneath his arm, he was on his knees on the floor, where an elaborate mosaic included a fanciful "W" for "Wandsbekstrasse." He placed his face to the hot tiles and gasped for a breath of clean air, to tap a last reservoir of strength to crawl five meters to the exit. It was agony and . . . he . . . couldn't . . . make . . . it. It was almost as bad as drowning.

The final thing Snakes heard before he passed out was the rasping voice of Max Vetter crying, "I found Him."

Apparently Ben Alef had been sitting on a bench on the narrow traffic island opposite the synagogue the entire while Max and Snakes and half the Hamburg police force were searching for Him. He was still there when Snakes opened his eyes and saw the four cast-iron feet of the bench guarding the hem of the Messiah's robe.

Snakes felt as if his head were filled with smoke. He turned and vomited a gray, clotted mess that reeked so intensely of charred carbon it seemed ready to ignite. "How did I get here?"

Max hunched his shoulders with modesty, and changed the subject. "What about Willy?"

Head sideways, Snakes saw the prone body of Willy Wilk in the grass. "I found him," he said.

The two heroes looked at each other.

"Stay down," Max urged him.

"Is he . . . ?"

Willy moaned.

Snakes sighed. "Thank God."

"Thank Ben Alef," Max corrected him.

The rest of the night until Snakes climbed onto the rooftop of the Kastrasse was a blur. An ambulance pulled up onto the sidewalk and gave him and Willy oxygen. The child revived easily, but Snakes still felt dizzy. Then Erich Langefeld, mid-roister, happened by—disciples were bouncing back and forth across the city like pinballs—and offered to escort Willy back to the bar. That was the word he used, "escort."

"Thank you," Max said. "I think the rest of us need to walk slowly."

They made their way away from Wandsbekstrasse, Max and Margot, who appeared from somewhere, guiding Snakes carefully over the tangled hoses from half a dozen fire trucks fruitlessly pumping streams of water that turned to ice midair before they dropped into the empty space where there had once been a roof, a resilient Willy scampering ahead with Erich, Ben Alef shuffling in solitary contemplation.

They walked as if they were invisible. Not once did any of the hooting bands of youths or any of the individuals sliding furtively in and out of shadows on errands of personal redemption recognize the Son of Man who had freed them. Even as He stepped like a wind between two quarreling members of a raging mob, they only peered quizzically at Max and Margot and Snakes.

Tinkling of glass, screeching of tires, raucous sailor chanties and carols, and the wailing of distant sirens.

"What's going to happen?" Max asked no one in particular.

"I don't know about you, but I've got to pee," Margot said, and skipped ahead to the welcome neon of the Kastrasse.

"It will play itself out, I suppose," Snakes replied, beginning to find his voice.

"But how? I mean, in history, or outside history, in . . ." Max struggled to convey his meaning. "In some sort of cosmic time?"

"Does it make a difference?"

"I think so. And also, not only how, but what. What is going to happen to us?"

Ben Alef turned, his skin aglow in the neon script, and said, "One of you will betray me."

Snakes and Max stood, frozen and alone. Margot had returned to walk Ben Alef inside.

Finally, Max could no longer bear the silence. Voice quavering as childishly as Bruno's up on the roof, he said, "I don't understand anything. You are Samuel, the interpreter. Explain."

"What?"

"Please," Max begged. He had never asked for anything but to serve. He brought the other disciples food; he cleaned their linens. He accompanied whoever required company on speaking engagements and sat quietly in the rear, grateful for the unique gift he had been vouchsafed. This was the first time Snakes could recall Max asking for anything. He spoke almost as little as Ben Alef.

"All right." Snakes took pity, and besides, he had to spool out the meaning for himself. He, too, was shocked. "Step by step. I think we know the word 'betray,' but the result of betrayal can be anything from insignificant to catastrophic." He thought of multiple betrayals in the Hamburg underworld—99.4 percent pure cocaine cut with baby powder—and they usually led to blood on the floor. "The real question is, Will it be remediable?"

"No," Max murmured apologetically, "the real question is, Who?"

"Yes, yes, that's very interesting." Snakes obviously didn't want to think anymore—he was tired of thinking; he didn't ever want to think again—but Max couldn't leave it alone. "He said, 'One of you will betray me.' "

"Well, all right, then, we know who the 'me' in that sentence is, but the complication I suppose you're referring to is the word 'you.' He could mean, well, there's no avoiding it . . . us . . ." Snakes paused to take in the lack of other human presence anywhere in sight. "But He could also mean any of the twelve, some of whom are more likely than others." He didn't have to name the suspect whose cackle suddenly burst forth from the roof ten meters above the door. "Or perhaps He means any one of the Alefites. Or maybe He just means someone, anyone, a person we don't know . . . out there." Snakes looked into the darkness, where Luther Huber and Father Immaculato were meeting beside a snow-dusted park bench, and shouted, "You!"

Max, however, was sure. "He means someone particular."

Snakes admitted, "Yes, I agree."

When they reached the Kastrasse they found Glucks and Langefeld leaning over the bar with Celia and Willy Wilk, plying the latter with medicinal liquor and listening to his story of entombment and rescue. Snakes was tempted to whisper a word of caution to his colleagues, but Glucks waved him and Max away—"They're waiting upstairs"—so the last two disciples hurried to join the rest. Already they could hear Anton smashing Eisenheim, Kiehr licking his lips, and the sound of endless fires crackling.

Placing one foot on the winding staircase to the mezzanine, Max said, "Wait."

Snakes turned, "Yes?"

"How do we stop it?"

"We watch Him. And them. We keep watching until we know who 'you' is. We keep watch from now on. Deal?"

Max nodded. "Deal, but . . ."

"Yes?"

"Let's keep this to ourselves."

Once again, Snakes agreed, but he looked at the simple fisherman who had been forced into the first dissembling in his life. The two men shook hands, making a pact right there to trust each other and distrust everyone else in the world.

And now they were on the roof, where the remaining *Farnhagen*ers echoed their placement in Cell #306, Ben Alef alone, Anton and Bruno at the corners, Eisenheim in the center; and Snakes felt a yearning for the hard bench that had been his bed during the storm that led to revelation. That bench was the last surface he could lie upon, uneasy perhaps about his own legal future, but entirely comfortable with his past. There, he had thought of his earthly father and of the world he knew, until the miracles of Ben Alef ushered in this strange, dangerous, and beatific new world.

Occasionally Kiehr climbed down the steep ladder to go to the bathroom and return with the latest news from the lonely television over the empty bar, broadcasting live from the latest hot spot.

Snakes and Max Vetter and Margot and the rest of the Messiah's innermost circle watched the burning city with increasing anxiety as Hamburg's citizens, automatically forgiven for any atrocity, seemed to forget their humanity and become citizens of another world that might have been inspired by Dietrich Eisenheim.

"Let's remember," Bruno said, "why we're here."

"I'll tell you why we're here," Eisenheim declared.

"It's your night," Kiehr said. "The Obersturmbannführer has been treating us to his philosophy," he explained to Snakes. "Let's hear another aria."

Eisenheim obliged. "We're here for God's sake. Literally. Call it His entertainment. God does two things to all of us. I've said it before and I'll say it again: He gives us life and He kills us. God sets you up like a house of cards and knocks you down. That's His pleasure. And the higher the house, the greater the fall. Don't you understand, you pathetic creatures, you live for seventy eighty ninety even a hundred years, and then you die forever."

"But—"

"Everything else is chance; some people are rich, some are poor, some happy, some sad, you name it, that's where variation comes in. But connection is two things, birth, otherwise, well, you aren't, and then death. God takes every one of his creatures and kills them. The lightness exists only to define the dark."

"Sounds like Nietzsche." The intellectual Kiehr remembered his days at the university.

"Almost, but not quite, O great mind: Nietzsche said that God is dead, not that God is death. Look at all His sacred imagery. It's red, the color of blood. That's the stuff He loves. Don't you?" He addressed Ben Alef for the first time, and didn't wait for a reply. "Look at Him, looking at them, out there. . . ." His arm swept the horizon. "That's what He really loves, isn't it. Admit it, you bastard."

"Lay off," Anton said.

"But He's here now. So it's different."

"Yes, until now it was all hypothetical. Now, it's actual. And what a gift for us, to witness the true nature of the deity. After thousands of years of fakery, here we are, at the moment of genuine truth. Thank you, Ben Alef. All hail the Messiah and His perfect universe!"

"So"—Max Vetter glanced up from his writing for the first time— "even you believe?"

"Of course, I believe. What else is there?"

Ben Alef had sat motionless throughout the entire oration, but at the end, when every eye was upon Him, when even Eisenheim acknowledged faith, the Messiah finally answered, without a word, but with a single tear that formed like a pearl in the corner of His left eye, and slid slowly down His grief-stricken face.

"Crocodile tears. I'm getting out of here," Eisenheim declared.

"Wait," Nazzarian said. "Me, too."

"But where are you going?" Max asked, worried.

"To bed," Nazzarian lied. "I have to dream."

Eisenheim winked. "I have an appointment."

"With who?"

"It's a secret." He laughed, and started down the ladder, humming a catchy tune they all knew though it had been forbidden for fifty years.

Elsewhere in the Kastrasse complex, others were in bed, too, and dreaming with their eyes open. Herbert Glucks couldn't believe his luck. After dancing in front of a burning seminary with the tartaned schoolgirls of Hamburg, he had straggled home and met Celia at the empty bar.

"Working?" he said.

"It's the first time I've been here when I'm not working," she said.

"Then let me pour you a drink," Herbert offered.

"Well, I don't know."

"Hey, how often do you get to be a customer?" Before she could reply, he ducked under the wooden gate and was standing between her and three rows of bottles, each row a hundred bottles long. "What'll it be?"

"Um, a Black Russian."

The former teacher, who had never been a big drinker, recalled the ingredients, found a glass, poured a generous helping of top-shelf Icelandic vodka, and tipped in a jigger of Kahlúa.

The syrupy liqueur spread through the clear liquor like a lava lamp. Celia gazed at the mixture. "It's beautiful."

"Not so beautiful as you," Herbert blurted, then blushed, and hurried to pour himself a drink, the same as Celia's without the Kahlúa. "To eternal love," he declared, and clinked glasses.

Celia looked at the older man with a jaundiced eye. She was used to older men who desired her slim frame and large eyes, but this one was different. For the others, passion was relative. Had they been unmarried or less physically or emotionally repulsive, they might have set their sights higher. But Herbert's yearning was absolute, fixed at a particular moment in time that was probably appropriate at that moment yet less and less so as time passed. Had they been eleventh-graders together, he would have loved her, and then shunned her by the time he taught eleventh-graders a dozen years later. Herbert would love eleventh-graders, or reasonable facsimiles thereof, like Celia, forever, as he crossed taboo after taboo.

"Is this a private party or is anybody welcome?" Langefeld asked as he walked a smudge-faced Willy Wilk in the door.

"Bar's open," Glucks replied, recognizing a kindred spirit.

"Good, we'll take whatever you're drinking. Right, Willy, my boy?"

Since his privileged entry into the innermost circle of Messiahdom, Willy Wilk had met many strange human beings and seen much strange behavior his straitlaced parents had never dreamed of. He learned how to speak to journalists and policemen, and had even addressed the assembly in front of the Hamburg jail. Tasting vodka and black coffee liqueur was just another initiation as far as he was concerned, and the eleven-year-old took it in stride, climbing up the leather-padded bar stool as if it were a jungle gym in his local playground. He drank the entire glass like soda and said, "It tastes sweet."

"Another?" Erich Langefeld asked.

"Sure."

And the four initiates lingered over the bar, discussing the events of the day, Glucks pouring with a heavy hand.

Celia was only slightly older, but infinitely more weathered, than Lorna Kirtchner, and lines creased her eyes. It took the liquor-blurred vision of Herbert Glucks to smooth away the lines and return him to the Rijksmuseum and the last night he saw Lorna alive. "You look tired," he suggested with teacherly solicitousness.

"All those paintings," Lorna had said.

"I am tired," Celia answered, and suddenly laughed.

The hint of a sophisticated double meaning aged her, but Herbert refused to listen to the evidence of his senses. He was a schoolteacher with the heart of an adolescent, and he was drunk. "But none of them are as beautiful as you."

"What?"

"I mean, Shall I escort you to your room?"

"My so-called room, my cubicle, my three square meters? Sure." She extracted a key from a tiny beaded bag and dangled it over the bar. Actually, the Peddler had offered Celia better accommodations after her status rose, but she had refused. After all, she had been reborn while in residence in the "girls' wing" of the Kastrasse complex, and she would remain there.

Glucks grabbed at the key.

"How about you?" Langefeld asked his own prey.

Wise in his own ways and up past his bedtime, the child wasn't yet at the point of multiple entendre and, unlike Celia, could not have imagined what was coming. "One for the road," he said, echoing the jukebox, and thrust his empty glass forward so eagerly and awkwardly that an ice cube rolled over the edge of the glass and clattered onto the bar.

"One for my baby," Langefeld sang to Glucks with a wink. Of all the disciples, these two knew each other's souls better than any of the rest, because, with a slight age and gender distinction, they were subject to the same mania.

There was a gentleness and a gentlemanliness about Herbert Glucks that Celia appreciated and there was a catlike quality to Celia that he adored. She promised nothing, but he could tell by the way her legs rubbed together that a biological reaction was occurring inside her as they walked the long corridor into the girls' quarters, which until recently had seen more men than girls, say a ratio of six to one, each and every night. She was boiling; he knew it—they were all alike—and he was so excited he could barely insert the key into the keyhole.

"Tired." Celia sighed, and lay down on the cot that occupied almost the entire floor area except for a single wooden chair and a narrow dresser topped with an array of lubricants and a roll of paper towels.

Glucks was disgusted. This was no Class B hotel room in Amsterdam. For a second he was tempted to flee, but the sight of Celia's thighs extending into the nether reaches below her skirt was irresistible. He lay down beside her, one leg on the mattress, one foot on the floor for balance. The tiny room was spinning, whether with alcohol or potential he couldn't tell and didn't care.

"Your father does not appreciate you, does he, little Kaiser?" Erich whispered into Willy's ear as the two of them entered the lad's more generous quarters, reserved for special visitors and private parties. The suite was as large as the entire Wilk family house, and decorated with a curved sectional sofa—easier to remove part of in case of ugly stains—and a glass coffee table and its own bar and an oversized television with access to special channels and, set in an alcove, a king-sized bed under a mirrored ceiling. "I know how to treat you, Willy. I know what boys want."

"Hmmmm," Willy murmured, not quite understanding what the older man was saying, but idly entertained by the tickling in his ear—was that a tongue?

Herbert's index finger slid up the stocking along the young woman's leg until it disappeared beneath the scant material of her dress.

Celia's toleration of the hand that squeezed and stroked her flesh was vaguely disappointing to Herbert, but he closed his eyes and imagined her only a year earlier, running away from some brutal, blue-collar father, nervous, afraid, alone in the big city until some guy on the streets—he pictured Snakes Hammurabi in dapper, peach-colored suit—gave her a neon-pink card and suggested, "Call this number. They have a position open."

"Open," he commanded, and pushed apart her legs.

Dizzy Willy giggled as he felt thick fingers unbuttoning his shirt.

"You'll be more comfortable this way," Erich cooed.

Willy's eyes popped open, and gazed up at the mirror laminated onto the ceiling. What a funny place for a mirror, and what a funny sight. He saw his own bemused expression and the curved back of Erich Langefeld and the creepy, crawly fingers spidering across his chest. The silver glass reminded him of the pails of water on his family's lawn, and the hands reminded him of Ben Alef's hands rubbing his forearm.

Unconsciously obliging, Celia arched her bottom off the cot to assist the man—more a conglomeration of parts, to her, than a human being—in liberating her left foot from the entanglement of pantyhose, but the effort was so exhausting that she—and he—ignored the right leg's stocking, which clung to her muscular thigh as it rode up to her crotch, into which he leaned, feasting on the fruit of her degradation. Like a small animal, his head nuzzled at her midsection and then explored her belly, licking a scar left by a previous customer.

Impatient now, Herbert stretched Celia's brassiere above her breasts rather than reach around her back to unclasp it. Pausing a moment to behold his triumph, savoring the moment, he unzipped his pants. Then he lay down, mouth pressing urgently upon her own slack and unmarred lips. "Lorna," he crooned.

"My Lord," she sighed.

"Now roll over," Erich said.

"Nooo." Willy enjoyed looking at the mirror and couldn't see it with his face pressed into the soft down pillow.

But Langefeld was ready to have his way. Unlike the shy teacher down the hall, he had traveled the waterfront, where delicacy was a notion reserved for squid. He flipped the boy over as easily as a pancake and yanked the slim-hipped kid's pants down to his ankles. He hadn't felt this eager since the death of Heinrich, who had betrayed him and suffered accordingly. Then he unzipped his own pants.

For the first time since their journey had begun, Snakes saw Ben Alef cry. The initial tear from His left eye was followed by one from His right; they established parallel routes over which drop after glistening drop slid down the hills and valleys of His cheeks to disappear in the scruff on His chin. "Showers," He said.

And Snakes thought of all the water he loathed and detested from the River Lyons to the open Baltic to the ink-stained bucket in front of the jail to Willy Wilk's plea for "Water" back on Wandsbekstrasse. Showers, indeed. Ben Alef was right, as always. The water from which life emerged always flowed toward death. Everything that cleansed really sullied. Everything beautiful on the synagogue stage had turned into dust. Only pee was true.

"Back to the *Farnhagen*," Anton pointed out, not without sympathy.

Ben Alef looked up at the sky through his reddened, furiously blinking eyes, and Snakes felt a drop of rain on his forehead. The snow had turned to drizzle.

"What's this?" Kiehr asked.

"Showers," Snakes explained as he inched toward the hatch to escape from them.

"It's too cold to rain," Anton said.

"Thank you, weatherman," Snakes replied, holding open his palms to feel the warm liquid pouring from somewhere in the dark.

"It's another miracle," Bruno blubbered.

Maybe it was, Snakes thought, as he and Anton and Bruno and Kiehr and Margot and even Max Vetter, fearful that the rain would ruin his precious notebook, descended the steep ladder to contemplate everything that had happened.

"Showers to wash away sin," Ben Alef said, smiling as He continued to sob, and the showers began to put out the fires, while His face streamed with—it was impossible to tell—rain or tears.

Immersed and ecstatic as he only had been once before in his life, the day he lost his virginity with the late Lorna, Herbert Glucks didn't hear the thin door of Celia's chamber open, while Celia, the majority of whose waking and sometimes sleeping hours had been spent with some man spending himself between her legs, wouldn't have cared if the Prussian army had marched in and started doing calisthenics. Thus neither of them noticed a man enter the barren cubicle, though he made no particular attempt at stealth. He stood there for a minute in the square meter of open floor space, looking down on their half-clad bodies, and then he reached out and picked up the empty leg of stocking that lay like a ghost limb on the mattress.

"Hey." Herbert roused himself. "What are you doing here?"

In one swift motion, the man wrapped the stocking about Herbert's neck and tied it into a knot. "This," he said and left the room just as Celia's eyes opened and widened and her nostrils flared and she began to shake with another, uncontrollable fit.

Because her other leg was secured to the stocking, every kick pulled the knot together.

Herbert bucked up, but the stocking pulled him back into Celia. She saw him and felt him there as the haze of vodka and Kahlúa dissipated. She wanted to stop, but couldn't. And the more he struggled to escape, the wider her legs spread, the tighter the noose.

Minutes later, the same man entered the considerably fancier room where Erich Langefeld, more expert in the avenues and varieties of human sexual endeavor than Herbert Glucks would ever be, vigorously pumped away at the moaning Willy Wilk. Again, neither of the participants in the performance noticed their audience until it was too late and the show almost over.

This time only Willy's one-size-fits-all orlon socks lay on the bed, but the man had brought the instrument of Herr Langefeld's punishment with him. He extracted a long, serrated knife from a leather holster.

Preoccupied, clasping the boy's waist with both hands, Eric suddenly felt an icy coolness tickle his own exposed anus. And as Herbert had bounced up when the stocking's softness touched his neck, so the cold metal compelled the pedophile to thrust deeper into the reluctant child, and he groaned with delight. But then he realized that the sensation was not a product of his imagination; it actually had a highly, and sharply, specific physical origin, and he turned.

"Hello," the intruder said, and showed Erich the weapon, like a housewares salesman displaying an especially useful domestic utensil—on sale today.

Erich remembered the kitchen knife he had used upon the faithless Heinrich and felt his penis wither.

"Relax," the man said.

Erich felt the smooth, blunt surface of the knife glide gently down his crack until the point poised at the opening. His organ grew hard in final salute just before that point, and the blade and its teeth, followed by a fist and forearm, rocketed straight up his rectum, tore through his stomach, severed muscles and tendons and vessels, and pierced his heart.

Langefeld screamed; he came; and a gout of blood poured forth onto the bed and the boy below.

Dear Frieda,

The events of this evening have been awful, worse than the inundation of Wieland, worse than anything I've ever seen—except for the faint, fifty-five-year-old memory of . . . you know.

Rank sex—forgive my candor—I've gotten used to; it's repulsive, but human. But the madness here, the violence—

people in flames and people inflamed with blood lust—I will never forget. All spurred by the scene in the synagogue. Such a beautiful building, and so grand. The church in Wieland would be like your dollhouse in the corner; the Jews must have all the money. So why, why can't such an intelligent people ever learn better? Once, two thousand years ago, they refused to see the light, and they suffered for two thousand years. Now, they are the most blessed of all, for Ben Alef comes from their seed, and He seeks their affirmation and still, still, the speaker for the tribe, this Asher Rose, looked the Lord in the eye and said Nay. I fail to understand this, Frieda.

Or don't they mind having their grand synagogue and their fancy shops burned, their women mistreated, their children witness their parents' humiliation? I saw Asher Rose as he said Nay, and that man knew what would occur. For a second, I thought that he wanted it.

Maybe they encourage our fury, because it keeps them strong. Like a field of wheat that's burnt to refertilize itself with a more potent strain. But they are devious, and cowardly; they cannot bring themselves to kill themselves—it goes against their sacred texts—so they deliberately compel us to murder them, then we reap the guilt while they sprout anew. And a few generations later, the whole cycle repeats.

Nothing ever changes.

No, that's wrong. This time they are wrong, This time Ben Alef is here, and their cunning will not be rewarded. All of the rules of history have changed. This time the punishment is forever. There will be no new Asher Rose to transform good people into killers. This time only the righteous will be reborn.

Five of the disciples are dead, and though I believe that we shall meet them soon we are nervous. Nazzarian thinks it is a plot. Bruno thinks it is a terrible coincidence. Enough people have met their Maker on this evil night for the latter to be true. On the other hand, great powers must be threatened by Ben Alef's existence. Does this mean I am in danger?

Or is He in danger? Ben Alef hinted as much. But as long as He is with me, I fear not. Great things are coming, yet I am tired, so tired. Please join us for the final revelation. Next week brings the end of days.

Yours,

Max

Came one clap of unforecast thunder in the perfectly clear sky and everything in Hamburg, the very stones and timbers, the marauding gangs and yipping dogs, was doused by the downpour, and tired, so tired.

Ten minutes after Snakes saw the first drop on Bel Alef's cheek and felt the first drop on his own palm, he practically threw himself down the Kastrasse hallway, groggy and desperate to find his room before he collapsed in the corridor. Outside, cars pulled over to the shoulder of the road. Mid-sex throughout the city, snores replaced sighs. Revelers glorying in the frigid industrial city's transformation into the capital of the millennium and mourners weeping for loved ones slaughtered in the hysteria shut their eyes. People curled up in doorways, and ten minutes later the only sounds to be heard were those of water sizzling on the dying embers.

The soporific rain extinguished all life as effectively, if not as permanently, as the first showers Ben Alef had witnessed fifty-six years earlier. Fires quenched, Hamburg fell to sleep. A steamy fog enshrouded the streets.

Chapter Twenty-one

ARLY THE NEXT MORNING, few people had yet risen when a solitary figure walked to the husk of the jail to which he had been summoned. He looked at the slumbering encampment of Neue Juden in the yard, and climbed a folding staircase into a police trailer.

Two other early risers sat inside, at opposite ends of a black metal desk covered with stacks of paper that reported events in the rest of the city. "Three of your friends are dead," the shorter man last seen by the park bench greeted the secret visitor.

"Your information is pathetic."

The man riffled the topmost sheaf of paper and read: " 'Log of the City Morgue, 1:15: Karl Blobel, dead on arrival due to massive trauma to head and body sustained in an automobile accident.'

" 'Memorial Hospital, 5:23: Franz Palitzsch, expired due to suspected narcotics overdose,' and . . . where do we have it—ah, here:

" 'Police Report from fire on Wandsbekstrasse, 6:02: Body found in organ chamber above pulpit, believed to be Martin Clauberg. Awaiting dental confirmation." He was proud of the efficiency of his information-gathering apparatus.

"Six oh two," the visitor repeated.

"Exactly."

"It's six-thirty now."

"Twenty-eight minutes."

"You can subtract. Congratulations."

The tall man at the end of the table tapped his finger, allowing the weight of a thick gold ring to beat the table with an ominously regular cadence. "More than three?" he asked.

The visitor tossed a small parcel wrapped in brownish butcher paper tied with twine onto the desk between the two men.

The shorter one drew the package toward him with the handle of his umbrella and unwrapped it with a tweezer from the desk. He had seen enough evidence in his life to know to treat it carefully. Pinching the corner, he let the object inside slide out of the paper onto the desk. It was a tongue.

The visitor didn't say a word.

Luther Huber, chief officer of the law in Germany's northernmost population center, looked at the clear proof of unspeakable crime, and swept it off his desk into the garbage can. "Very good," he said. "But is it the one we want?"

"Not yet."

"Soon."

"At the right time."

"And when will that be?"

"Trust me."

"He's right," interposed the taller man, whose ring bore the insignia of an eagle. "It's Christmas, after all, and we don't want irony."

"Just effect."

"Yes."

"But won't it also be ironic a few days from now, at the turn of His millennium?"

"Not ironic. Appropriate."

"Hmm." The General mulled over the information. Used to making decisions on the indictability quotient of given evidence, he didn't like the decision he had to make now. If this was what political office required, he rather wished he had followed his father's advice and become a furniture salesman; people always needed sofas. Who or what besides the state needed to be saved from salvation? And what a strange battle to have to fight. And no possible personal benefit to be gained except for the dubious satisfaction of knowing that he had personally protected secular authority from deity. But he had received his orders, and he would follow them. He turned toward his companion and lifted his chin as if to say, Your call.

Unlike the attorney, the priest either had no doubts, or he transcended them. Father Immaculato handed Dietrich Eisenheim a gun. "You can choose your moment."

"Who needs a gun?" replied the man, who might or might not have murdered his companions by means of knife, poison, automobile, stocking, and fire, but surely didn't mind taking credit for all of the above.

"Take it anyway," Immaculato said. "We have faith in technology."

"You will be granted immunity," Huber said, adding the only gift he could offer.

"I am already immune," Eisenheim scoffed. "You can't hurt me. You've tried for how many decades? It doesn't make a shit of difference unless you think that maybe your buddy's God gives a shit. What's He gonna do, damn me?"

"Will you do it?"

"Only because I want to." He took the gun.

Snakes Hammurabi thought he was the first to rise, but of course Eisenheim had long since preceded him, and so had Ben Alef. Or perhaps Ben Alef had stopped sleeping again. Snakes padded in cantaloupe-colored socks down the spiral staircase to find the Messiah sitting alone at the bar with the great, padded front door of the Kastrasse wide open, motes of ash and the scent of char permeating the beams of dawn air.

"Good morning." Snakes greeted his Lord just as he had often greeted the Peddler in the same room following innumerable nights of inebriated debauchery. Always, the Peddler was first in the room, always the last to shut off the lights, but he had seemed so dejected after the debacle in the synagogue that Snakes wasn't surprised that he had chosen to sleep late.

"Good night," Ben Alef replied.

But it *was* morning, and Snakes desperately sought meaning. Did Ben Alef intend to imply that the night before, when so many innocent people and several guilty disciples died, was good? Was He, in his own ineffable way, affirming the truth of Dietrich Eisenheim's nihilistic philosophy? Or was He . . .

"It is time to go," Ben Alef declared.

Good night to the third phase of the journey. The first quarter took place asea with the twelve (eleven walkers, one witness), the second en route to Hamburg with the first followers from Kaltenhaven and Warnemünde, the third, here concluded, in the metropolis. Now the fourth and ultimate passage was about to commence. Five days until the calendar turned. But where? And for what reason? To what end? Snakes had so many questions that he dared not ask.

Instead, he set off to Max Vetter's room, because he figured that the former fisherman was the most likely to keep early hours. He was right. Max was already awake, and writing at his desk with such concentration that he didn't hear Snakes enter. "Hello," Snakes said, and Max awkwardly tried to slip the notebook under a towel.

What was it—poetry, a chronicle of the season, a laundry list? Snakes didn't care. He rather hoped that somebody was keeping a diary of the day-to-day occurrences that would remake the world, even though such a document would be entirely superfluous once the world was remade. "Get ready," he said, "we're going."

"Where?"

"On," Snakes answered. Normally he would have played his information close to the vest, leaving whoever he was speaking to uncomfortably aware of Herr Hammurabi's special, superior position, but instead he explained that he didn't really have any private knowledge. "Ben Alef is ready to move again."

"Thank God."

"Yes."

"I meant . . . well, I guess I did mean that." Max smiled. After a lifetime of hard work and few words, he had made his first pun. The world was changing indeed. Max was happy.

Snakes smiled back kindly. Of all the disciples the simple fisherman, furthest from the criminal's natural iniquity, most deeply appealed to Snakes. Max was the template of the Messiah's new man. Soon, everyone would be as simple and straightforward as he. "But you also meant something else."

"Right, I also meant that I . . . I hate this city. I know it's your home, and I apologize for any insult, but this"—he gestured to encompass the sensual double bed in the Mata Hari suite and the rest of the Kastrasse complex and all of Hamburg—"doesn't seem to be the way people are meant to live."

Of course, Snakes had read one of Max's private letters to his sister,

Frieda, so he knew quite well what Max thought of Hamburg, but he didn't mind. He, too, was changing. "Well, Max, we're on the road to someplace else. You want to help me get everyone else up?"

"Sure."

The two men headed off in different directions, Max to fetch Celia, Margot, and Willy—those who, like himself, encountered Ben Alef after His first appearance—while Snakes roused Anton, Omar, and Bruno, shaking the slumbering giant, who was curled into a ball, lips sucking at something only he could see. After those three, however, Snakes searched, fruitlessly, for the rest of the disciples from the *Farnhagen*. Glucks, Langefeld, Kiehr, and Eisenheim were not in their rooms.

Therefore Max found the next two dead disciples. Celia, who hardly realized that her epileptic thrashings had strangled her last lover, lay sleeping beside the blue-faced body of Herbert Glucks, one free stocking still snug to her right leg. At first, Max was embarrassed by the sight of the half-naked girl, but he had become a man of the world in the past few weeks, and swiftly overcame his naive shame to help disentangle the groggy and disoriented Celia from her inadvertent victim. Then he led the dazed young woman down the hall, until both of them heard a faint whimpering coming from behind the door of the suite assigned to Willy Wilk.

Immediately, Max knew. "Wait here," he told Celia in a tone of newly attained authority, and entered, prepared for the worst.

Willy's head was buried in the pillow, the body of Erich Langefeld sprawled atop him.

Max stared at their coiled legs, like a double helix, crimson and brown from the waist down, the stained hasp of a kitchen knife protruding from Langefeld's anus. Again, this time without a hint of a double meaning, he gasped, "My God."

Together, Max and his shaken companions went downstairs, where Omar Nazzarian was already pouring himself a breakfast Bloody Mary. The fisherman called the police just as Snakes brought in the pajamaed Bruno and Anton, rubbing his flawed eyes.

"I called the police," Max said.

"Where is He?" Snakes cried.

"No, it's Herbert and Erich."

"I left Ben Alef here half an hour ago. Where is He?"

The enormous room was empty.

One heart-stopping second later, Celia pointed. "There!"

The Messiah stood in the doorway, bathed in light. He turned and looked at the last four disciples and two beneficiaries of His touch. Then He extended an arm and beckoned.

"I guess we're going," Snakes announced.

"But what about Herbert and Erich?"

"You said they're dead," Snakes said, realizing that it was all the more imperative that they leave immediately. Once again, Ben Alef knew before any of them.

"And Georg? And Dietrich?"

"They are where they are."

"And so am I," Nazzarian announced. He had followed along willingly enough, but some long introspective process had finally come to a resolution.

"What?"

"You may be going, but I've had enough. I should have left as soon as we hit the shore, but I was weak. I was weak, but I'm not weak anymore. You can go where you want, but I'm staying." He laid a dark-skinned hand on the bar.

"Omar," Bruno pleaded.

"He's staying," Ben Alef said, and started for the door.

That was it; there was no time for discussion. Celia and Willy were ready, Margot shambled downstairs brushing her hair, and Snakes whispered to Max, "Don't let Him out of your sight."

There was a hurried rush to pack a few hard-boiled eggs, and five minutes later they were gone.

By the time the would-be assassin returned to the Kastrasse, the bar was empty. No customers, no girls, no disciples, no Alefites, no one. It was spooky. Obersturmbannführer Eisenheim had spent his entire life since 1945 in company, and he found the solitude unnerving. He ran a finger over the lip of the bar, which, like every other horizontal surface in Hamburg, was coated with a thin layer of ash. Usually it would have been swabbed down with a wet cloth by now, but none of the regular procedures mattered any longer.

He started up the stairs to the mezzanine, and then stopped. There was at least one body on the premises. The Kommandant had seen it two hours before when, waking early for his appointment, he looked around the kitchen for breakfast. Before the Kastrasse's menu was changed to corn, corn, and more corn, the Peddler had always laid out a free dinner buffet of cheap chicken wings or a large ham to lure the after-work crowd with something besides liquor and the flesh trade. The cost was minimal, the advantage significant.

Aside from corn-cooking facilities, most of the kitchen had been converted into storage for bar supplies and music and video equipment, but the huge walk-in freezer to the left of an industrial range, maple chopping block, and stainless-steel washing equipment with detachable spray hose had been left intact, since it was too much trouble to remove the thing. Eisenheim had thought he might find leftovers from the previous day's corn fritters, but instead a residue of meat lay on the chopping board beside a cleaver that the cook had forgotten to place in the washing tray, and the hungry early riser anticipated finding a nice roast beef sandwich in the freezer. He put two hands to the talon-shaped pull, opened the heavy wooden door, and enjoyed the blast of wintry air, more seasonable than the obnoxious and unnatural spring that had descended with the previous night's rain.

The freezer occupied ten-plus cubic meters, filled with shelves of canned goods and gallon jugs of mustard, ketchup, sauerkraut, and pickles. But straight ahead hung the carcass that the exposed cleaver had neatly divided. The torso floated on a metal chain, independent of the legs and arms, which flanked it rather like those of a toy doll ripped apart by an angry child, undressed and ripped apart and flayed so that the muscles' bright red sheen drew every ray of light from outside the freezer and reflected it in a satanic glow. Long, torn strips of skin littered the grimy, sawdust-strewn floor.

And on one of the shelves, there, between the mustard and a large tin of corn "niblets," where Eisenheim had left it not quite fully intact before striding off to his meeting with Luther Huber and Father Immaculato, the head of Georg Kiehr cast one last sophisticated and lugubrious glance at the world.

"Can't talk anymore, I suppose," the Kommandant addressed his former cellmate, glad nonetheless for the company.

"Why not?" a voice replied.

Surprised but not scared—he had spent three years in the land of the dead—Eisenheim tried to explain, "Um, well, because I gave your tongue to the cops."

"That's no reason," the vaguely familiar voice said. "After all, if I'm dead I don't need a tongue."

"True enough," Eisenheim conceded. Always ready to argue anything with anyone, he felt as if this disembodied head and decapitated voice were the first bona fide other he could ever respect. But for the first time in his career he also couldn't help but wonder if he was really crazy. Even Anton called him a psycho, and the U.S. Army psychiatrists who examined him back in the autumn of '45 knew that the Obersturmbannführer was not as well-adjusted as his peers and was therefore of no possible use to the postwar dispensation.

What defined sanity? Probably the inability—or unwillingness—to think for oneself. A craven concession to commonly accepted reality. In 1999 anyone who said the world was flat was insane, but in 1299 anyone who said the world was round was insane. Reason was relative, and bore no necessary relationship to truth.

After 1945, anyone who believed what everyone in Germany had believed from 1933 to 1945 was insane. Eisenheim, however, stuck to his guns and continued to believe that killing every Jew on earth was good; like the Alefites, he suffered not so much for his actions as for his faith. In the *Farnhagen*, he took beating after beating when he continued to reveal unpleasant truths. But now: a gruesomely severed head conversing as easily as any other head that happened to be attached to breathing and circulatory and muscular and nervous system apparatuses, this went against the empirical, earthbound evidence of all Eisenheim's own senses.

"Of course I'm real," the voice said, answering the Kommandant's unspoken question. "A tongue is only a tool, and what one tool can do, another tool can do even better. That's progress." This definitely wasn't some weird gurgling of dishwasher or knocking or hissing of steam pipes that, very loosely interpreted, could be imagined as a voice. Besides, aside from the voice, it was absolutely silent in the freezer, insulated from the outside world by ten centimeters of steel-clad concrete. The voice was real all right, yet it didn't sound like Georg Kiehr; it didn't have his aristocratic Prussian accent, although it was familiar.

Eisenheim ignored the logical incongruities. He was ecstatic. While the rest of the world listened to the all-too-alive pronouncements of Ben Alef as reiterated by the disciples and recapitulated by the media, here was the ultimate proof of the inviolability of death. He stepped forward to gaze into Georg Kiehr's bloodshot eyes and the gaping hole from which he had personally torn the missing tongue hours before to present to the various authorities of church and state. The auditory apparition may have been miraculous, but it was definitely real. Oh, yes, the end was coming, and not as the rest of the world expected. Now, now would arrive the era when Death ruled.

And he, Dietrich Eisenheim, was the prophet. The Kommandant fell to his knees before the head and, like Louis XVI at the guillotine, let his own head sink beneath the weight of destiny.

"Looks familiar," the voice said.

Suddenly, the believer discerned the source of the voice. His eyes popped open to a knothole in the midst of a plank of blood-soaked, fat-drenched pine floorboard. Eisenheim jerked upright, spun around, and ducked as the cleaver Omar Nazzarian held whistled above his scalp, barbered off a hank of white hair, and landed with a thud several inches inside the carcass of Georg Kiehr.

"Christ!" Eisenheim explained.

"Not quite," Nazzarian replied, and he wrenched the cleaver out of the bloody slab.

"That's not what I meant, you dark little bastard!"

Nazzarian smiled. "That's what I'll miss about you, Dietrich—or aren't you on a first-name basis with dark little bastards?—your honesty. Too bad you weren't born in America; you could have had whole Harlems full of dark little bastards to hate. Or, better yet, Africa. Instead, you've had to make do with Jews and, of late, the occasional Turk." He used the word that represented all the impoverished Auslanders who had come to the land of cleanliness and opportunity. "But you've always let us know where we stand, and there's something to be said for that. Now I stand here, and you are about to become history." He raised the cleaver.

But Eisenheim was uncowed. Nazzarian was right. The pure German never denied himself, and wasn't going to start in the face of the blood-smeared blade. "I *am* history, past and future. And you're jealous."

"You don't know how jealous I am."

"Jealous enough to do this?"

"Did I say that I did . . . this?" Nazzarian patted the top of Kiehr's head.

"Didn't you?"

"Didn't *you?*"

Presumably one of the two men was responsible for Georg Kiehr's open-mouthed cadaver as well as for the corpses of Palitzsch, Blobel, Glucks, and Langefeld, some reposing in the Hamburg morgue, some about to be discovered by the police hastening in response to Max Vetter's call, and also for the incinerated shell of Martin Clauberg in the wreckage on Wandsbekstrasse, yet here, at this moment of undeniable conclusion, the guilty party was loath to admit his crime—be it murder or heresy.

"How jealous are you?" Eisenheim asked.

"Are you playing for time?"

"Hey, you know me, I'm just playing." The man on his knees smirked. He *was* insane, but he was also courageous.

"Well, then, let's speak frankly."

"You're no Frank." Even here, possibly, probably, breathing his last mortal mouthfuls of air, Eisenheim couldn't resist putting the intruder in his place.

"Precisely, and that is the problem. So what, then, is the solution?"

"The final solution?"

"Oh, a temporary one will do." Nazzarian lifted the cleaver.

"Killing every white man in sight."

"Only some, the same ones you can't abide. You see, Dietrich, we do have something in common."

And the light dawned. "Jews!"

Nazzarian nodded, the truth glittering in his nervous eyes. He had grown up with a resentment that his parents could not understand. They were grateful for European opportunity at any price, but their son saw the invisible yet absolute line beyond which he could not cross. Still, the one value shared by the young assassin and the older generation was that ancient, atavistic hatred for a different set of outsiders—"Old Jews, New Jews, they're all the same to me"—some of whom had migrated to Mitteleuropa a thousand years earlier from the eastern shore of the Mediterranean, and some of whom still lived there in the Zionist heaven. And now the Jewish Messiah was bringing news of His Jewish heaven to the rest of the world, and it was intolerable.

Eisenheim filled in the rest. "You're jealous of me for wanting to kill Ben Alef. Your boiling Arab—no, sorry, Muslim—blood cannot bear that the credit for this will go elsewhere. And you have no interest whatsoever in going into partnership with me." He was getting sly, maybe worried, at least implying the possibility of negotiation.

"None whatsoever," Nazzarian replied, recalling the swastika on his parents' front door.

"So you will help them by killing me in order to prevent me from killing them, so that you can do it yourself."

"Crazy you are, stupid you're not, dead you'll be." Nazzarian had had enough of analysis. He was a man of action. Nonetheless, something inhibited him. Not the killing; Lord, no, he had been the most professional murderer on board the *Farnhagen*. But he had never looked into a victim's eyes. Not that he felt pity; if guilt was foreign to Eisenheim, then pity was the one emotion utterly foreign—or European—to Omar Nazzarian. No, it was the sheer unusualness of the situation. Nazzarian specialized in the sneak attack: the sniper's bullet at sixty yards, the explosives wired into a car's ignition, the ice pick in the neck. He had one last task to accomplish, but he had to do it his way, and then he would finally escape the Western madhouse he had been locked in since his parents made their unfortunate journey from Iran. Perhaps Omar would return to the Islamic republic where he truly belonged. "Turn around," he commanded.

Eisenheim saw the slim youth's weakness, saw an opportunity, and grinned. "Why don't *you?*"

But Nazzarian ignored the advice—good advice it was—and a moment later an enormous cast-iron skillet, swung like a baseball bat, smashed into the back of his skull, flattening the cerebellum against the spinal cord and sending his instantaneously lifeless body sprawling against the torso of Georg Kiehr, whose head seemed to laugh.

"Why did you say that?" the Peddler practically screamed at the ingrate he had rescued from certain death.

Eisenheim shrugged. "Hey, I had to give him a fighting chance."

"About as much of a chance as he was going to give you?"

"Call me an old softie. So, Mr. Chief Yid, where's the minyan?" The Kommandant put a hand to his ear to pantomime listening to the silence that surrounded them. Nothing.

"They left."

"What do you mean, 'left'?"

"Gone. Vamoosed. Scotto. Before I woke up. I'm surprised you aren't with them. But I guess nobody counted heads."

"I had an appointment."

"Seems like you had several appointments. What a clean-up." The Peddler looked around the awful room and then back at the one disciple he had always shunned.

Still on his knees, Eisenheim took a few moments to understand. The man was looking for gratitude. But Nazzarian's cleaver had missed the Aryan head on its first swipe, and the Kommandant did have a gun inside his pocket. He felt certain that, somehow, he would have eluded the dark little bastard, and that no gratitude was required, least of all for yet another one of the tribe of Jacob.

The world was rife with them, and worst were those Eisenheim had not managed to kill half a century earlier. Only fifty thousand–odd survivors, yet they had infiltrated banks, media, bars. Scratch a business and you found a Yid. He rose from his kneeling position, disdaining the Peddler's extended hand.

Dietrich Eisenheim didn't have to look beyond the grasping fingers to visualize the sign on the Peddler's forearm beneath his shirt. That was the reason they had ended up in this cesspool, because Ben Alef had an infallible homing instinct for his own.

Eisenheim guessed that a six-digit number was tattooed between the Peddler's wrist and elbow, or at least the digits with a letter that late arrivals received. The future owner of the Kastrasse was not the type to come at first call. He had been in hiding, rounded up late in the war, the devious type, the type that should have been the first forced to walk a last mile.

The Peddler, formerly known as Chaim Rosenthal, thought of the single blurry photograph he kept in his private office, which looked through a one-way mirror into an anteroom where business was conducted at an elephant-foot coffee and cocaine table surrounded by three chairs. Only three chairs, two for the good guys, one for the competition. "Never allow them to outnumber you," he once told Snakes.

Nobody outnumbered the Peddler beyond the locked door to the inner sanctum. Nobody entered the Holy of Holies. There lay accommodations so spartan as to be unprofessional: a desk with a telephone, an accounts ledger, and a single photograph in a simple frame that almost disappeared against the one human touch in the room, custom-made and custom-installed rose-patterned wallpaper.

Centered in the frame, an elderly man with a long gray beard and a plump elderly woman whose knees always ached sat in formal dress on two wing chairs. Behind them, rigidly posed against the rose-patterned wallpaper in the photographer's studio, stood three young women and two young men. The women were the elderly couple's daughters, Sarah, Malka, and Ruth; the men were Sarah and Malka's husbands, Moshe Rosenthal, a promising rabbinical scholar with thinning hair, and Mordecai Luster, an aspiring dry goods merchant. Arranged in front of the chairs, kneeling or sitting cross-legged, pudgy thighs pressing against short pants, were six children, ranging in age from eight to sixteen.

The real story in the photograph was not merely genealogical, but also characterological. If one examined the blurry image carefully—the original was ten centimeters square and it had been blown up to forty, gaining in size while losing in definition—one could note a more than physical weariness in the matriarch's expression and a slight swelling that would never see fruition in Malka's belly and an envious yearning in the un-married Ruth's eyes. If one looked even more carefully, perhaps one could perceive something in the eldest boy's sheer cliff of brow that resembled the man who owned and still treasured the image. He had carried it with him through years of running and scrounging burnt potatoes and Wiener schnitzel gristle from the garbage cans of Berlin, and worse.

Early in the war, grandparents, parents, aunts, uncle and all but one sibling destined for extermination, the boy had run away from the Łódź ghetto by sneaking through a sewer pipe. But once he stood on the far side of the barbed wire, in which direction should he travel? Even then he knew that the best place to hide was in the heart of the beast, so west he fled, against the flow of advancing brown uniforms. Any soldier basking in the Polish sun from the open turret of a rolling Panzer tank might have used him for target practice, but he arrived in the German capital safe and starving.

Gradually the prematurely worldly child adjusted himself to the wartime economy. He sold individual cigarettes on the black market, and by the time the calendar clicked over into 1944, when everyone knew what the end would be if not how long it would take to arrive, he was running errands for a brothel. Wounded soldiers back from the Eastern Front, to-gether with bureaucrats who conducted the war via telegraphic fiat from Berlin, drained their pensions in a furious quest for one last moment of pleasure, and the boy who had renamed himself Christian Ruehr saw what really mattered.

It was one such wounded soldier who betrayed him, although betrayal implies prior allegiance. Perhaps the one-eyed soldier was a testament to loyalty that night, when, with drunken generosity, he invited the Hot Haus gofer to share a kohl-eyed girl not much older than himself.

"No, thank you," Christian demurred.

"For the Fatherland," the soldier insisted, and laughingly tugged Christian's baggy trousers off his skinny frame, and blinked his one good eye when he noticed the shriveled, circumcised organ.

Arriving on the last transport, Chaim returned to Poland only long enough to present his forearm to the camp tattooist, and then he was ordered to march back to Germany. Two thousand people started on the march; two hundred finished. And then the war was over. Christian hooked up with a gang of black marketeers who smuggled cigarettes and forged currency until the group split up, some to America, some to Palestine. Then he was on his own until, astonishingly, he saw his brother's face staring at him out of a newspaper.

The youngest Rosenthal, the least likely to survive, had not only eked his way through Hell, but had become a emblem for survival itself, and there he was, interviewed by the Joint Distribution Committee's weekly rag, *Liberation*.

Chaim, or Christian, or whatever his nom de post-guerre was, hastened to the DP camp at Feldafing to find his brother. It was a miracle. They embraced and swore to remain together forever, but already the baby was in the midst of the inexorable process that would carry him off into a better life with no room for his smuggling, pandering, conniving older brother. "Come to France with me," the baby begged. "If you don't go, I don't go. I don't care what they offer me."

The future Peddler knew that his destiny was in Germany. He said good-bye to his brother, and didn't see his only blood relative in the world again in the flesh, though much in print, until that week. That week, the Peddler sat in his private office staring at the photo on his credenza, into the eight-year-old eyes of Asher Rose.

Alone now, bereft, the Peddler saw his dreams for anything from vulgar prosperity to divine redemption on the road to some ultimate destination where he could no more go than he could follow his brother in '47. But instead of looking back toward Asher's past or forward toward Ben Alef's future, he remained anchored precisely where he was, and spoke to the man in the freezer. "And where have you been?"

"Out," Eisenheim answered like a petulant teenager.

"They're gone."

"You already told me that."

"Oh." After finding and losing his brother, after the Son of God and His diminished troop of disciples had walked away, after the effort he had put into one massive swing of the four-kilo skillet, the Peddler felt as depleted as shorn Samson in the ruins of the Philistine temple.

"Where?" Eisenheim asked again.

"The way that crew travels, they shouldn't be hard to find."

"Although if this dump is any indication, then wherever they are doesn't seem like the safest place in the world to be."

The Peddler shrugged. "If that's what you care about."

"Yes, you're right, I don't care about safety." Eisenheim knew himself better than that, and he also knew this situation. He felt as desperate and lost as the Peddler, as if the glorious war were ending once more, and fat green Allied planes were buzzing out of the sky and dropping bombs upon his beloved chambers. He reached into his breast pocket, pulled forth the revolver. He wasn't sure if it was loaded, but didn't bother to check. He aimed.

"I should have known that saving you was a mistake. And I should have known that you're not allowed any mistakes in this life."

"Your mistake was being born."

"What about a fighting chance?"

"The hell with that," the German said, and pulled the trigger.

A third eye opened in the center of the Peddler's forehead. Sirens rang in the distance.

"It's for wisdom," Eisenheim giggled as the dead merchant lurched into Kiehr's cadaver, which swung wildly upon its clanking chain. "Damn Jew."

Book IX
Glory

Chapter   Twenty - two

"**E**XTRA. EXTRA. READ ALL ABOUT IT. Bodies in Brothel. Souls at Large." The Kommandant brought the dawn procession the bad news before they were fully out of the municipality's southernmost precinct. Deposited by a white limousine at a crossroads, he waited for the ragged troupe, which consisted of Ben Alef Himself and Snakes and Max Vetter and Anton and Bruno and Margot and Celia, the last two each holding a hand of wee Willy Wilk. "Get your *Daily Zeitung*."

Almost everyone Ben Alef touched died. Yes, at least one had returned from the land beyond—rheumy eyes blinking, a crust of preservative salt rimed in a wave across the breast of his ancient brown tunic—but the resurrected one had already inhabited the valley of the shadow during its incarnation in Europe; he carried a passport.

No matter that the rumors had yet to be fulfilled beyond the Baltic shore. Expectations of universal revival rippled out from Hamburg to the rest of the world. Since the Night of Conflagration, ecstasy had inextricably commingled with doom. Friends and families of those massacred on Christmas Eve celebrated their loved ones' demise and took comfort in images of tombs in cemeteries popping open like crocuses on the first warm day of spring.

Yet if the dead were reprieved from any obligation but to rise, the small band of living who left Hamburg on the morning of the twenty-fifth of December, 1999, proceeded on their earthly mission, counting down the days—and their own numbers. They knew about Clauberg and Blobel and Palitzsch and Glucks and Langefeld, and weren't surprised to hear about Kiehr and Nazzarian.

Word had leaked directly from a trailer outside the jail to the newspaper ("Just be sure you refer to the excellent police work," Luther Huber told Fritz Hofmann), which changed its front-page layout (featuring a dramatic photo of the Wandsbekstrasse fire, which Martin Clauberg would have loved) to include a banner that painted the broad strokes of the most recent deaths in forty-point type and left details pending for the late city edition. But Eisenheim, the witness who knew more than any journalist, drew his own conclusion from the sketchy "rumors." Forget about the approximately two hundred city-wide casualties, including Asher Rose and the Peddler; he counted only disciples. "First there were twelve," he said, "And now there are five." He looked at Snakes Hammurabi, glanced over Max and Anton and Bruno, and asked the approaching group, "Who's next?"

Snakes looked at Max, nodded, and turned back to Eisenheim. "What are you doing here?"

"Where else do I belong?"

"In Hell."

"Already been." Eisenheim chortled and joined the march. "To your left, hup, two, left, hup two. Just along for the ride, sailor, hup two. Follow the header, hup two. How you been, Maxie, keeping late hours? Charter member of the club. Walking tour of the continent. It's a free country, and a beautiful day. That is, if you're breathing."

The greater Eisenheim's giddy extremity, the more keenly the rest of the group suffered from their lack of multitude. None of them needed the pulsing horde of Alefites or press, but the overnight loss of more than half the original disciples was devastating. A month ago, the presence of Blobel and Clauberg, endlessly discussing finer points of criminal technique, had provided a distraction, and Glucks's scholarship and Langefeld's sophistication a buffer. Now the former Obersturmbannführer dominated the thinned ranks of disciples as arrogantly as he might have a 1940s mess of junior recruits. Even with Celia and Margot and Willy, the band composed a smaller tune than had straggled over the dunes from the wreck of the *Farnhagen* on Day 1 of the new dispensation.

Snakes Hammurabi thought about the difference between marches. Four weeks earlier, the survivors of the disaster at sea had emerged from a physical hardship so brutal they were barely able to perceive the miracles that saved them; the lightning, the walk across the waves. Indeed, it could have been a dream; but then came the wedding party at Kaltenhaven, in

one young journalist's fortuitous presence, and reality immediately intervened. From the moment a couple's bridal canopy collapsed under the
weight of a silo's worth of corn from the blue, they had endured a strange
modern ordeal: trial by celebrity. Now seven men whose deaths in prison,
natural or unnatural, by stroke or a shiv in the dark, wouldn't have created
a hiccup of attention anywhere but potter's field were front-page news,
and Snakes's terror was personal.

"Hup two. Hup two, where are we going, Lithuania? No, the sun is
behind us. Hup two, hup two, Gay Paree? We'll show De Gaulle a thing
or two. What, he's dead? Who killed Mon Général? You?" He gaped at
Bruno, who blushed. "You?" he looked at Max Vetter, who ignored him.
"Well, keep marching. To your left, to your left. We had twelve good men,
but one left, he left . . ."

Like a mosquito distracting a dying man from his cancer, the incessant babble almost made Snakes forget his larger fears.

"Eleven good men, but one left, he left. Ten . . ."

So metronomic was the song that it finally lost all meaning, and
Snakes discovered his own legs moving to the beat. It felt good to be on the
road again, air cleansed by the unseasonal, summery storm of the night before, blossoms of bearded lilies and whistling hydrangeas by the shoulder
glistening, en route to who knew where for the final, most momentous
transfiguration.

Just strolling into the countryside, with the last of Hamburg's mercantile towers receding into the morning mist ten kilometers away, Snakes
felt as bizarrely comfortable as he had a month earlier when the sea had so-
lidified for his benefit. He couldn't say why, but this walk, available as air
in the democratic republic, seemed as miraculous as God's own gift. Was
it possible that human legs, those crude mechanisms, alternately thick or
scrawny, pale, hairy, awkwardly knobbed at the pivot and mapped with
varicose veins, were stronger than gravity, more sensuous than clouds, and
intrinsically capable of superseding all natural or divine phenomena?

"Hup two, hup two. Seven good men, but one left, he left."

Nor was Snakes alone in his nostalgia. Anton's eyes twitched and
Max Vetter gazed across a field of waving, black-tipped tar grass as if expecting to see the surreal image of his dead companions in the distance.
Even Bruno recognized the echoes of the situation, but the shy wrestler was
disturbed rather than pensive and lagged behind the beat. He couldn't shake
off one possibility that none of the others saw in their private reveries.

Finally, unable to contain himself any longer, but not daring to address Ben Alef directly, he blurted, "Couldn't we turn around and, uh, bring them back?"

"Six—" Suddenly Eisenheim stopped counting.

Ben Alef sat on a stump. Five days to go and all the time in the world.

"Good question." Eisenheim clucked, impressed despite himself at the dumb beast's unexpected wisdom. "I'd like to turn around myself, travel in time, bring them back, *all* of them . . . and kill them again, for good this time, and, of course, for evil."

"My, it's hot." Margot sighed, and indolently pushed some air around with a Venetian fan she had picked up in her travels.

"I don't know." Ben Alef reached down to remove a leather sandal and rub his feet.

"Something's wrong with your friend," the Kommandant addressed Snakes. "He doesn't really have a capacity to enjoy himself. Maybe he doesn't like it here."

"He like it any better where you knew him?" Snakes returned.

But Eisenheim was correct. The bland expression that had been on Ben Alef's thin features within the *Farnhagen* remained throughout the entire march to and now from Hamburg. There was life in Him, life that He gave to His followers, but there wasn't any joy. Only life itself, pure and perfect and including a more than passing familiarity with death. That and, apparently, aching feet. He sat on a stump.

Willy Wilk threw himself to the ground, uncapped the scout canteen slung like a bandolier over his shoulder, and splashed its contents across the Messiah's dusty, callused toes.

"Here, let me help." Celia joined the boy. "I know how to give a massage." She began to knead the balls of Ben Alef's feet.

"Thank you," He said. "That feels good."

One by one, the rest of the small crew arranged themselves in a semi-circle around the stump, and one by one they took turns bathing their Lord's feet in holy water except for Eisenheim, who took a swig when the canteen passed his way, and Max Vetter, who shook his head.

Though hardly steeped in Bible studies, Max knew that something was wrong with the picture. Something structural, something basic. Of course. In the Bible, God washed His people's feet. Now the situation was reversed.

"But," Celia answered as if she could read Max's mind, "it's only right that I help Him, because He helped me."

"Me, too," Willy Wilk chimed in.

"Did I?"

"Yes." Max answered his Lord politely but firmly. "We all saw it."

"Then it must be true." Ben Alef nodded to His last disciple's higher wisdom.

"But now . . ." Max hesitated. He didn't wish to be accusatory, but curious. "Now you're not helping." Whether he was referring merely to the Messiah's feet or the load of dead back in Hamburg was unclear.

"Yes."

"Why?" Max choked.

"Mr. Hammurabi knows, don't you?" Eisenheim interrupted the dialogue as the canteen passed to Snakes.

"Yes, Samuel knows," Ben Alef agreed. It seemed as if He would agree to anything any of them said.

Still holding the canteen filled with the fluid he despised, Snakes once again became Ben Alef's interpreter. "Every time a story is told it's different," he explained. The dead schoolteacher, Glucks, might have referred to as variations on a theme. "It plays itself out as the circumstances it takes place within require." As Snakes continued, he felt more and more at ease. Words flowed off his tongue like water over a Niagara, and water, as he idly unscrewed the canteen's metal cap held in place by a short chain of flat oval links, flowed over his hands onto the glistening ridge of Ben Alef's left foot. At first its cool amorphousness shocked Snakes, who had only the night before fled before God's own water, but then, before he could pull his hands away it soothed him, soothed his flesh and his soul and his entire past. Without once mentioning his father or the River Lyons aloud, Snakes forgave the elder Hammurabi for the fear that man had placed in his son's heart like a stone, through his own misguided search for holiness. "If we knew the answer to the question, it wouldn't be worth asking. If we knew the end in advance, it wouldn't be authentic."

So comfortable was Snakes that he didn't mind when Eisenheim tried to confuse the issue and incite jealousy in the others by breaking in: "That's why Mr. Messiah over there chose this dark little brother for his mouthpiece, but do you believe this mumbo-jumbo? No, if you've got a God here, of course He can do whatever He wants. He just doesn't want to.

Either He's no God and you're marching to doom, or He hates you and you're marching to doom—take your pick."

No, the day was beautiful, and their faith secure. Snakes's march-weary feet felt soothed, too, as if Celia's professional fingers had reached sympathetically beneath the leather lip of his shoes and caressed his own perfectly manicured, snipped, emeried, and chamois-buffed extremities. But there was still much to accomplish. Snakes watched the last holy water from the canteen cascade into the earth, and concluded, "We must go on."

Bruno was about to ask another question, but Snakes had said they must go, so go they must. Instead, he looked at his companions around the stump and saw the same uncertainty mixed with confidence he felt. None of them had any idea where they were heading. He stood, wiped his wet hands on his trousers, leaving palm prints the size of a soccer ball, and picked up Margot's suitcase.

Margot lovingly strapped Ben Alef's sandals back onto his painfully roughened but clean feet.

Celia returned the canteen to Willy, who ducked to allow the strap over his small head and blinked quizzically when he felt its weight. He unscrewed the cap and peeked inside, and couldn't help himself. He yelped, "It's full."

Ben Alef shrugged. The Son of . . . Someone . . . never claimed the mantle His followers insisted on laying on His frail shoulders. However reluctantly, He had also made it clear that the dead disciples would not be resurrected, at least not this week, and yet incredible events occurred in His presence. Maybe He didn't make miracles; but nonetheless they happened. Wherever He was going, they were prepared to follow.

Only that morning was peaceful. By noon, when it became obvious that Ben Alef, together with his five remaining disciples and three closest associates had left—or "fled"—Hamburg, leaving five bodies at the Kastrasse for retrieval by the coroner's wagon, the hounds of ink and pixel were back sniffing on the trail. Lesser reportorial mutts remained in the city to follow up on the Night of Conflagration, which might have been juicy enough on a normal news day, but was strictly a sideshow to the main event. The guys with bylines and expense accounts rented every available vehicle in town and caravaned straight ahead on the Messiah beat. They, too, knew the countdown.

The Peddler had been right when he told Eisenheim that Ben Alef's crew would not be difficult to find. Witnessed by an unseasonable crow that flapped enormous black wings with serrated feathers and cawed with delight at its discovery of a crust from a sandwich Anton left next to the stump, neither Snakes nor any of the others realized that the crow had been chased across the waist-high tar grass by two tenth-grade boys on winter vacation. The boys hid behind the supports of a billboard advertising Eurodisney, and rushed home to tell their mothers what they had seen. Word percolated back from Route 17, and, regular as the 12:19 commuter train outbound from Wilhelmy Terminal, Fritz Hofmann and the rest of the press arrived in a mobile jam of media vans and chartered buses.

The vehicles' doors hissed open and spewed journalists. Waving pens, pads, mikes, and cameras, they were as inescapable as a swarm of summer gnats.

"No comment," Snakes cried, even as his mind's eye saw the next day's headline—accompanied by a photograph of a canteen—as clearly as a crow pecking at a crescent of stale pumpernickel.

But the reporters wouldn't stop. Ignoring Snakes, the storm of press descended upon the hapless half-dozen like rats on a wounded kitty. Some went for the head—"Did you see anything?"—and some for the heart—"What did you feel when you first heard the news?"

"What about the murders?"

"Sir, here, for the photogravure!"

"Any ideas who could have done this?"

"Do you think it's a conspiracy?"

"What about the murders?"

"Is that why you left Hamburg?"

"And where are you going?"

"What's this about another miracle, where's the kid with the canteen?"

Fritz Hofmann, unofficial spokesman for the fourth estate, elbowed his way to the front of the cluster. Ever since breaking the story of Ben Alef's tattoo, which led to the Day of the Three Miracles, which led to the Night of Conflagration, Fritz didn't know if he was a reporter or a believer, and every time he contemplated the mass of Alefites, either quietly holding hands at an assembly or fiercely fucking at midnight or raging through the streets, tearing and burning any structure in sight, he half disdained, half envied them. Nonetheless he stifled his conflict and filed his reports, which appeared on page one, above the fold, morning after morning. In the world of ink and pulp, he was a star, so a respectful pause now greeted him as primus inter pares. Yet even as the assembled royal inquisitors parted for the cub majesty, Fritz quivered in the balmy weather, heart fluttering.

Struck dumb, Fritz felt like throwing himself flat at Ben Alef's clean feet, begging the same boon He had given to His followers, begging forgiveness, begging redemption, begging the tattoo that might allow him to forget the sins he and his family had committed in a more naive age before the glimmer or hint of a better world alit on the Baltic shore. Nonetheless he summoned forth one last reserve of neutrality and stammered the exact same question that had already been asked, repeating the old as if it were new. "What about the murders?"

Ben Alef's gaze pierced Fritz's chest like a needle, and then He responded, answering a question with a question, the most astonishing question Fritz could have imagined: "Which murders?"

As if He didn't know that more than half of His disciples had been slaughtered by knife, poison, fire, car, stocking, and frying pan, as if He didn't know the sun came up in the east, as if He didn't know who He was, Ben Alef held Fritz's eyes with the same gaze the former stringer had first witnessed binding together an innocent couple under the canopy at Kaltenhaven, and said, "Tell me."

"I . . . I don't know," Fritz stammered.

Which murders, indeed: the seven disciples or the two hundred victims of the Night of Conflagration or the six million European Jews or the sixty or was it six hundred or more million who had paid the price for some belief that belied their murderers' over the meager several thousand years of human history? As Fritz didn't have the courage to bow, neither did he have the courage to confront the Son of Man he ought to have bowed to with the bad news the journalist and his peers had been slapping on the front page of the *Zeitung* and the *Zeitungs* of the ages, whether print or papyrus or bytes of satellite transmission. He couldn't answer the question.

"We all die."

Was it a voice from the sky? The words floated among them like a slow snow in a lazy storm, like big, wet flakes that fell on one's cheek meltingly evanescent as a kiss. A reporter from America stifled a sob. Did this mean that the Messiah was refusing to accept His place in the divine drama that even the cynical reporters had assigned Him?

Or was He only—only!—referring to Himself? Snakes Hammurabi remembered the words uttered on the doorstep of the seedy bar destined to become a charnel house: "One of you shall betray me."

"You heard Him," Snakes heard himself saying.

"But . . ."

"Enough questions for now. Besides, we have company." Snakes pointed into the visible distance, toward a faint cloud of dust raised by the tramping army of Alefites in pursuit of their Lord.

The parking lot outside the Hamburg Municipal Jail was empty of people, vehicles, and tents, and only the detritus of a week's encampment remained to greet the General, who was used to clarity and cleanliness in every corner of his life. "Look at this filth," Luther Huber muttered angrily to his aide as he strode over the acres of shredded cornhusks and squashed grains of brown rice that speckled the macadam. He threaded a path between heaps of garbage, rain-sodden cardboard, and items of discarded clothing—a scarf like a snake wriggling out from a clogged sewer catch basin, a torn windbreaker, a black T-shirt with Ben Alef's image serenely contemplating the gutter.

He reached the edge of the lot and gazed sadly at the fire-scarred jail, his domain, in ruins. Smashed windows leered at each level like jagged-toothed grins, and a streak of black ran up the façade from the third to the seventh floor. Two policemen stood at the taped-off entrance to the complex guarding . . . what?

All discipline had disappeared from the city over the course of the savior's week-long stay, and a return to order was not going to be simple. After the people had eaten of the tree of desire—or of multiple desires, desire for flesh and desire for faith, neither of which the urban charter could grant—the other human desire, for order, that Luther Huber had based his life upon seemed quaint.

Fortunately, Ben Alef was gone from Hamburg, for good. Huber had received word that his hunter had met his quarry. He had also been the first to hear about the cache of bodies in the Kastrasse, although the initial conversation with the captain at the scene was confusing.

"What other hot tips do you have for me?" Huber barked at the captain. " 'Extra. Extra. Read all about it. 'Columbus Discovers America.' You dolt. We know about them." The General was, of course, referring to the two elderly sex fiends found uncovered with their pants down and long, rigid strands of semen mixed with blood. Huber himself had taken the initial phone call from Max Vetter, which, though frantic, was specific regarding the discovery of *two* bodies. "No doubt what Glucks and Langefeld were doing when they met their unmaker," Huber said. "No particular loss to the world, either."

"I don't mean those, sir," the captain replied. "We have three more."

"What? I mean who?"

"Two more from the *Farnhagen*, Georg Kiehr and Omar Nazzarian, the Arab, and also an old friend of the force."

Huber was in no mood for guessing games. "I said, Who?"

"The last body was identified as one Christian Ruehr, né Chaim Rosenthal, alias the Peddler."

"Oh, shit!" The normally subdued Huber could not restrain himself, then turned professional. "Details."

"In the freezer, all of them, sir. The Peddler, shot, a single bullet to the forehead. Nazzarian apparently bludgeoned with a frying pan. Kiehr . . ."

"What?"

"Well, it's hard to determine the cause of death, sir, because he was cut into pieces. . . ."

Huber remembered the tongue, or about four inches of it, still sitting at the bottom of the dented metal can under his desk. He had assumed it belonged to either Glucks or Langefeld and hadn't imagined more killings. Nice. Really nice. Better than a smoking gun. The man Immaculato and Huber had chosen was perfect for the job, and these little preliminary murders were his way of proving himself—how sweet. But the maniac was so stupid that he didn't realize he had presented Herr Huber with an ancillary gift, to be opened on January 1, the sixth day after Christmas. Huber saw the entire situation, nifty as an Advent calendar, clean as the parking lot used to be.

The moment Eisenheim fulfilled his role, a certain Generalstaatsanwalt's brilliant investigative work might come into play. What might happen if someone, say Huber himself, mopping up after the police, discovered the crucial evidence those slobs had missed, and thus put that ghoul back in *Farnhagen II* for the rest of his unnatural life. Bingo!

No, better yet, the culprit might be shot while attempting to escape, or, best of all, resisting arrest—an entirely likely scenario, resulting in no messy trial. Who could blame a servant of the law for putting down a mad dog? There was nothing the public needed more than a gun-toting order man after the riotousness tolerated—no, encouraged—under the current Chancellor. Of course, the Chancellor had been the one to compel the General to join forces with that strange priest to set Plan B in motion, but the beautiful thing was that Grabner could never admit it and the voters didn't know it. The voters were fed up with Berlin's incompetence at this delicate hour. Come the millennium, it was time to boot out the old. Ring in the new.

"Are you still there, sir?" asked the police captain on the end of the line.

"Yes, yes." Enough delightful anticipation for one day. In the meantime there was the tedium of process to be undergone, mitigated only by the opportunity to meet more press. Yes, he would personally promise a solution within a week. Berlin would call that grandstanding, but Berlin didn't know that he had the proof. First, he had to retrieve the loathsome human morsel from the trash and put it on ice, literally. "Don't anyone touch anything," he commanded the captain. "I'll be right there."

Vaguely, persistently, the procession meandered southwest through Buchholtz, Soltau, and Nienburg, as if they had all the time in the world. Ben Alef led, flanked sometimes by Margot and Celia, the two women in his life, sometimes by Anton and Bruno, sometimes by Snakes and Max Vetter, sometimes by the remorseless gnawing rasp of Dietrich Eisenheim, whom only He could abide, sometimes by reporters. And everywhere they went, new Neue Juden swelled the multiheaded, single-minded creature the group had become. Each night, new converts sneaked out after dusk to celebrate the illicit pleasures of the Alefite flesh, and come the day, they marched, too.

December 27. Twenty-four hours. Forty kilometers.

During the first delirious parade toward Hamburg, each day had brought forth new tests and new anxieties; but now they felt a dizzy sense of infinite possibility everywhere, in Melle, Ibbenbüren, and Münster. Everywhere, people left food along with utensils on their doorsteps, canned goods with can openers and bottles of mineral water and orange juice, and some cooked hearty casseroles of stew and huge cast-iron pots of bean soup, emptying larders and pantries as they had when, fifty-five years earlier, Allied soldiers marched in the opposite direction.

December 28. Twenty-four hours. Eighty kilometers.

Onward they moved from one town into the countryside, into the orbit of another town, through suburbs and out again across the fertile farmland of the north German plain and up into the highlands approaching the urban sprawl between Düsseldorf and Cologne. They passed smokestacks and gray stone factories, each the size of a lesser municipality, and rows of tenements occupied by generations of gray-lunged drones. They crossed the Rhine on a rickety bridge, from underneath which an armada of motorboats waved them forward. The entire country was abuzz with hope, and also with fear of judgment for the excesses of the Night of Conflagration and worse, much worse, and with the frail prayer that remorse and contrition would purify them as the last grain of sand slid down the clean, transparent slope toward the neck of the hourglass, and history abruptly halted.

People of every occupation and class followed, with one exception. Nowhere did they meet any form of authority. In Bergheim and Alsdorf, post offices were closed; in Ubach-Palenberg, school was canceled. Despite the bodies left behind in Hamburg, the only faint whiff of jurisdiction came from the exhaust pipe of a ghostly white limousine that several people claimed to witness skimming the horizon parallel to the procession. Otherwise, not a uniform was in sight, and police stations were as dark as London during the blackout. Perhaps the forces of this-worldly rule were stunned into a narcoleptic, Snow White–like slumber by the approach of the Redeemer whose dominion was heralded only by chaos and death, or maybe they hid in their basements as they had when, fifty-five years earlier, Allied soldiers marched in the opposite direction.

"Come out, come out, wherever you are," Eisenheim taunted his beloved Volk on the afternoon of the twenty-ninth of December as they approached a silent border station from Germany to Belgium near Aachen, free as he hadn't been since long before the *Farnhagen* docked.

"I'm here," Anton Bartsch replied. He stood between Margot and Willy Wilk, eyes unnaturally focused on the mother and child. A tiny kiosk hung with white, triangular flags and bunting that might have been the derelict guards' emblem of goodwill stood beside the raised bar between nations. Standing beneath the bar, on the slim shadow that defined sovereignty, Anton suddenly realized that Ben Alef did have a specific destination in mind.

It was clear because Anton's eyes refocused onto the separate sides of the border. Facing north, his left, westward eye gazed longingly eastward to the country of his own birth and the death of his Lord back in '44 when the factories of the Ruhr worked overtime to produce the ovens that Ben Alef's first body had been tossed into like a log. But Anton's right, eastward eye aimed west, toward Belgium and France, where something momentous was going to occur in forty-eight hours. He calculated with the same crackpot ideology the Neue Juden attached to every incident in Ben Alef's history: if the Messiah had died in Germany and been reborn in France, then Anton himself, born in Germany, could only anticipate his own demise in France. He froze to the spot.

Unafraid in the *Farnhagen*, unafraid through the previous week's murders of most of his peers, the cop killer couldn't bring himself to inch across the line. He knew why the authorities refused to witness the procession of the last few days: because they too, even without the benefit of Dietrich Eisenheim's vicious diatribes, grasped the kernel of truth that underlay the officer's rants: that it was not toward eternal light that the Alefites, who no longer had any choice, marched, but perpetual darkness, and that they might as well have been a parade of skeletons, led by the representative of the six million skeletons that were the final product of their century's labor.

Anton hovered there, until a thin, tapered hand led him to the other side.

On through precious little Belgium on the twenty-ninth. Sky still blue-gray. Temperature still unseasonably warm.

One man of indeterminate age. Four former criminals. Two women, one approximately fifty, the other about twenty. One child, male, weak. Several dozen newspaper and television reporters. Several thousand followers. And a partridge in a pear tree. Fifty kilometers.

Into France on the thirtieth, past another silent border station.

"The last two times this many Germans entered France at once there was hell to pay," Richard Federman said to Fritz Hofmann.

"And one hell of a story," Fritz replied.

"Front page for six years."

"We have two days."

"The world's a shabbier place."

"Unless, of course . . ." Fritz let his last thought go unsaid. Like Anton Bartsch, he had begun to intuit their direction.

Fifty kilometers.

At first the Germanic atmosphere extended across the border, casting a gray penumbra and the guttural accents of its language and the angst of its history onto another nation's soil, but gradually the land became less and less industrial, more and more agricultural. The Alefites passed between terraced hills cluttered with idiosyncratically shaped and ramshackle greenhouses that produced flowers for the daily dinner tables of a more joyous people. At this point, tulip farmers popped their heads out of the greenhouses and waved freely to the procession, and several children on bicycles accompanied them, shouting "Bonjour!"

"Alors!" Willy Wilk yelled back, and nobody even heard the defiant "Heil!" of Eisenheim.

For a moment, they were in an undisturbed, prelapsarian world in which it made perfect sense for a buxom young woman to bound exuberantly down a terrace, pause to brush a few escaped strands of sun-bleached hair under a kerchief, and hand Snakes a bouquet. Then suddenly, inexplicably, just the far side of a massive concrete overpass, everything changed again. The road widened from two empty lanes to six lanes jammed with traffic. The young woman returned to her greenhouse, the bicycles peeled off, and a thousand station wagons and minivans crammed with screaming offspring curved off an exit ramp into a district whose entire raison d'être appeared to be the headlong pursuit of a particularly modern form of "fun."

These people had planned their vacations months in advance, but their timing could not have been more superlative. They gaped at the procession as they slowed down on their way to celebrate the last night of the millennium in one of a score of enormous hotels that sprouted like steel-and-glass mushrooms on the horizon, huge sprawling installations constructed in the last decade by multinational corporations, their neon logos brilliantly ablaze in the daylight. No need for names: the S, the H, the orange, ersatz-tiled roof were as familiar as a hammer and sickle in Communist Russia.

Family farms immediately gave way to multiplex movie theaters and fast-food concessions and shopping centers advertising international name brands from Makita to Norsk to Ralph Lauren to Lord Jolly's Bun Corner. Billboards advertised a sporting complex complete with roller rink, batting cage, basketball courts, skateboard ramps, artificial rock-climbing cliffs, and a virtual Grand Prix. The road widened again, from six to eight lanes, divided by a median containing pine trees of uniform height and uniform width and set in a line so straight they must have been planted by a surveyor instead of a landscaper. With cars turning in the entrance to one mall and turning out the next exit, backing up on the shoulders, and crossing the highway at every designated intersection, the median was the only place to walk.

"Look!" Bruno shouted with glee, and pointed at a miniature golf course sporting elaborate hazards along its Astroturfed greens: sand pits, moving streams, and windmills the size of giants, their blades slowly turning and glinting in the late-millennium sun.

Kilometer by kilometer, the commercial agglomeration grew denser and denser until one could hardly imagine any form of humanly devised entertainment not represented a dozen times over on the stretch of Route 7. Finally, Ben Alef declared, "There."

Hemmed in by a regional mall to the left and a trapezoidal blue-glass office building to the right, set back from the highway, a modest two-story box stood shaded by a single chestnut tree of enormous dimensions. A leftover, forgotten during the region's massive transformation to late-twentieth-century leisure society, the building's dun stucco façade broken by narrow, lead-paned windows flanked by slanted shutters reminded Bruno of his days at La Petite Ecole. But this was no school, nor did it still serve as the bourgeois farmhouse it must once have been. Removed in time from their surroundings, the building's owners made one pathetic attempt to concede to modernity: at the entrance to their graveled drive hung a rusted metal sign that read "Vacancy."

"Vacancies" was more likely, since, aside from an arrogantly angled white limousine, the only vehicle in the circular drive under the chestnut tree was an incapacitated Mercedes on cinder blocks. Unless swarms of more prosperous guests had temporarily departed to enjoy the multiple attractions of the region, the inn probably had the only vacancy within a ten-kilometer radius from the center of the vicious pond that had to be Ben Alef's destination.

Yes, by now most of the surviving disciples and the press and the Alefites realized where they would arrive come the morrow. Unless another miracle intervened and they were all transported to Jerusalem or the North Pole, only one landmark lay ahead. And yes, even the bucolic former farmhouse's paneled front door was indelibly marred with its image. There, painted or pasted beneath a translucent fanlight, lay the familiar black silhouette composed of three circles, a larger one in the center and two smaller ones overlapping it left and right at the top, like a pair of three-quarter moons partially obscured by a planet, or ears.

Chapter Twenty-three

THE SILHOUETTE SWUNG WIDE, revealing a musty interior of heavy black walnut and quarter oak furniture, an oversized rocking chair and couch with faded purple damask cushions lit by a standing lamp with a yellow parchment shade. Nothing in the room appeared to have been touched for ages, except the proprietor, a spry elderly man with a grizzle of white hair cut to equal length over his chin, upper lip, and head, so he looked like a desiccated albino peach. Behind him, peeking over his slumped shoulder, stood an elderly woman, her own white hair tied in a bun behind her wrinkled face. She dressed rather like Margot, Mother of God, in a scoop-necked peasant blouse and long, pleated peasant skirt that came down to a pair of tiny feet clad in black leather ballet slippers. Unlike Margot, however, whose hippie-dippie garb had been out of style when she first adopted it back in the late 1960s, this elfin old lady wore the antiquated clothes as if she had been born in them. She leaned over, cupped her frail right hand to her mouth and whispered into the old man's ear, "Who is it, Dodie?"

"No one," he rasped while his own keener eyes scanned the half-dozen faces in the front of the crowd and the endless mass of Neue Juden beyond, some carrying banners aloft with bright yellow and blue six-pointed stars. He started to close the door.

"I can hear something, Dodie," the old lady whimpered.

"She's blind," whispered Anton, always aware of flaws of the eyes.

"Wait here, and I will check," the old man said as he stepped forward and shut the door behind him, the black ears of the silhouette poking up over his own semi-shaven scalp.

"Please go away. My wife is very . . . sensitive."

"Yes." Dietrich Eisenheim practically clicked his heels, absolutely obedient as none of the disciples had ever seen him before. "Yes," he repeated, his entire face bathed in the light from the old man's countenance, eyes aglow with the bliss of a cow in a pasture or the Neue Juden assembled at the feet of their divine master.

"But we need a place to stay," Snakes insisted. "At least, our"—he looked at Ben Alef—"friend does. The rest of us can sleep outside, but He's exhausted. We must have a room."

"Damn *Him*," Eisenheim hissed, "this man also needs peace for once in his life. Can't you leave *him* alone?"

Snakes looked quizzically at the Kommandant, and then back at the shabby proprietor, who nodded at Eisenheim's plea, as if he expected no less. But just as Snakes was about to pursue his curiosity or his demand on Ben Alef's behalf, the door opened again.

A tall, elegantly garbed young man with jet-black hair stood on the threshold.

"You!" Dietrich Eisenheim's eyes nearly popped out of his head.

"Shah," the proprietor commanded.

Snakes looked back and forth. Multiple forms of communication were going on here.

"Come in," the man said easily. Surely this was not the older couple's son; his accent and complexion were southern, theirs Teuton. Snakes glanced toward the sleek white car in the yard. The young man continued, "I've explained the situation and made reservations for a party of seven." He might have been the doorman at a fancy club, lifting the velvet rope for VIPs.

"But what about my people?" Ben Alef gestured to the multitude of Alefites making their way off the highway and down the long, derelict drive.

"You need it more than they do," Snakes implored.

"Come in." Max Vetter gently guided Ben Alef's arm. "They won't mind. They've spent the last month out in the open, and from what I hear, they like it." He blushed at his own reference to the Alefites' activities among themselves. "Also, I'm sure that no one would have it any other way."

"Do you think they're hungry?"

"There are abundant places to eat along the highway," the man in the door said. "And I've ordered in for supper."

. . .

"May I use the, um, facilities?" Fritz Hofmann asked, needing the privacy to take notes.

"Surely," the suddenly polite proprietor replied, and led Fritz down a dim hallway, decorated with faded prints of hound dogs and men with shotguns cradled in their arms, to a W.C. that contained a toilet, a crazed porcelain washstand, and a brass rack hung with towels bearing the red-stamped initial "B."

One framed photograph over the bowl hinted at the meaning of the "B." In it, a young woman wearing a low-cut peasant blouse cavorted on a balustraded terrace with a range of hills in the background. She must have been in motion when the camera snapped, dancing or playfully pirouetting in the spirit of the moment, because her blond and gaily ribboned pigtails were flung out from her head, parallel to the ground. Beside her, a familiar man in a uniform was caught mid-clap.

"This is very nice," Ben Alef said of the dingy, countrified hovel. But His only known prior residences were the prison ship *Farnhagen* and the camp at Bergen-Belsen, neither of which was famous for comfort or hygiene.

Max and Snakes accompanied Ben Alef to His room, while Father Immaculato escorted the women and Willy Wilk and two of the other three disciples. "Are you coming?" he asked a laggardly Dietrich Eisenheim.

"No, no thank you," the shockingly mild and polite Kommandant replied. He wished to remain downstairs with the proprietor and his wife, to see if they needed any help in setting up a table for dinner.

It was the attic, where dinner was served, that the survivors recalled. The room sat above the parlor, under the dormered roof, reachable only through a narrow opening in the kitchen that looked more like a broom closet than a door. Fitted with a false back, its shelving crammed with string, rubber bands, household cleansers, lightbulbs, batteries, and insect repellent, the closet led to a ladderlike staircase up to a hidden space seven meters long, three wide, containing nothing but one long, planked pine farm table, a sideboard, and chairs.

An attempt had been made to clean the room during the afternoon, and damp spots from a hasty mopping still glistened in spots where the beams had sunk and floorboards dipped to produce minor ponds, like the drain on the *Farnhagen,* but dust balls remained in the corners and a spider-web where the ceiling met the wall. The space felt less like a dining room than a secret shrine, into which the visitors ascended one by one by way of the steep, banisterless staircase. "Oh my!" Bruno gasped.

"What?" Anton demanded.

"It's just, just that I thought I'd been here before." Bruno's knuckles almost started to bleed in sympathetic recollection of a faded print of a famous painting he had seen in Monsieur LeClerc's class.

"Sit down, please," Father Immaculato encouraged the shaken wrestler.

By common consent, a place was left in the center of the table for Ben Alef, and the rest arrayed themselves accordingly. Snakes and Max Vetter, the voice from inside and the first witness from outside, sat beside their Lord, Bruno and Anton together on the left, Margot and Celia and Willy Wilk across from Ben Alef, Father Immaculato, the unofficial host, nearest the trap door where the stairs emerged, and, at the far end, the proprietor of the inn stuck in time and his wife and Dietrich Eisenheim, who hovered beside the only man in the room older than himself the way the rest attached themselves to Ben Alef.

An ethereal tintinnabulation filled the room, and Snakes looked around for the source. It was the old lady, standing, not much taller than the table, shoulders hunched, no longer capable of dance, rapping an empty goblet with a spoon. When she had everyone's attention, she announced, "Dodie will speak."

The proprietor stood, shrunken and diminished from whatever stature he once had occupied, yet imperial still, master of this minor domain. "Welcome." His voice quavered. "I apologize for my earlier inhospitality, but we're not really used to strangers, haven't had any visitors for a long time. How long, Evie?"

"Many years."

"I said, 'How many?' " He was used to speaking with authority.

Snakes imagined the old man out on the rusty ornamental *Romeo and Juliet* balcony of the farmhouse addressing the horde of strangers who filled every inch of his yard—but the only citizen currently under his rule was his tiny, blind wife. And maybe, strangely, Dietrich Eisenheim.

"I believe the doctor was our last guest, and he must have gone abroad in '52 or '53."

"Which?"

"Nineteen fifty-three."

Satisfied, Dodie continued, "A long time, in any case. But the house was busy, attachés coming and going, reports from the front. No, that's not what I mean. That was the early days. At Berchtesgaden. Later, when we moved here, after . . . it was just old friends remembering the good times. Surely you can understand that. Why, I recall . . ."

"Long time, Dodie." Evie interrupted, with caution.

"Hmm. Quite right. No need to bore our new guests with old stories." But Snakes could tell from Dodie's fond expression that he was deep inside those untold stories, and that, like the Peddler on rare occasions, the proprietor lived partially in the past. Snakes might have thought that the old man lived entirely in the past, if he hadn't suddenly awakened to the moment and asked, "And where have you come from?"

"Hamburg," Bruno answered.

"A good, strong city. The rock of the north, we used to call it. Ruined by the new government, but aren't they all? Evie?"

"Yes, Dodie."

"Sometimes I read the newspapers, and I don't like what I read. Terrible trials."

The old man collapsed into his seat.

Eisenheim was up in a second.

But Dodie lifted his head again, as if he had died and returned.

"I didn't come from Hamburg," Ben Alef said.

The disciples, momentarily mesmerized by the old man's display, turned back to their Lord.

"Where did you come from?" Evie, the good hostess, asked, as if nothing was wrong and she was filling out a sheet at the concierge's desk in the lobby.

"I came from God."

Father Immaculato stiffened, but Evie chatted away as convivially as if the Messiah had said He'd just spent a week at the Sad Baden Spa. "Oh, how nice."

But none of the disciples moved. They heard every word of Ben Alef's pronouncement, and even Bruno understood the complication there. The key was in the grammar, in the ostensibly least important word of the sentence, the locational preposition "from." In this, maybe his first outright statement of divine origin, Ben Alef did not claim that He was God. No, according to His own words, He came *from* God. He might be the Son of

God, or God's messenger, but the form of the sentence distinguished Him *from* the Other.

From.

Beyond identification, that simple word evoked another question, one of motivation. Think of the disciples; they came from Hamburg and escaped from the *Farnhagen*. Perhaps Ben Alef was a runaway *from* the heavenly house. Indeed, perhaps He had escaped before, but the Romans caught Him and crucified Him; escaped again, but the Germans caught Him, gassed Him, burned Him. In fact, this meant that centurions and storm troopers—and probably Tartar warriors and Conquistadors and Cossacks and British majors on the Indian subcontinent, and American soldiers in Colorado, too—were God's troops, sent out to retrieve the wayward boy before He could fulfill the mission which His Dad, master of all but His rebellious scion, did not approve.

"Don't we all?" Dodie's eyes glittered with understanding shading to sadness. He had served God once this century, had done so with enthusiasm and the passion of a lifetime, but, alas, he was too old, too worn, to be enlisted once again in the divine chase for the dangerous offspring who refused to stay dead.

"Jews do," Snakes said.

It was the first time the "J" word had entered the house, and Eisenheim twitched as if a needle had just struck a nerve in his neck.

But if the Kommandant had been able to maintain his passion—or unable to relinquish it—over his decades in the *Farnhagen*, the proprietor could not. For him, isolation bred resignation. "Yes," the latter sighed. "They are adaptable."

Credit having been given where it was due, the conversation turned to the people of eternal exile. Anton recalled a Jewish lawyer and Bruno remembered Genser the wrestling impresario and even Snakes described one raucous party that spanned several days until the Peddler cut it short because that particular sundown ushered in Yom Kippur. Only Ben Alef, whose body displayed the sign of the covenant from eight days after His first birth, did not participate.

Father Immaculato uncorked a bottle of wine. Something about his role as steward irked him as he leaned over each person at the table, poured, moved a foot to his left, and poured again, but he used those moments of physical closeness to try to understand what had brought these people together. It was not only Ben Alef but the deep need they had felt for a Ben Alef before they met Him. Over the chess table in Vatican City, Urban IX had taught Immaculato that to understand was to conquer.

Most of the diners had already been given whatever they needed: Margot her lost child, Willy Wilk his own miracle, Max Vetter a vision, Eisenheim the final, grand hatred of his hate-filled existence. At this juncture it was Anton, oddly, who seemed most needy, least satisfied. His eyes were like pinballs in a penny arcade machine, jumping wildly off the human bumpers to his left and right. Before anyone could ask him, he asked them, "You know what I want?"

"What?" the Father, in his confessional mode, replied.

"To see straight."

"You mean to see the truth?" asked Bruno, who often confounded the literal and the metaphorical, though usually in the opposite direction.

"No," Anton corrected with rare gentleness. "I mean to see straight, for once in my life. If that's the truth, then good, but mostly I'd just like to be able to see what everyone else sees. I asked a doctor once, but I didn't have the money for the surgery, and that was a long time ago."

"That's all you want?" Ben Alef spoke again, smiling at a request so simple it could be granted as easily as dropping a coin in a beggar's cup.

"Yes."

"Okay."

Anton blinked, and in the fraction of a second in which his eyelids descended, he felt the orbs beneath the fleshy curtain pop out of the warp they had been locked in since his birth. For a moment he was disoriented. But then he understood that the lank Son of Man he had abused in Cell #306 had truly forgiven him personally; then he opened his eyes, expecting to behold the blazing vision.

Yet each story was different. Sometimes He was born in Bethlehem, sometimes Paris. Sometimes He washed the people's feet; sometimes they washed His. Maybe this time the Lord would betray the disciples, or at least Anton Bartsch, whose need seemed so modest after everything that preceded it and was nonetheless denied. Anton's warped vision remained unchanged.

"You, you didn't do anything," Anton cried like the child he had been before he discovered how to fight. He rose awkwardly, staggered across the floor as if he were as blind as Evie, and hurled himself down the steep staircase two or three risers at a time, nearly knocking over a hesitant delivery boy coming up.

Suddenly the line that had never fully left Snakes's consciousness came back to him: "One of you will betray me."

"Like I said, blackness thou art and blackness thou shalt remain," Eisenheim crowed.

The delivery boy announced, "Pizza's here!"

"I ordered plain, pepperoni, and an onion-and-pepper combination for the vegetarians." Father Immaculato extracted a plain slice for himself from one of the three shallow cardboard boxes, while trying to avoid noticing that the wine in his glass had been mysteriously replenished; someone else must have poured while he paid the kid from Domino's.

The Father had deliberately chosen the most ludicrous possible menu to undermine any attempts at retroactive sanctification by the Neue Juden after Dietrich Eisenheim fulfilled his mission. The deal struck back in Wannsee was that Luther Huber and the forces of law would seek and destroy all messianic nonsense in the secular world, while the power of Rome and Jerusalem together would repudiate heresy from within the church bunker. Last Supper, indeed: takeout pizza. Try Leonardo on that! "There's also chips and soda," he added.

Nonetheless, the Father's first face-to-face encounter with Ben Alef was trying. This fraud whose meanderings he had tracked at a safe distance, whose alleged miracles he derided as cheap parlor tricks, was nothing like what he had expected. Ben Alef did not seem to care if He was the Messiah—which could have been the most deviously convincing sham of all, but wasn't. Immaculato felt as if he were on the edge of a precipice, dizzy and tempted to leap. Given, gifted with, granted, or grabbing an ounce more faith, he could step off the precipice and float. Disturbingly, it was this precise yearning that initially led him to the church. So if this was what he and Urban and the College of Cardinals and all good, God-fearing people across the globe were waiting for, why couldn't they just admit it and rejoice?

Because it was false, he silently catechized, sipping at the wine, which infuriatingly stayed at the same height in his goblet.

Because he lived in the real world while awaiting the ideal.

Father Immaculato tried to make himself believe his rational, Jesuit-ical logic as the rest of the people at the table partook of his junk food, joke food, as solemnly as if celebrating mass. "How do we know God?" he asked before he knew what he was saying. The last thing he wanted was to enter into a theological discussion here, but the question just blurted out, and the door was open.

Willy Wilk raised his hand as if he were in school. "Miracles."

Well, corn from the skies and disappearing tattoos and reappearing water or wine were persuasive evidence for a lay audience, but, like most other myths and mysteries, easily debunkable by experts. Think of locked-room puzzlers like "The Speckled Band." With a little imagination, the impossible became obvious. Several years earlier, researchers provided plausible geological and biological scenarios for the Ten Plagues of the Bible: algae turning the Red Sea red; the algae leading to insect infestation; the infestation to disease, straight on to the slaying of the firstborn, which was probably just exaggeration or poetic license. Couldn't this whole sea-son's mania be an illusion, smoke and mirrors enough to fool anyone?

"Besides," Snakes said, more to himself than to Willy, "what isn't a miracle? Take the telephone. You speak into a piece of plastic, wires carry your voice, and it comes out next door or a thousand kilometers away; that's pretty miraculous. Or an electric lightbulb. Flick a switch and . . . let there be light. I don't have the faintest idea how that works. Or gravity, why when I let go of"—he fumbled in his breast pocket—"this pencil"—it dropped to the table—"does it fall? It makes more sense to me for it to stay put, but there's gravity, and that's a miracle too. As far as I'm concerned, I don't understand anything, and the whole world is a miracle."

"Nice," Ben Alef agreed. He didn't understand anything, either.

No, miracles were not sufficient proof. Besides, the disciples had al-ready learned that inner transformations were far more fantastic than trans-mutation of matter. Magic tricks were only the tip of the divine iceberg that allowed flawed, skeptical beings to accept the transcendence of everyday life.

"Yes, Willy." Snakes nodded. "But there's also a change in ourselves. We know Him when we see the divinity within."

The boy picked at a strand of melted cheese in the box of pepperoni pizza.

"Ask Anton Bartsch." Eisenheim took the floor, revivified in this house of amber. "If he could see straight, he'd see the divinity within; that's what allows us to kill, to rape, and to burn."

"Don't scare the child," Margot reprimanded him.

"Pardon, but Herr Bartsch wanted the truth."

"I didn't say that divinity meant that everything was good." Snakes took on the objection. "God teaches us that it's our decision whether to do good or evil."

"So God is the snake in the Garden of Eden. Unless, of course, *you* are . . . Samuel." Eisenheim stared directly at Hammurabi.

Snakes ignored the bait. "He allows us to make our own mistakes. He tolerates human freedom, but then He redeems."

"But first He kills." Eisenheim reiterated. "That's where He starts. He struck down Moses, His prophet in the wilderness; He nailed Jesus to the cross."

Bruno cringed under the onslaught of Eisenheim's relentless logic.

"Look what He did to . . ." Eisenheim halted and reached out to cut the old man's slice of onion-and-pepper pizza into bite-sized chunks small enough for his shrunken gums to chew.

"How do you know this?" Dodie suddenly asked.

"What?"

"You heard me," the proprietor repeated with an ominous echo, the timber of yore rolling up his corded throat. "How do you know this?" German soldiers were not encouraged to quote scripture, because—contrary to the Kommandant's elegant use of Holy Writ—most were tainted and turned sentimental by the ancient documents. No, their Bible was written in a Munich beer hall. But then, perhaps thinking of those grand beer-hall days, the ferocious old man turned sentimental. "Besides," he said, "why can't we forgive them? Yes, that never occurred to me before. If we forgive the Jews who have held their silly grudge for all these years, then we show that we are truly superior to them."

Stunned, Eisenheim didn't have a chance to answer, and gave silent thanks when Father Immaculato, now immersed, pursued the theological questing he had begun. "Well, it certainly happened that way the first time. . . ." He stopped, because his own grammar had implied a second time, which, yes, was supposed to occur, but not this way, not in this place.

"That's it." Snakes jumped in. "All stories are different the second time." Variations on a theme had become his message to the tribe. The narrator had grown infatuated with the idea of narrative, and had forgotten the plot. They couldn't expect a duplication of a two-thousand-year-old story; to be authentic *now* it had be rewritten in the modern vernacular.

"Once more, with feeling!" Eisenheim cried.

And to himself, Father Immaculato couldn't help but feel his plans crumbling. Once more, with pizza?

"We—" Snakes continued.

"And who are we?" the old man asked.

"It's obvious." Eisenheim, back to his old self, bowed, honored to repeat the twentieth-century catechism to the man who wrote it. "We are the people who betray God."

Max Vetter gagged on his pizza and coughed up a chunk of crust.

Snakes recalled Ben Alef's words to Asher Rose. Denied by the Jew— "*You* are no God!"—the Jewish Messiah had looked down upon his denier's expiring shell and begged forgiveness. Yet less than an hour later, He had told Snakes and Max, "One of you will betray me." Perhaps He was confused, and mixed up his clear and public betrayer with his closest disciples.

"And"—Dodie followed his line of thought—"how do we know God?"

Eisenheim looked around the table at the company and grinned. "Do all of you want to know that, too?"

They couldn't help themselves. They wanted to know. Whatever lack of empathy for anything outside themselves had led to their various criminal careers, they had—through Ben Alef—discovered curiosity.

"You sure?" Eisenheim teased.

"Tell us, you bastard."

"Well you know how we really, really, really know God? It's the deepest secret of all. Only one other person knew this, and now he's dead." He referred obliquely to Asher Rose. Then he leaned forward and whispered, "We know Him when we kill Him."

Champagne corks popped and fireworks burst in the midnight sky from the international date line eastward, a chain reaction linking Tokyo, Shanghai, Bombay, even sullen Baghdad, then pell-mell, modernizing Moscow, and traveling with the moon into Europe in secular concord based on a single, historically inaccurate date with religious implications. Only the Alefites— those at the inn, those left in Hamburg, and those gathered in almost every major city in the world—waited to go beyond the happy hysteria that exploded when the silver ball dropped in the capital of the twentieth century, Times Square, New York.

"A New Beginning or The End?" Fritz Hofmann typed by flashlight in a small niche he had claimed under the eaves of Dodie's inn. "As people the globe over wildly celebrated the arrival of mankind's third millennium, followers of Ben Alef, whom they believe to be the Messiah, rested comfortably outside this modest French farmhouse. These 'New Jews' sang hymns of praise on the eve of the day in which their savior's mission must finally prove true or false. Inside the dwelling, Mr. Alef and His closest associates remained incommunicado. . . ."

Fritz read over his copy and pressed a button to zap it off to the press by cellular modem, just as Anton Bartsch tottered onto the crumbling stoop. The Alefites occupied the patch of parched land in front of Dodie's inn as completely as a pond its bed. Every available inch was filled with sleeping bags and small fires over which the faithful roasted the ears of corn they had carried all the way from Hamburg in sympathetic communion with the supper occurring in the hidden room at the top of the hidden ladder. A few children skipped back and forth, tripping over their elders, trying to catch fireflies that flickered on and off like tiny, mobile, close, and benign stars, while the glow of house-sized neon signs and the mechanical rumble of traffic filtered in from the distant entertainment complex along Route 7 where more dozens of thousands of people celebrated the last tick of the clock.

"Herr Bartsch. Herr Bartsch!" Fritz called, again the first reporter on the story. "Can you tell me what's happening inside?"

The familiar crossed eyes twitched in their sockets, and Bartsch tried to look at his questioner. "What?"

"Say, are you all right?"

"All right?" repeated the man who had looked a policeman in the face and cold-bloodedly pulled the trigger. For half a second, when his eyes were closed amid the scent of pizza and the gurgle of wine, he had thought he was all right for the first time in his life, but he had been wrong. "No," he said, and before Fritz could offer to help him, turned around and slammed the door.

Anton no longer had any faith in the future. Like a bank robber whose only chance of escape was murder, like a prisoner condemned to a sentence without parole, he woke from a dream of salvation to discover himself back in the present. Betrayed for the last time, he determined to set the record straight if he couldn't see straight. No use pretending he was anything but what he was. A stone killer born and bred, with only one talent and one destiny he could honestly fulfill, Anton found his way to his room to detail plans of revenge.

But there, lying rigid as a corpse on the single bed that hadn't seen an occupant for half a century, head propped on the pillow that hadn't known a scalp for half a century, eyes closed in the midst of fantasies of flowing blood, he fell asleep, crying. Unaffected by rains, showers, springs, founts, freshets, and oceans, Anton Bartsch, cop killer, was blinded by an unstoppable torrent of waters from within which, though he couldn't know it, healed him.

Cheeks glistening with the salty liquid that seeped out from under his lids to dampen his pillow, Anton dreamed multiple scenes of mayhem from the early, vicious playgrounds of his youth to the Düsseldorf branch of Deutsche Bank, and everywhere he saw eyes. Eyes, everywhere eyes—the shocked eyes of a six-year-old child whom the five-year-old Anton pushed off the top strut of a jungle gym, tumbling out into space, and the fear in the eyes of a guard who had stupidly stepped on the bank's alarm button.

"I can't fucking believe you did that!" Anton said as he put his gun's barrel to the man's face.

The child landed flat on his back on the macadam with a heavy thunk, and his eyes closed.

It wasn't the danger the guard's move put Anton in that infuriated the robber, but the clarity of that guard's eyes, wide and blue and true as a straight line, that made him pull the trigger.

Then he was in the *Farnhagen*, on a night that never occurred, lying in his corner bunk, eyes closed, crying. Still, he could sense the presence of the strange and silent prisoner from the center bunk nearest the latrine hovering above him. He turned over in his sleep, murmured, "Keep away," and in his dream he turned over in his sleep and murmured, "Keep away." But the presence remained and he turned face up again, in his dream and in his sleep.

The Ben Alef figure leaned over, extended two fingers of his right hand in the gesture of a peace sign, and touched Anton's eyes. A cymbal crash of thunder and a bright flash of lightning. Anton blinked and woke for real, and looked straight—straight! straight!—into the eyes of a man standing above him.

Anton's mouth was filled with a cool, rigid object, not the penile tissue of jailhouse rapes—shit, man, the king of Cell #306 had been the rapist, never the rapee. No, the thing was steel, and the last time he had felt an object like that it had been in his hands, not his mouth.

Was he still dreaming? Would the next scene take place back in the bank, the dead cop sprawled on the floor, eyes closed?

Or was he one step further removed, dreaming back in the *Farnhagen*, in a safe, secure, floating cell, and had the last month been but a nocturnal journey building to this strange culmination?

No, Anton knew the difference between a dream and reality. He was definitely conscious now, lying in a bed in a farmhouse, and a person he recognized stood above him, pushing a gun into his mouth—loaded, no doubt—in his mouth. Yet above all, he knew that he could see this man and this gun in this room exactly the same way anyone else could, which was all he ever really wanted. If Ben Alef in the flesh had refused him, Ben Alef's touch in a dream had finally straightened Anton's eyes in one last miracle.

Used to turning right to look left, and vice versa, he stared in the wrong direction at first and then focused directly ahead. And then the tears of sorrow for himself ceased and new tears of gratitude cascaded out from his furiously blinking eyes. Even with the weapon in his mouth, the transformed killer gave thanks and garbled out a gleeful "I want to, I have to, see . . . everything . . ."

The last thing he saw, straight as an arrow, was a finger pulling the trigger.

Dear Frieda,

Almost nobody heard the shot amid the racket from the highway, New Year's, cars honking, a universal shouting that even affected some of the Alefites. We have lost another disciple. Anton, whom Snakes tells me was the leader in the cell, was the eighth to go, an ugly, bloody scene. Perhaps the pause over the last few days in transit made us relax. Now there is no doubt that the murderer is among us. There is also hardly any doubt who he is. But as long as Ben Alef accepts him into our midst, everyone else's hands are tied. Four disciples remain, and I am not at all certain that all of us shall make it the last hours and the last kilometers down the road to the final event. The boy, Willy, named I suppose for our great Kaiser of yore, and Celia and Margot are safe, I think, unless they get in the way. As for the rest of the disciples, we must believe that this is not Russian roulette; death cannot be random; it is in accordance with a plan. Do not worry for me, however; I go where I must.

Complicated, complicated, my darling sister. Currents so dense and so dark that I cannot begin to comprehend them. Every situation implies its opposite; every sentence uttered is a paradox.

For perhaps the last time, let me try to lay out the facts as this weak, human fisherman's mind understands them:

Ben Alef is the Messiah.
He is a Jew.
We killed the Jews.
He has come to redeem us.

At first, I might have asked how, but that is only idle curiosity; it shall be revealed. That is His question to answer as He will. Yet His answer requires a response. Remember, we are not not talking about the Lord at the creation, when all was void. Ben Alef has not merely come; He has come to *us*. We have a role in this drama. Not to be vain, but not to be naive either, I have a role, but I have not been given a script. And I am not an improviser by nature. I am standing on the great stage, blinded by the lights. What experience do I have? I took my boat out of the same harbor into the same waters every day for decades. I hauled my catch to the same market every afternoon. I caulked and sanded and repainted every season. I learned my job, but I did not invent it. Now, I have the most important job of my life, and I must invent it.

Luckily, Snakes is working with me to assure that everything will occur as it must, but even he is fearfully uneasy. This is bad, because we have all come to rely upon him. Not only as Ben Alef's interpreter, but as the only one who can contend with Eisenheim. And now, somehow, the demented one has gotten to him through something that happened at supper—not the *last* supper; Snakes says that every story is different. Try as hard as I can, I cannot help pondering the conundrum myself.

Dawn, I'm in a fever, been scribbling all night, and could use a shot of schnapps. I still know nothing and the sun doesn't look any different; it still rises in the east. Yet sometime today, the impossible shall occur. And I know where. The evidence is clear. The trajectory of our path, speed, direction—it doesn't take a Jew to figure out—is impossible to ignore. If miracles can happen, this must be the new Jerusalem, the setting for the story this time around, the necessary fable for our time.

The Alefites are stirring—how did they sleep? A police unit has come to examine Anton's body, but they dare not interrogate the suspects. Getting ready to march. The route blocked off and flag-marked. The ranks arrayed. I will attempt to write the final chapter on the road. There will be an answer. On to Calvary.

I am a good German.

Max

Book X
Dominion

Chapter Twenty-four

APINNACLE PIERCED THE SKY. A thin, stainless needle jabbing up over the horizon. And immediately, at that precise second, the crass hubbub of Route 7 ceased, as if an invisible boundary had been crossed.

Behind the ragtag army of the saved lay the hotels, motels, movie theaters, sporting complexes, and shopping centers that battled for the billion-dollar scraps beneath the table of the Enchantment Empire.

Ahead lay a vast meadow shaven to a military crew. Even the roads changed here, into baby-flesh-smooth ribbons of concrete. Tended by a power superior to the antiquated nation's, they efficiently funneled all the cars that had jammed the vicinity beyond the boundary into vast parking lots that made the urban macadam outside the Hamburg jail look as pocked and pathetic as a teenager's complexion.

A snub-nosed bullet train whisked past on unseen rails to deposit more people at a gleaming, modern station. So clear was the hundred-meter glass vault over the station that it had had to be etched at frequent intervals to keep pedestrians from walking into its panes and hurting themselves. And the pattern etched into the glass, meter after meter, endlessly self-replicating, was identical to the pattern on the door of the farmhouse the messianic contingent had just left: three overlapping circles.

The same three circles appeared beneath the apex of this new world they approached, but the abstract pattern was three-dimensional here, a black spherical head, from which extended two smaller, black, and spherical ears, the unmistakable icon of the ultimate mouse, regnant.

Bruno sighed. "I've always dreamed of this."

Willy Wilk gaped. He knew he was on a delegation of cosmic urgency, and he was duly amazed by the miracles in which he participated, but the pastel-colored castle that seemed to grow down from the sky with every step he took took his breath away.

Here was heaven, or perhaps Oz, the shining city in the distance, across the grass that sparkled as if minuscule mirrors had been affixed to the individual blades to catch the morning rays of midwinter sun. The very sun seemed to beam on command from the mouse head, which wore a delicate spike—like a Prussian war helmet.

Dream land, candy land, the residence of the modern imagination: turrets and towers of pink and pale yellow, designed and crafted with every iota of art and skill available to man—the Sphinx, Chartres, the Taj Mahal, and Angkor Wat had nothing on this—the castle and its city sprawled forth as the marchers crested a gentle knoll to behold it. The castle ruled amid perfect streets lined with perfectly deciduous trees that gave off an aroma of sugar, and perfectly contoured lakes and pools of perfectly blue water that emitted their own misty froth.

Some of the village surrounding the castle echoed images they had seen before: gingerbread cottages with gables and porches out of an ideal American past that must have been ferried intact across the Atlantic to conquer the Old World, and then a Middle Eastern bazaar, all intricately patterned arches, dense, even at a distance, with arabesques as a Persian carpet. And wasn't that a Persian carpet, hovering . . .

A roller coaster shot out of the mouth of a tunnel and spiraled down from the peak of an artificial mountain, trailing the shrieks of delighted children.

Dramatic variations of landscape and architecture and character occurred in incestuous proximity throughout the realm: a cowboy in a ten-gallon hat and an astronaut in a silver helmet walked in identical strides on opposite sides of a brick wall, while glistening banana-tree fronds cast shadows on a superfuturistic submarine set to plunge into and explore the depths of an artificial lagoon.

Only two features united every section, niche, and centimeter of the empire. First, the relentless perfection. Not a tile was out of place, not a smudge or speck of dust allowed to mar the pristine, multicultural surface. Every night the streets were steam cleaned, and every day a regiment of inconspicuous "helpers" fanned out to buff the marble, burnish the brass, tend the tens of thousands of flowers, and sweep away the detritus the public had left behind. Snakes swore he saw one of the helpers swoop in to catch a child's discarded candy wrapper before it hit the ground, like a hawk on its prey.

Second, whatever the style of any given corner of the empire—the cowboy and astronaut were, after all, hermetically sealed into their separate environments—a distinct and endemic form of animal life that none of the marchers had ever encountered in the flesh inhabited this place. Wherever the Alefites' eyes alit, they saw animals beside the pirates and sheiks and castanet-clicking señoritas in long, flounced dresses, and not the kind you'd see on a *National Geographic* tour, either. All of them—bears and penguins and dogs and ducks and, omnipresent, mice—bore some likeness to their ancestors—beaks or stripes, or perfectly circular ears—but they were all approximately the same somewhat-larger-than-human size, and most of them wore clothes to chastely protect their private, animal parts, and all of them were smiling.

Converging now with the stream of "visitors" from the parking lots, and the train station, and the heliport for VIPs, Ben Alef and His disciples stood at the front of the mass of Alefites, the last straggling few of whom had just reached the tiny crest from which their communal "Oooh" drifted forward along with another sound that came from yet farther away, so distant, so faint, it might have been a scent rather than a sound. It was the delicate tintinnabulation of a spoon striking a glass goblet.

Ahead, above the gigantic gate to the empire, topped by a wrought-iron arch set with wrought-iron silhouettes of the famous animal profiles, a banner unfurled by means of a hidden motor. A rainbow of silk fluttered in a breeze calibrated by a hidden wind machine. A band marching out to greet them played a bright, brass tune, the tuba emphasizing a prominent beat: *ump ump ump—ump ump ump—M-O-U-S-E!*

And the banner itself—every day a new banner, stitched at night in the underground workshops of the empire, hailing "Foreign Legion Day" or "Free Admission for AIDS Victims" or "Greetings to Handlers of Nuclear Waste"—bore the last two words any of the group would have expected except for Ben Alef, who had led them here, because it was the place He knew He had to be on this special day. On this, the first morning of the new millennium, January 1, 2000, the two words read, "WELCOME MESSIAH."

. . .

Loved, shunned, and loved again, Ben Alef and His disciples and followers had no way of telling what the response to their divine embassy might be in any given locale, but this all-out hosanna from the greatest worldly domain of its age—more extensive than the Commonwealth, more devious than the Kremlin, more enduring than the Middle Kingdom, more powerful than the Pentagon, the Empire of the Mouse was the only temporal institution with the raw might to transform environment and the manipulative psychological know-how to twist human behavior to its will—was pretty strange.

Representatives from every region in the Empire poured forth in joyous community, a bespectacled pharmacist from Ye Olde Phosphate Shoppe on Center Street, one-eyed, peg-legged pirates from Excitementland, happy, three-headed aliens from Futuropolis, along with more, many recognizable, animals by the score.

"Get your fucking . . . paws . . . off me." Eisenheim slapped wildly at a friendly chipmunk, who tried to get him to dance in the street.

The former Kommandant was the only one who did not succumb to the ecstatic fuss.

"You must be Willie!" The cluster of dwarves designated to attend the lad formed a tight circle and drew him from Celia and Margot, each with her own escort, Prince Charming for the former and a hirsute but kindly and masculine Beast for the latter.

"Well," the onetime Little Sister said, giggling, "this is just how I remember Paris."

Cinderella and her retinue curtsied in front of Bruno while a genial blue genie prostrated himself before Snakes and intoned, "Your wish is my command."

Ben Alef was hoisted atop the shoulders of two fullbacklike bears and carried through the gates.

Giddy with the delight of living for a moment in an entire world appropriate to his mental age, Bruno gazed about rapturously and repeated, "I always dreamed of this," but then he turned serious for one second and turned to Snakes, and said, "You know that I'm next."

Immediately, Snakes understood that Bruno did not mean next to be swept up, presented with his own flock of obeisant ducks or princesses, but next after Clauberg, Blobel, Palitzsch, Langefeld, Glucks, Kiehr, Nazzarian, and Bartsch: next to be slaughtered.

"No," Snakes said. "We're home now," but he tried and failed to make eye contact with the man with whom he shared a secret pact. Surrounded by an animated crowd of walking lobsters and mischievously spouting whales, a befuddled Max Vetter was being led away for adorning prior to the official ceremony, a white satin cape draped across his shoulders in the interim.

"Yes," Bruno insisted, "but that's all right. I believe you; we're home."

"Home," Snakes murmured.

"This way, mortal." The genie winked, and a red carpet unrolled under the gates into the Empire.

Nor were the Alefites ignored by the minions of the Mouse. Hundreds of grinning creatures of the jungle, the forest, and, breathing freely, the ocean, mixed among them in a festive party atmosphere. "This way," they cried, waving hands or limbs over their heads in exaggerated gestures of welcome when they weren't distributing tri-scooped ice cream cones and chocolate bars molded to a tri-circled pattern that appeared by the freezerful out of the kitchens of the realm.

"Look, there's Davy Crockett!"

"And Mary Poppins!"

"And Jiminy Cricket!"

The dapper insect adjusted his monocle and tipped his umbrella, while the frontiersman ripped off his coonskin cap, swung it in a circle around his head, and cried, "Yippeee!"

And for the journalists who presumably had a need for information that, say, the hundred-plus-strong pack of spotted, human-sized, bipedal Dalmatian pups couldn't provide, a phalanx of publicity men and women poured out of the main administration building. They wore brown pants or skirts and identical beige blazers bearing the sign of the mouse upon their breast pockets, and attached themselves to the journalists like barnacles to a sunken prison barge.

Publicity had done its homework well. No matter what country a reporter came from, each was assigned a publicity person who spoke his or her native language.

"Three hundred people work in our costume shops, which hold over half a million yards of material in eighty different fabrics. Costumes are changed daily and cleaned in our on-site laundering facilities."

Packages containing facts, figures, maps, diagrams, free passes to all the major attractions, and whatever else anyone who might conceivably say anything nice about Mouse World might desire were stacked on the press table.

But most of the press was as enthralled by the show that surrounded them as the most susceptible of Alefites. "Look, there's Winnie-le-Pooh."

"And Pinocchio!"

"E Bambi, triste bambino."

Waving a smokeless cigarette, Cruella De Ville smiled as cheerfully as Snow White, who also appeared, atop an elaborate float, a real-life girl with raven-black hair, alabaster complexion, and carmine lips, pivoting left and right as regularly as a pendulum.

A stocky, middle-aged man wearing the most expensive head of hair money could buy stood behind the press desk, clasping a single leather folder to his chest and making sure that everything went as planned. He was Myron Karnovsky, chief of all Mouseland publicity, and had been dispatched from international headquarters to oversee the millennial jamboree on a private jet with a special cargo.

"There's Fritz Hofmann," Karnovsky's aide whispered in his ear.

"Mr. Hofmann?" He addressed the one journalist who did not seem agog at the 360-degree show performed for his benefit. Instead, Fritz's eyes remained focused on Ben Alef.

"Yes."

"I have a document that I think you should see." The Californian Karnovsky was used to conducting his business schmoozing over top-shelf Scotch at movie premiere parties, but his directions here were explicit. Let the blazer-clad corps take care of the feature-writing wretches. This was serious. He opened the precious folder to reveal a single page of single-spaced legal paper perfectly preserved under a transparent cover. It was titled: "Last Will and Testament."

"What?" Fritz stammered.

"Ignore the financial details," Karnovsky said. "Read the codicil." He pointed a tanned finger at the last paragraph.

"Being of sound mind and frail body . . ." Fritz read to himself until he came to the relevant instructions, to be followed to the letter. He read them again. "You're kidding."

"This is no joke. At least, we don't think so, and neither do they." He nodded to the horde of Alefites passing through the gates. Then he gazed at the sky, a sunny, temperate blue that might have extended across the continent and the Atlantic and the next continent to the Pacific, as far as they knew. "He said that when the day came when . . . it . . . was possible, we were to do everything, I mean everything, we could to bring him back. And now, well, it's a beautiful day for a miracle."

"Yes," Fritz agreed, "they always are."

"There's Pluto!" cried a small boy, child of one of the Alefites.

Snakes shivered, the fantasy shattered, and memory took over. Once again, he was with his father, not on an army base and not at the River Lyons, but in a mountain village on the Spanish slopes of the Pyrénées. A crumbling medieval version of Mouseland's castle loomed above them. An enormous door creaked open and a procession of dark-robed figures emerged, carrying torches. They chanted a fractured, ancient Latin, and the multilingual diplomat, out on yet another search for life's hidden truths, chanted, too.

"You are ready?" The head of the procession addressed the elder Hammurabi in a somber voice that came from deep within the folds of his robe.

"Yes, Master."

"You must don the appropriate garb."

"Yes, Master."

The figure's bony, skeletal hands extended two additional gowns from his enormous sleeves.

"Yes, Master." Mr. Hammurabi accepted the gowns along with their implicit mandate. A moment later he drew the first garment, black and woven of a rough, burlaplike material, like those worn by the rest of the sect, over his secular clothes. Then he took the second, smaller gown—this one red—and handed it to his son.

Suddenly Samad, or Esteban this season, noticed a figure shrinking behind the men in their strange uniforms. It was another boy, older than he, maybe five, dressed in ragged shorts and an oversized T-shirt silk-screened with the smiling face of the mouse, and he had followed the procession to the door, holding its key on a large tarnished-brass ring. In an urgent, private communication between the two boys, the older one shook his head.

Samad felt the harsh fabric, but noticed spots and streaks of some hardened liquid that caught the flickering light of the torches.

"This is Isaac," the Master said, conferring upon Samad a new ceremonial name.

But before Mr. Hammurabi could affirm this by repeating yet again, "Yes, Master"—these would have been the only two words he had uttered since he and his son heard the door open—Samad cried out, "No!"

"Hush," Mr. Hammurabi hissed.

"I don't want to." It was Samad's first act of rebellion, and the child could see his father tensing.

Then the Master spoke in a kind, low tenor. "Don't you wish to meet Pluto, my son?"

Samad stammered his regrets. "N-n-no. I don't think so, sir."

"But He only comes to the surface once a year, for a special occasion. It is a very great honor. You wouldn't want to miss that, would you?"

The more the voice spoke, the more Samad very much wished to miss the event. He cringed.

"Enough!" the Master declared.

"Enough?" Mr. Hammurabi echoed meekly.

"The gift must be willing, or the ceremony is void." The Master raised his long, emaciated fingers to his cowl, threw it back, and boomed, "Begone!"

Samad had just a fraction of a second in which to glimpse the awful image of—was it the eerie light, the ominous shadows?—a skull topped by a round, black, yarmulkelike cap with two gigantic black ears before he shut his eyes and fled. Only once, midway down the pebbled hill in his headlong flight to the inn in the village, did he turn to see the evil figure himself turning toward the lad in the doorway with a crooked, beckoning finger.

Pluto was a hound with a bright orange, semihuman body, legs, arms, etc., that seemed to be composed of links of sausage. He had long, floppy black ears, great, sentimental, parabolic eyes, dewlapped cheeks, and a protuberant, whiskered nose that ended in a bulbous black honk-me horn at the tip. All he wore was a bright red collar that hung loosely about his skinny neck, and all he carried was a bone.

Snakes looked at the bone and tried to imagine the size of the femur of a boy he had once seen in an Iberian doorway.

But all Pluto did was yawn and stretch exaggeratedly, and then he chased his whippish tail in a circle, to the delight of the crowd of lucky tourists who hadn't quite expected to alight from their bullet trains and station wagons in the midst of such a brilliant fantasia.

"Everyone has their role." The chief of public relations was quite pleased with himself for so impeccably following the bizarre orders from the den atop the empire.

"Yes, I suppose so," Snakes replied noncommittally. Worried by the sight of Pluto, he looked around for the only other person he could communicate with, but Max Vetter was no longer in sight. The procession had moved on, and Myron Karnovsky was holding Snakes's elbow in a vise grip, urging him to catch up.

"We have a great deal planned, and I'm sure you have an announcement to make."

"Yes, I'm sure." With an eye to hidden reality, Snakes perceived the amazing brilliance of this place. It was clearly designed with one essential transaction in mind, to empty the pockets of anyone within fifty kilometers in return for fulfilling their souls. Several hours after arrival, people would depart with a surfeit of simulated experience and, to prove it to themselves, a shopping bag full of one-size-fits-all mouse caps and dog ears and duck beaks and snowshake paperweights and pennants and souvenirs of every imaginable variety.

The Peddler would have been envious. He, who dealt in physical experience, chemical or, as it were, aesthetic, in flesh and smoke and alcohol and grains of white powder in the bloodstream, had never made the step to the produce of the imagination. Once in his life he had tried, by attaching himself to Ben Alef and the idea of salvation, but all his own conceptual leap had gained him was an all too palpable ounce of steel alloy in the brain.

Suddenly Snakes understood why Ben Alef had brought them here. This ultimately man-made world, where not a thread in a clown's costume was immaterial, where not a brick of path was laid without a plan, where not a flower failed to serve as part of a larger pattern—note the enormous, festive mouse head of irises and lilies and tulips and gladioli inlaid in the slanted mound of earth beside the gate—was the locus of belief in His age. If Ben Alef's predecessor had had to contend with the ramparts of Jerusalem, His own Via must lie between Futuropolis and Excitementland where Cora the Cow and the Spanish señorita and the German mädchen and the fire-breathing dragon puppet on the ten-meter float were the priests—and so were Myron Karnovsky and the anonymous lackeys who sold tickets and Goofy Dogs and Donald Cola and Frisbees in the shape of their Lord's ears, because Mouseland was the twentieth century's Holy Land.

But did the acolytes of this particularly modern faith understand that? Or were they just in it, like the Peddler, for the loot?

"Rest assured," Karnovsky said, "today everything is free. Admissions, food, souvenirs. Today it's not about money. Look, the booths are shuttered, and all the ticket takers are here anyway. They wouldn't miss it for the world, because they know, too. This is the day we've been waiting for. It only comes once in a very long while."

Once, again, Snakes heard the echo of a gory, sacrificial night in the Pyrénées, and again the faintest possible hint of a spoon tapping a goblet ten kilometers away.

"One might even say that today was the day for which this entire land was made."

A sea of people and cartoon characters filled the Mouseland Town Square behind the band as the tuba thumped a final, resounding *ump ump ump— ump ump ump—M-O-U-S-E!*

Finally, the band stopped in front of a stage rimmed with swags of satin upon which a ten-foot object stood covered with a white cloth held in place by ropes guarded by the park's security force. People jammed the railings of the verandas and porches of the olde-fashioned ice cream parlour and gift shoppes surrounding the square and more people and cameras peered down from balconies over the square. More people, more than could fit, converged by way of the five major avenues that met at the square, but enormous video monitors were set up to broadcast the ceremony at the corners, so that they could watch from the spokes of the radii.

"This way," Karnovsky said to Snakes, taking out a key on a brass ring and unlocking an unmarked door between twin bathrooms, one marked with the image of the master of the realm and the word for "Men" in a dozen languages and the other with the mistress and the same dozen versions of "Women."

Inside, a staircase led directly down to a world equivalent to and just as perfect in its own purely functional way as the world above. There were corridors instead of streets, and anonymous storerooms instead of well-designed shoppes, and changing and staging areas for the permanent festival up top, and all of them were just as clean as above, but without any attendant image. No need for display here.

Just below the ceiling of the fluorescent-lit passage, rows of ducts and pipes and conduits stretched and branched to serve the upper world. If the Town Square was the public face of the beast, these were its guts. Mouseland was an organism, complete with the same air-filtration, arterial transport, neurological and waste-removal systems a real live rodent required.

Snakes paced behind Karnovsky's clacking heels—he had the body of a man who spent a lot of time on golf courses—until they approached an intersection in the underground maze. Ben Alef stood in the center with his inner circle of followers, Celia and Margot and Willy and, as of the night before, Father Immaculato, although Bruno was the only disciple in sight. Both Eisenheim and Max Vetter were missing.

"Don't worry," Karnovsky said. "There's a companion assigned to each of you. They're probably a little ahead, maybe in the green room, but everyone will get on the stage. We're scheduled for noon. A couple of other groups are on now. Look." He pointed to a video monitor broadcasting the events outside.

Warming up the crowd, "Ur shud I say coolin' yu down?" a famous middle-aged singer with lank gray hair to his belt joshed in the Liverpudlian accent of his youth, "Here's a little number I wrote an eon ago, for a dif'rent god oot frum a dif'rent continent. But rilly, mates, all gods are good, what hey? But now we've got the real one." He started strumming familiar chords on a six-string guitar, bent over, glanced up, said, "This one's fer Ben Alef," and began humming:

"My sweet Lord."

Farther down the utilitarian corridor, Snakes caught a glimpse of Pluto entering another room.

And then Goofy exited through the same door. He, too, was a dog, with the same floppy ears and the same wrinkled and whiskered nose that came down to the same round rubber bulb, but, unlike Pluto, he was dressed. Instead of orange fur, he wore pants and a vest over a T-shirt with wide red and yellow horizontal stripes. Covering his paws, he wore puffy white gloves.

Something was odd here, and disturbing. Of course, all seven dwarves went to the same tailor (though some were happy with his work and others grumpy), but Donald Duck and his nephews all wore the same sailor outfits, and all the bears in the park, whether lumbering behemoths or cute-as-a-button cubs, sported small, conical dunce caps atop their brown, furry heads. Yes, there was a hierarchy that separated those in the footlights from the chorus, and those employees who donned gigantic, sweaty animal suits from those who had their hair coiffed and nails buffed in the park salon, but Goofy and Pluto: here were two creatures clearly of the same species, practically twins, who had by no means had the same opportunities.

Pluto was several years older than Goofy, and a heck of a lot more mature. Damm it, Pluto was there at the beginning, when the Master still had stick legs and before Donald's beak job, but Pluto hadn't evolved. He hadn't been allowed to evolve, because Goofy showed up on the lot one day with a hobo's bundle over his upright shoulder and a bogus aw-shucks, just-off-the-farm sincerity you could cut with a knife—and promptly usurped Pluto's rightful position. The hand-cranked cameras they were still using in those days loved him. The mutt had star quality.

It was the worst possible timing for Pluto. Father was beginning to feel his creative oats in those days, the Master was starting to compose symphonies, and Donald strutted around the studio with his patented duck-of-the-walk waddle, followed by those obnoxious nephews, quacking "Yeth, Unca Donna. Yeth, Unca Donna," no matter what came into his bird brain. Those runts knew where the power was. And the money! Contracts were being renegotiated left and right. Minnie moved into a hacienda next to Jack Warner and attended auctions with Mrs. Mayer. Oh, she was a real society doll.

Worst of all, everyone loved the Goofster. He could open a film on his own, and Father knew it. And boy did he love the Life. After a day on the set, throwing tantrums, demanding expensive reshoots to catch his better profile, and scarfing Purina's top-of-the-line chow—nothing else was good enough for him, private waiter, private bowl with his name scripted on the side, never ate at the commissary like the rest of the cast— he relaxed by playing poker with Gable, Cagney, and the Coop . . . and won. Baggy pockets filled with their cash, he yukked, "See you bums around the poorhouse," tipped that stupid ersatz baker's hat he always wore, and set off to sniff around the musical sound stages for a flock of chorines to invite over to the Brown Derby for drinks . . . and later they did it doggie style. Not for print, the columnists called him the biggest cock in Hollywood.

But did any of them bother to check out Pluto's tool? No, they just scratched him on the head. Typecast, woebegone Pluto was relegated to running around in blurred circles and carrying that bloody bone, while Goofy got to hobnob with Tinseltoon royalty. Goofy was a peer, Pluto just . . . a pet.

Call it canine rivalry, Pluto seethed with envy. And Goofy, for all his hail-hound-well-met manner, knew it; he couldn't meet his co-speciean's eyes when he insisted that they never appear in the same reel. He was the star; he did features, Pluto shorts. But they both knew the unfair truth. They were the same under the skin.

Now, however, they were together, all the big shots were here, because Father had decreed it in his Last Will and Testament.

But while Goofy had been whooping it up through the decades—the columnists marveled at his ageless joie de vivre—Pluto had found his own reason for being. It came about one lonely night after another bad party at some shack in Malibu rented by one of the junior animators. Pluto had had a bit too much to drink and made a pass at a French poodle in town for a screen test. He should have known better. Fi-Fi, Chi-Chi, whatever, thought she was hot stuff, and shunned him.

The humiliation was intense. If he couldn't make this tutued tootsie, he really had lost everything. Desperate, Pluto slunk out to the beach and relapsed into primitive atavism; he howled at the moon.

Then came the moment Pluto hadn't known he was waiting for.

Rejected herself by Goofy, who had plugged her that afternoon and already forgotten—he was all eyes now for some silent Swedish babe said to be the Next Big Thing—Fi-Fi trotted onto the beach.

Pluto halted mid-howl and watched the pathetic wannabe sniffing sorrowfully and digging in the sand like a pup. "Need a pail and shovel, hon?" he asked.

"Oh, Monsieur Pluto, you surprised me," Fi-Fi said, and coyly revealed her hindquarters.

So now he was Monsieur Pluto; now his casting basket was tempting. But it was too late for that. It was too late for Fi-Fi. Impelled by a vigor he hadn't known since his first two-reelers, Pluto ambled over to the bitch, mounted her from behind, and clamped his teeth about her curly-haired neck.

"Ooooh!" Fi-Fi moaned. "Not so sharp, Monsieur, I feel your teeth."

Cribbing a line from one of Father's other works, Pluto loosed his grip only long enough to explain, "All the better to rip your throat out, my dear."

"Oh, zir, pleeze. Zis should be heaven."

"But, Madame, you have been misinformed," Pluto growled through a mouthful of fur. "I am Pluto, the God of the Underworld."

Now Fi-Fi was frightened. She squirmed for release and yowled madly, but Pluto's teeth had been drawn large by Father, and he didn't let go. The more she struggled, the more excited he grew. He could feel her arteries pulsing, and tearing; he drank the blood.

Sated, Pluto tossed Fi-Fi's lifeless carcass over his shoulder like a rag.

Oh, the studio flacks hushed up the scandal and made an anonymous contribution to the Parisian pound, because Pluto was still a valuable property—not so valuable as the Goof, but beloved by kids of all ages. Father gave him a stern lecture, but from then on, the pet was no longer interested in the Hollywood Mouse Race. Let Father build his dream; let Goofy hog all the glory; Pluto had bigger things in mind. He had made his bones.

Nor did he have to work hard to find his natural milieu. Word spread, and those with a need figured out how to reach Pluto. A little ceremony, a little hocus-pocus, a pentacle drawn in the dirt with a sharp stick, and sure enough he would come loping over the hill just like any other dog summoned by a silent whistle.

Wherever a cult worshipped dark deities, Pluto was there. Austria, '39. A witness at the Moscow Doctors' Trial. In Cambodia. In Chile. In Memphis with a satchel of pills in return for a song. Back to Hollywood for an appointment with a longhaired loony, leaving a bloody paw print on the wall underneath the human-scrawled legend "Helter Skelter." He was careful not to overexpose himself, but showed up now and again, making rare and special appearances, often marked by the disappearance of a child, and another notch on his bone. At a monastery at the base of the Pyrénées.

Pluto caught a glimpse of Snakes looking at him, and winked. His human eyes were entirely hidden in the costume mesh beneath permanently goggly plastic dog eyes, but still there was something expressive in that wink that established a communion. Then he threw an arm across Father Immaculato's shoulders.

Other cartoon figures and people in beige blazers held intense conversations on cell phones and rushed back and forth on various last minute errands before the big show commenced. When two engineers muttering about "melt point" ran up another staircase that led backstage, the speeches of several local dignitaries already on the stage filtered down into the corridor, and Snakes could hear the usual "a new age beginning" etc. etc. etc.

He had heard enough pat oratory in the last six weeks so that it ceased to have any meaning. Somehow the wonder he had experienced on the Baltic Shore had been packaged into one more tin speech fit for consumption. Suddenly, Snakes despised his surroundings, their clever and well-oiled machinery of imagery without substance to back it up. Suddenly, he felt the kind of anger welling up in him that had seemed so irrational in the mouth of Dietrich Eisenheim—and where was the creep, anyway? And where was Ben Alef? He stood silent and ignored as a tree in the forest amidst the bustling Empire officials.

Despite Hammurabi's cynicism, the speeches had their effect on almost everyone else. A few bunnies dabbed at their eyes with their ears, and one of the publicity people pressed her cell phone to her chest to block out any other sounds. Up top, the mass must have been swaying by now, because the underground chamber felt like the hold of an ocean liner. Then a wet spot appeared on the ceiling, and a drop fell toward Snakes's feet.

Karnovsky noted the spot immediately, looked up toward the moisture spreading from a seam in the concrete, and immediately shouted into a speaker mounted on the wall. "Melt point reached. Melt point reached."

Bruno looked confused, but Bruno always looked confused. Where was Glucks when you needed a scientific explanation?

"I hadn't expected it this early," Karnovsky said to the group. "But the weather must be even warmer than we thought. We'd all better rise." He pressed a button and the entire floor of the green room commenced a slow ascent as the twin sections of ceiling on either side of the crack gently slid open, allowing a further stream of strangely scented liquid to drip through.

The sky was a searing blue light in the widening crack. Not a cloud in sight. Clouds were prohibited from marring this occasion.

"Going up," Richard Federman cracked, unable to resist one last joke. "Ladies' lingerie on three."

Up they rose into the view of the Alefites—it was only an elevator, nineteenth-century technology, but it seemed as miraculous as an apparition in the desert—who responded with an ovation so thunderous their applause obliterated any sound made by the band at the base of the stage.

The first figure Snakes saw was the Master himself. Back to the rising elevator, gigantic ears erect and slightly aquiver, he was dressed for the occasion in tails, waving a baton and conducting the band that proclaimed him its leader, while his moll stepped onto the square with the honored guests. "Mickey almost never conducts anymore," she mouthed to Snakes. "This is very special."

Snakes looked at the musicians. The tuba player's cheeks expanded and contracted like a blowfish, and the cymbalist's hands vibrated on impact with the halves of his instrument, but they were inaudible amid the roar that kept rolling in from the far perimeter of the square and the avenues beyond, where further crowds watched on the video monitors. So contagious was the applause that Karnovsky and the rest of the people and animals on the lift clapped immodestly for themselves.

Minnie lifted the hems of her red polka-dotted dress and performed a little dance.

Pluto cupped his hands to Father Immaculato's ears. The two of them slipped off the side of the stage. Snakes warned himself to keep an eye out for them later on, as well as for Eisenheim, who didn't seem to be among the tiered rows of dignitaries. Once again, Snakes wished he had Max Vetter's eyes to help him, but Max, too, was missing, although Celia and Margot and Willy Wilk had been given seats in the front row.

Finally, the cheers abated, allowing the band to be heard. By now they had shifted from their most famous show tunes, "Zip-A-Dee Doo-Dah" and "Um-Boogah-Woogah" to a more abstract classical repertoire, heavy with oboes and strings and highlighted by an enormous golden harp played by an imposing dark-haired woman who fingered the instrument on a signal from the Master. His baton was awhir, jabbing the air like a lightning bolt, defining the tempo, and constantly refining the mix—a little stronger on the flutes, a shade more delicate on the timpani—and whatever musicians he pointed at instantaneously responded with a virtuosity they hadn't known they possessed. Talent turned to genius at his decree.

The band built to crescendo after crescendo, arriving successively at peaks that could not possibly be surmounted, yet surmounting them, until Mickey spun around in a single magnificent pirouette, eyes flashing, and pointed his baton at the ranks of mayors and governors and corporate sponsors of the event who concluded as one, "Hallelujah! Hallelujah!"

Spent, as if every ounce of energy had been drained from his soul, the Maestro bowed his head, and the crowd erupted again.

Only Ben Alef and Snakes Hammurabi were unmoved, the latter growing more suspicious of his hosts and more questioning of his Lord by the moment. Surely Ben Alef hadn't brought them out of Germany into this new promised land of cash and plastic only to allow Himself to be used by the worldly powers He had once given hope of superseding. His passivity, which originally appeared noble and divine, now seemed craven if not base. Was this . . . this . . . this sham His apotheosis?

Snakes looked at his Lord with sorrow and regret. Ben Alef seemed shrunken on the stage. His pale countenance looked unhealthy compared with the vigorous tans of the men and women in the blazers, and even his breaths seemed to come in slow motion.

"Sit here," Karnovsky said to the Messiah, leading Him to a throne beneath the gigantic object, still covered with its white cloth, from the bottom of which the liquid, smelling worse and worse, leaked and spread.

"Hi, everyone!" peeped the Maestro and Master of Ceremonies from his podium. "Wasn't that fun?"

The crowd screamed agreement.

"You bet." Mickey pumped his white, balloonlike fist. "But gosh my golly, you know, we're here today for more than fun. We're here for a very serious reason." He looked down at his notes. "We're here to greet a very special visitor. For the first time in this new minnellium—oops, that's millennium, I guess I was thinking of the little lady over there. . . ." He nodded to his consort who bobbed her big head up and down with pleasure at the recognition.

"For the first time in this new mil-len-ni-um, long word that, we've got the Messiah here. Let's have a hearty welcome for Him, ladies and gents and kids."

While the audience cheered again until their throats were hoarse, Mickey puttered about inside his lectern, and removed a large gold key, then turned directly to Ben Alef. Underneath his tux and bow tie, he still wore his trademark red lederhosen with the two white buttons big and round as his eyes. "Mr. Ben Alef, we're proud to have you here, and, before your big number"—he pointed the implement like a wand at the cloth-covered obelisk—"please accept the Key to the Empire."

Like a zombie in thrall, Ben Alef stood and shuffled across the stage.

"Stop!" Snakes wanted to scream, to rage like Eisenheim, good riddance to him. "Don't You know where You are anymore? Look around. There isn't an honest face here, not one that isn't grinning in rigid, costumed delight. It's the survival of the cutest here, and woe be to anyone who doesn't fit the agenda. This is eugenics. No room for dark-skinned folks, no room for circumcisions, and no room for You. Dammit, You've been here before. Don't You recognize the Kingdom of Death!"

Snakes smelled death. He remembered it from a hotel room where he was supposed to meet a courier from Pakistan. When he opened the door, the fecal smell hit him before he saw a slim man in boxer shorts sprawled across the bed beside an attaché case that was open and empty as the man's rigor-mortis'ed mouth. He also remembered it from an alley behind an army barracks. And Stephan remembered it from a sunny river. And Esteban remembered it suffusing the stained clothes of his father one morning in the Pyrénées. Now Samuel knew it.

"Is that you in there, Dietrich?"

"I am that I am."

Father Immaculato knew his Bible and recognized the words that God spoke to Moses out of the burning bush.

"But my identity is irrelevant," said the costumed figure, whose voice was muffled by layers of fabric. "The question you should be concerned with is who that *man* is." The figure sneered.

Pluto had led Immaculato up a winding spiral inside the tower to a tiny balcony atop the castle, just below the gigantic black ears and the Junker's antenna. They were both tired from the climb and somewhat dizzy as they looked down at the spectacle below: the stage, the band, the crowd, with yet more bodies coming in from the entrance, and more from the train station and more along the highways that ribboned into the horizon.

"I know who He is; that's why I'm here. But you should be down there doing something."

"So I'm up here doing something else." Pluto laughed.

"Eisenheim!"

"Not precisely. But I know him well. One of my favorite adjuncts. Tireless in pursuit of the goal."

Immaculato was confused, and suddenly worried.

"You, too, are valuable, dear Salvatore."

Immaculato froze. Nobody outside the innermost chambers of the Holy See knew his birth name.

But Pluto hardly noticed the reaction he had created. He went on. "The only difference between you and your rabid little lap dog, no offense intended, is that he knows whom he is serving and you don't. For a bright boy, you're very ignorant."

"Urban sent you."

"Alas, he couldn't."

"Rosare then, or Bardolino?" The young priest named two high level cardinals who might have known about his mission.

"No, neither of those good men."

Then one of the words Pluto used a moment earlier struck Immaculato. "What do you mean 'couldn't'?"

"So perhaps you are an observant bambino after all. I can see why Giuseppe invited you to play."

Forget about the implicit denigration of the office of the Pontiff in the description of his activities as "play." Nobody referred to Urban by his pre-papal name, not in jest, not in private. Nobody. The weather might have been balmy enough to melt the object under the white cloth, its stain spreading like a shadow across the stage, but Immaculato started to feel rapidly oscillating hot flashes.

"None of you wops really knows anything, not you, Salvatore, not your boss of bosses, Giuseppe, not even Benito during the good old days."

This was too offensive, too weird, too scary for Immaculato to take any longer. "I'm going down."

"Yes," Pluto agreed, "I suppose you are." He peered over the edge of the balcony, twenty, thirty meters to the lesser peaks that were also as sharp as the spikes in a Vietnamese bamboo pit.

Before he left, Immaculato tried once more to reassert his authority. "I asked you a question. What do you mean 'couldn't'?"

"Perhaps you didn't see the newspapers today. I suppose you were too busy making last-minute arrangements with Dietrich. And perhaps Rome didn't bother to call you. Tsk. Tsk. Alas, poor Giuseppe."

"What the hell are you saying?" Immaculato gripped Pluto by the collar.

"That's more like it," Pluto growled amiably. "Late last night we were sitting in his room, you know the room . . ." Pluto described the Vatican's most private chamber, down to the pattern of inlay in Urban's marble table, and Immaculato backed off. "We were playing a friendly game of chess and discussing exactly what you and I are discussing now, or will be soon, and he was eating one of those disgusting little treats of his, and he choked. Checkmate."

Immaculato felt his own throat tighten, so that he could barely gasp, "Choked?"

"To death. Oh, look, the Maestro is going to conduct. He only does that on very special occasions."

Sounds of the band rose to the tower while Pluto thumped his tail to the beat. After a song or two, he turned to the pale and stricken emissary, leaning against the balcony. "And you know the strangest coincidence? At almost the exact same moment, that fellow in Hamburg, your partner, what's his name, Herr Law and Order?"

"Huber," Immaculato said weakly.

"Yes, that's the one. He had a heart attack."

"And he's . . . ?"

"Yup. Too much pressure. Not enough fun. Guy stood up at his desk, I think he was planning to call you. Clutched his chest." Pluto acted it out, paws raised. "Dead before he hit the ground. Hey, long way down." He leaned dangerously over the edge.

Immaculato slumped against the pink terra-cotta ornamentation.

Pluto persisted, "Hey, listen, you haven't even heard the bad news."

But Immaculato *was* the smartest acolyte in Vatican City, and by then he already knew the bad news, the worst possible news for him and the best possible news for the world. Ben Alef *was* the Messiah. And Immaculato had set in motion the events leading inexorably to the second death of God.

"Didn't you suspect?" the Lord of the Underworld asked, curious now what made these people tick. "Not even a teeny, tiny prick of doubt in yourself and your church?"

"No," Immaculato moaned.

"Not after the corn? Not after the Day of the Three Miracles?"

"No, no, no. It was a fake. I could have sworn it was a fake."

"Tsk, tsk." Pluto wagged a stubby paw. "Oh, ye unfaithful."

"Too faithful!" the Father cried. "I believed, but . . . just . . . not . . . in . . . Him."

"Too late," Pluto declared, and took out his golden key, the exact same key in miniature that the Maestro was delivering to Ben Alef down below.

Was it too late? Maybe Immaculato could redeem himself, save his Lord. "Stop!" he shrieked over the balcony. *"STO-O-O-OP!"*

"Oh, there's no way they can hear you. There's no way to stop events now," Pluto said calmly, idly nibbling one of his paws. "You only have two choices. You can watch, or . . . not. *Capisce?*"

"Yes," Immaculato murmured.

"Well, it's time for me to leave. Have to catch the final curtain." He unlocked the door.

"Wait!" Immaculato cried.

"Yes?"

"Just one more thing."

"Yes, of course, anything at all for a loyal soldier. Just name it."

Having forfeited all hopes of God, Immaculato knew his true Lord at last. "Forgive me."

"Of course, my son." Only then, acknowledged by the miserable plea of the wrecked believer, did the voice attain specificity and character. Immaculato had heard it recently—but where?—as a whisper, a faint echo of years, glorious years, of envenomed idealism. Impossible.

Suddenly Immaculato saw himself as a young novitiate, a student of clerical history hunkered down in a cubicle in the stacks of the Vatican Library, earphones clamped to his head, listening to an indexed tape of a meeting between two men long dead, one in purple, the other in brown. Impossible.

More recently, that same voice—decayed and degenerated, but nonetheless the same—couldn't have welcomed him to a forgotten country farmhouse lost in time. Or could it? Yes! Everything connected. Immaculato spun around, but Pluto had left, and locked the door behind him, leaving only the reticent tintinnabulation of a spoon rapping a glass. There was only one place for Immaculato. Down. To meet his master. Delicately, as if wading into the sea, he poked a toe over the edge of the balcony, and then he dove.

Arms open to the healing climate, palms extended, Ben Alef said, "No showers today." After weeks of public life, this was essentially Ben Alef's first public address, yet all he could do was repeat Himself, this time with a different inflection: "No showers today?"

"What is he, a weatherman?" Richard Federman nudged Fritz Hofmann.

"Hssh."

"Touchy. Hey, you think this place has a bar?"

Fritz had had enough cynicism and inwardly resolved that today's would be the last "story" he would report. Nonetheless, he was responsible to the organization, and wouldn't leave the *Zeitung* and its readers in the drunken hands of Richard Federman. He would do his job today, but his dispatch would be accompanied by his resignation.

"Or"—Ben Alef looked toward the horizon—"is there a hint of rain in the air?"

It was a rhetorical question, but the crowd had been so primed by the Maestro to respond that they screamed in unison, "No-o-o!" thereby blotting out the sound of Father Immaculato's body landing on the lesser spires of the castle.

Was a shower coming? Snakes felt a glimmer of hope. When Ben Alef sensed showers, He was not entirely pleased. Perhaps He disliked His display here, like a rare beast at a zoo, as much as Snakes did. In the midst of the Enchantment Empire's bogus exaltation of divinity, Snakes yearned for humanity. He was thirsty. He craved all the filth of water.

But if there wasn't rain in the transparent air, there was more and more moisture on the stage as rivulets of liquid from the soaked cloth ran off the edge of the subtly raked platform onto the band.

The water smelled disgusting, but all Ben Alef said was, "There is water from above and water from below . . . water from within and water from without . . . clouds and glaciers . . . gases and solids . . . water from the east, the west, the north, and the south . . . the water that flows and the water that gathers. . . ."

The crowd hung on every word, but without Snakes's interpretation they were mystified by their Messiah's allegory. Were the droplets meant to represent individual souls, and the clouds nations or history, or were they just . . . clouds? Was Ben Alef Himself the seafarer He referred to—they all knew the story of the *Farnhagen*—or was each and every one of the Alefites a lost mariner, standing in the prow of a pilotless vessel, scanning the endless ocean for a lighthouse?

Baffled, they were nonetheless satisfied as deeply as the depths beneath their imaginary ships. The modest assembly was not there to understand, but merely to behold the maker of miracles, the speaker of ineffable truth. Whatever He *meant*, more vitally He *was.*

And yet, a lingering disquietude affected the crowd. Not a spiritual complaint—no, their souls swayed on waves of ecstasy—but a physical one so awkward no one dared mention it. In fact, it was virtually undetectable where the avenues met the perimeter of the square, faint enough to be denied in the center, but unpleasantly potent anywhere near the band pit. Among the dignitaries on the stage, it was too grossly palpable to be ignored. A scent infected the air.

With every moment that passed, the odor grew stronger. Imagine a drop of oil in a barrel of rainwater; it taints the pristine supply, but more in the mind than in the palate. De minimis. Now imagine a second drop and a third. Still, they're insignificant, but imagine another drop and another, until even the least observant eye can tell that the water is gray, and then imagine more drops sullying the now slick and iridescent surface until any tongue can tell that the water is poison.

The water on the stage had gone beyond gray; its odor was mephitic, its very texture a slow and jellied ooze, its source embarrassingly obvious. One or two dignitaries subtly dabbed scented handkerchiefs to their nostrils, while others tried to keep from breathing more than absolutely necessary. Even Mickey's heavy mouse head provided imperfect protection against the fumes writhing around the sopping and shrinking and stinking cloth, and the Master glanced sideways for help—as covertly as possible, since the event was being simultaneously, and scentlessly, broadcast to Enchantment Empires in Hollywood and Tokyo, and therefrom released to the press everywhere.

Myron Karnovsky, the PR man whose plans—and career—were suddenly going disastrously awry, pulled a finger across his throat.

Impolitely maybe, the Maestro had to intervene. He stood, shook his head clear of the noxious vapors, thick now as a fog, and grabbed the microphone from Ben Alef at the Messiah's next pause. "Thank you. Thank you," he cried, slapping his absolutely white gloves together. As perennial Master of Ceremonies, Mickey knew how to work a show. "But you know, there is one single task. . . ."

He perused his lines, staggered back from a fresh, nauseating gust, and jettisoned the script entirely. Another minute, and half the people onstage would keel over. He paraphrased, "A miracle, a favor, a proof. Aw, shit, Goofy, please!"

Without a moment's hesitation, Goofy whipped a long, serrated knife out of his pants pocket and cut the ropes that bound the tarpaulin draped over the mysterious obelisk to the stage.

It was supposed to flutter up like a billowing sail, but instead it sat, sodden, drenched, reeking.

"Allow me, bucko," the returning Pluto said as he gripped the miserable sheet between his teeth, dug in his heels, and tugged. Gradually the sheet separated itself from the object beneath, which finally stood unveiled. What had started as a two-meter-tall, one-meter-square, opaque block of ice shipped aboard a refrigerated plane from a cryogenics warehouse in California according to explicit directions in "Last Will and Testament" had melted enough so that everyone could see the outline of an elderly man inside the shell of ice. The crowd gasped to see the cracks on his skin and his thin mustache through the cracks in the ice.

Mickey demanded, "Bring back our Father."

Even if medical science had lived up to its promises, this was no easy task. But the putrid scent told everyone that something had gone drastically wrong. Whatever state the body was supposed to be suspended in had long since gone to rot.

Exposed now, without the modest benefit of the white garment he had worn in transit, the Founder and Father of Mouseland was a mass of festering red caries with finger bones showing through where the flesh was thinnest.

"Please," Mickey whimpered in a small, rodently voice.

Ben Alef raised His arms.

"No!"

The denial burst from a voice in the heart of the crowd, but Snakes's first reaction was to shoot a glance at Pluto. Why had he ever thought that some jerk in a costume was the man he feared? He knew who was coming. The dog shrugged.

"Out of my way!" Eisenheim insisted, creating a small flurry of activity around him, but no space. "Lebensraum!" he shrieked.

Bruno looked at Snakes, and Snakes remembered the wrestler's sad, resigned "I'm next," but didn't have time to reflect.

"Damn, did I say out of my way, raus, move it, or—"

People tried to avoid the crazy man, but they were locked into the pattern of humanity in the square, like chips of tile in a mosaic grid. When he pulled a gun out of his inside pocket, however, the grid buckled.

"Peace, brothers, peace," gentle Neue Juden said, trying to soothe both Eisenheim and the nervous crowd, but their ranks had been alloyed by tourists who didn't share the extremity of their faith, and hysteria began to mount.

Like ripples emanating from a rock dropped in a pond, people in the ring pushed against those behind them who pushed at those behind them in turn until the furthermost circle pushed at those filling the spokes that radiated out beyond the perimeter of the square. Those people, however, were more unrelenting than any shoreline; they pressed inward out of curiosity to see what was happening. Gradually those in the vise between the competing pressures of the center and the radii felt the air forcibly expelled from their lungs. A child lay panting for breath against the picket fence in front of the General Store.

"Help him!" the mother cried, before she, too, was crushed under the stampeding feet.

"Peace!" cried the Alefites. "Allow the Lord to do His good will."

Ignoring salvation in their haste to get to safety, people fell over each other as randomly as ears of corn tumbling out of a bridal canopy, while Eisenheim egged them on. "Peace! Allow the Lord to do His will!" he mocked, and took aim at the first familiar face he saw—it was butcher Hossler from Warnemünde, still holding the hand-painted placard with a six-pointed star he had carried from home—and fired. "If you're New Jews, you can die just like the old Jews; that's His will for you." He fired again, into the crowd.

"Stop him!" people cried, sobbing, as they shrank before the avenger's fury, but their words had as little effect as Father Immaculato's earlier, equally futile plea.

"You can't stop God." Eisenheim moved toward the stage, pausing to reload. "That's the point. You can't stop Him. His time has come. Can't you see Him? Can't you hear Him? Can't you smell Him?"

Maybe the word "smell" terrified the frozen elite on the stage more than the gun, because the mayors and dignitaries suddenly clambered to escape. Some jumped into the crowd; others hid behind the rapidly melting block of ice, from which rancid water now streamed like a fountain of death.

"Cowards!" Eisenheim shrieked, and shot wildly, one bullet piercing Minnie's ear, another Myron Karnovsky's heart. "Got one," he said, and paused again to reload, calmly fitting another clip of bullets into his revolver, as confident and competent as he had when organizing the assembly line that moved the first incarnation of Ben Alef to His first fate.

That reminded him of the good old days, and he started singing a ditty that he remembered or maybe made up on the spot:

"People pushin',
people shovin',
shovin' people
in the oven."

Quiet and strangely contemplative after the Last Supper in the farmhouse inn that now seemed a thousand miles and fifty years away, Eisenheim was back in form, revived and reinvigorated, and ready to fulfill the assignment that Father Immaculato would have spared him. But the cleric was dead, and had Salvatore been alive he would have had no more chance of halting the man he thought was his tool—wrong!—than Eisenheim did of recalling the bullets he sprayed delightedly, catching a woman climbing atop another woman in the spine.

None of them understood. Most were too young, the rest too stupid. They knew the Messiah was Jewish, the way they knew He performed miracles, but they didn't think historically or theologically. They just wore the garb, sang the Psalms, waited for God, and took the bullets. Not so resignedly as their mid-century ancestors—no panic in the cattle cars—but just as lethally.

"You wonder why we did it," Eisenheim explained—to whom: Snakes? Ben Alef? Himself? The world? "You say we were hypnotized. Not true. Bang," he echoed his weapon like a child at play. "Nice shot, if I do say so. You say we were carried away by the craziness of the war itself. Not true. Bang." He shot a hole in the castle window. "Drat. Bang." He nailed the postman from Rerike. "Much better. You say we were poor after the first war; we were bitter. True, but irrelevant. Bang. Bang. New Jews, my ass! Take what the old Jews got. Not as efficient as a gas chamber, but it will have to do. Bang. I'll tell you why we did it, if you really want to know. We did it because we wanted to!"

The time for language was over. Everything that could have been said was. Done with the square, Eisenheim strode toward the stage.

And the crowd parted like the Red Sea.

Cowards! Snakes wanted to throttle these people. Just as they made way for Ben Alef at Hamburg, now they made way for His assassin. Didn't they see what they were doing? Or did they see with the same 20/20 vision they saw with in Hamburg and Frankfurt and Aachen and Berlin and Munich in the 1940s, the vision that led them to bow to the face of power no matter what costume it wore, be it a straight or twisted cross?

Ben Alef had not sold his soul to Mouseland after all. No, the Messiah had deliberately brought Himself here, because this was where His destiny lay. But He could succeed only with the people's help. Or at least some people's, or someone's. This time Snakes was determined that God would not have to sacrifice Himself again. This time, a real son of man would save God, and sacrifice himself if he must.

Here came the moment Snakes had been waiting for. All his lingering doubts were forgotten in the final light of Ben Alef's superior wisdom, as he and Bruno, the last two disciples except for the missing Max Vetter, hurled themselves into the action. Snakes leapt in front of Ben Alef.

Everything happened at once.

One bullet whistled past Snakes's head and fractured the brittle and glistening ice veneer encasing the Empire's Father. Like a ram's-horn blast atop the Matterhorn, the short, sharp shot set off an avalanche. The figure trembled and toppled forward, landing with the clatter of a million shards of ice—like glass breaking at a Jewish wedding, or the shattering of a synagogue's stained-glass windows—and a burst of liquefied flesh exploded across the stage.

Running forward at the same moment, Bruno slipped in the puddle of loathsome human fluid and also fell. He slammed into the orchestra pit amid a clatter of abandoned cymbals and brass, and broke his neck as cleanly as he had broken the neck of his last professional opponent in the Allenberger arena a decade earlier.

Only Snakes stood between his God and tragedy. He jumped over Bruno's body and set to face the fury of the enemy straight on, like a Warsaw Ghetto fighter about to throw himself under a German tank declaring, "You can kill me, but you can't kill what I believe in."

Then, finally, Mouseland security, second to none at apprehending turnstile jumpers and pickpockets and finding and comforting lost children, found its courage. A pack of chipmunks and six out of the seven dwarves (Sleepy was taking a nap in the Excitementland garden) and an army of movie extras and theme-park stars swarmed out of the wings and buried Eisenheim.

He thrashed and managed to pull his trigger two or three more times, but the sheer mass of animality was too great for him. Dumbo pinned him to the ground while Minnie cried, "You beast!" and swatted him with her pearl-handled mirror, and a pair of crows pecked at his eyes.

Safe, at last.

Standing over his subdued adversary, Snakes felt the profoundest relief he had ever known in his life. He had lived an epoch in the last six weeks, gone from petty criminal to escaped convict to disciple to savior of the Savior. He had outlived all of the other sons of men and women from the *Farnhagen* and finally conquered all that was evil in the name of all that was good. Ben Alef was saved and so, too—perhaps the greater miracle— was Snakes. He turned around to seek his Lord's eyes.

The Messiah stood on the stage, bare feet pinkened by the swirling waters of a different Father. His mother sat cross-legged on the floor beside him, Celia shook uncontrollably at the left, and Goofy, alone of all the Enchantment Empire's characters, remained where he had last been seen, still holding the long, serrated knife he had used to cut the ropes that bound the white sheet to earth.

It was the same kind of knife fishermen used to slice and gut their catch.

"No!" Snakes shrieked.

Too late.

Goofy stepped forward and plunged the knife into Ben Alef's back; its point emerged from His navel.

The Messiah staggered sideways, a froth of red foam bubbling at the corner of His pale lips, before He slumped into Margot's lap. There He lay, trying, trying to get out one last message, trying, in vain.

Margot's arms spread out from her body like extended wings, and her hands fluttered as uselessly as two white doves until they alit to clasp and embrace her dying son.

Immediately and too late the minions of authority knocked Goofy to the ground, but that was easy; he didn't resist. He didn't care. He just lay there until Snakes walked slowly back onto the stage, wrestled off his stupid dog head, and threw it aside. The head bounced on its rubber nose and landed flop-eared at the feet of another dog.

"Fetch," Pluto had said to the dog in human dress, and Goofy fetched, because that was what dog-faced people did. Whenever a strong voice gave orders, they followed.

But Snakes Hammurabi no longer noticed Pluto, upright now and triumphant, dancing an obscene little jig at the side of the stage. Snakes hardly noticed anything, not the murderer and not even the martyr, and surely not the insipid mourners already keening. The pain was finally too great, so great that Snakes—not Samad, not Stephan, not Esteban, not Samuel—couldn't and wouldn't ever again give a fuck about God. No, he had touched Heaven with his elegant loafers and found it wanting. If the glorious Son of Man couldn't save Himself, how could people expect Him to save them? Nothing to regret, because that was just the way it was. Just another weakling, just another failure. Snakes knelt and immersed his hands in the cold and putrid mix of divine and human fluid, glad that he was alive.

From here on, Snakes resolved to confine his interest to this world. In his mind, he was already back in Hamburg; the Kastrasse needed a boss. But for the record, in one last foredoomed effort to comprehend, he looked into the innocent human eyes on the grizzled face extending out from the dog's body. Snakes knew who it was—the best among them, the good one—yet he still didn't begin to understand, and though he didn't expect any answer—No answers ever again! And no unanswerable questions either!—he said, "You?"

The killer made his statement. "We did it because we wanted to."

Not another word escaped his lips, but tucked inside his dog suit, next to his heart, lay a folded piece of paper that contained all the explanation anyone would ever get.

Fritz Hofmann, still young enough to feel grief but old enough so that a faint shadow darkened his upper lip, extracted the paper. Together he and Snakes read the two words that would appear on the front of the next day's newspaper: "Dear Frieda."

About the Author

Melvin Jules Bukiet's books include *After, While the Messiah Tarries*, and *Stories of an Imaginary Childhood*, which received the Edward Lewis Wallant Award for the best American-Jewish Fiction of 1992. His stories have appeared in *Antaeus, Paris Review*, and elsewhere. He teaches writing at Sarah Lawrence College and lives in New York City with his wife and three children.